Praise for *After the Plague* by T.C. Boyle

"Boyle has always been a peculiar voice, particularly in the short story form, which he has worked like a master trickster, the jester of the butt end of the twentieth-century . . . life is different now, and the twenty-first century Boyle is different too . . . his new stories confront us with hard problems and modern hypocrises . . . curiosity and passion have drawn him towards the weightier, more complex dilemmas."

—*Los Angeles Times*

"At their best Boyle's most recent stories bring to mind the surreal juxtapositions of F. Scott Fitzgerald . . . the title story is best and most improbable of all: a tale of apocalypse with a happy ending. If (as seems likely) the world is going to hell in a handbasket, it would be a good idea to pack Boyle's latest book, so you'll have something to read on the way."

—*The Washington Post*

"*After the Plague* is both searing anthropology and literary fiction at the highest level. Beyond depicting the way we live now, Boyle locates with breathtaking skill the conflux between the way people represent themselves and the ugly selfish violence sitting beneath the surface."

—*The Baltimore Sun*

"Shows once again T.C. Boyle's power to be funny, deep, quirky, relentless, painful, and all too real." —*The Oregonian* (Portland)

"This new collection proves that Boyle is nowhere near running out of ideas . . . all exemplify his trademark blend of entertainment and insight." —*The Seattle Times*

"Stories that seem ripped from the headlines . . . Boyle has lent his considerable imaginative muscle to the cause of explaining modern life."

—*St. Petersburg Times*

"Dazzling . . . an absolute must read for anyone who loves great fiction."
—*The Miami Herald*

"The narratives almost seemed to be lifted from the pages of the *New York Post* . . . as this collection proves, Boyle is a writer who can take any topic and spin a yarn too good to put down."

—*Men's Journal*

"People do such mean and sneaky things to each other in T.C. Boyle's latest collection of stories that reading them all at once may be enough to sour you on humanity. But the stories are so good, you'll want to read them all at once anyway . . . even if the cumulative effect of these stories is to make you feel that humanity may not be worth saving, there's the paradoxical consolation of art: After all, if people can write with the wit and insight and passion that T.C. Boyle possesses, they must be worth something, right?" —*San Jose Mercury News*

"Boyle has something new on display—a finer interest in the subtleties of character—and the result is a collection with more texture and depth than any that preceded it." —*The Hartford Courant*

"Air rage, first love, Internet porn, abortion and the apocalypse are all fodder for master storyteller T.C. Boyle in *After the Plague* . . . his intense style and trademark narrative twists are, if anything, more effective than ever." —*Playboy*

"The stories in *After the Plague* won't disappoint anyone looking for graceful sentences expressing witty sentiments about memorable characters." —*St. Louis Post-Dispatch*

"The satire, irony, and dark humor the reader expects from Boyle are all here, but there's also compassion and a sense of redemption. Each story is multilayered, tackling love, rage, isolation, fear, passion. They're microcosms of life and death." —*Rocky Mountain News*

"Boyle is not only a master literary craftsman but also profoundly attuned to the here and now, writing with sharp wit, supple imagination, and acute emotional sensitivity about the peculiarities of our densely populated, technology addled, and precarious world . . . here Boyle burrows deeply into the psyches of disparate characters in crisis, balancing his gift for vigorous description with insights into seemingly inexplicable behavior, moments when a person crashes through the guardrail of reason." —*Booklist*

"Boyle's talent for crafting amusing and startling short stories has never been in doubt . . . his imagination and zeal for storytelling are in top form here, making this collection a smash." —*Publishers Weekly*

PENGUIN BOOKS

AFTER THE PLAGUE

T. C. Boyle is the author of the novels *A Friend of the Earth*, *Riven Rock*, *The Tortilla Curtain*, *The Road to Wellville*, *East Is East*, *World's End* (winner of the PEN/Faulkner Award), *Budding Prospects*, and *Water Music*. His short story collections include *Descent of Man*, *Greasy Lake*, *If the River Was Whiskey*, *Without a Hero*, and *T. C. Boyle Stories*. His short fiction regularly appears in major American magazines, including *The New Yorker*, *Harper's*, *The Paris Review*, *Playboy*, *Esquire*, and *The Atlantic Monthly*. Boyle was the recipient of the 1999 PEN/Malamud Award for Excellence in Short Fiction. He lives near Santa Barbara, California. T. C. Boyle's Web site is www.tcboyle.com. His new novel, *Drop City*, will be published by Viking in March of 2003.

To request Great Books Foundation Discussion Guides by mail (while supplies last), please call (800) 778-6425 or E-mail reading@penguinputnam.com.
To access Great Books Foundation Discussion Guides online, visit our Web site at www.penguinputnam.com or the foundation Web site at www.greatbooks.org.

AFTER THE PLAGUE

STORIES BY

T. CORAGHESSAN BOYLE

PENGUIN BOOKS

PENGUIN BOOKS

Published by the Penguin Group
Penguin Putnam Inc., 375 Hudson Street, New York, New York 10014, U.S.A.
Penguin Books Ltd, 80 Strand, London WC2R 0RL, England
Penguin Books Australia Ltd, 250 Camberwell Road,
Camberwell, Victoria 3124, Australia
Penguin Books Canada Ltd, 10 Alcorn Avenue, Toronto, Ontario, Canada M4V 3B2
Penguin Books India (P) Ltd, 11 Community Centre,
Panchsheel Park, New Delhi – 110 017, India
Penguin Books (N.Z.) Ltd, Cnr Rosedale and Airborne Roads,
Albany, Auckland, New Zealand
Penguin Books (South Africa) (Pty) Ltd, 24 Sturdee Avenue,
Rosebank, Johannesburg 2196, South Africa

Penguin Books Ltd, Registered Offices:
Harmondsworth, Middlesex, England

First published in the United States of America by Viking Penguin,
a member of Penguin Putnam Inc. 2001
Published in Penguin Books 2003

10 9 8 7 6 5 4 3 2 1

Grateful acknowledgment is made to the following magazines, in which these stories first
appeared: *Esquire*, "Peep Hall"; *GQ*, "Death of the Cool"; *Granta*, "Rust"; *The New Yorker*,
"She Wasn't Soft," "Killing Babies," "Captured by the Indians," "Achates McNeil," "Mexico," "The Love of My Life," "Friendly Skies," "My Widow," and "The Underground Gardens"; *The Paris Review*, "Going Down"; *Playboy*, "Termination Dust," "The Black and
White Sisters," and "After the Plague."

"Killing Babies" also appeared in *The Best American Stories 1997*, edited by E. Annie
Proulx (Houghton Mifflin); "The Underground Gardens," in *Prize Stories 1999: The O.
Henry Awards*, edited by Larry Dark (Anchor Books); "The Love of My Life," in *Prize Stories 2001: The O. Henry Awards*, edited by Larry Dark (Anchor Books); and "Mexico," in
somewhat different form, in *T. C. Boyle Stories* (Penguin).

THE LIBRARY OF CONGRESS HAS CATALOGED THE HARDCOVER EDITION AS FOLLOWS:
Boyle, T. Coraghessan.
After the plague : stories / by T. Coraghessan Boyle.
p.   cm.
ISBN 0-670-03005-8 (hc.)
ISBN 0 14 20.0141 4 (pbk.)
1. United States—Social life and customs—20th century—Fiction.   I. Title.
PS3552.O932 A68 2001
813'.54—dc21   2001026585

Printed in the United States of America
Set in Janson Text

For Paul Slovak and Bettina Schrewe

Language is like a cracked kettle on which we beat our tunes to dance to, while all the time we long to move the stars to pity.

—Gustave Flaubert, *Madame Bovary*

CONTENTS

AFTER THE PLAGUE

TERMINATION DUST

There were a hundred and seven of them, of all ages, shapes and sizes, from twenty-five- and thirty-year-olds in dresses that looked like they were made of Saran Wrap to a couple of big-beamed older types in pantsuits who could have been somebody's mother—and I mean somebody grown, with a goatee beard and a job at McDonald's. I was there to meet them when they came off the plane from Los Angeles, I and Peter Merchant, whose travel agency had arranged the whole weekend in partnership with a Beverly Hills concern, and there were a couple other guys there too, eager beavers like J. J. Hotel, and the bad element, by which I mean Bud Withers specifically, who didn't want to cough up the hundred fifty bucks for the buffet, the Malibu Beach party and the auction afterward. They were hoping for maybe a sniff of something gratis, but I was there to act as a sort of buffer and make sure that didn't happen.

Peter was all smiles as we came up to the first of the ladies, Susan Abrams, by her nametag, and started handing out corsages, one to a lady, and chimed out in chorus, "Welcome to Anchorage, Land of the Grizzly and the True-Hearted Man!" Well, it was pretty corny—it was Peter's idea, not mine—and I felt a little foolish with the first few (hard-looking women, divorcées for sure, maybe even legal secretaries or lawyers into the bargain), but when I saw this little one with eyes the color of glacial melt about six deep in the line, I really began to perk up. Her nametag was done in calligraphy, hand-lettered instead of computer-generated

1

like the rest of them, and that really tugged at me, the care that went into it, and I gave her hand a squeeze and said, "Hi, Jordy, welcome to Alaska," when I gave her the corsage.

She seemed a little dazed, and I chalked it up to the flight and the drinks and the general party atmosphere that must certainly have prevailed on that plane, one hundred and seven single women on their way for the Labor Day weekend in a state that boasted two eligible bachelors for every woman, but that wasn't it at all. She'd hardly had a glass of chablis, as it turned out—what I took to be confusion, lethargy, whatever, was just wonderment. As I was later to learn, she'd been drawn to the country all her life, had read and dreamed about it since she was a girl growing up in Altadena, California, within sight of the Rose Bowl. She was bookish—an English teacher, in fact—and she had a new worked-leather high-grade edition of *Wuthering Heights* wedged under the arm that held her suitcase and traveling bag. I guessed her to be maybe late twenties, early thirties.

"Thank you," she said, in this whispery little voice that made me feel about thirteen years old all over again, and then she squinted those snowmelt eyes to take in my face and the spread of me (I should say I'm a big man, one of the biggest in the bush around Boynton, six-five and two-forty-two and not much of that gone yet to fat), and then she read my name off my nametag and added, in a deep-diving puff of a little floating wisp of a voice, "Ned."

Then she was gone, and it was the next woman in line (with a face like a topographic map and the grip of a lumberjack), and then the next, and the next, and all the while I'm wondering how much Jordy's going to go for at the auction, and if a hundred and twenty-five, which is about all I'm prepared to spend, is going to be enough.

The girls—women, ladies, whatever—rested up at their hotel for a while and did their ablutions and ironed their outfits and put on their makeup, while Peter and Susan Abrams fluttered around making sure all the little details of the evening had been worked out. I sat at the bar drinking Mexican beer to get in the mood. I'd barely finished my first when I looked up and who did I see but J.J. and Bud with maybe half a dozen local types in tow, all of them looking as lean and hungry as a winter cat. Bud ignored me and started chatting up the Anchorage boys with his eternal line of bullshit about living off the land in his cabin in the bush outside Boynton—which was absolutely the purest undiluted nonsense, as anybody who'd known him for more than half a minute could testify—but J.J. settled in beside me with a combination yodel and sigh and offered to buy me a drink, which I accepted. "Got one picked out?" he said, and he had this mocking grin on his face, as if the whole business of the Los Angeles contingent was a bad joke, though I knew it was all an act and he was as eager and sweetly optimistic as I was myself.

The image of a hundred and seven women in their underwear suddenly flashed through my mind, and then I pictured Jordy in a black brassiere and matching panties, and I blushed and ducked my head and tried on an awkward little smile. "Yeah," I admitted.

"I'll be damned if Mr. Confidence down there"—a gesture for Bud, who was neck-deep in guano with the weekend outdoorsmen in their L. L. Bean outfits—"doesn't have one too. Says he's got her room number already and told her he'd bid whatever it takes for a date with her, even if he had to dip into the family fortune."

My laugh was a bitter, strangled thing. Bud was just out of jail, where he'd done six months on a criminal mischief charge for shooting out the windows in three cabins and the sunny side of my store on the main street—the only street—in downtown Boynton, population 170. He didn't have a pot to piss in, except what he got from the VA or welfare or whatever it was—it was hard to say, judging from the way he seemed to confuse fact and fiction. That and the rattrap cabin he'd built on federal land along the Yukon River, and that was condemned. I didn't even know what he'd done with his kid after Linda left him, and I didn't want to guess. "How'd he even get here?" I said.

J.J. was a little man with a bald pate and a full snow-white beard, a widower and a musician who cooked as mean a moose tri-tip with garlic and white gravy as any man who'd come into the country in the past ten years. He shrugged, set his beer mug down on the bar. "Same as you and me."

I was incredulous. "You mean he drove? Where'd he get the car?"

"All I know's he told me last week he had this buddy was going to lend him a brand-new Toyota Land Cruiser for the weekend and that furthermore, he was planning on going home to Boynton with the second Mrs. Withers, even if he did have to break down and shell out the one fifty for the party and all. It's an investment, he says, as if any woman'd be crazy enough to go anyplace with him, let alone a cabin out in the hind end of nowhere."

I guess I was probably stultified with amazement at this point, and I couldn't really manage a response. I was just looking over the top of my beer at the back of Bud's head and his elbow resting on the bar and then the necks of his boots as if I could catch a glimpse of the plastic feet he's got stuffed in there. I'd seen them once, those feet, when he first got back from the hospital and he came round the store for a pint of something, already half drunk and wearing a pair of shorts under his coat though it was minus thirty out. "Hey, Ned," he said to me in this really nasty, ac-cusatory voice, "you see what you and the rest of them done to me?," and he flipped open the coat to show his ankles and the straps and the plastic feet that were exactly like the pink molded feet of a mannequin in a department store window.

I was worried. I didn't want to let on to J.J., but I knew Bud, I knew how smooth he was—especially if you weren't forewarned—and I knew women found him attractive. I kept thinking, What if it's Jordy he's after?, but then I told myself the chances were pretty remote, what with a hundred and seven eager women to choose from, and even if it was—even if it *was*—there were still a hundred and six others and one of them had to be for me.

/ / / / /

Statistics:

There were thirty-two women out of a population of 170 in Boynton, all of them married and all of them invisible, even when they were sitting around the bar I run in the back room of the store. Average winter temperature was minus twelve, and there was a period of nearly two months when we hardly saw the sun. Add to that the fact that seven out of ten adults in Alaska have a drinking problem, and you can imagine what life was like on the bad days.

I was no exception to the rule. The winter was long, the nights were lonely, and booze was a way to take the edge off the loneliness and the boredom that just slowed you down and slowed you down till you felt like you were barely alive. I was no drunk, don't get me wrong—nothing like Bud Withers, not even close—and I tried to keep a check on myself, going without even so much as a whiff of the stuff every other day at least and trying my best to keep a hopeful outlook. Which is why I left the bar after two beers to go back to Peter's place and douse myself with aftershave, solidify the hair round my bald spot with a blast of hair spray and slip into the sport coat I'd last worn at Chiz Peltz's funeral (he froze to death the same night Bud lost his feet, and I was the one who had to pry him away from the back door of the barroom in the morning; he was like a bronze statue, huddled over the bottle with his parka pulled up over his head, and that was how we had to bury him, bottle and all). Then I made my way back through the roaring streets to the hotel and the ballroom that could have contained all of Boynton and everybody in it, feeling like an overawed freshman pressed up against the wall at the weekly social. But I wasn't a freshman anymore, and this was no social. I was thirty-four years old and I was tired of living like a monk. I needed someone to talk to—a companion, a helpmeet, a wife—and this was my best chance of finding one.

As soon as I saw Jordy standing there by the hors d'oeuvres table, the other hundred and six women vanished from sight, and I knew I'd been fooling myself back there at the bar. She was the one, the only one, and the longing for her was a continuous ache that never let up from that moment on. She was with another woman, and they had their heads together, talking, but I couldn't have honestly told you whether this other woman was tall or short, blond, brunette, or redhead: I saw Jordy, and nothing more. "Hi," I said, the sport coat gouging at my underarms and clinging to my back like a living thing, "remember me?"

She sure did. And she reached up to take hold of my hand and peck a little kiss into the outer fringe of my beard. The other woman—the invisible one—faded away into the background before she could be introduced.

I found myself at a loss for what to say next. My hands felt big and cumbersome, as if they'd just been stapled on as I came through the door, and the sport coat flapped its wings and dug its talons into my neck. I wanted a drink. Badly.

"Would you like a drink?" Jordy whispered, fracturing the words into tiny little nuggets of meaning. She was holding a glass of white wine in one hand and she was wearing a pair of big glittery dangling earrings that hung all the way down to the sculpted bones of her bare shoulders.

I let her lead me up to the long folding table with the four bartenders hustling around on one side and all the women pressed up against the other while the rawboned bush crazies did their best to talk them to death, and then I had a double scotch in my hand and felt better. "It's beautiful country," I said, toasting her, it, the ballroom and everything beyond with a clink of our glasses, "especially out my way, in Boynton. Peaceful," I said, "you know?"

"Oh, I know," she said, and for the first time I noticed a hint of something barely contained bubbling just below the surface of that smoky voice, "or at least I can imagine. I mean, from what I've read. That's in the Yukon watershed, isn't it—Boynton?"

This was my cue, and I was grateful for it. I went into a rambling five-minute oration on the geographic and geological high points of the bush around Boynton, with sidelights on the local flora, fauna and human curiosities, tactfully avoiding any reference to the sobering statistics that made me question what I was doing there myself. It was a speech, all right, one that would have done any town booster proud. When I was through with it, I saw that my glass was empty and that Jordy was squirming in her boots to get a word in edgewise. "Sorry," I said, dipping my head in apology, "I didn't mean to talk your ear off. It's just that"—and here I got ahead of myself, my tongue loosened by the seeping burn of the scotch—"we don't get to talk much to anybody new, unless we make the trek into Fairbanks, and that's pretty rare—and especially not to someone as good-looking, I mean, as attractive, as you."

Jordy managed to flush prettily at the compliment, and then she was off on a speech of her own, decrying the lack of the human dimension in city life, the constant fuss and hurry and hassle, the bad air, the polluted beaches, and—this really got my attention—the lack of men with old-fashioned values, backbone and grit. When she delivered this last line—I don't know if that's how she phrased it exactly, but that was the gist of it—she leveled those glaciated eyes on me and I felt like I could walk on water.

We were standing in line at the buffet table when Bud Withers shuffled in. It was surprising how well he managed to do on those plastic feet—if you didn't know what was wrong with him, you'd never guess. You could see something wasn't quite right—every step he took looked like a recovery, as if he'd just been shoved from behind—but as I say, it wasn't all that abnormal. Anyway, I maneuvered myself in between Jordy and his line of sight, hunkering over her like an eagle masking its kill, and went on with our conversation. She was curious about life in Boynton, really obsessing over the smallest details, and I'd been telling her how much freedom you have out in the bush, how you can live your life the way you want, in tune with nature instead of shut up in some stucco box next to a shopping mall. "But what about you?" she said. "Aren't you stuck in your store?"

"I get antsy, I just close the place down for a couple days."

She looked shocked, or maybe skeptical is a better word. "What about your customers?"

I shrugged to show her how casual everything was. "It's not

like I run the store for the public welfare," I said, "and they do have The Nougat to drink at, Clarence Ford's place." (Actually, Clarence meant to call it The Nugget, but he's a terrible speller, and I always go out of my way to give it a literal pronunciation just to irritate him.) "So anytime I want, dead of winter, whatever, I'll just hang out the Gone Trappin' sign, dig out my snowshoes, and go off and run my trapline."

Jordy seemed to consider this, the hair round her temples frizzing up with the steam from the serving trays. "And what are you after—" she said finally, "mink?"

"Marten, lynx, fox, wolf." The food was good (it ought to have been for what we were paying), and I heaped up my plate, but not so much as to make her think I was a hog or anything. There was a silence. I became aware of the music then, a Beach Boys song rendered live by a band from Juneau at the far end of the room. "With a fox," I said, and I didn't know whether she wanted to hear this or not, "you come up on him and he's caught by the foot and maybe he's tried to gnaw that foot off, and he's snarling like a chainsaw . . . well, what you do is you just rap him across the snout with a stick, like this"—gesturing with my free hand—"and it knocks him right out. Like magic. Then you just put a little pressure on his throat till he stops breathing and you get a nice clean fur, you know what I mean?"

I was worried she might be one of those animal liberation nuts that want to protect every last rat, tick and flea, but she didn't look bothered at all. In fact, her eyes seemed to get distant for a minute, then she bent over to dish up a healthy portion of the king crab and straightened up with a smile. "Just like the pioneers," she said.

That was when Bud sniffed us out. He butted right in line, put a hand round Jordy's waist and drew her to him for a kiss, full plate and all, which she had to hold out awkwardly away from her body or there would have been king crab and avocado salad all down the front of that silky black dress she was wearing. "Sorry I'm late, babe," Bud said, and he picked up a plate and began mounding it high with cold cuts and smoked salmon.

Jordy turned to me then, and I couldn't read her face, not at all, but of course I knew in that instant that Bud had got to her and though the chances were a hundred and seven to one against it, she was the one who'd given him her room number. I was dazed by the realization, and after I got over being dazed, I felt the anger coming up in me like the foam in a loose can of beer. "Ned," she murmured, "do you know Bud?"

Bud gave me an ugly look, halfway between a "fuck you" and a leer of triumph. I tried to keep my cool, for Jordy's sake. "Yeah," was all I said.

She led us to a table in back, right near the band—one of those long banquet-type tables—and Bud and I sat down on either side of her, jockeying for position. "Bud," she said, as soon as we were settled, "and Ned"—turning to me and then back to him again— "I'm sure you can both help me with this, and I really want to know the truth of it because it's part and parcel of my whole romance with Alaska and now I've read somewhere that it isn't true." She had to raise her voice to be heard over the strains of "Little Deuce Coupe"—this was the Malibu Beach party, after all, replete with the pile of sand in the corner and a twenty-foot-high poster of Gidget in a bikini—and we both leaned in to hear her better. "What I want to know is, do you really have seventy-two different words for snow—in the Eskimo language, I mean?"

Bud didn't even give me a glance, just started in with his patented line of bullshit, how he'd spent two years with the Inuit up around Point Barrow, chewing walrus hides with the old ladies and dodging polar bears, and how he felt that seventy-two was probably a low estimate. Then he fell into some dialect he must have invented on the spot, all the while giving Jordy this big moony smile that made me want to puke, till I took her elbow and she turned to me and the faux Eskimo caught like a bone in his throat. "We call it termination dust," I said.

She lifted her eyebrows. Bud was on the other side of her, looked bored and greedy, shoveling up his food like a hyperphagic bear. It was the first moment he'd shut his mouth since he'd butted in. "It's because of the road," I explained. "We're at the far end of it, a two-lane gravel road that runs north from the Alaska Highway and dead-ends in Boynton, the last place on the continent you can drive to."

She was still waiting. The band fumbled through the end of the song and the room suddenly came alive with the buzz of a hundred conversations. Bud glanced up from his food to shoot me a look of unadulterated hate. "Go on," she said.

I shrugged, toyed with my fork. "That's it," I said. "The first snow, the first good one, and it's all over till spring, the end, it's all she wrote. If you're in Boynton, you're going to stay there—"

"And if you're not?" she asked, something satirical in her eyes as she tucked away a piece of crab with a tiny two-pronged fork.

Bud answered for me. "You're not going to make it."

The auction was for charity, all proceeds to be divided equally among the Fur Trappers' Retirement Home, the AIDS Hospice and the Greater Anchorage Foodbank. I had no objection to that— I was happy to do my part—but as I said, I was afraid somebody would outbid me for a date with Jordy. Not that the date was anything more than just that—a date—but it was a chance to spend the better part of the next day with the woman of your choice, and when you only had two and a half days, that was a big chunk of it. I'd talked to J.J. and some of the others, and they were all planning to bid on this woman or that and to take them out on a fishing boat or up in a Super Cub to see the glaciers east of town or even out into the bush to look over their cabins and their prospects. Nobody talked about sex—that would demean the spirit of the thing—but it was there, under the surface, like a burning promise.

The first woman went for seventy-five dollars. She was about forty or so, and she looked like a nurse or dental technician, somebody who really knew her way around a bedpan or saliva sucker. The rest of us stood around and watched while three men exercised their index fingers and the auctioneer (who else but Peter?) went back and forth between them with all sorts of comic asides until they'd reached their limit. "Going once, going twice," he chimed, milking the moment for all it was worth, "sold to the man in the red hat." I watched the guy, nobody I knew, an Anchorage type, as he mounted the three steps to the stage they'd set up by the sandpit, and I felt something stir inside me when this dental technician of forty smiled like all the world was melting and gave him a kiss right out of the last scene of a movie and the two of them went off hand in hand. My heart was hammering like a broken piston. I couldn't see Bud in the crowd, but I knew what his intentions were, and as I said, a hundred twenty-five was my limit. There was no way I was going past that, no matter what.

Jordy came up ninth. Two or three of the women that preceded her were really something to look at, secretaries probably or cocktail waitresses, but Jordy easily outclassed them. It wasn't only that she was educated, it was the way she held herself, the way she stepped up to the platform with a private little smile and let those unquenchable eyes roam over the crowd till they settled on me. I stood a head taller than anyone else there, so I guess it wasn't so hard to pick me out. I gave her a little wave, and then immediately regretted it because I'd tipped my hand.

The first bid was a hundred dollars from some clown in a lumberjack shirt who looked as if he'd just been dragged out from under a bush somewhere. I swear there was lint in his hair. Or worse. Peter had said, "Who'll start us off here, do I hear an opening bid?," and this guy stuck up his hand and said, "A hundred," just like that. I was stunned. Bud I was prepared for, but this was something else altogether. What was this guy thinking? A lumberjack shirt and he was bidding on *Jordy*? It was all I could do to keep myself from striding through the crowd and jerking the guy out of his boots like some weed along the roadside, but then another hand popped up just in front of me, and this guy must have been sixty if he was a day, the back of his neck all rutted and seamed and piss-yellow hairs growing out of his ears, and he spoke up just as casually as if he was ordering a drink at the bar: "One twenty." I was in a panic, beset on all sides, and I felt my tongue thickening in my throat as I threw up my arm. "One—" I gasped. "One twenty-five!"

Then it was Bud's turn. I heard him before I saw him slouching there in the second row, right up near the stage. He didn't even bother raising his hand. "One fifty," he said, and right away the old bird in front of me croaked out, "One seventy-five." I was in a sweat, wringing my hands till I thought the left would crush the right and vice versa, the sport coat digging into me like a hairshirt, like a straitjacket, too small under the arms and across the shoulders. One twenty-five was my limit, absolutely and unconditionally, and even then I'd be straining to pay for the date itself, but I felt my arm jerking up as if it was attached to a wire. "One seventy-six!" I shouted, and everybody in the room turned around to stare at me.

I heard a laugh from the front, a dirty sniggering little stab of a laugh that shot hot lava through my veins, Bud's laugh, Bud's mocking hateful naysaying laugh, and then Bud's voice crashed through the wall of wonder surrounding my bid and pronounced my doom. "Two hundred and fifty dollars," he said, and I stood there stupefied as Peter called out, "Going once, going twice," and slammed down the gavel.

I don't remember what happened next, but I turned away before Bud could shuffle up to the stage and take Jordy in his arms and receive the public kiss that was meant for me, turned away, and staggered toward the bar like a gutshot deer. I try to control my temper, I really do—I know it's a failing of mine—but I guess I must have gotten a little rough with these two L. L. Bean types that were blocking my access to the scotch. Nothing outrageous, nothing more than letting them know in no uncertain terms that they were in my path and that if they liked the way their arms still fit in their sockets, they'd dance on out of there like the sugarplum fairy and her court, but still, I regretted it. Nothing else that night rings too clear, not after Jordy went to Bud for the sake of mere money, but I kept thinking, over and over, as if a splinter was implanted in my brain, *How in Christ's name did that unemployed son of a bitch come up with two hundred and fifty bucks?*

/ / / / /

I rang Jordy's room first thing in the morning (yes, there was that, at least: she'd given me her room number too, but now I wondered if she wasn't just playing mind games). There was no answer, and that told me something I didn't want to know. I inquired at the desk and the clerk said she'd checked out the night before, and I must have had a look on my face because he volunteered that he didn't know where she'd gone. It was then that the invisible woman from the cocktail party materialized out of nowhere, visible suddenly in a puke-green running suit, with greasy hair and a face all pitted and naked without a hint of makeup. "You looking for Jordy?" she said, and maybe she recognized me.

The drumming in my chest suddenly slowed. I felt ashamed of myself. Felt awkward and out of place, my head windy and cavernous from all that sorrowful scotch. "Yes," I admitted.

She took pity on me then and told me the truth. "She went to some little town with that guy from the auction last night. Said she'd be back for the plane Monday."

Ten minutes later I was in my Chevy half ton, tooling up the highway for Fairbanks and the gravel road to Boynton. I felt an urgency bordering on the manic and my foot was like a cement block on the accelerator, because once Bud got to Boynton I knew what he was going to do. He'd ditch the car, which I wouldn't doubt he'd borrowed without the legitimate owner's consent, whoever that might be, and then he'd load up his canoe with supplies and Jordy and run down the river for his trespasser's cabin. And if that happened, Jordy wouldn't be making any plane. Not on Monday. Maybe not ever.

I tried to think about Jordy and how I was going to rescue her from all that and how grateful she'd be once she realized what kind of person she was dealing with in Bud and what his designs were, but every time I summoned her face, Bud's rose up out of some dark hole in my consciousness to blot it out. I saw him sitting at the bar that night he lost his feet, sitting there drinking steadily though I'd eighty-sixed him three times over the course of the past year and three times relented. He was on a tear, drinking with Chiz Peltz and this Indian I'd never laid eyes on before who claimed to be a full-blooded Flathead from Montana. It was January, a few days after New Year's, and it was maybe two o'clock in the afternoon and dark beyond the windows. I was drinking too—tending bar, but helping myself to the scotch—because it was one of those days when time has no meaning and your life drags like it has brakes on it. There were maybe eight other people in the place: Ronnie Perrault and his wife, Louise, Roy Treadwell, who services snow machines and sells cordwood, Richie Oliver, and some others—I don't know where J.J. was that day, playing solitaire in his cabin, I guess, staring at the walls, who knows?

Anyway, Bud was on his tear and he started using language I don't tolerate in the bar, not anytime, and especially not when ladies are present, and I told him to can it and things got nasty. The upshot was that I had to pin the Indian to the back wall by his throat and rip Bud's parka half off him before I convinced the three of them to finish up their drinking over at The Nougat, which is where they went, looking ugly. Clarence Ford put up with them till around seven or so, and then he kicked them out and barred the door and they sat in Chiz Peltz's car with the engine running and the heater on full, passing a bottle back and forth till I don't know what hour. Of course, the car eventually ran out of gas with the three of them passed out like zombies and the overnight temperature went down to something like minus sixty, and as I said, Chiz didn't make it, and how he wound up outside my place I'll never know. We helicoptered Bud to the hospital in Fairbanks, but they couldn't save his feet. The Indian—I've never seen him since—just seemed to shake it off with the aid of a dozen cups of coffee laced with free bourbon at The Nougat.

Bud never forgave me or Clarence or anybody else in town. He was a sorehead and griper of the first degree, the sort of person who blames all his miseries on everybody but himself, and now he had Jordy, this sweet dreamy English teacher who probably thought Alaska was all *Northern Exposure* and charmingly eccentric people saying witty things to each other. I knew Bud. I knew how he would have portrayed that ratty illegal tumbledown cabin to her and how he would have told her it was just a hop, skip and jump down the river and not the twelve miles it actually was—and what was she going to do when she found out? Catch a cab?

These were my thoughts as I passed through Fairbanks, headed southeast on the Alaska Highway, and finally turned north for Boynton. It was late in the afternoon and I still had a hundred and eighty miles of gravel road to traverse before I even hit Boynton, let alone caught up with Bud—I could only hope he'd stopped off at The Nougat for his usual fix of vodka, but the chances of that were slim because he'd want to hustle Jordy down the river before she got a good idea of who he was and what was going on. And that was another thing: I just didn't understand her. Just didn't. He'd put in the highest bid and she was a good sport, okay—but to drive all night with that slime? To put up with his bullshit for all those crippling hours, maybe even fall for it? Poor Jordy. Poor, poor Jordy.

I pulled into Boynton in record time, foot to the floor all the way, and skidded to a halt in the gravel lot out front of my store. There were only three other cars there, each as familiar as my own, and Ronnie Perrault, who I'd asked to help out for the weekend, was presiding over a very quiet bar (half the men in town had gone to Anchorage for the big event, thanks to Peter and his unflagging salesmanship). "Ronnie," I said, coming into the bar to the strains of Lyle Lovett singing "Mack the Knife" like he was half dead, "you seen Bud?"

Ronnie was hunched lovingly over a cigarette and a Meyers and Coke, holding hands with Louise. He was wearing a Seattle Mariners cap backwards on his head, and his eyes were distant, the eyes of a man in rum nirvana. Howard Walpole, seventy years old and with a bad back and runny eyes, was at the far end of the bar, and Roy Treadwell and Richie Oliver were playing cards at the table by the stove. Ronnie was slow, barely flowing, like the grenadine in the back pantry that hardly gets any heat. "I thought," he said, chewing over the words, "I thought you wasn't going to be back till Tuesday?"

"Hey, Neddy," Doug shouted, squeezing out the diminutive until it was like a screech, "how many you bring back?"

"Bud," I repeated, addressing the room at large. "Anybody seen Bud?"

Well, they had to think about that. They were all pretty hazy, while the cat's away the mice will play, but it was Howard who came out of it first. "Sure," he said, "I seen him," and he leaned so far forward over his drink I thought he was going to fall into it, "early this morning, in a brand-new Toyota Land Cruiser, which I don't know where he got, and he had a woman with him." And then, as if remembering some distant bit of trivia: "How was that flesh bazaar, anyway? You married yet?"

Louise snickered, Ronnie guffawed, but I was in no mood. "Where'd he go?" I said, hopeful, always hopeful, but I already knew the answer.

Howard did something with his leg, a twitch he'd developed to ease the pain in his back. "I didn't talk to him," he said. "But I think he was going downriver."

The river wasn't too rough this time of year, but it was still moving at a pretty good clip, and I have to admit I'm not exactly an ace with the canoe. I'm too big for anything that small—give me a runabout with an Evinrude engine any day—and I always feel awkward and top-heavy. But there I was, moving along with the current, thinking one thing and one thing only: Jordy. It would be a bitch coming back up, but there'd be two of us paddling, and I kept focusing on how grateful she was going to be for getting her out of there, more grateful than if I'd bid a thousand dollars for her and took her out for steak three nights in a row. But then the strangest thing happened: the sky went gray and it began to snow.

It just doesn't snow that early in the year, not ever, or hardly ever. But there it was. The wind came up the channel of the river and threw these dry little pellets of ice in my face and I realized how stupid I'd been. I was already a couple miles downriver from town, and though I had a light parka and mittens with me, a chunk of cheese, loaf of bread, couple Cokes, that sort of thing, I really hadn't planned on any weather. It was a surprise, a real surprise. Of course, at that point I was sure it was only a squall, something to whiten the ground for a day and then melt off, but I still felt stupid out there on the river without any real protection, and I began to wonder how Jordy would see it, the way she was worried about all the names for snow and how sick at heart she must have been just about then with Bud's shithole of a cabin and no escape and the snow coming down like a life sentence, and I leaned into the paddle.

It was after dark when I came round the bend and saw the lights of the cabin off through the scrim of snow. I was wearing my parka and mittens now, and I must have looked like a snowman propped up in the white envelope of the canoe and I could feel the ice forming in my beard where the breath froze coming out of my nostrils. I smelled woodsmoke and watched the soft tumbling sky. Was I angry? Not really. Not yet. I'd hardly thought about what I was doing up to this point—it all just seemed so obvious. The son of a bitch had gotten her, whether it was under false pretenses or not, and Jordy, sweet Jordy with Emily Brontë tucked under her arm, couldn't have imagined in her wildest dreams what she was getting into. No one would have blamed me. For all intents and purposes, Bud had abducted her. He had.

Still, when I actually got there, when I could smell the smoke and see the lamps burning, I felt shy suddenly. I couldn't just burst in and announce that I'd come to rescue her, could I? And I could hardly pretend I just happened to be in the neighborhood . . . plus, that was Bud in there, and he was as purely nasty as a rattlesnake with a hand clamped round the back of its head. There was no way he was going to like this, no matter how you looked at it.

So what I did was pull the canoe up on the bank about a hundred yards from the cabin, the scrape of the gravel masked by the snow, and crept up on the place, as stealthy as a big man can be—I didn't want to alert Bud's dog and blow the whole thing. But that was just it, I realized, tiptoeing through the snow like an ice statue come to life—what thing would I blow? I didn't have a plan. Not even a clue.

In the end, I did the obvious: snuck up to the window and peered in. I couldn't see much at first, the window all smeared with grime, but I gingerly rubbed the pane with the wet heel of my mitten, and things came into focus. The stove in the corner was going, a mouth of flame with the door flung open wide for the fireplace effect. Next to the stove was a table with a bottle of wine on it and two glasses, one of them half full, and I saw the dog then—a malamute-looking thing—asleep underneath it. There was some homemade furniture—a sort of couch with an old single mattress thrown over it, a couple of crude chairs of bent aspen with the bark still on it. Four or five white plastic buckets of water were lined up against the wall, which was festooned with the usual backcountry junk: snowshoes, traps, hides, the mangy stuffed head of a caribou Bud must have picked up at a fire sale someplace. But I didn't see Bud. Or Jordy. And then I realized they must be in the back room—the bedroom—and that made me feel strange, choked up in the pit of my throat as if somebody was trying to strangle me.

It was snowing pretty steadily, six inches on the ground at least, and it muffled my footsteps as I worked my way around the cabin to the back window. The night was absolute, the sky so close it was breathing for me, in and out, in and out, and the snow held everything in the grip of silence. A candle was burning in the back window—I could tell it was a candle from the way the light wavered even before I got there—and I heard the music then, violins all playing in unison, the sort of thing I wouldn't have expected from a lowlife like Bud, and voices, a low, intimate murmur of voices. That almost stopped me right there, that whispery blur of Jordy's voice and the deeper resonance of Bud's, and for a moment everything hung in the balance. A part of me wanted to back away from that window, creep back to the canoe, and forget all about it. But I didn't. I couldn't. I'd seen her first—I'd squeezed her hand and given her the corsage and admired the hand-lettered nametag—and it wasn't right. The murmur of those voices rose up in my head like a scream, and there was nothing more to think about.

My shoulder hit the back door just above the latch and blew the thing off the hinges like it was a toy, and there I was, breathing hard and white to the eyebrows. I saw them in the bed together and heard this little birdlike cry from Jordy and a curse from Bud, and then the dog came hurtling in from the front room as if he'd been launched from a cannon. (And I should say here that I like dogs and that I've never lifted a finger to hurt any dog I've ever owned, but I had to put this one down. I didn't have any choice.) I caught him as he left the floor and slammed him into the wall behind me till he collapsed in a heap. Jordy was screaming now, actually screaming, and you would have thought that I was the bad guy, but I tried to calm her, her arms bare and the comforter pulled up over her breasts and Bud's plastic feet set there like slippers on the floor, telling her a mile a minute that I'd protect her, it was all right, and I'd see that Bud was prosecuted to the fullest extent, the fullest extent, but then Bud was fumbling under the mattress for something like the snake he was, and I took hold of his puny slip of a wrist with the blue-black .38 Special in it and just squeezed till his other hand came up and I caught that one and squeezed it too.

Jordy made a bolt for the other room and I could see she was naked, and I knew right then he must have raped her because there was no way she'd ever consent to anything with a slime like that, not Jordy, not my Jordy, and the thought of what Bud had done to her made me angry. The gun was on the floor now and I kicked it under the bed and let go of Bud's wrists and shut up his stream of curses and vile foul language with a quick stab to the bridge of his nose, and it was almost like a reflex. He went limp under the force of that blow and I was upset, I admit it, I was furious over what he'd done to that girl, and it just seemed like the most natural thing in the world to reach out and put a little pressure on his throat till the raw-looking stumps of his legs lay still on the blanket.

That was when I became aware of the music again, the violins swelling up and out of a black plastic boombox on the shelf till they filled the room and the wind blew through the doorway and the splintered door groaned on its broken latch. Jordy, I was thinking, Jordy needs me, needs me to get her out of this, and I went into the front room to tell her about the snow and how it was coming down out of season and what that meant. She was crouched in the corner across from the stove and her face was wet and she was shivering. Her sweater was clutched up around her neck, and she'd got one leg of her jeans on, but the other leg was bare, sculpted bare and white all the way from her little painted toenails to the curve of her thigh and beyond. It was a hard moment. And I tried to explain to her, I did. "Look outside," I said. "Look out there into the night. You see that?"

She lifted her chin then and looked, out beyond the doorway to the back room, beyond Bud on his bed and the dog on the floor and into the gaping hole where the door had been. And there it was, coming down like the end of everything, snow, and there was only one name for it now. I tried to tell her that. Because we weren't going anywhere.

SHE WASN'T SOFT

She wasn't tender, she wasn't soft, she wasn't sweetly yielding or coquettish, and she was nobody's little woman and never would be. That had been her mother's role, and look at the sad sack of neuroses and alcoholic dysfunction she'd become. And her father. He'd been the pasha of the living room, the sultan of the kitchen, and the emperor of the bedroom, and what had it got him? A stab in the chest, a tender liver, and two feet that might as well have been stumps. Paula Turk wasn't born for that sort of life, with its domestic melodrama and greedy sucking babies—no, she was destined for something richer and more complex, something that would define and elevate her, something great. She wanted to compete and she wanted to win—always, shining before her like some numinous icon was the glittering image of triumph. And whenever she flagged, whenever a sniffle or the flu ate at her reserves and she hit the wall in the numbing waters of the Pacific or the devilish winds at the top of San Marcos Pass, she pushed herself through it, drove herself with an internal whip that accepted no excuses and made no allowances for the limitations of the flesh. She was twenty-eight years old, and she was going to conquer the world.

On the other hand, Jason Barre, the thirty-three-year-old surf-and-dive shop proprietor she'd been seeing pretty steadily over the past nine months, didn't really seem to have the fire of competition in him. Both his parents were doctors (and that, as much as anything, had swayed Paula in his favor when they first met), and they'd set him up in his own business, a business that had continuously lost money since its grand opening three years ago. When the waves were breaking, Jason would be at the beach, and when the surf was flat he'd be stationed behind the counter on his tall swivel stool, selling wax remover to bleached-out adolescents who said things like "gnarly" and "killer" in their penetrating adenoidal tones. Jason liked to surf, and he liked to breathe the cigarette haze in sports bars, a permanent sleepy-eyed, widemouthed California grin on his face, flip-flops on his feet, and his waist encircled by a pair of faded baggy shorts barely held in place by the gentle sag of his belly and the twin anchors of his hipbones.

That was all right with Paula. She told him he should quit smoking, cut down on his drinking, but she didn't harp on it. In truth, she really didn't care all that much—one world-beater in a relationship was enough. When she was in training, which was all the time now, she couldn't help feeling a kind of moral superiority to anyone who wasn't—and Jason most emphatically wasn't. He was no threat, and he didn't want to be—his mind just didn't work that way. He was cute, that was all, and just as she got a little frisson of pleasure from the swell of his paunch beneath the oversized T-shirt and his sleepy eyes and his laid-back ways, he admired her for her drive and the lean, hard triumph of her beauty and her strength. She never took drugs or alcohol—or hardly ever—but he convinced her to try just a puff or two of marijuana before they made love, and it seemed to relax her, open up her pores till she could feel her nerve ends poking through them, and their lovemaking was like nothing she'd ever experienced, except maybe breaking the tape at the end of the twenty-six-mile marathon.

It was a Friday night in August, half past seven, the sun hanging in the window like a piñata, and she'd just stepped out of the shower after a two-hour tuneup for Sunday's triathlon, when the phone rang. Jason's voice came over the wire, low and soft. "Hey, babe," he said, breathing into the phone like a sex maniac (he always called her babe, and she loved it, precisely because she wasn't a babe and never would be—it was their little way of mocking the troglodytes molded into the barstools beside him). "Listen, I was just wondering if you might want to join me down at Clubber's for a while. Yeah, I know, you need your sleep and the big day's the day after tomorrow and Zinny Bauer's probably already asleep, but how about it. Come on. It's my birthday."

"Your birthday? I thought your birthday was in December?"

There was the ghost of a pause during which she could detect the usual wash of background noise, drunken voices crying out as if from the netherworld, the competing announcers of the six different games unfolding simultaneously on the twelve big-screen TVs, the insistent pulse of the jukebox thumping faintly beneath it all. "No," he said, "my birthday's today, August twenty-sixth—it is. I don't know where you got the idea it was in December . . . but come on, babe, don't you have to load up on carbohydrates?"

She did. She admitted it. "I was going to make pancakes and penne," she said, "with a little cheese sauce and maybe a loaf of that brown-and-serve bread. . . ."

"I'll take you to the Pasta Bowl, all you can eat—and I swear I'll have you back by eleven." He lowered his voice. "And no sex, I know—I wouldn't want to drain you or anything."

She wasn't soft because she ran forty-five miles a week, biked two hundred and fifty, and slashed through fifteen thousand yards of the crawl in the Baños del Mar pool. She was in the best shape of her life, and Sunday's event was nothing, less than half the total distance of the big one—the Hawaii Ironman—in October. She wasn't soft because she'd finished second in the women's division last year in Hawaii and forty-fourth over all, beating out a thousand three hundred and fifty other contestants, twelve hundred of whom, give or take a few, were men. Like Jason. Only fitter. A whole lot fitter.

She swung by Clubber's to pick him up—he wasn't driving, not since his last D.U.I., anyway—and though parking was no problem, she had to endure the stench of cigarettes and the faint sour odor of yesterday's vomit while he finished his cocktail and wrapped up his ongoing analysis of the Dodgers' chances with an abstract point about a blister on somebody or other's middle finger. The guy they called Little Drake, white-haired at thirty-six and with a face that reminded her of one of those naked drooping dogs, leaned out of his Hawaiian shirt and into the radius of Jason's gesticulating hands as if he'd never heard such wisdom in his life. And Paula? She stood there at the bar in her shorts and Lycra halter top, sucking an Evian through a straw while the sports fans furtively admired her pecs and lats and the hard hammered musculature of her legs, for all the world a babe. She didn't mind. In fact, it made her feel luminous and alive, not to mention vastly superior to all those pale lumps of flesh sprouting out of the corners like toadstools and the sagging abrasive girlfriends who hung on their arms and tried to feign interest in whatever sport happened to be on the tube.

But somebody was talking to her, Little Drake, it was Little Drake, leaning across Jason and addressing her as if she were one of them. "So Paula," he was saying. "Paula?"

She swivelled her head toward him, hungry now, impatient. She didn't want to hang around the bar and schmooze about Tommy Lasorda and O.J. and Proposition 187 and how Phil Aguirre had broken both legs and his collarbone in the surf at Rincon; she wanted to go to the Pasta Bowl and carbo-load. "Yes?" she said, trying to be civil, for Jason's sake.

"You going to put them to shame on Sunday, or what?"

Jason was snubbing out his cigarette in the ashtray, collecting his money from the bar. They were on their way out the door—in ten minutes she'd be forking up fettucine or angel hair with black olives and sun-dried tomatoes while Jason regaled her with a satiric portrait of his day and all the crazies who'd passed through his shop. The little man with the white hair didn't require a dissertation, and besides, he couldn't begin to appreciate the difference between what she was doing and the ritualistic farce of the tobacco-spitting, crotch-grabbing "athletes" all tricked out in their pretty unblemished uniforms up on the screen over his head, so she just smiled, like a babe, and said, "Yeah."

Truly, the race was nothing, just a warm-up, and it would have been less than nothing but for the puzzling fact that Zinny Bauer was competing. Zinny was a professional, from Hamburg, and she was the one who'd cranked past Paula like some sort of machine in the final stretch of the Ironman last year. What Paula couldn't fathom was why Zinny was bothering with this small-time event when there were so many other plums out there. On the way out of Clubber's, she mentioned it to Jason. "Not that I'm worried," she said, "just mystified."

It was a fine, soft, glowing night, the air rich with the smell of the surf, the sun squeezing the last light out of the sky as it sank toward Hawaii. Jason was wearing his faded-to-pink 49ers jersey and a pair of shorts so big they made his legs look like sticks. He gave her one of his hooded looks, then got distracted and tapped at his watch twice before lifting it to his ear and frowning. "Damn thing stopped," he said. It wasn't until they were sliding into the car that he came back to the subject of Zinny Bauer. "It's simple, babe," he said, shrugging his shoulders and letting his face go slack. "She's here to psych you out."

He liked to watch her eat. She wasn't shy about it—not like the other girls he'd dated, the ones on a perpetual diet who made you feel like a two-headed hog every time you sat down to a meal, whether it was a Big Mac or the Mexican Plate at La Fondita. No "salad with dressing on the side" for Paula, no butterless bread or child's portions. She attacked her food like a lumberjack, and you'd better keep your hands and fingers clear. Tonight she started with potato gnocchi in a white sauce puddled with butter, and she ate half a loaf of crusty Italian bread with it, sopping up the leftover sauce till the plate gleamed. Next it was the fettucine with Alfredo sauce, and on her third trip to the pasta bar she heaped her plate with mostaccioli marinara and chunks of hot sausage—and more bread, always more bread.

He ordered a beer, lit a cigarette without thinking, and shovelled up some spaghetti carbonara, thick on the fork and sloppy with sauce. The next thing he knew, he was staring up into the hot green gaze of the waitperson, a pencil-necked little fag he could have snapped in two like a breadstick if this weren't California and everything so copacetic and laid back. It was times like this when he wished he lived in Cleveland, even though he'd never been there, but he knew what was coming and he figured people in Cleveland wouldn't put up with this sort of crap.

"You'll have to put that out," the little fag said.

"Sure, man," Jason said, gesturing broadly so that the smoke fanned out around him like the remains of a pissed-over fire. "Just as soon as I"—puff, puff—"take another drag and"—puff, puff—"find me an ashtray somewhere . . . you wouldn't happen"—puff, puff—"to have an ashtray, would you?"

Of course the little fag had been holding one out in front of him all along, as if it were a portable potty or something, but the cigarette was just a glowing stub now, the tiny fag end of a cigarette—fag end, how about that?—and Jason reached out, crushed the thing in the ashtray and said, "Hey, thanks, dude—even though it really wasn't a cigarette but just the *fag* end of one."

And then Paula was there, her fourth plate of the evening mounded high with angel hair, three-bean salad, and wedges of fruit in five different colors. "So what was that all about? Your cigarette?"

Jason ignored her, forking up spaghetti. He took a long swig of his beer and shrugged. "Yeah, whatever," he said finally. "One more fascist doing his job."

"Don't be like that," she said, using the heel of her bread to round up stray morsels on her plate.

"Like what?"

"You know what I mean. I don't have to lecture you."

"Yeah?" He let his eyes droop. "So what do you call this then?"

She sighed and looked away, and that sigh really irritated him, rankled him, made him feel like flipping the table over and sailing a few plates through the window. He was drunk. Or three-quarters drunk anyway. Then her lips were moving again. "Everybody in the world doesn't necessarily enjoy breathing through a tube of incinerated tobacco, you know," she said. "People are into health."

"Who? You maybe. But the rest of them just want to be a pain in the ass. They just want to abrogate my rights in a public place"—abrogate, now where did that come from?—"and then rub my nose in it." The thought soured him even more, and when he caught the waitperson pussyfooting by out of the corner of his eye he snapped his fingers with as much pure malice as he could manage. "Hey, dude, another beer here, huh? I mean, when you get a chance."

It was then that Zinny Bauer made her appearance. She stalked through the door like something crossbred in an experimental laboratory, so rangy and hollow-eyed and fleshless she looked as if she'd been pasted onto her bones. There was a guy with her— her trainer or husband or whatever—and he was right out of an X-Men cartoon, all head and shoulders and great big beefy biceps. Jason recognized them from Houston—he'd flown down to watch Paula compete in the Houston Ironman, only to see her hit the wall in the run and finish sixth in the women's while Zinny Bauer, the Amazing Bone Woman, took an easy first. And here they were, Zinny and Klaus—or Olaf or whoever—here in the Pasta Bowl, carbo-loading like anybody else. His beer came, cold and dependable, green in the bottle, pale amber in the glass, and he downed it in two gulps. "Hey, Paula," he said, and he couldn't keep the quick sharp stab of joy out of his voice—he was happy suddenly and he didn't know why. "Hey, Paula, you see who's here?"

The thing that upset her was that he'd lied to her, the way her father used to lie to her mother, the same way—casually, almost as a reflex. It wasn't his birthday at all. He'd just said that to get her out because he was drunk and he didn't care if she had to compete the day after tomorrow and needed her rest and peace and quiet and absolutely no stimulation whatever. He was selfish, that was all, selfish and unthinking. And then there was the business with the cigarette—he knew as well as anybody in the state that there was an ordinance against smoking in public places as of January last, and still he had to push the limits like some cocky immature chip-on-the-shoulder surfer. Which is exactly what he was. But all that was forgivable—it was the Zinny Bauer business she just couldn't understand.

Paula wasn't even supposed to be there. She was supposed to be at home, making up a batch of flapjacks and penne with cheese sauce and lying inert on the couch with the remote control. This was the night before the night before the event, a time to fuel up her tanks and veg out. But because of him, because of her silver-tongued hero in the baggy shorts, she was at the Pasta Bowl, carbo-loading in public. And so was Zinny Bauer, the last person on earth she wanted to see.

That was bad enough, but Jason made it worse, far worse—Jason made it into one of the most excruciating moments of her life. What happened was purely crazy, and if she hadn't known Jason better she would have thought he'd planned it. They were squabbling over his cigarette and how unlaid-back and uptight the whole thing had made him—he was drunk, and she didn't appreciate him when he was drunk, not at all—when his face suddenly took on a conspiratorial look and he said, "Hey, Paula, you see who's here?"

"Who?" she said, and she shot a glance over her shoulder and froze: it was Zinny Bauer and her husband Armin. "Oh, shit," she said, and she lowered her head and focussed on her plate as if it were the most fascinating thing she'd ever seen. "She didn't see me, did she? We've got to go. Right now. Right this minute."

Jason was smirking. He looked happy about it, as if he and Zinny Bauer were old friends. "But you've only had four plates, babe," he said. "You sure we got our money's worth? I could go for maybe just a touch more pasta—and I haven't even had any salad yet."

"No joking around, this isn't funny." Her voice withered in her throat. "I don't want to see her. I don't want to talk to her. I just want to get out of here, okay?"

His smile got wider. "Sure, babe, I know how you feel—but you're going to beat her, you are, no sweat. You don't have to let anybody chase you out of your favorite restaurant in your own town—I mean, that's not right, is it? That's not in the spirit of friendly competition."

"Jason," she said, and she reached across the table and took hold of his wrist. "I mean it. Let's get out of here. Now."

Her throat was constricted, as if everything she'd eaten was about to come up. Her legs ached, and her ankle—the one she'd sprained last spring—felt as if someone had driven a nail through it. All she could think of was Zinny Bauer, with her long muscles and the shaved blond stubble of her head and her eyes that never quit. Zinny Bauer was behind her, at her back, right there, and it was too much to bear. "*Jason,*" she hissed.

"Okay, okay," he was saying, and he tipped back the dregs of his beer and reached into his pocket and scattered a couple of rumpled bills across the table by way of a tip. Then he rose from the chair with a slow drunken grandeur and gave her a wink as if to indicate that the coast was clear. She got up, hunching her shoulders as if she could compress herself into invisibility and stared down at her feet as Jason took her arm and led her across the room—if Zinny saw her, Paula wouldn't know about it because she wasn't going to look up, and she wasn't going to make eye contact, she wasn't.

Or so she thought.

She was concentrating on her feet, on the black-and-white checked pattern of the floor tiles and how her running shoes negotiated them as if they were attached to somebody else's legs, when all of a sudden Jason stopped and her eyes flew up and there they were, hovering over Zinny Bauer's table like casual acquaintances, like neighbors on their way to a P.T.A. meeting. "But aren't you Zinny Bauer?" Jason said, his voice gone high and nasal as he shifted into his Valley Girl imitation. "The great triathlete? Oh, God, yes, yes, you are, aren't you? Oh, God, could I have your autograph for my little girl?"

Paula was made of stone. She couldn't move, couldn't speak, couldn't even blink her eyes. And Zinny—she looked as if her plane had just crashed. Jason was playing out the charade, pretending to fumble through his pockets for a pen, when Armin broke the silence. "Why don't you just fock off," he said, and the veins stood out in his neck.

"Oh, she'll be so thrilled," Jason went on, his voice pinched to a squeal. "She's so adorable, only six years old, and, oh, my God, she's not going to believe this—"

Armin rose to his feet. Zinny clutched at the edge of the table with bloodless fingers, her eyes narrow and hard. The waiter—the one Jason had been riding all night—started toward them, crying out, "Is everything all right?" as if the phrase had any meaning.

And then Jason's voice changed, just like that. "Fuck you too, Jack, and your scrawny fucking bald-headed squeeze."

Armin worked out, you could see that, and Paula doubted he'd ever pressed a cigarette to his lips, let alone a joint, but still Jason managed to hold his own—at least until the kitchen staff separated them. There was some breakage, a couple of chairs overturned, a whole lot of noise and cursing and threatening, most of it from Jason. Every face in the restaurant was drained of color by the time the kitchen staff came to the rescue, and somebody went to the phone and called the police, but Jason blustered his way out the door and disappeared before they arrived. And Paula? She just melted away and kept on melting until she found herself behind the wheel of the car, cruising slowly down the darkened streets, looking for Jason.

She never did find him.

When he called the next morning he was all sweetness and apology. He whispered, moaned, sang to her, his voice a continuous soothing current insinuating itself through the line and into her head and right on down through her veins and arteries to the unresisting core of her. "Listen, Paula, I didn't mean for things to get out of hand," he whispered, "you've got to believe me. I just didn't think you had to hide from anybody, that's all."

She listened, her mind gone numb, and let his words saturate her. It was the day before the event, and she wasn't going to let anything distract her. But then, as he went on, pouring himself into the phone with his penitential, self-pitying tones as if he were the one who'd been embarrassed and humiliated, she felt the outrage coming up in her: didn't he understand, didn't he know what it meant to stare into the face of your own defeat? And over a plate of pasta, no less? She cut him off in the middle of a long digression about some surfing legend of the fifties and all the adversity he'd had to face from a host of competitors, a blood-sucking wife and a fearsome backwash off Newport Beach.

"What did you think," she demanded, "that you were protecting me or something? Is that it? Because if that's what you think, let me tell you I don't need you or anybody else to stand up for me—"

"Paula," he said, his voice creeping out at her over the wire, "Paula, I'm on your side, remember? I love what you're doing. I want to help you." He paused. "And yes, I want to protect you too."

"I don't need it."

"Yes, you do. You don't think you do but you do. Don't you see: I was trying to psych her."

"Psych her? At the Pasta Bowl?"

His voice was soft, so soft she could barely hear him: "Yeah." And then, even softer: "I did it for you."

It was Saturday, seventy-eight degrees, sun beaming down unmolested, the tourists out in force. The shop had been buzzing since ten, nothing major—cords, tube socks, T-shirts, a couple of illustrated guides to South Coast hot spots that nobody who knew anything needed a book to find—but Jason had been at the cash register right through lunch and on into the four-thirty breathing spell when the tourist mind tended to fixate on ice-cream cones and those pathetic sidecar bikes they pedalled up and down the street like the true guppies they were. He'd even called Little Drake in to help out for a couple of hours there. Drake didn't mind. He'd grown up rich in Montecito and gone white-haired at twenty-seven, and now he lived with his even whiter-haired old parents and managed their two rental properties downtown—which meant he had nothing much to do except prop up the bar at Clubber's or haunt the shop like the thinnest ghost of a customer. So why not put him to work?

"Nothing to shout about," Jason told him, over the faint hum of the oldies channel. He leaned back against the wall on his high stool and cracked the first beer of the day. "Little stuff, but a lot of it. I almost had that one dude sold on the Al Merrick board—I could taste it—but something scared him off. Maybe mommy took away his Visa card, I don't know."

Drake pulled contemplatively at his beer and looked out the window on the parade of tourists marching up and down State Street. He didn't respond. It was that crucial hour of the day, the hour known as cocktail hour, two for one, the light stuck on the underside of the palms, everything soft and pretty and winding down toward dinner and evening, the whole night held out before them like a promise. "What time's the Dodger game?" Drake said finally.

Jason looked at his watch. It was a reflex. The Dodgers were playing the Mets at five-thirty, Astacio against the Doc, and he knew the time and channel as well as he knew his A.T.M. number. The Angels were on Prime Ticket, seven-thirty, at home against the Orioles. And Paula—Paula was at home too, focussing (do not disturb, thank you very much) for the big one with the Amazing Bone Woman the next morning. "Five-thirty," he said, after a long pause.

Drake said nothing. His beer was gone, and he shuffled behind the counter to the little reefer for another. When he'd cracked it, sipped, belched, scratched himself thoroughly, and commented on the physique of an overweight Mexican chick in a red bikini making her way up from the beach, he ventured an opinion on the topic under consideration: "Time to close up?"

All things being equal, Jason would have stayed open till six, or near six anyway, on a Saturday in August. The summer months accounted for the lion's share of his business—it was like the Christmas season for everybody else—and he tried to maximize it, he really did, but he knew what Drake was saying. Twenty to five now, and they had to count the receipts, lock up, stop by the night deposit at the B. of A., and then settle in at Clubber's for the game. It would be nice to be there, maybe with a tall tequila tonic and the sports section spread out on the bar, before the game got under way. Just to settle in and enjoy the fruits of their labor. He gave a sigh, for form's sake, and said, "Yeah, why not?"

And then there was cocktail hour and he had a couple of tall tequila tonics before switching to beer, and the Dodgers looked good, real good, red hot, and somebody bought him a shot. Drake was carrying on about something—his girlfriend's cat, the calluses on his mother's feet—and Jason tuned him out, ordered two soft chicken tacos, and watched the sun do all sorts of amazing pink and salmon things to the storefronts across the street before the gray finally settled in. He was thinking he should have gone surfing today, thinking he'd maybe go out in the morning, and then he was thinking of Paula. He should wish her luck or something, give her a phone call at least. But the more he thought about it, the more he pictured her alone in her apartment, power-drinking her fluids, sunk into the shell of her focus like some Chinese Zen master, and the more he wanted to see her.

They hadn't had sex in a week. She was always like that when it was coming down to the wire, and he didn't blame her. Or yes, yes, he did blame her. And he resented it too. What was the big deal? It wasn't like she was playing ball or anything that took any skill, and why lock him out for that? She was like his overachieving, straight-arrow parents, Type A personalities, early risers, joggers, let's go out and beat the world. God, that was anal. But she had some body on her, as firm and flawless as the Illustrated Man's—or Woman's, actually. He thought about that and about the way her face softened when they were in bed together, and he stood at the pay phone seeing her in the hazy soft-focus glow of some made-for-TV movie. Maybe he shouldn't call. Maybe he should just . . . surprise her.

She answered the door in an oversized sweatshirt and shorts, barefooted, and with the half-full pitcher from the blender in her hand. She looked surprised, all right, but not pleasantly surprised. In fact, she scowled at him and set the pitcher down on the book-case before pulling back the door and ushering him in. He didn't even get the chance to tell her he loved her or to wish her luck before she started in on him. "What are you doing here?" she demanded. "You know I can't see you tonight, of all nights. What's with you? Are you drunk? Is that it?"

What could he say? He stared at the brown gloop in the pitcher for half a beat and then gave her his best simmering droopy-eyed smile and a shrug that radiated down from his shoulders to his hips. "I just wanted to see you. To wish you luck, you know?" He stepped forward to kiss her, but she dodged away from him, snatching up the pitcher full of gloop like a shield. "A kiss for luck?" he said.

She hesitated. He could see something go in and out of her eyes, the flicker of a worry, competitive anxiety, butterflies, and then she smiled and pecked him a kiss on the lips that tasted of soy and honey and whatever else was in that concoction she drank. "Luck," she said, "but no excitement."

"And no sex," he said, trying to make a joke of it. "I know."

She laughed then, a high girlish tinkle of a laugh that broke the spell. "No sex," she said. "But I was just going to watch a movie if you want to join me—"

He found one of the beers he'd left in the refrigerator for just such an emergency as this and settled in beside her on the couch to watch the movie—some inspirational crap about a demi-cripple who wins the hurdle event in the Swedish Special Olympics—but he was hot, he couldn't help it, and his fingers kept wandering from her shoulder to her breast, from her waist to her inner thigh. At least she kissed him when she pushed him away. "Tomorrow," she promised, but it was only a promise, and they both knew it. She'd been so devastated after the Houston thing she wouldn't sleep with him for a week and a half, strung tight as a bow every time he touched her. The memory of it chewed at him, and he sipped his beer moodily. "Bullshit," he said.

"Bullshit what?"

"Bullshit you'll sleep with me tomorrow. Remember Houston? Remember Zinny Bauer?"

Her face changed suddenly and she flicked the remote angrily at the screen and the picture went blank. "I think you better go," she said.

But he didn't want to go. She was his girlfriend, wasn't she? And what good did it do him if she kicked him out every time some chickenshit race came up? Didn't he matter to her, didn't he matter at all? "I don't want to go," he said.

She stood, put her hands on her hips, and glared at him. "I have to go to bed now."

He didn't budge. Didn't move a muscle. "That's what I mean," he said, and his face was ugly, he couldn't help it. "I want to go to bed too."

Later, he felt bad about the whole thing. Worse than bad. He didn't know how it happened exactly, but there was some resentment there, he guessed, and it just snuck up on him—plus he was drunk, if that was any excuse. Which it wasn't. Anyway, he hadn't meant to get physical, and by the time she'd stopped fighting him and he got her shorts down he hadn't even really wanted to go through with it. This wasn't making love, this wasn't what he wanted. She just lay there beneath him like she was dead, like some sort of zombie, and it made him sick, so sick he couldn't even begin to apologize or excuse himself. He felt her eyes on him as he was zipping up, hard eyes, accusatory eyes, eyes like claws, and he had to stagger into the bathroom and cover himself with the noise of both taps and the toilet to keep from breaking down. He'd gone too far. He knew it. He was ashamed of himself, deeply ashamed, and there really wasn't anything left to say. He just slumped his shoulders and slouched out the door.

And now here he was, contrite and hungover, mooning around on Ledbetter Beach in the cool hush of 7:00 A.M., waiting with all the rest of the guppies for the race to start. Paula wouldn't even look at him. Her mouth was set, clamped shut, a tiny little line of nothing beneath her nose, and her eyes looked no farther than her equipment—her spidery ultra-lightweight bike with the triathlon bars and her little skullcap of a helmet and water bottles and what-not. She was wearing a two-piece swimsuit, and she'd already had her number—23—painted on her upper arms and the long bur-nished muscles of her thighs. He shook out a cigarette and stared off past her, wondering what they used for the numbers: Magic Marker? Greasepaint? Something that wouldn't come off in the surf, anyway—or with all the sweat. He remembered the way she looked in Houston, pounding through the muggy haze in a sheen of sweat, her face sunk in a mask of suffering, her legs and but-tocks taut, her breasts flattened to her chest in the grip of the clinging top. He thought about that, watching her from behind the police line as she bent to fool with her bike, not an ounce of fat on her, nothing, not even a stray hair, and he got hard just looking at her.

But that was short-lived, because he felt bad about last night and knew he'd have to really put himself through the wringer to make it up to her. Plus, just watching the rest of the four hun-dred and six fleshless masochists parade by with their Gore-Tex T-shirts and Lycra shorts and all the rest of their paraphernalia was enough to make him go cold all over. His stomach felt like a fried egg left out on the counter too long, and his hands shook when he lit the cigarette. He should be in bed, that's where he should be—enough of this seven o'clock in the morning. They were crazy, these people, purely crazy, getting up at dawn to put themselves through something like this—one mile in the water, thirty-four on the bike, and a ten-mile run to wrap it up, and this was a walk compared to the Ironman. They were all bone and long, lean muscle, like whippet dogs or something, the women in-distinguishable from the men, stringy and titless. Except for Paula. She was all right in that department, and that was genetic—she re-ferred to her breasts as her fat reserves. He was wondering if they shrank at all during the race, what with all that stress and water loss, when a woman with big hair and too much makeup asked him for a light.

She was milling around with maybe a couple hundred other

spectators—or sadists, he guessed you'd have to call them—
waiting to watch the crazies do their thing. "Thanks," she breathed,
after he'd leaned in close to touch the tip of his smoke to hers.
Her eyes were big wet pools, and she was no freak, no bone
woman. Her lips were wet too, or maybe it was his imagination.
"So," she said, the voice caught low in her throat, a real smoker's
rasp, "here for the big event?"

He just nodded.

There was a pause. They sucked at their cigarettes. A pair of
gulls flailed sharply at the air behind them and then settled down
to poke through the sand for anything that looked edible. "My
name's Sandra," she offered, but he wasn't listening, not really, because it was then that it came to him, his inspiration, his moment
of grace and redemption: suddenly he knew how he was going to
make it up to Paula. He cut his eyes away from the woman and
through the crowd to where Paula bent over her equipment, the
take-no-prisoners look ironed into her face. And what does she
want more than anything? he asked himself, his excitement so intense he almost spoke the words aloud. What would make her
happy, glad to see him, ready to party, celebrate, dance till dawn
and let bygones be bygones?

To win. That was all. To beat Zinny Bauer. And in that moment, even as Paula caught his eye and glowered at him, he had a
vision of Zinny Bauer, the Amazing Bone Woman, coming into
the final stretch with her legs and arms pumping, in command, no
problem, and the bright green cup of Gatorade held out for her by
the smiling volunteer in the official volunteer's cap and T-shirt—
yes—and Zinny Bauer refreshing herself, drinking it down in mid-
stride, running on and on until she hit the wall he was already
constructing.

Paula pulled the red bathing cap down over her ears, adjusted her
swim goggles, and strode across the beach, her heartbeat as slow
and steady as a lizard's. She was focussed, as clearheaded and certain as she'd ever been in her life. Nothing mattered now except
leaving all the hotshots and loudmouths and macho types behind

in the dust—and Zinny Bauer too. There were a couple of pros competing in the men's division and she had no illusions about beating them, but she was going to teach the rest of them a hard lesson, a lesson about toughness and endurance and will. If anything, what had happened with Jason last night was something she could use, the kind of thing that made her angry, that made her wonder what she'd seen in him in the first place. He didn't care about her. He didn't care about anybody. That was what she was thinking when the gun went off and she hit the water with the great thundering herd of them, the image of his bleary apologetic face burning into her brain—date rape, that's what they called it—and she came out of the surf just behind Zinny Bauer, Jill Eisen, and Tommy Roe, one of the men's pros.

All right. Okay. She was on her bike now, through the gate in a flash and driving down the flat wide concourse of Cabrillo Boulevard in perfect rhythm, effortless, as if the blood were flowing through her legs and into the bike itself. Before she'd gone half a mile she knew she was going to catch Zinny Bauer and pass her to ride with the men's leaders and get off first on the run. It was preordained, she could feel it, feel it pounding in her temples and in the perfect engine of her heart. The anger had settled in her legs now, a bitter, hot-burning fuel. She fed on the air, tucked herself into the handlebars, and flew. If all this time she'd raced for herself, for something uncontainable inside her, now she was racing for Jason, to show him up, to show him what she was, what she really was. There was no excuse for him. None. And she was going to win this event, she was going to beat Zinny Bauer and all those hundreds of soft, winded, undertrained, crowing, chest-thumping jocks too, and she was going to accept her trophy and stride right by him as if he didn't exist, because she wasn't soft, she wasn't, and he was going to find that out once and for all.

By the time he got back to the beach Jason thought he'd run some sort of race himself. He was breathing hard—got to quit smoking—and his tequila headache was heating up to the point where he was seriously considering ducking into Clubber's and slamming a shot or two, though it was only half past nine and all the tourists would be there buttering their French toast and would you pass the syrup please and thank you very much. He'd had to go all the way out to Drake's place and shake him awake to get the Tuinal—one of Drake's mother's six thousand and one prescriptions to fight off the withering aches of her seventy-odd years. Tuinal, Nembutal, Dalmane, Darvocet: Jason didn't care, just so long as there was enough of it. He didn't do barbiturates anymore—probably hadn't swallowed a Tooey in ten years—but he remembered the sweet numb glow they gave him and the way they made his legs feel like tree trunks planted deep in the ground.

The sun had burned off the fog by now, and the day was clear and glittering on the water. They'd started the race at seven-thirty, so that gave him a while yet—the first men would be crossing the finish line in just under three hours, and the women would be coming in at three-ten, three-twelve, something like that. All he needed to do now was finesse himself into the inner sanctum, pick up a stray T-shirt and cap, find the Gatorade and plant himself about two miles from the finish. Of course there was a chance the Amazing Bone Woman wouldn't take the cup from him, especially if she recognized him from the other night, but he was going to pull his cap down low and hide behind his Ray-Bans and show her a face of devotion. One second, that's all it would take. A hand coming out of the crowd, the cup beaded with moisture and moving right along beside her so she didn't even have to break stride—and what was there to think about? She drinks and hits the wall. And if she didn't go for it the first time, he'd hop in the car and catch her a mile farther on.

He'd been watching one of the security volunteers stationed outside the trailer that served as a command center. A kid of eighteen maybe, greasy hair, an oversized cross dangling from one ear, a scurf of residual acne. He was a carbon copy of the kids he sold wetsuits and Killer Beeswax to—maybe he was even one of them. Jason reminded himself to tread carefully. He was a businessman, after all, one of the pillars of the downtown community, and somebody might recognize him. But then so what if they did? He was volunteering his time, that was all, a committed citizen doing his civic best to promote tourism and everything else that was right in the world. He ducked under the rope. "Hey, bro," he said to the kid, extending his hand for the high five—which the kid gave him. "Sorry I'm late..Jeff around?"

The kid's face opened up in a big beaming half-witted grin. "Yeah, sure—I think he went up the beach a ways with Everardo and Linda and some of the press people, but I could maybe look if you want—"

Jeff. It was a safe bet—no crowd of that size, especially one consisting of whippets, bone people and guppies, would be without a Jeff. Jason gave the kid a shrug. "Nah, that's all right. But hey, where's the T-shirts and caps at?"

Then he was in his car, and forget the D.U.I., the big green waxed cup cold between his legs, breaking Tuinal caps and looking for a parking space along the course. He pulled in under a huge Monterey pine that was like its own little city and finished doctoring the Gatorade, stirring the stuff in with his index fingers. What would it take to make her legs go numb and wind up a Did Not Finish without arousing suspicion? Two? Three? He didn't want her to pass out on the spot or take a dive into the bushes or anything, and he didn't want to hurt her, either, not really. But four—four was a nice round number, and that ought to do it. He sucked the finger he'd used as a swizzle stick to see if he could detect the taste, but he couldn't. He took a tentative sip. Nothing. Gatorade tasted like such shit anyway, who could tell the difference?

He found a knot of volunteers in their canary-yellow T-shirts and caps and stationed himself a hundred yards up the street from them, the ice rattling as he swirled his little green time bomb around the lip of the cup. The breeze was soft, the sun caught in the crowns of the trees and reaching out to finger the road here and there in long, slim swatches. He'd never tell Paula, of course, no way, but he'd get giddy with her, pop the champagne cork, and let her fill him with all the ecstasy of victory.

A cheer from the crowd brought him out of his reverie. The

first of the men was cranking his way round the long bend in the road, a guy with a beard and wraparound sunglasses—the Finn. He was the one favored to win, or was it the Brit? Jason tucked the cup behind his back and faded into the crowd, which was pretty sparse here, and watched the guy propel himself past, his mouth gaping black, the two holes of his nostrils punched deep into his face, his head bobbing on his neck as if it wasn't attached right. Another guy appeared round the corner just as the Finn passed by, and then two others came slogging along behind him. Somebody cheered, but it was a pretty feeble affair.

Jason checked his watch. It would be five minutes or so, and then he could start watching for the Amazing Bone Woman, tireless freak that she was. And did she fuck Klaus, or Olaf, or whoever he was, the night before the big event, or was she like Paula, all focus and negativity and no, no, no? He fingered the cup lightly, reminding himself not to damage or crease it in any way— it had to look pristine, fresh-dipped from the bucket—and he watched the corner at the end of the street till his eyes began to blur from the sheer concentration of it all.

Two more men passed by, and nobody cheered, not a murmur, but then suddenly a couple of middle-aged women across the street set up a howl, and the crowd chimed in: the first woman, a woman of string and bone with a puffing heaving puppetlike frame, was swinging into the street in distant silhouette. Jason moved forward. He tugged reflexively at the bill of his hat, jammed the rims of the shades back into his eyesockets. And he started to grin, all his teeth on fire, his lips spread wide: Here, take me, drink me, have me!

As the woman closed, loping, sweating, elbows flailing and knees pounding, the crowd getting into it now, cheering her, cheering this first of the women in a man's event, the first Ironwoman of the day, he began to realize that this wasn't Zinny Bauer at all. Her hair was too long, and her legs and chest were too full—and then he saw the number clearly, No. 23, and looked into Paula's face. She was fifty yards from him, but he could see the toughness in her eyes and the tight little frozen smile of triumph and superiority. She was winning. She was beating Zinny Bauer and Jill Eisen and all those pathetic jocks laboring up the hills and down the blacktop streets behind her. This was her moment, this was it.

But then, and he didn't stop to think about it, he stepped forward, right out on the street where she could see him, and held out the cup. He heard her feet beating at the pavement with a hard merciless slap, saw the icy twist of a smile and the cold, triumphant eyes. And he felt the briefest fleeting touch of her flesh as the cup left his hand.

KILLING BABIES

When I got out of rehab for the second time, there were some legal complications, and the judge—an old jerk who looked like they'd just kicked him out of the Politburo—decided I needed a sponsor. There was a problem with some checks I'd been writing for a while there when all my resources were going up the glass tube, and since I didn't have a record except for traffic infractions and a juvenile possession when I was fifteen, the court felt inclined to mercy. Was there anybody who could speak up for me, my attorney wondered, anybody financially responsible? Philip, I said, my brother Philip. He's a doctor.

So Philip. He lived in Detroit, a place I'd never been to, a place where it gets cold in winter and the only palm trees are under glass in the botanical gardens. It would be a change, a real change. But a change is what I needed, and the judge liked the idea that he wouldn't have to see me in Pasadena anymore and that I'd have a room in Philip's house with Philip's wife and my nephews, Josh and Jeff, and that I would be gainfully employed doing lab work at Philip's obstetrical clinic for the princely sum of six dollars and twenty-five cents an hour.

So Philip. He met me at the airport, his thirty-eight-year-old face as trenched with anal-retentive misery as our father's was in the year before he died. His hair was going, I saw that right away, and his glasses were too big for his head. And his shoes—he was wearing a pair of brown suede boatlike things that would have had people running for the exits at the Rainbow Club. I hadn't seen him in six years, not since the funeral, that is, and I wouldn't have even recognized him if it wasn't for his eyes—they were just like mine, as blue and icy as a bottle of Aqua Velva. "Little brother," he said, and he tried to gather a smile around the thin flaps of his lips while he stood there gaping at me like somebody who hadn't come to the airport specifically to fetch his down-on-his-luck brother and was bewildered to discover him there.

"Philip," I said, and I set down my two carry-on bags to pull him to me in a full-body, back-thumping, chest-to-chest embrace, as if I was glad to see him. But I wasn't glad to see him. Not particularly. Philip was ten years older than me, and ten years is a lot when you're a kid. By the time I knew his name he was in college, and when I was expressing myself with my father's vintage Mustang, a Ziploc baggie of marijuana, and a can of high-gloss spray paint, he was in medical school. I'd never much liked him, and he felt about the same toward me, and as I embraced him there in the Detroit airport I wondered how that was going to play out over the course of the six months the judge had given me to stay out of trouble and make full restitution or serve the next six in jail.

"Have a good flight?" Philip asked when I was done embracing him.

I stood back from him a moment, the bags at my feet, and couldn't help being honest with him; that's just the way I am. "You look like shit, Philip," I said. "You look like Dad just before he died—or maybe after he died."

A woman with a big shining planetoid of a face stopped to give me a look, then hitched up her skirt and stamped on by in her heels. The carpeting smelled of chemicals. Outside the dirt-splotched windows was snow, a substance I'd had precious little experience of. "Don't start, Rick," Philip said. "I'm in no mood. Believe me."

I shouldered my bags, stooped over a cigarette, and lit it just to irritate him. I was hoping he'd tell me there was a county ordinance against smoking in public places and that smoking was slow suicide, from a physician's point of view, but he didn't rise to the bait. He just stood there, looking harassed. "I'm not starting," I said. "I'm just . . . I don't know. I'm just concerned, that's all. I mean, you look like shit. I'm your brother. Shouldn't I be concerned?"

I thought he was going to start wondering aloud why *I* should be concerned about *him*, since I was the one on the run from an exasperated judicial system and twelve thousand and some-odd dollars in outstanding checks, but he surprised me. He just shrugged and shifted that lipless smile around a bit and said, "Maybe I've been working too hard."

Philip lived on Washtenaw Street, in an upscale housing development called Washtenaw Acres, big houses set back from the street and clustered around a lake glistening with black ice under a weak sky and weaker sun. The trees were stripped and ugly, like dead sticks rammed into the ground, and the snow wasn't what I'd expected. Somehow I'd thought it would be fluffy and soft, movie snow, big pillows of it cushioning the ground while kids whooshed through it on their sleds, but it wasn't like that at all. It lay on the ground like a scab, clots of dirt and yellow weed showing through in mangy patches. Bleak, that's what it was, but I told myself it was better than the Honor Rancho, a whole lot better, and as we pulled into the long sweeping driveway to Philip's house I put everything I had into feeling optimistic.

Denise had put on weight. She was waiting for us inside the door that led from the three-car garage into the kitchen. I didn't know her well enough to embrace her the way I'd embraced Philip, and I have to admit I was taken aback by the change in her—she was fat, there was nothing else to say about it—so I just filtered out the squeals of welcome and shook her hand as if it was something I'd found in the street. Besides which, the smell of dinner hit me square in the face, so overpowering it almost brought me to my knees. I hadn't been in a real kitchen with a real dinner in the oven since I was a kid and my mother was alive, because after she died, and with Philip away, it was just my father and me, and we tended to go out a lot, especially on Sundays.

"You hungry?" Denise asked while we did an awkward little

dance around the gleaming island of stainless steel and tile in the middle of the kitchen. "I'll bet you're starved," she said, "after all that bachelor cooking and the airplane food. And look at you—you're shivering. He's shivering, Philip."

I was, and no denying it.

"You can't run around in a T-shirt and leather jacket and expect to survive a Michigan winter—it might be all right for L.A. maybe, but not here." She turned to Philip, who'd been standing there as if someone had crept up on him and nailed his shoes to the floor. "Philip, haven't you got a parka for Rick? How about that blue one with the red lining you never wear anymore? And a pair of gloves, for God's sake. Get him a pair of gloves, will you?" She came back to me then, all smiles: "We can't have our California boy getting frostbite now, can we?"

Philip agreed that we couldn't, and we all stood there smiling at one another till I said, "Isn't anybody going to offer me a drink?"

Then it was my nephews—red-faced howling babies in dirty yellow diapers the last time I'd seen them, at the funeral that had left me an orphan at twenty-three, little fists glomming onto the cold cuts while drool descended toward the dip—but here they were, eight and six, edging up to me in high-tops and oversized sweatshirts while I threw back my brother's scotch. "Hey," I said, grinning till I thought my head would burst, "remember me? I'm your Uncle Rick."

They didn't remember me—how could they?—but they brightened at the sight of the two yellow bags of M&M's peanut candies I'd thought to pick up at the airport newsstand. Josh, the eight-year-old, took the candy gingerly from my hand, while his brother looked on to see if I was going to sprout fangs and start puking up black vomit. We were all sitting around the living room, very clean, very *Home & Garden*, getting acquainted. Philip and Denise held on to their drinks as if they were afraid somebody was going to steal them. We were all grinning. "What's that on your eyebrow?" Josh said.

I reached up and fingered the thin gold loop. "It's a ring," I said. "You know, like an earring, only it's in my eyebrow."

No one said anything for a long moment. Jeff, the younger one, looked as if he was going to start crying. "Why?" Josh said finally, and Philip laughed and I couldn't help myself—I laughed too. It was all right. Everything was all right. Philip was my brother and Denise was my sister-in-law and these kids with their wide-open faces and miniature Guess jeans were my nephews. I shrugged, laughing still. "Because it's cool," I said, and I didn't even mind the look Philip gave me.

Later, after I'd actually crawled into the top bunk and read the kids a Dr. Seuss story that set off all sorts of bells in my head, Philip and Denise and I discussed my future over coffee and home-made cinnamon rolls. My immediate future, that is—as in tomorrow morning, 8 A.M., at the clinic. I was going to be an entry-level drudge despite my three years of college, my musical background and family connections, rinsing out test tubes and sweeping the floors and disposing of whatever was left in the stainless-steel trays when my brother and his colleagues finished with their "procedures."

"All right," I said. "Fine. I've got no problem with that."

Denise had tucked her legs up under her on the couch. She was wearing a striped caftan that could have sheltered armies. "Philip had a black man on full time, just till a week ago, nicest man you'd ever want to meet—and bright too, very bright—but he, uh, didn't feel . . ."

Philip's voice came out of the shadows at the end of the couch, picking up where she'd left off. "He went on to something better," he said, regarding me steadily through the clear walls of his glasses. "I'm afraid the work isn't all that mentally demanding—or stimulating, for that matter—but, you know, little brother, it's a start, and, well—"

"Yeah, I know," I said, "beggars can't be choosers." I wanted to add to that, to maybe soften it a bit—I didn't want him to get the idea I wasn't grateful, because I was—but I never got the opportunity. Just then the phone rang. I looked up at the sound—it wasn't a ring exactly, more like a bleat, *eh-eh-eh-eh-eh*—and saw that my brother and his wife were staring into each other's eyes in shock, as if a bomb had just gone off. Nobody moved. I counted two more rings before Denise said, "I wonder who that could be at this hour?" and Philip, my brother with the receding hairline and the too-big glasses and his own eponymous clinic in suburban Detroit, said, "Forget it, ignore it, it's nobody."

And that was strange, because we sat there in silence and listened to that phone ring over and over—twenty times, twenty times at least—until whoever it was on the other end finally gave up. Another minute ticked by, the silence howling in our ears, and then Philip stood, looked at his watch, and said, "What do you think—time to turn in?"

I wasn't stupid, not particularly—no stupider than anybody else, anyway—and I was no criminal, either. I'd just drifted into a kind of thick sludge of hopelessness after I dropped out of school for a band I put my whole being into, a band that disintegrated within the year, and one thing led to another. Jobs came and went. I spent a lot of time on the couch, channel-surfing and thumbing through books that used to mean something to me. I found women and lost them. And I learned that a line up your nose is a dilettante's thing, wasteful and extravagant. I started smoking, two or three nights a week, and then it was five or six nights a week, and then it was every day, all day, and why not? That was how I felt. Sure. And now I was in Michigan, starting over.

Anyway, it wouldn't have taken a genius to understand why my brother and his wife had let that phone ring—not after Philip and I swung into the parking lot behind the clinic at seven forty-five the next morning. I wasn't even awake, really—it was four forty-five West Coast time, an hour that gave me a headache even to imagine, much less live through. Beyond the misted-up windows, everything was gloom, a kind of frozen fog hanging in air the color of lemon ice. The trees, I saw, hadn't sprouted leaves overnight. Every curb was a repository of frozen trash.

Philip and I had been making small talk on the way into town, very small talk, out of consideration for the way I was feeling. Denise had given me coffee, which was about all I could take at that hour, but Philip had gobbled a big bowl of bran flakes and sunflower seeds with skim milk, and the boys, shy around me all over again, spooned up Lucky Charms and Frosted Flakes in silence. I came out of my daze the minute the tires hit the concrete apron separating the private property of the lot from the public space of the street: there were people there, a whole shadowy mass of shoulders and hats and steaming faces that converged on us with a shout. At first I didn't know what was going on—I thought I was trapped in a bad movie, *Night of the Living Dead* or *Zombies on Parade*. The faces were barking at us, teeth bared, eyes sunk back in their heads, hot breath boiling from their throats. "Murderers!" they were shouting. "Nazis!" "Baby-killers!"

We inched our way across the sidewalk and into the lot, working through the mass of them as if we were on a narrow lane in a dense forest, and Philip gave me a look that explained it all, from the lines in his face to Denise's fat to the phone that rang in the middle of the night no matter how many times he changed the number. This was war. I climbed out of the car with my heart hammering, and as the cold knife of the air cut into me I looked back to where they stood clustered at the gate, lumpish and solid, people you'd see anywhere. They were singing now. Some hymn, some self-righteous churchy Jesus-thumping hymn that bludgeoned the traffic noise and the deep-frozen air with the force of a weapon. I didn't have time to sort it out, but I could feel the slow burn of anger and humiliation coming up in me. Philip's hand was on my arm. "Come on," he said. "We've got work to do, little brother."

That day, the first day, was a real trial. Yes, I was turning over a new leaf, and yes, I was determined to succeed and thankful to my brother and the judge and the great giving, forgiving society I belonged to, but this was more than I'd bargained for. I had no illusions about the job—I knew it would be dull and diminishing, and I knew life with Philip and Denise would be one long snooze—but I wasn't used to being called a baby-killer. Liar, thief, crackhead— those were names I'd answered to at one time or another. Murderer was something else.

My brother wouldn't talk about it. He was busy. Wired. Hurtling around the clinic like a gymnast on the parallel bars. By nine I'd met his two associates (another doctor and a counsellor, both female, both unattractive); his receptionist; Nurses Tsing and Hempfield; and Fred. Fred was a big rabbity-looking guy in his early thirties with a pale reddish mustache and hair of the same color climbing up out of his head in all directions. He had the official title of "technician," though the most technical things I saw him do were drawing blood and divining urine for signs of pregnancy, clap, or worse. None of them—not my brother, the nurses, the counsellor, or even Fred—wanted to discuss what was going on at the far end of the parking lot and on the sidewalk out front. The zombies with the signs—yes, signs, I could see them out the window, ABORTION KILLS and SAVE THE PREBORNS and I WILL ADOPT YOUR BABY—were of no more concern to them than mosquitoes in June or a sniffle in December. Or at least that was how they acted.

I tried to draw Fred out on the subject as we sat together at lunch in the back room. We were surrounded by shadowy things in jars of formalin, gleaming stainless-steel sinks, racks of test tubes, reference books, cardboard boxes full of drug samples and syringes and gauze pads and all the rest of the clinic's paraphernalia. "So what do you think of all this, Fred?" I said, gesturing toward the window with the ham-and-Swiss on rye Denise had made me in the dark hours of the morning.

Fred was hunched over a newspaper, doing the acrostic puzzle and sucking on his teeth. His lunch consisted of a microwave chili-and-cheese burrito and a quart of root beer. He gave me a quizzical look.

"The protesters, I mean. The Jesus-thumpers out there. Is it like this all the time?" And then I added a little joke, so he wouldn't think I was intimidated: "Or did I just get lucky?"

"Who, them?" Fred did something with his nose and his upper teeth, something rabbity, as if he were tasting the air. "They're nobody. They're nothing."

"Yeah?" I said, hoping for more, hoping for some details, some explanation, something to assuage the creeping sense of guilt and shame that had been building in me all morning. Those people had pigeonholed me before I'd even set foot in the door, and that hurt. They were wrong. I was no baby-killer—I was just the little brother of a big brother, trying to make a new start. And Philip was no baby-killer, either—he was a guy doing his job, that was all. Shit, somebody had to do it. Up to this point I guess I'd never really given the issue much thought—my girlfriends, when there were girlfriends, had taken care of the preventative end of things on their own, and we never really discussed it—but my feeling was that there were too many babies in the world already, too many adults, too many suet-faced Jesus-thumping jerks ready to point the finger, and didn't any of these people have better things to do? Like a job, for instance? But Fred wasn't much help. He just sighed, nibbled at the wilted stem of his burrito, and said, "You get used to it."

I wondered about that as the afternoon crept by, and then my mind went numb from jet lag and the general wash of misery and I let my body take over. I scrubbed out empty jars and test tubes with Clorox, labelled and filed the full ones on the racks that lined the walls, stood at Fred's elbow and watched as he squeezed drops of urine onto strips of litmus paper and made notations in a ledger. My white lab coat got progressively dirtier. Every once in a while I'd come to and catch a glimpse of myself in the mirror over the sinks, the mad scientist exposed, the baby-killer, the rinser of test tubes and secreter of urine, and have an ironic little laugh at my own expense. And then it started to get dark, Fred vanished, and I was introduced to mop and squeegee. It was around then, when I just happened to be taking a cigarette break by the only window in the room, that I caught a glimpse of one of our last tardy patients of the day hurrying up the sidewalk elbow to elbow with a grim middle-aged woman whose face screamed *I am her mother!*

The girl was sixteen, seventeen maybe, a pale face, pale as a bulb, and nothing showing on her, at least not with the big white doughboy parka she was wearing. She looked scared, her little mouth clamped tight, her eyes fixed on her feet. She was wearing black leggings that seemed to sprout from the folds of the parka and a pair of furry white ankle boots that were like house slippers. I watched her glide through the dead world on the flowing stalks of her legs, a spoiled pouty chalk-cheeked sweetness to her face, and it moved something in me, something long buried beneath a mountain of grainy little yellow-white rocks. Maybe she was just coming in for an examination, I thought, maybe that was it. Or she'd just become sexually active—or was thinking of it—and her mother was one step ahead of her. Either way, that was what I wanted to believe. With this girl, with her quick fluid step and downcast eyes and all the hope and misery they implied, I didn't want to think of "procedures."

They'd almost reached the building when the zombies began to stir. From where I was standing I couldn't see the front of the building, and the Jesus-thumpers had already begun to fade out of my consciousness, dim as it was. But they came crashing back into the picture now, right there at the corner of the building, shoulders and heads and placards, and one in particular. A shadow that separated itself from the mass and was instantly transformed into a hulking bearded zealot with snapping teeth and eyes like hardboiled eggs. He came right up to the girl and her mother, rushing at them like a torpedo, and you could see how they shied away from him and how his head raged back on his shoulders, and then they ducked past the corner of the building and out of my line of sight.

I was stunned. This wasn't right, I was thinking, and I didn't want to get angry or depressed or emotional—keep on an even keel, that's what they tell you in rehab—but I couldn't help snuffing the cigarette and stepping quietly out into the hallway that ran the length of the building and gave me an unobstructed view of the front door. I moved forward almost against my will, my feet like toy cars on a track, and I hadn't got halfway down the hall before the door opened on the dwindling day and the dead sticks of the trees, and suddenly there she was, pale in a pale coat and her face two shades paler. We exchanged a look. I don't know what she saw in my eyes—weakness, hunger, fear—but I know what I saw in hers, and it was so poignant and so everlastingly sad I knew I'd never have another moment's rest till I took hold of it.

In the car on the way home Philip was so relaxed I wondered if he wasn't prescribing something for himself. Here was the antithesis of the ice man who'd picked me up at the airport, watched me eat pork chops, read to his children, and brush my teeth in the guest bathroom, and then thrown me to the wolves at the clinic. "Sorry about all that commotion this morning," he said, glancing at me in the glowing cubicle of the car. "I would have warned you, but you can never tell when they're going to pull something like that."

"So it gets better, is that what you're saying?"

"Not much," he said. "There's always a couple of them out there, the real hard-core nuts. But the whole crew of the walking dead like you saw today, that's maybe only once a week. Unless they go on one of their campaigns, and I can't figure out what provokes them—the weather, the tides in the lake, the phases of the moon—but then they go all out, theater in the street, schoolchildren, the works. They throw themselves under the wheels, handcuff themselves to the front door—it's a real zoo."

"But what about the cops? Can't you get a restraining order or something?"

He shrugged, fiddled with the tape player—opera, he was listening to opera, a thin screech of it in the night—and turned to me again, his gloved hands rigid on the wheel. "The cops are a bunch of pro-lifers, and they have no objection to those people out there harassing my patients and abridging their civil rights, and even the women just coming in for an exam have to walk the gauntlet. It's hell on business, believe me. And it's dangerous too. They scare me, the real crazies, the ones that shoot people. You've heard of John Britton? David Gunn? George Tiller?"

"I don't know," I said. "Maybe. You've got to realize I've been out of touch for a while."

"Shot down by people like the ones you saw out there today. Two of them died."

I didn't like hearing that. The thought of one of those nutballs attacking my brother, attacking me, was like throwing gasoline on a bed of hot coals. I'd never been one to turn the other cheek, and I didn't feature martyrdom, not at all. I looked out on a blur of brake lights and the crust of ice that seemed to narrow the road into a funnel ahead of us. "Why don't you shoot them first?" I said.

My brother's voice was hard. "Sometimes I wish I could."

We stopped to pick up a few things at the market, and then we were home, dinner stabbing at my salivary glands, the whole house warm and sugary with it, and Philip sat down to watch the news and have a scotch with me. Denise was right there at the door when we came in—and now we embraced, no problem, sister- and brother-in-law, one big happy family. She wanted to know how my day was, and before I could open my mouth, she was answering for me: "Not much of a challenge, huh? Pretty dull, right? Except for the crazies—they never fail to liven things up, do they? What Philip goes through, huh, Philip? Philip?"

I was beat, but the scotch smoked through my veins, the kids came and sat beside me on the couch with their comics and coloring books, and I felt good, felt like part of the family and no complaints. Denise served a beef brisket with oven-roasted potatoes, carrots, and onions, a fresh green salad, and coconut creme pie for dessert. I was planning on turning in early, but I drifted into the boys' room and took over the *Winnie-the-Pooh* chores from my brother because it was something I wanted to do. Later, it must have been about ten, I was stretched out on my own bed—and again I had to hand it to Denise, because the room was homey and private, done up with little knickknacks and embroidery work and whatnot—when my brother poked his head in the door. "So," he said, mellow with the scotch and whatever else, "you feeling okay about everything?"

That touched me. It did. Here I'd come into the airport with a chip on my shoulder—I'd always been jealous of Philip, the great shining success my father measured me against—thinking my big brother was going to be an asshole and that assholery would rule the day, but it wasn't like that at all. He was reaching out. He was a doctor. He knew about human foibles and addictions and he knew about his little brother, and he cared, he actually cared. "Yeah," was all I could manage, but I hoped the quality of my voice conveyed a whole lot more than that.

"Good," he said, framed in the light from the hallway, his sunken orbits and rucked face and flat, shining eyes giving him a look of wisdom and calm that reminded me of our father on his good days.

"That girl," I said, inspired by the intimacy of the moment, "the last one that came in today?"

His expression changed. Now it was quizzical, distant, as if he were looking at me through the wrong end of a telescope. "What girl? What are you talking about?"

"The young-looking one in the white parka and furry boots? The last one. The last one in. I was just wondering if, uh, I mean, what her problem was—if she was, you know, coming in for a procedure or whatever. . . ."

"Listen, Rick," he said then, and his voice was back in the deep freeze, "I'm willing to give you a chance here, not only for Dad's sake but for your own sake too. But there's one thing I ask—stay away from the patients. And I'm not really asking."

It was raining the next morning, a cold rain that congealed on the hood of the car and made a cold pudding of the sidewalk out front of the house. I wondered if the weather would discourage the Jesus-thumpers, but they were there, all right, in yellow rain slickers and green gum boots, sunk into their suffering with gratitude. Nobody rushed the car when we turned into the lot. They just stood there, eight of them, five men and three women, and looked hate at us. As we got out of the car, the frozen rain pelting us, I locked eyes across the lot with the bearded jerk who'd gone after the girl in the white parka. I waited till I was good and certain I had his attention, waited till he was about to shout out some hoarse Jesus-thumping accusation, and then I gave him the finger.

We were the first ones at the clinic, what with the icy roads, and as soon as my brother disappeared into the sanctum of his office I went straight to the receptionist's desk and flipped back the page of the appointment book. The last entry, under four-thirty the previous day, was staring me in the face, neat block letters in blue metalpoint: "Sally Strunt," it read, and there was a phone number jotted beneath the name. It took me exactly ten seconds, and then I was in the back room, innocently slipping into my lab coat. Sally Strunt, I whispered to myself, Sally Strunt, over and over. I'd never known anyone named Sally—it was an old-fashioned name, a hokey name, Dick and Jane and Sally, and because it was old-fashioned and because it was hokey it seemed perfect for a teenager in trouble in the grim sleety washed-out navel of the Midwest. This was no downtown Amber, no Crystal or Shanna—this was Detroit Sally, and that really appealed to me. I'd seen the face attached to the name, and the mother of that face. *Sally, Sally, Sally.* Her name sang through my head as I schmoozed with Fred and the nurses and went through the motions of the job that already felt as circumscribed and deadening as a prison sentence.

That night, after dinner, I excused myself and strolled six cold wintry blocks to the convenience store. I bought M&M's for the boys, some white chocolate for Denise, and a liter of Black Cat malt liquor for myself. Then I dialled Sally's number from the phone booth out front of the store.

A man answered, impatient, harassed. "Yeah?"

"Sally there?" I said.

"Who's this?"

I took a stab at it: "Chris Ryan. From school?"

Static. Televised dialogue. The roar of Sally's name and the sound of approaching feet and Sally's approaching voice: "Who is it?" And then, into the receiver: "Hello?"

"Sally?" I said.

"Yes?" There was hope in that voice, eagerness. She wanted to hear from me—or from whoever. This wasn't the voice of a girl concealing things. It was open, frank, friendly. I felt expansive suddenly, connected, felt as if everything was going to be all right, not only for me but for Sally too.

"You don't know me," I said quickly, "but I really admire you. I mean, your courage. I admire what you're doing."

"Who is this?"

"Chris," I said. "Chris Ryan. I saw you yesterday, at the clinic, and I really admire you, but I just wanted to know if, uh, if you need anything."

Her voice narrowed, thin as wire. "What are you talking about?"

"Sally," I said, and I didn't know what I was doing or what I was feeling, but I couldn't help myself, "Sally, can I ask you something? Are you pregnant, or are you—?"

Click. She hung up on me. Just like that.

I was frozen through by the time I got back with the kids' M&M's and Denise's white chocolate, and I'd finished off the beer on the way and flung the empty bottle up under a squat artificial-looking spruce on the neighbor's lawn. I'd tried Sally twice more, after an interval of fifteen or twenty minutes, but her father answered the first time and when I dialled again the phone just rang and kept on ringing.

A week went by. I scrubbed out test tubes and jars that smelled powerfully of the urine of strange women and learned that Fred didn't much care for Afro-Americans, Mexicans, Haitians, Cubans, Poles, or Hmong tribesmen. I tried Sally's number three more times and each time I was rebuffed—threatened, actually—and I began to realize I was maybe just a bit out of line. Sally didn't need me—she had her father and mother and maybe a gangling big-footed slam-dunking brother into the bargain—and every time I glanced through the blinds in the back room I saw another girl just like her. Still, I was feeling itchy and out of sorts despite all Denise and Philip and my nephews were doing for me, and I needed some sort of focus, a plan, something to make me feel good about myself. They'd warned us about this in rehab, and I knew this was the trickiest stage, the time when the backsliders start looking up their old friends and hanging out on the street corner. But I didn't have any old friends, not in Detroit, anyway, and the street corner was about as inviting as the polar ice cap. On Saturday night I went out to a bar that looked as if it had been preserved under Plexiglas in a museum somewhere, and I came on to a couple of girls and drank too much and woke up the next morning with a headache.

Then it was Monday and I was sitting at the breakfast table with my brother and my two nephews and it was raining again. Sleeting, actually. I wanted to go back to bed. I toyed with the idea of telling Philip I was sick, but he'd probably insist on inserting the rectal thermometer himself. He sat across from me, expressionless, crunching away at his bran flakes and sunflower seeds, the newspaper spread out before him. Denise bustled around the kitchen, brewing coffee and shoving things into the microwave while the boys and I smeared Eggo waffles with butter and syrup. "So," I said, addressing my nephews over the pitcher of pure Grade A maple syrup, "you know why the California kids have it all over the Midwestern kids when it comes to baseball?"

Josh looked up from his waffles; Jeff was still on dreamtime.

"Because of this," I said, gesturing toward the dark windows and the drooling panes. "In L.A. now it's probably seventy degrees, and when the kids wake up they can go straight out and play ball."

"After school," Josh corrected.

"Yeah," I said. "Whatever. But that's the reason your California and Arizona players dominate the big leagues."

"The Tigers suck," Josh said, and his brother glanced up to add his two cents. "They *really* suck," he said.

It was then that I became aware of the background noise, a thin droning mewl from beyond the windows as if someone were drowning kittens in the street. Philip heard it then too, and the boys and Denise, and in the next moment we were all at the window. "Oh, shit," Philip hissed. "Not again. Not today, of all days."

"What?" I said. "What is it?" And then I saw, while my nephews melted away and Denise gritted her teeth and my brother swore: the zombies were out there at the edge of the lawn, a hundred of them at least. They were singing, locked arm in arm and swaying to the beat, stretched across the mouth of the driveway in a human chain.

Philip's face was drawn tight. He told Denise to call the police, and then he turned to me. "Now you're going to see something, little brother," he said. "Now you're going to see why I keep asking myself if I shouldn't just close down the clinic and let the lunatics take over the asylum."

The kitchen was gray, a weak, played-out light pasted on every surface. Sleet rattled the windows and the conjoined voices mewled away in praise of mercy and forgiveness. I was about to ask him why he didn't do just that—close up and move someplace friendlier, someplace like California, for instance—but I already knew the answer. They could harass all the chalk-faced Sallys and thump all the Bibles they wanted, but my brother wasn't going to bow down to them—and neither was I. I knew whose team I was on, and I knew what I had to do.

It took the police half an hour to show up. There were three squad cars and a bus with wire mesh over the windows, and the cops knew the routine. They'd been here before—how many times you could guess from the deadness in their eyes—and they'd arrested these very people, knew them by name. Philip and I waited in the house, watching the *Today* show at an uncomfortable volume, and the boys stayed in their room, already late for school. Finally, at quarter past eight, Philip and I shuffled out to the garage and climbed into the car. Philip's face was like an old paper sack with eyes poked in it. I watched him hit the remote for the garage door and watched the door lift slowly on the scene.

There they were, right there on the street, the whole bug-eyed crew from the clinic, and ninety more. I saw squat, brooding mothers with babies, kids who should have been in school, old people who should have known better. They jerked their signs up and down and let out with a howl when the door cranked open, and though the cops had cleared them from the mouth of the drive they surged in now to fill the gap, the big Jesus-thumper with the beard right in front. The cops couldn't hold them back, and before we'd got halfway down the drive they were all over us, pounding on the windows and throwing themselves down in the path of the car. My brother, like a jerk, like the holy fool who automatically turns the other cheek, stepped on the brake.

"Run them over," I said, and all my breath was gone. "Run the fuckers over."

Philip just sat there, hanging his head in frustration. The cops peeled them away, one by one, zipped on the plastic cuffs and hauled them off, but for every one they lifted out of the way another dove in to take his place. We couldn't go forward, we couldn't back up. "Your neighbor kills babies!" they were shouting. "Dr. Beaudry is a murderer!" "Kill the butchers, not the babies!" I tried to stay calm, tried to think about rehab and jail and the larger problems of my life, but I couldn't. I couldn't take this. I couldn't.

Before I knew what I was doing I was out of the car. The first face I saw belonged to a kid of eighteen maybe, a tough guy with veins standing out in his neck and his leather jacket open to the sleet to show off a white T-shirt and a gold cross on a gold chain. He was right there, right in my face, shouting, "Jesus! Jesus!" and he looked genuinely surprised when I pitched into him with everything I had and shoved him back into a pair of dumpy women in matching scarves and earmuffs. I went right for the next guy—a little toadstool who looked as if he'd been locked in a closet for the last forty years—and flung him away from the car. I heard shouts, saw the cops wading through the crowd, and then I was staring into the face of the big guy, the king yahoo himself— Mr. Beard—and he was so close I knew what he'd had for breakfast. In all that chaos he just stood there rigid at the bumper of the car, giving me a big rich phony Jesus-loving smile that was as full of hate as anything I'd ever seen, and then he ducked down on one knee and handcuffed himself to the bumper.

That put me over the line. I wanted to make a martyr out of him, wanted to kick him to death right there, right in the driveway and with the whole world looking on, and who knows what would have happened if Philip hadn't grabbed me from behind. "Rick!" he kept shouting. "Rick! Rick!" And then he wrestled me up the walk and into the house, Denise's scared white face in the door, the mob howling for blood and then lurching right into another weepy, churchy song as if they were in a cathedral somewhere.

In the safety of the hallway, the door closed and locked behind us, my brother turned on me. "Are you crazy?" he shouted, and you would have thought *I* was the enemy. "You want to go back to jail? You want lawsuits? What were you thinking, anyway—are you stoned on something, is that it?"

I looked away from him, but I wanted to kill him too. It was beating in my veins, along with the Desoxyn I'd stolen from the clinic. I saw my nephews peeking out of their room down the hall. "You can't let these people push you around," I said.

"Look at me, Rick," he said. "Look at me."

I was dodging around on my feet, tight with it, and I lifted my eyes grudgingly. I felt like a kid all over again, Rick the shoplifter, the pothead, the fuckup.

"You're just playing into their hands, don't you see that? They want to provoke you, they want you to go after them. Then they put you back in jail and they get the headlines." His voice broke. Denise tried to say something, but he shut her up with a wave of his hand. "You're back on the drugs, aren't you? What is it— cocaine? Pot? Something you lifted from the clinic?"

Outside I could hear them, "We Shall Overcome," and it was a cruel parody—this wasn't liberation, it was fascism. I said nothing.

"Listen, Rick, you're an ex-con and you've got to remember that, every step you take. I mean, what did you think, you were protecting me out there?"

"Ex-con?" I said, amazed. "Is that what you think of me? I can't believe you. I'm no ex-con. You're thinking of somebody in the movies, some documentary you saw on PBS. I'm a guy who made a mistake, a little mistake, and I never hurt anybody. I'm your brother, remember?"

That was when Denise chimed in. "Philip," she said, "come on, Philip. You're just upset. We're all upset."

"You keep out of this," he said, and he didn't even turn to look at her. He just kept his Aqua Velva eyes on me. "Yeah," he said finally, "you're my brother, but you're going to have to prove it to me."

I can see now the Desoxyn was a mistake. It was exactly the sort of thing they'd warned us about. But it wasn't coke and I just needed a lift, a buzz to work behind, and if he didn't want me to be tempted, then why had he left the key to the drug cabinet right there in the conch-shell ashtray on the corner of his desk? *Ex-con.* I was hurt and I was angry and I stayed in my room till Philip knocked at the door an hour later to tell me the police had cleared the mob away. We drove to work in silence, Philip's opera chewing away at my nerves like a hundred little sets of teeth.

Philip didn't notice it, but there was something different about me when I climbed back into that car, something nobody could notice unless they had X-ray vision. I was armed. Tucked inside the waistband of my gray Levi's, underneath the flap of my shirt where you couldn't see it, was the hard black stump of a gun I'd bought from a girl named Corinne at a time when I was feeling especially paranoiac. I had money lying around the apartment then and people coming and going—nobody desperate, nobody I didn't know or at least know through a friend—but it made me a little crazy. Corinne used to drop by once in a while with my roommate's girlfriend, and she sold me the thing—a .38 Special—for three hundred bucks. She didn't need it anymore, she said, and I didn't want to know what that meant, so I bought it and kept it under my pillow. I'd only fired it once, up a canyon in Tujunga, but it made me feel better just to have it around. I'd forgotten all about it, actually, but when I got my things out of storage and shipped them to Philip's house, there it was, hidden away in a box of CDs like some poisonous thing crouching under a rock.

What I was feeling is hard to explain. It had to do with Philip, sure—ex-con, that really hurt—and with Sally and the clinic and the whole Jesus-thumping circus. I didn't know what I was going to do—nothing, I hoped—but I knew I wasn't going to take any shit from anybody, and I knew Philip didn't have it in him to protect himself, let alone Denise and the kids and all the knocked-up grieving teenage Sallys of the world. That was all. That was it. The extent of my thinking. I walked into the clinic that morning just as I had for the past week and a half, and nobody knew the difference.

I cleaned the toilets, washed the windows, took out the trash. Some blood work came back from an outside lab—we only did urine—and Fred showed me how to read the results. I discussed the baseball strike with Nurse Tsing and the prospects of an early spring with Nurse Hempfield. At noon I went out to a deli and had a meatball wedge, two beers, and a breath mint. I debated dialling Sally just once more—maybe she was home from school, headachy, nauseous, morning sickness, whatever, and I could get past the brick wall she'd put up between us and talk to her, really talk to her for the first time—but when I got inside the phone booth, I just didn't feel like it. As I walked back to the clinic I was wondering if she had a boyfriend or if it was just one of those casual encounters, blind date, back seat of the car—or rape, even. Or incest. Her father's voice could have been the voice of a child abuser, easily—or who even knew if he was her father? Maybe he was the stepfather. Maybe he was a Humbert Humbert type. Maybe anything.

There were no protesters out front when I got back—they were all in jail—and that lightened my mood a bit. I even joked with Fred and caught myself whistling over my work. I forgot the morning, forgot the gun, forgot Pasadena and the life that was. Coffee kept me awake, coffee and Diet Coke, and I stayed away from the other stuff just to prove something to myself—and to Philip too. For a while there I even began to suffer from the delusion that everything was going to work out.

Then it was late, getting dark, and the day was almost done. I pictured the evening ahead—Denise's cooking, *Winnie-the-Pooh*, my brother's scotch, six windblown blocks to the store for a liter of Black Cat—and suddenly I felt like pulling out the gun and shooting myself right then and there. Uncle Rick, little brother, ex-con: who was I kidding? I would have been better off in jail.

I needed a cigarette. Badly. The need took me past the waiting room—four scared-looking women, one angry-looking man—through the lab, and into the back corner. The fluorescent lights hissed softly overhead. Fred was already gone. I stood at the window, staring into the nullity of the drawn blinds till the cigarette was a nub. My hands were trembling as I lit another from the butt end of the first, and I didn't think about the raw-looking leftovers in the stainless-steel trays that were like nothing so much as skinned frogs, and I didn't think about Sally or the fat-faced bearded son of a bitch shackling himself to the bumper, either. I tried hard to think nothing, to make it all a blank, and I was succeeding, I was, when for some reason—idle curiosity, boredom, fate—I separated two of the slats and peered out into the lot.

And there she was, just like that: Sally.

Sally in her virginal parka and fluffy boots, locked in her mother's grip and fighting her way up the walk against a tide of chanting zombies—and I recognized them too, every one of them, the very ones who'd been dragged away from my brother's door in the dark of the morning. Sally wasn't coming in for an exam—there weren't going to be any more exams. No, Sally meant business. You could see that in the set of her jaw and in the way she lowered her head and jabbed out her eyes like swords, and you could see it in every screaming line of her mother's screaming face.

The light was fading. The sky hung low, like smoke. And then, in that instant, as if some god had snapped his fingers, the streetlights went on, a sudden artificial burst of illumination exploding in the sky above them. All at once I felt myself moving, the switch turned on in me too, all the lights flaring in my head, burning bright, and I was out the door, up the corridor, and pushing through the double glass doors at the front entrance.

Something was blocking the doors—bodies, deadweight, the zombies piled up on the steps like corpses—and I had to force my way out. There were bodies everywhere, a minefield of flesh, people stretched out across the steps, obliterating the sidewalk and the curb in front of the clinic, immobilizing the cars in the street. I saw the punk from this morning, the teenage tough guy in his leather jacket, his back right up against the door, and beside him one of the dumpy women I'd flung him into. They didn't learn, these people, they didn't know. It was a game. A big joke. Call people baby-killers, sing about Jesus, pocketful of posies, and then the nice policeman carries you off to jail and Mommy and Daddy bail you out. I tried to kick them aside, lashing out with the steel toes of my boots till my breath was coming in gasps. "Sally!" I cried. "Sally, I'm coming!"

She was stalled at the corner of the building, standing rigid with her mother before the sea of bodies. "Jesus loves you!" somebody cried out and they all took it up till my voice was lost in the clamor, erased in the everlasting hiss of Jesus. "We're going to come looking for you, brother," the tough guy said then, looking up at me out of a pair of seething blue eyes. "You better watch your back."

Sally was there. Jesus was there. Hands grabbed at me, snaked round my legs till I couldn't move, till I was mired in flesh. The big man came out of nowhere, lithe on his feet, vaulting through the inert bodies like the shadow of something moving swiftly overhead, and he didn't so much as graze me as he went by. I was on the third step down, held fast, the voices chanting, the signs waving, and I turned to watch him handcuff himself to the door and flash me a tight little smile of triumph.

"Sally!" I shouted. "Sally!" But she was already turning around, already turning her back to me, already lost in the crowd.

I looked down at my feet. A woman was clutching my right leg to her as if she'd given birth to it, her eyes as loopy as any crackhead's. My left leg was in the grip of a balding guy who might have been a clerk in a hardware store and he was looking up at me like a toad I'd just squashed. "Jesus," they hissed. "Jesus!"

The light was burning in my head, and it was all I needed. I reached into my pants and pulled out the gun. I could have anointed any one of them, but the woman was first. I bent to her where she lay on the unyielding concrete of the steps and touched that snub-nose to her ear as tenderly as any man of healing. The noise of it shut down Jesus, shut him down cold. Into the silence, and it was the hardware man next. Then I swung round on Mr. Beard.

It was easy. It was nothing. Just like killing babies.

CAPTURED BY THE INDIANS

At the lecture that night they learned that human life was expendable. Melanie had sat there in shocked silence—the silence of guilt, mortification and paranoia (what if someone should see her there in the crowd?)—while Dr. Toni Brinsley-Schneider, the Stanford bioethicist, had informed them that humans, like pigs, chickens and guppies, were replaceable. In the doctor's view, the infirm, the mentally impaired, criminals, premature infants and the like were non-persons, whose burden society could no longer be expected to support, especially in light of our breeding success. "We're hardly an endangered species," she said with a grim laugh. "Did you know, all of you good and earnest people sitting here tonight, that we've just reached the population threshold of six billion?" She was cocked back from the lectern in a combative pose, her penurious little silver-rimmed reading glasses flinging fragments of light out into the audience. "Do any of you really want more condominiums, more shantytowns and favelas, more cars on the freeway, more group homes for the physically handicapped right around the corner from you? On your street? Next door?" She leveled her flashing gaze on them. "Well, do you?"

People shifted in their seats, a muted moist surge of sound that was like the timid lapping of waves on a distant shore. No one responded—this was a polite crowd, a liberal crowd dedicated to free expression, a university crowd, and besides, the question had been posed for effect only. They'd have their chance to draw blood during the Q&A.

Sean sat at attention beside Melanie, his face shining and smug. He was midway through the Ph.D. program in literary theory, and the theoreticians had hardened his heart: Dr. Brinsley-Schneider was merely confirming what he already knew. Melanie took his hand, but it wasn't a warm hand, a hand expressive of comfort and love—it was more like something dug frozen from the earth. She hadn't yet told him what she'd learned at two thirty-three that afternoon, special knowledge, a secret as magical and expansive as a loaf of bread rising in a pan. Another sort of doctor had brought her the news, a doctor very different from the pinched and angry-looking middle-aged woman at the podium, a young dark-haired sylph of a woman, almost a girl, with a wide beatific face and congratulatory eyes, dressed all in white like a figure out of a dream.

They walked to the car in silence, the mist off the ocean redrawing the silhouettes of the trees, the streetlights softly glowing. Sean wanted a burger—and maybe a beer—so they stopped off at a local bar and grill the students hadn't discovered yet and she watched him eat and drink while the television over the bar replayed images of atrocities in the Balkans, the routine bombing of Iraq and the itinerary of the railroad killer. In between commercials for trucks that were apparently capable of scaling cliffs and fording rivers, they showed the killer's face, a mug shot of a slightly built Latino with an interrupted mustache and two dead eyes buried like artifacts in his head. "You see that?" Sean said, nodding at the screen, the half-eaten burger clenched in one hand, the beer in the other. "That's what Brinsley-Schneider and these people are talking about. You think this guy worries much about the sanctity of human life?"

Can we afford compassion? Melanie could hear the lecturer's droning thin voice in the back of her head, and she saw the dour pale muffin of a face frozen in the spotlight when somebody in back shouted *Nazi!* "I don't know why we have to go to these lectures, anyway," she said. "Last year's series was so much more—do I want to say 'uplifting' here? Remember the woman who'd written that book about beekeeping? And the old professor—what was his name?—who talked about Yeats and Maud Gonne?"

"Stevenson Elliot Turner. He's emeritus in the English Department."

"Yeah," she said, "that's right, and why can't we have more of that sort of thing? Tonight—I don't know, she was so depressing. And so wrong."

"Are you kidding me? Turner's like the mummy's ghost—that talk was stupefying. He was probably giving the same lecture in English 101 thirty years ago. At least Brinsley-Schneider's controversial. At least she keeps you awake."

Melanie wasn't listening, and she didn't want to argue—or debate, or discuss. She wanted to tell Sean—who wasn't her husband, not yet, because they had to wait till he got his degree—that she was pregnant. But she couldn't. She already knew what he would say, and it was right on the same page with Dr. Toni Brinsley-Schneider.

She watched his eyes settle on the screen a moment, then drift down to the burger in his hand. He drew back his lips and took a bite, nostrils open wide, the iron muscles working in his jaw. "We live by the railroad tracks," Melanie said, by way of shifting the subject. "You think we have anything to worry about?"

"What do you mean?"

"The train killer."

Sean gave her a look. He was in his debating mode, his put-down mode, and she could see it in his eyes. "He doesn't kill trains, Mel," he said, "—he kills people. And yes, everybody has something to worry about, everybody on this planet. And if you were listening to half of what Brinsley-Schneider was saying tonight, I wouldn't be surprised if every third person out there on the street was a serial killer. There's too many of us, Mel, let's face it. You think things are going to get better? You think things are better now than when we were kids? When our parents were kids? It's over. Face it."

Something corny and ancient was on the jukebox—Frank Sinatra, Tony Bennett, somebody like that—because the place smacked of the kind of authenticity people were looking for, the kind of authenticity that cried out from the fallen arches, ravaged faces and sclerotic livers of the regulars, to whom she and Sean—at twenty-nine and thirty respectively—were as inauthentic as newborns.

At home, she changed into a cotton nightgown and got into bed with a book. She wasn't feeling anything, not elation or pain or disappointment, only the symptoms of a headache coming on. The book was something she'd discovered at a yardsale two days earlier—*Captured by the Indians: 15 Firsthand Accounts, 1750–1870*—and the minute she opened it she was swept up into a voyeuristic world of pain and savagery that trumped any horror she could conceive of. It wasn't a good thing to be captured by the Indians, as Sean had snidely observed on seeing her poised behind the cover the night before last, not good at all. There were no notions here of the politically correct, of revisionist history or the ethics of one people forcibly displacing another: no, it was the hot flash of murder and reprisal, the thump of the musket ball hitting home, the operation of knife and tomahawk on unresisting flesh. To die, to be murdered, to be robbed of your life and consciousness and being, that was the stuff of morbid fascination, and she couldn't get enough of it.

Sean was in his underwear, the briefs he preferred over boxers, the sort of thing she'd always associated with boys—little boys, children, that is—and as she watched him pad across the carpet on his way to the bathroom and his nightly ritual of cleansing, clipping, flossing, brushing, tweezering and shaving, it struck her that she'd never in her life been in an intimate situation with a man—or boy—in boxers. "The last they heard," Sean was saying, and he paused now to gaze at her over the mound of the bedspread and her tented knees, "he was in the Midwest someplace—after leaving Texas, I mean. That's a long ways from California, Mel, and besides, his whole thing is so random—"

"He rides freight trains—or hops them, isn't that the terminology?" she said, peering over the cover of the book. "He hops freight trains, Sean, and that means he could be anywhere in twenty-four hours—or forty-eight. How long does it take to drive from Kansas to Isla Vista? Two days? Three?" She wanted to tell him about the doctor, and what the doctor had said, and what it was going to mean for them, but she didn't want to see the look on his face, didn't want to have to fight him, not now, not yet. He'd go pale and tug involuntarily at the grown-over hole in his left earlobe where the big gold hoop used to reside before he got serious about his life, and then he'd tell her she couldn't have her baby for the same reason she couldn't have a dog or even a cat—at least until he'd done his dissertation, at least until then.

"I don't know, Mel," he said, all the tiredness and resignation in the world crept into his voice, as if a simple discussion could martyr him, "what do you want me to say? He's coming through the window tonight? Of the two hundred seventy million potential victims in the country, he's singled us out, zeroed right in on us like a homing pigeon—?"

"Statistics," she said, and she was surprised at her own vehemence. "That's like saying you have about the same chance of getting attacked by a shark as you do of getting hit by lightning, and yeah, sure, but anybody anywhere can get hit by lightning, but how many people live by the ocean, how many actually go in it, and of them, how many are crazy enough—or foolhardy, that's the word I want here—how many are foolhardy enough to go out where the sharks are? Probably a hundred percent of *them* get eaten, and we live right by the tracks, don't we?"

As if in answer, there was the sudden sharp blast of the northbound's whistle as it neared the intersection two blocks away, and then the building thunder of the train itself, the fierce clatter of the churning wheels and everything in the room trembling with the rush of it. Sean rolled his eyes and disappeared into the bathroom. When the thunder subsided and he could be heard again, he poked his head round the doorframe. "It's the Indians," he said.

"It has nothing to do with the Indians." She wouldn't give him this, though he was right, of course—or partially, anyway. "It's Brinsley-Schneider, who you seem to think is so great. Brinsley-Schneider and eugenics and euthanasia and all the rest of the deadly *u*'s."

He was smiling the smile of the literary theorist in a room full of them, the smile that made him look like a toad with an over-sized insect clamped in its jaws. "The deadly *u*'s?" he repeated. And then, softening, he said, "All right, if it'll make you feel any better I'll check the doors and windows, okay?"

Her eyes were on the book. Way off in the night she could hear the dying rattle of the last car at the end of the train. Her life was changing, and why couldn't she feel good about it—why shouldn't she?

He was in the doorway still, his face settling into the lines and grooves he'd dug for it over the past two and a half years of high seriousness. He looked exactly like himself. "Okay?" he said.

She didn't have to be in at work till twelve the next day—she was an assistant to the reference librarian at the university library, and her schedule was so flexible it was all but bent over double—and after Sean left for class she sat in front of the TV with the sound off and read the account of Lavina Eastlick, who was twenty-nine and the mother of five when the Sioux went on a rampage near Acton, Minnesota, in the long-forgotten year of 1862. There was a moment's warning, no more than that. A frightened neighbor shouting in the yard, first light, and suddenly Lavina Eastlick—a housewife, a hopeful young woman her own age rudely jolted from sleep—was running barefooted through the wet grass, in her nightgown, herding her children before her. The Indians soon overtook them and cut down her husband, her children, her neighbors and her neighbors' children, taking the women captive. She'd been shot twice and could barely stand, let alone walk. When she stumbled and fell, a Sioux brave beat her about the head and shoulders with the stock of his rifle and left her for dead. Later, when they'd gone, she was able to crawl off and hide herself in the brush through the long afternoon and in-terminable night that followed. The wounded children—hers and her neighbors'—lay sprawled in the grass behind her, crying out for water, but she couldn't move to help them. On the second afternoon the Indians returned to dig at the children's wounds with sharpened sticks till the terrible gargling cries choked off and the locusts in the trees filled the void with their mindless chant.

And what would Dr. Toni Brinsley-Schneider have thought of that? She'd probably applaud the Indians for eliminating the useless and weak, who would only have grown up crippled around their shattered limbs in any case. That was what Melanie was thinking as she closed the book and glanced up at the casual violence scrolling across the TV screen, but once she was on her feet she realized she was hungry and headed off in the direction of the kitchen, thinking tuna fish on rye with roasted sunflower seeds and red bell pepper. She supposed she'd be putting on weight now, eating for two, and wouldn't that be the way to announce the baby to Sean six months down the road, like the prom mom who hid it till the last fatal minute: *And you thought I was just going to fat, didn't you, honey?*

Outside, beyond the windows, the sun washed over the flowers in the garden, all trace of the night's mist burned off. There were juncos and finches at the feeder she shared with the upstairs neighbor, a dog asleep at the curb across the street, pure white fortresses of cloud building over the mountains. It was still, peaceful, an ordinary day, no Indians in sight, no bioethicists, no railroad killers hopping off freight trains and selecting victims at random, and she chopped onions and diced celery with a steady hand while something inexpressibly sad came over the radio, a cello playing in minor key, all alone, until it was joined by a single violin that sounded as if a dead man were playing it, playing his own dirge—and maybe he was dead, maybe the recording was fifty years old, she was thinking, and she had a sudden image of a man with a long nose and a Gypsy face, serenading the prisoners at Auschwitz.

Stop it, she told herself, *just stop it.* She should be filled with light, shouldn't she? She should be knitting, baking, watching the children at the playground with the greedy intensity of a connoisseur.

The sunflower seeds were in the pan, the one with the loose handle and the black non-stick surface, heat turned up high, when the doorbell rang. The violin died at that moment—literally—and the unctuous, breathless voice of the announcer she hated (the one who always sounded as if he were straining over a bowel movement) filled the apartment as she crossed the front room and stepped into the hall. She was about to pull open the door—it would be the mailman at this hour, offering up a clutch of bills and junk mail and one of Sean's articles on literary theory (or Theory, as he called it, "Just Theory, with a capital *T*, like Philosophy or Physics"), returned from an obscure journal with postage due—but something stopped her. "Who is it?" she called from behind the door, and she could smell the sunflower seeds roasting in the pan.

There was no answer, so she moved to the window beside the door and parted the curtains. A man stood on the concrete doorstep, staring at the flat plane of the door as if he could see through it. He was small and thin, no more than five-five or -six, tanned to the color of the copper teakettle on the stove and dressed in the oily jeans and all-purpose long-sleeved shirt of the bums who lined Cabrillo Boulevard with their styrofoam cups and pint bottles—or should she call them panhandlers or the homeless or the apartmentally challenged? Sean called them bums, and she guessed she'd fallen into the habit herself. They said crude things to you when you walked down the street, gesturing with fingers that were as black as the stubs of cigars. They were bums, that was all, and who needed them?

But then the man turned to her, saw her there at the window and turned to her, and she had a shock: he was Hispanic, a Latino just like the man on TV, the killer, with the same dead cinders for eyes. He put three fingers together and pushed them at his open mouth, and she saw then that he had no mustache—no, no mustache, but what did that mean? Anybody could shave, even a bum. "What do you want?" she called, feeling trapped in her own apartment, caught behind the wall of glass like a fish in an aquarium.

He looked surprised by the question. What did he want? He wanted food, money, sex, booze, drugs, her car, her baby, her life, her apartment. "Hungry," he said. And then, when she didn't respond: "You got work?"

She just shook her head—No, she didn't have any work—and all the time she had to give this man, this stranger, this bum, had already been used up, because there was smoke in the kitchen and the seeds were burning in the pan.

It was past eight when she drove home from work, feeling exhausted, as if she were in her eighth month instead of the second. The day was softening into night, birds dive-bombing the palms along the boulevard, joggers and in-line skaters reduced to shadows on the periphery of her vision. All through the afternoon the mist had been rolled up like a carpet on the horizon, but it was moving closer now and she could smell it on the air—it was going to be another dense, compacted night. She parked and came up the walk and saw that the upstairs neighbor—Jessica, Jessica-something, who'd been there only a month and was so pathologically shy she cupped both hands to her face when she talked to you as if a real live moving mouth were somehow offensive—had been doing something in the flower garden. The earth was raw in several spots, as if it had been turned over, and there was a spade leaning against the side of the house. Not that it mattered to Melanie—she'd never had a green thumb and plants were just plants to her. If Jessica wanted to plant flowers, that was fine; if she wanted to dig them up, that was fine too.

Sean was in the kitchen, banging things around and singing—bellowing—along with one of Wagner's operas, the only music he ever listened to. And which one was it?—she'd heard them all a thousand times. There it was, yes, Siegfried going down for the count: *Götterdämmerung*. Sean was making his famous shrimp and avocado salad, and he was in the throes of something—Wagner, Theory, some sort of testosterone rush—and he barely glanced up at her as she trudged into the bedroom. Her mistake was in taking off her shoes, the flats she wore for the sake of her feet while propping up an automatic smile behind the reference desk, because once her shoes were off she felt out of balance and had to rest her head on the pillow, just for a minute.

The gods of Valhalla had been laid to rest and the house was silent when she awoke to the soft click of the bedroom door. Sean was standing there framed in the doorway, the tacky yellow globe of the hallway light hanging over his shoulder like a captive moon. It was dark beyond the windows. "What," he said, "are you sick or something?"

Was she? Now was her chance, now was the time to tell him, to share the news, the joyous news, pop the cork on the bottle of champagne and let's go out to a nice place, a really nice place, and save the famous shrimp and avocado salad for tomorrow. "No," she said. "No. Just tired, that's all."

At dinner—Sean and Lacan and a scatter of papers, the shrimp salad, lemonade from the can and an incongruous side dish of Ranch Style barbecue beans, also from the can—she did tell him about the man at the door that morning. "He said he wanted work," she said, waving a forkful of shrimp and beans in an attempt to delineate the scene for the third time, "and I told him I didn't have any work for him. That was it. The whole thing."

Sean had begun to develop a groove just over the bridge of his nose, a V-shaped gouge that might have been a scar or the mark of a hot branding iron. It vanished when he was asleep or sunk into the couch with a beer and the *New York Times*, but it was there now, deeper than ever. "You mean he was Mexican?"

"I don't know," she said, "he was a Latino. I was scared. He really scared me."

There was a long silence, the clock her mother had given her ticking dramatically from atop the brick-and-board bookcase in the hall, someone's sprinklers going on outside, the muted rumble of Jessica-something's TV seeping down through the ceiling—Melanie half-expected to hear the blast of the train's whistle, but it was too early yet. "It could be," Sean said finally, "—I mean, why not? You're right. The guy takes a train, he could be anywhere. And then there's the aleatory factor—"

She just stared at him.

"Chance. Luck. Fate. You can't buck fate." And then a look came over his face: two parts high seriousness, one part vigilante. "But you can be ready for it when it comes—you can be prepared."

Suddenly he was on his feet. "You just wait here, just sit tight"—and his voice had an edge to it, as if she'd been arguing with him, as if she had to be restrained from running off into the night like one of the screaming teenagers in a cheap horror film—"I'll be right back."

She wanted a glass of wine, but she knew she couldn't drink anymore, not if she was going to keep the baby, and if she hadn't known, the doctor had taken her down a smiling anfractuous road full of caveats and prohibitions, the sort of thing she—the doctor—must go through ten times a day, albeit tailoring her tone to the educational level of the patient. Outside, the sprinklers switched off with an expiring wheeze. She could hear Sean in the bedroom, rummaging around for something. Tonight, she would tell him tonight.

Because the knowledge was too big for her to contain, and she wanted to call her mother and have a long, confidential chat, and call her sisters too—but before that, before there could be any possibility of that, she had to tell Sean, and Sean had to say the things she needed to hear. During her five o'clock break, she'd confided in one of the girls she worked with, Gretchen Mohr, but it did nothing to reassure her. Gretchen was only twenty-three, in no way serious about the guy she was dating, and Melanie could tell from the way she squeezed her eyes shut over the news that the idea of a baby was about as welcome to her as paraplegia or epilepsy. Oh, she tried to cover herself with a flurry of congratulations and a nonstop barrage of platitudes and one-liners, but the final thing she said, her last and deepest thought, gave her away. "I don't know," she sighed, staring down into the keyhole of her Diet Coke can as if she were reading tea leaves, "but I just don't think I'd be comfortable bringing a baby into a world like this."

When Melanie looked up, Sean was standing over her. He was wearing a T-shirt with a picture of Freud on it, over a legend that read "Dr. Who?" His hair was slicked down, and the left side of his face, up to and encircling the ear, was inflamed with the skin condition he was forever fighting. But that was ordinary, that was the way he always looked. What was different were his eyes—

proud, incandescent, lit up like fireworks—and his hands, or what was in his hands. Swaddled in coarse white cloth that was stained with what might have been olive oil lay an object she recognized from the movies, from TV and pawnshop display cases: a gun.

"What is that?" she said, edging away from him. "What are you showing me?"

"Come on, Mel, give me a break."

"It's a gun, isn't it?"

"We're on the ground floor here, and we're going to lock the windows tonight, even if it's hot, which I doubt because already the fog's coming in, and we're going to keep this by the bed, on the night table, that's all."

She'd drawn up her legs and hugged them to her, as far away from him on the couch as she could manage to be. "I don't *believe* you," she said, and she could hear the thin whine of complaint in her own voice. "You know what my father would say if he saw you now? Where did you get it? Why didn't you tell me?" she demanded, and she couldn't help herself—her voice broke on the final syllable.

He drew the thing back, took it from its cradle and raised it up in one hand till it grazed the ceiling. The muscles of his forearm flexed, the soiled rag dropped to the carpet. "Son of a bitch," he said, "son of a fucking bitch. Tell me this," he said, "would you rather be the killer or the killee?"

She was asleep and dreaming the image of a baby floating in amniotic fluid, the cord attached, eyes shut tight—a big baby, an enormous glowing baby floating free like the interstellar embryo of *2001*—when a sudden sharp explosion of noise jolted her awake. It took her a moment, heart pounding, breath coming quick, to understand what it was—it was a scream, a woman's scream, improvised and fierce. The room was dark. Sean was asleep beside her. The scream—a single rising note tailing off into what might have been a sob or gasp—seemed to have come from above, where Jessica-something lived alone with her potted plants and two bloated pampered push-faced cats that were never allowed out of the apartment for fear of the world and its multiplied dangers. Melanie sat up and caught her breath.

Nothing. The alarm clock on the night table flashed 1:59 and then 2:00.

Earlier, after a dessert of tapioca pudding with mandarin orange slices fresh from the can, she and Sean had watched a costume drama on the public station that gave her a new appreciation for the term *mediocre* (*mediocre,* as she observed to Sean, didn't come easy—you had to work at it), and then she'd slipped into bed with her book while the station went into pledge-break mode and Sean sat there paralyzed on the couch. She hadn't read two paragraphs before he tiptoed into the room, naked and in full amatory display. She left the light on, the better to admire him, but the book dropped to the floor, and then it didn't matter. She felt new, re-created. His body was so familiar, but everything was different now—she'd never been so aroused, rising up again and again to hold him deep inside her in the place where the baby was. Afterward, immediately afterward, almost as if he'd been drugged, he fell asleep with his head on her breast, and it was left to her to reach up awkwardly and kill the lamp. They hadn't discussed a thing.

But now—now there was chaos, and it erupted all at once. There was a thump overhead, the caustic burn of a man's voice, and then another scream, and another, and Melanie was out of bed, the walls pale and vague, the dark shadow that was Sean lurching up mechanically, and "What?" he was saying. "What is it?"

Footsteps on the stairs. More screams. Melanie flicked on the light, and there was Sean, dressed only in his briefs, the long muscles of his legs, all that skin, and the gun in his hand, the pistol, the nasty gleaming black little thing he'd bought at a gun show six months ago and never bothered to tell her about. "Sean," she said, "Sean, don't!" but he was already out the door, racing down the hall in the sick yellow wash of the overhead light, already at the front door, the screams from above rising, rising. She was in her nightgown, barefooted, but she had no thought for anything but to get out that door and put an end to whatever this was.

There was a streetlight out front, but the fog had cupped a hand over it and blotted the light from the windows and the stairway too. Melanie shot a glance up the stairs to where Jessica stood bracing herself against the railing, in nothing but panties and a brassiere torn off one shoulder, and then she saw the glint of Sean's back across the lawn where the cars threw up a bank of shadow against the curb. He was shouting something, ragged, angry syllables that could have made no sense to anyone, even a Theorist, and she saw then that there was somebody else there with him, a dark, shifting figure rallying round a shuffle of feet on the pavement. She was closer now, running, Sean's feet glowing in the night, the long white stalks of his legs and expanse of his back—he seemed to be wrestling with a shadow, but no, it was an animate thing, a man, a dark little man in bum's clothes with a shovel clenched in both hands and Sean fighting him for it. Where was the gun? There was no gun. Both Sean's hands were on the shovel and both the little man's, and now Jessica was screaming again. "The gun," Sean said. "In the grass. Get the gun."

In that moment the little man managed to wrench the shovel free, and in the next—it happened so quickly she wasn't sure she actually saw it—he caught Sean under the chin with the haft, and then the blade, and Sean was on the ground. She never hesitated. Before the man could bring the blade down—and that was what he meant to do, no mistake about it, his arms already raised high for a savage stabbing thrust—she took hold of the haft with all the strength in her and pulled it tight to her chest.

She could smell him. She could feel him. He hung on, the little man, the bum, the one who'd been on the doorstep that afternoon with his reeking breath and greasy clothes, and then he jerked so violently at the shovel she almost pitched headlong into him, into the spill of his flesh and the dankness of the grass. But she didn't. She jerked back, and Jessica screamed, and Sean, reeling like a drunk, began to pick himself up off the lawn, and for the instant before the man let go of the shovel and flung himself into the shadows across the street she was staring him full in the face— yes, but she wasn't seeing the man on the TV or the man on the porch or any one of the army of bums lined up along the street in their all-purpose shirts and sweat-stained caps, she was seeing Dr. Toni Brinsley-Schneider, Dr. Brinsley-Schneider the bioethicist, just her.

There were two policemen. From where she was sitting at the end of the couch, Melanie could see their cruiser reined in at the curb, the interior a black pit, the slowly revolving light on top chopping up the night over and over again. They were built like runners or squash players, both of them—crisp, efficient men in their thirties who looked away from her bare legs and feet and into her eyes. "So you heard screams, and this was about what time?"

They'd already taken Jessica-something's statement—Jessica Fortgang, and she had a name now: *Ms.* Fortgang, as the policemen referred to her—and Sean, hunched in the armchair with an angry red weal under his chin, had given his version of events too. The man in the night, the bum, the one who'd been the cause of all this, had escaped, at least for the time being, and they were denied the satisfaction of seeing him handcuffed in the back of the cruiser, bowed and contrite. Sean had been in a state when the police arrived, clenching his jaws as if he were biting down hard on something, gesturing with a closed fist and wide sweeps of his arm. "The railway killer, it was him, the railway killer," he kept repeating, till the policeman with the mustache, the taller one, told him the railway killer had turned himself in at the Mexican border some fifteen hours earlier. "That was the Texas border," he added, and then his partner, in a flat professional voice, said that they were treating this as an assault in any case, possibly an attempted rape. "Your neighbor, Ms. Fortgang? She apparently hired this individual to do some yard work this afternoon and then invited him in for iced tea and a sandwich when he was done. Then he comes back at night—and this is a cultural thing, you understand, a woman looks at one of these guys twice and he expects a whole lot more. He's a transient, that's all, nobody from around here. But we'll get him."

Melanie answered their questions patiently, though her heart was still jumping in her chest, and she kept glancing at Sean, as if for guidance. But Sean was sullen, distant, withdrawn into some corner of himself—the gun was an embarrassment, the man had knocked him down, he'd been involved in an ordinary altercation with an ordinary bum, and the railway killer had already given himself up. She saw the lines in his face, saw the way his lower lip pushed his chin down into the soft flesh beneath it. Theory couldn't help here. Theory deconstructs, theory has no purpose, no point, no overview or consolation—it was a kind of intellectual masturbation. If she hadn't known it before, she knew it now.

The police thanked them, tried on the briefest of smiles, and then Sean showed them to the door and Melanie got up from the couch with the vague idea of making herself a cup of herbal tea to help her unwind. Just as the door closed, she called Sean's name aloud, and she almost said it, almost said, "Sean, there's something I've been wanting to tell you," but there was no use in that now.

Sean turned away from the door, shoulders slumped, the corners of his mouth drawn down. After the skirmish on the lawn, he'd shrugged into a pair of jeans and the first shirt he could find—a Hawaiian print, festive with palm fronds and miniature pineapples—and she saw that he'd misbuttoned it. He looked hopeless. He looked lost in his own living room.

She held that picture of him, and then she was thinking, unaccountably, of another captive of the Sioux, a young woman taken from her husband to be bride to a chief, the business settled in the smoke and confusion of a desperate fight, her daughter crying out over the cacophony of shouts and curses and the rolling thunder of a hundred rifles firing at once. Months later, fleeing with her captors after a loss in battle, she watched a brave from another party come up to them on his pony, in full regalia, trailing the shawl she'd knitted for her daughter and a tiny shrunken scalp with the hair—the blond shining hair—still attached.

ACHATES McNEIL

My father is a writer. A pretty well-known one too. You'd recognize the name if I mentioned it, but I won't mention it, I'm tired of mentioning it—every time I mention it I feel as if I'm suffocating, as if I'm in a burrow deep in the ground and all these fine grains of dirt are raining down on me. We studied him in school, in the tenth grade, a story of his in one of those all-purpose anthologies that dislocate your wrists and throw out your back just to lift them from the table, and then again this year, my freshman year, in college. I got into a Contemporary American Lit class second semester and they were doing two of his novels, along with a three-page list of novels and collections by his contemporaries, and I knew some of them too—or at least I'd seen them at the house. I kept my mouth shut though, especially after the professor, this blond poet in her thirties who once wrote a novel about a nymphomaniac pastry maker, made a joke the first day when she came to my name in the register.

"Achates McNeil," she called out.

"Here," I said, feeling hot and cold all over, as if I'd gone from a sauna into a snowbank and back again. I knew what was coming; I'd been through it before.

She paused, looking up from her list to gaze out the window on the frozen wastes of the campus in the frozen skullcap of New York State, and then came back to me and held my eyes a minute. "You wouldn't happen by any chance to be a relation of anybody on our reading list, would you?"

I sat cramped in the hard wooden seat, thinking about the faceless legions who'd sat there before me, people who'd squirmed over exams and unfeeling professorial remarks and then gone on to become plastic surgeons, gas station attendants, insurance salesmen, bums and corpses. "No," I said. "I don't think so."

She gave me a mysterious little smile. "I was thinking of Teresa Golub or maybe Irving Thalamus?" It was a joke. One or two of the literary cretins in back gave it a nervous snort and chuckle, and I began to wonder, not for the first time, if I was really cut out for academic life. This got me thinking about the various careers available to me as a college dropout—rock and roller, chairman of the board, center for the New York Knicks—and I missed the next couple of names, coming back to the world as the name Victoria Roethke descended on the room and hung in the air like the aftershock of a detonation in the upper atmosphere.

She was sitting two rows up from me, and all I could see was her hair, draped in a Medusan snarl of wild demi-dreadlocks over everything within a three-foot radius. Her hair was red—red as in pink rather than carrot-top—and it tended to be darker on the ends but running to the color of the stuff they line Easter baskets with up close to her scalp. She didn't say here or present or yes or even nod her amazing head. She just cleared her throat and announced, "He was my grandfather."

I stopped her in the hallway after class and saw that she had all the usual equipment as well as a nose ring and two eyes the color of the cardboard stiffeners you get as a consolation prize when you have to buy a new shirt. "Are you really—?" I began, thinking we had a lot in common, thinking we could commiserate, drown our sorrows together, have sex, whatever, but before I could finish the question, she said, "No, not really."

"You mean you—?"

"That's right."

I gave her a look of naked admiration. And she was looking at me, sly and composed, looking right into my eyes. "But aren't you afraid you're going to be on Professor What's-Her-Face's shitlist when she finds out?" I said finally.

Victoria was still looking right into me. She fiddled with her hair, touched her nose ring and gave it a quick squeeze with a nervous flutter of her fingers. Her fingernails, I saw, were painted black. "Who's going to tell her?" she said.

We were complicitous. Instantly. Half a beat later she asked me if I wanted to buy her a cup of ramen noodles in the Student Union, and I said yeah, I did, as if it was something I had any choice about.

We ran through a crust of dead snow in a stiff wind and temperatures that hadn't risen above minus ten in the past two weeks, and there were a lot of people running with us, a whole thundering herd—up here everybody ran everywhere; it was a question of survival.

In the Union she shook out her hair, and five minutes after we'd found a table in the corner and poured the hot water into the styrofoam containers of dehydrated mystery food I could still smell the cold she'd trapped there. Otherwise I smelled the multi-layered festering odors of the place, generic to college cafeterias worldwide: coffee, twice-worn underwear, cream of tomato soup. If they enclosed the place in plastic and sealed it like a tomb, it'd smell the same two thousand years from now. I'd never been in the kitchen, but I remembered the kitchen from elementary school, with its big aluminum pots and microwave ovens and all the rest, and pictured them back there now, the cafeteria ladies with their dyed hair and their miserable small-town loutish-husband lives, boiling up big cauldrons of cream of tomato soup. Victoria's nose was white from the cold, but right where the nose ring plunged in, over the flange of her left nostril, there was a spot of flesh as pink as the ends of her hair.

"What happens when you get a cold?" I said. "I mean, I've always wondered."

She was blowing into her noodles, and she looked up to shoot me a quick glance out of her cardboard eyes. Her mouth was small, her teeth the size of individual kernels of niblet corn. When she smiled, as she did now, she showed acres of gum. "It's a pain in the ass." Half a beat: that was her method. "I suffer it all for beauty."

And of course this is where I got all gallant and silver-tongued and told her how striking it was, she was, her hair and her eyes and—but she cut me off. "You really are his son, aren't you?" she said.

There was a sudden eruption of jock-like noises from the far end of the room—some athletes with shaved heads making sure everybody knew they were there—and it gave me a minute to compose myself, aside from blowing into my noodles and adjusting my black watchcap with the Yankees logo for the fourteenth time, that is. I shrugged. Looked into her eyes and away again. "I really don't want to talk about it."

But she was on her feet suddenly and people were staring at her and there was a look on her face like she'd just won the lottery or the trip for two to the luxurious Spermata Inn on the beach at Waikiki. "I don't believe it," she said, and her voice was as deep as mine, strange really, but with a just detectable breathiness or hollowness to it that made it recognizably feminine.

I was holding onto my styrofoam container of hot noodles as if somebody was trying to snatch it away from me. A quick glance from side to side reassured me that the people around us had lost interest, absorbed once again in their plates of reheated stir fry, newspapers and cherry Cokes. I gave her a weak smile.

"You mean, you're like really Tom McNeil's son, no bullshit?"

"Yes," I said, and though I liked the look of her, of her breasts clamped in the neat interwoven grid of a blue thermal undershirt and her little mouth and the menagerie of her hair, and I liked what she'd done in class too, my voice was cold. "And I have a whole other life too."

But she wasn't listening. "Oh, my God!" she squealed, ignoring the sarcasm and all it was meant to imply. She did something with her hands, her face; her hair helicoptered round her head. "I can't believe it. He's my hero, he's my god. I want to have his baby!"

The noodles congealed in my mouth like wet confetti. I didn't have the heart to point out that I *was* his baby, for better or worse.

/ / / / /

It wasn't that I hated him exactly—it was far more complicated than that, and I guess it got pretty Freudian too, considering the way he treated my mother and the fact that I was thirteen and having problems of my own when he went out the door like a big cliché and my mother collapsed into herself as if her bones had suddenly melted. I'd seen him maybe three or four times since and always with some woman or other and a fistful of money and a face that looked like he'd just got done licking up a pile of dogshit off the sidewalk. What did he want from me? What did he expect? At least he'd waited till my sister and brother were in college, at least they were out of the house when the cleaver fell, but what about me? I was the one who had to go into that classroom in the tenth grade and read that shitty story and have the teacher look at me like I had something to share, some intimate little anecdote I could relate about what it was like living with a genius—or having lived with a genius. And I was the one who had to see his face all over the newspapers and magazines when he published *Blood Ties*, his postmodernist take on the breakdown of the family, a comedy no less, and then read in the interviews about how his wife and children had held him back and stifled him—as if we were his jailers or something. As if I'd ever bothered him or dared to approach the sanctum of his upstairs office when his genius was percolating or asked him to go to a Little League game and sit in the stands and yabber along with the rest of the parents. Not me. No, I was the dutiful son of the big celebrity, and the funny thing was, I wouldn't have even known he was a celebrity if he hadn't packed up and left.

He was my father. A skinny man in his late forties with kinky hair and a goatee who dressed like he was twenty-five and had a dead black morbid outlook on life and twisted everything into the kind of joke that made you squirm. I was proud of him. I loved him. But then I saw what a monster of ego he was, as if anybody could give two shits for literature anymore, as if he was the center of the universe while the real universe went on in the streets, on the Internet, on TV and in the movie theaters. Who the hell was he to reject me?

So: Victoria Roethke.

I told her I'd never licked anybody's nose ring before and she asked me if I wanted to go over to her apartment and listen to music and have sex, and though I felt like shit, like my father's son, like the negative image of something I didn't want to be, I went. Oh, yes: I went.

She lived in a cramped drafty ancient wreck of a nondescript house from the wood-burning era, about five blocks from campus. We ran all the way, of course—it was either that or freeze to the pavement—and the shared effort, the wheezing lungs and burning nostrils, got us over any awkwardness that might have ensued. We stood a minute in the superheated entryway that featured a row of tarnished brass coathooks, a dim hallway lined with doors coated in drab shiny paint and a smell of cat litter and old clothes. I followed her hair up a narrow stairway and into a one-room apartment not much bigger than a prison cell. It was dominated by a queen-size mattress laid out on the floor and a pair of speakers big enough to double as end tables, which they did. Bricks and boards for the bookcases that lined the walls and pinched them in like one of those shrinking rooms in a Sci-Fi flick, posters to cover up the faded nineteenth-century wallpaper, a greenish-looking aquarium with one pale bloated fish suspended like a mobile in the middle of it. The solitary window looked out on everything that was dead in the world. Bathroom down the hall.

And what did her room smell like? Like an animal's den, like a burrow or a hive. And female. Intensely female. I glanced at the pile of brassieres, panties, body stockings and sweatsocks in the corner, and she lit a joss stick, pulled the curtains and put on a CD by a band I don't want to name here, but which I like—there was no problem with her taste or anything like that. Or so I thought.

She straightened up from bending over the CD player and turned to me in the half-light of the curtained room and said, "You like this band?"

We were standing there like strangers amidst the intensely personal detritus of her room, awkward and insecure. I didn't know her. I'd never been there before. And I must have seemed like some weird growth sprung up on the unsuspecting flank of her personal space. "Yeah," I said, "they're hot," and I was going to expand on that with some technical praise, just to let her see how hip and knowing I was, when she threw out a sigh and let her arms fall to her sides.

"I don't know," she said, "what I really like is soul and gospel—especially gospel. I put this on for you."

I felt deflated suddenly, unhip and uncool. There she was, joss stick sweetening the air, her hair a world of its own, my father's fan—my absent famous self-absorbed son of a bitch of a father actually pimping for me—and I didn't know what to say. After an awkward pause, the familiar band slamming down their chords and yowling out their shopworn angst, I said, "Let's hear some of your stuff then."

She looked pleased, her too-small mouth pushed up into something resembling a smile, and then she stepped forward and enveloped me in her hair. We kissed. She kissed me, actually, and I responded, and then she bounced the two steps to the CD player and put on Berna Berne and the Angeline Sisters, a slow thump of tinny drums and an organ that sounded like something fresh out of the muffler shop, followed by a high-pitched blur of semi-hysterical voices. "Like it?" she said.

What could I say? "It's different," I said.

She assured me it would grow on me, like anything else, if I gave it half a chance, ran down the other band for their pedestrian posturing, and invited me to get into her bed. "But don't take off your clothes," she said, "not yet."

I had a three o'clock class in psychology, the first meeting of the semester, and I suspected I was going to miss it. I was right. Victoria made a real ritual of the whole thing, clothes coming off with the masturbatory dalliance of a strip show, the covers rolling back periodically to show this patch of flesh or that, strategically revealed. I discovered her breasts one at a time, admired the tattoo on her ankle (a backward *S* that proved, according to her, that she was a reincarnated Norse skald), and saw that she really was a redhead in the conventional sense. Her lips were dry, her tongue was unstoppable, her hair a primal encounter. When we were done, she sat up and I saw that her breasts pointed in two different directions, and that was human in a way I can't really express, a very personal thing, as if she was letting me in on a secret that was more intimate than the sex itself. I was touched. I admit it. I looked at those mismatched breasts and they meant more to me than her lips and her eyes and the deep thrumming instrument of her voice, if you know what I mean.

"So," she said, sipping from a mug of water she produced from somewhere amongst a stack of books and papers scattered beside the mattress, "what do I call you? I mean, Achates—right?—that's a real mouthful."

"That's my father," I said. "One of his bullshit affectations— how could the great one have a kid called Joe or Evan or Jim-Bob or Dickie?" My head was on the pillow, my eyes were on the ceiling. "You know what my name means? It means 'faithful companion,' can you believe that?"

She was silent a moment, her gray eyes locked on me over the lip of the cup, her breasts dimpling with the cold. "Yeah," she said, "I can see what you mean," and she pulled the covers up to her throat. "But what do people call you?"

I stared bleakly across the room, fastening on nothing, and when I exhaled I could see my breath. Berna Berne and the Angeline Sisters were still at it, punishing the rhythm section and charging after the vocals till you'd think somebody had set their dresses on fire. "My father calls me Ake," I said finally, "or at least he used to when I used to know him. And in case you're wondering how you spell that, that's Ake with a *k*."

Victoria dropped out of the blond poet-novelist's lit class, but I knew where she lived and you couldn't miss her hair jogging across the tundra. I saw her maybe two or three times a week, especially on weekends. When things began to get to me—life, exams, too many shooters of Jack or tequila, my mother's zombielike voice on the telephone—I sank into the den of Victoria's room with its animal funk and shrinking walls as if I'd never climb back out, and it was nothing like the cold, dry burrow I thought of when I thought of my father. Just the opposite: Victoria's room, with Victoria in it, was positively tropical, whether you could see your breath or not. I even began to develop a tolerance for the Angeline Sisters.

I avoided class the day we dissected the McNeil canon, but I was there for Delmore Schwartz and his amazing re-creation of his parents' courtship unfolding on a movie screen in his head. In dreams begin responsibilities—yes, sure, but whose responsibility was I? And how long would I have to wait before we got to the se-quel and *my* dreams? I'd looked through the photo albums, my mother an open-faced hippie in cutoffs and serape with her seam-less blond hair and Slavic cheekbones and my father cocky and staring into the lens out of the shining halo of his hair, everything a performance, even a simple photograph, even then. The sperm and the egg, that was a biological concept, that was something I could envision up there on the big screen, the wriggling clot of life, the wet glowing ball of the egg, but picturing them coming together, his coldness, his arrogance, his total absorption in him-self, that was beyond me. Chalk it up to reticence. To DNA. To the grandiosity of the patriarchal cock. But then he was me and I was him and how else could you account for it?

It was Victoria who called my attention to the poster. The posters, that is, about six million of them plastered all over every stationary object within a two-mile orbit of the campus as if he was a rock star or something, as if he really counted for anything, as if anybody could even read anymore let alone give half a shit about a balding, leather-jacketed, ex-hippie wordmeister who wor-ried about his image first, his groin second, and nothing else after that. How did I miss it? A nearsighted dwarf couldn't have missed it—in fact, all the nearsighted dwarves on campus had already seen it and were lining up with everybody even vaguely ambulatory for their $2.50 Student Activities Board–sponsored tickets:

TOM McNEIL
READING FROM ELECTRONIC
ORPHANS & BLOOD TIES
FEB. 28, 8:00 P.M.
DUBOFSKY HALL

Victoria was right there with me, out front of the Student Union, the poster with his mugshot of a photo staring out at me from behind the double-insulated glass panel that reflected the whole dead Arctic world and me in the middle of it, and we had to dance on our toes and do aerobics for a full two minutes there to stave off hypothermia while I let the full meaning of it sink in. My first response was outrage, and so was my second. I bundled Victoria through the door and out of the blast of the cold, intimately involved in the revolution of her hair, the smell of her gray bristling fake fur coat that looked like half a dozen opossums dropped on her from high, even the feel of her breasts beneath all that wintry armament, and I howled in protest.

"How in Christ's name could he do this to me?" I shouted across the echoing entranceway, pink-nosed idiots in their hooded parkas coming and going, giving me their eat-shit-and-die looks. I was furious, out of control. Victoria snatched at my arm to calm me, but I tore away from her.

"He planned this, you know. He had to. He couldn't leave well enough alone, couldn't let me get away from him and be just plain nobody up here amongst the cowflops in this podunk excuse for a university—no, it's not Harvard, it's not Stanford, but at least I didn't take a nickel of his money for it. You think he'd ever even consider reading here even if the Board of Regents got down and licked his armpits and bought him a new Porsche and promised him all the coeds in Burge to fuck one by one till they dropped dead from the sheer joy of it?"

Victoria just stood there looking at me out of her flat gray eyes, rocking back and forth on the heels of her red leather boots with the cowgirl filigree. We were blocking the doors and people were tramping in and out, passing between us, a trail of yellow slush dribbling behind them in either direction. "I don't know," Victoria said over the heads of two Asian girls wrapped up like corpses, "I think it's kind of cool."

A day later, the letter came. Personalized stationery, California address. I tore it open in the hallway outside the door of my overheated, overlit, third-floor room in the sad-smelling old dorm:

Querido Ake:

I know it's been a while but my crazy life just gets crazier what with the European tour for *Orphans* and Judy and Josh, but I want to make it up to you however I can. I asked Jules to get me the gig at Acadia purposely to give me an excuse to see how you're getting along. Let's do dinner or something afterward—bring one of your girlfriends along. We'll do it up. We will.

  Mucho,
  Dad

This hit me like a body blow in the late rounds of a prizefight. I was already staggering, bloodied from a hundred hooks and jabs, ten to one against making it to the bell, and now this. Boom. I sat down on my institutional bed and read the thing over twice. Judy was his new wife, and Josh, six months old and still shitting in his pants, was my new brother. Half brother. DNA rules. Shit, it would have been funny if he was dead and I was dead and the whole world a burnt-out cinder floating in the dead-black hole of the universe. But I wasn't dead, and didn't want to be, not yet at least. The next best thing was being drunk, and that was easy to accomplish. Three Happy Hours and a good lip-splitting, sideburn-thumping altercation with some mountainous asshole in a pair of Revo shades later, and I was ready for him.

You probably expect me to report that my father, the genius, blew into town and fucked my lit professor, Victoria, the cafeteria ladies and two or three dogs he stumbled across on the way to the reading, but that's not the way it fell out. Not at all. In fact, he was kind of sorry and subdued and old-looking. Real old-looking, though by my count he must have been fifty-three or maybe fifty-four. It was as if his whole head had collapsed like a rotten jack-o'-lantern, his eyes sucked down these volcanoes of wrinkles, his hair standing straight up on his head like a used toilet brush. But I'm getting ahead of myself. According to my roommate, Jeff Heymann, he'd called about a hundred times and finally left a message saying he was coming in early and wanted to have lunch too, if that was okay with me. It wasn't okay. I stayed away from the telephone, and I stayed away from my room. In fact, I didn't even go near the campus for fear of running into him as he long-legged his way across the quad, entourage in tow. I blew off my classes and sank into Victoria's nest as if it was an opium den, sleep and forgetfulness, Berna Berne and the Angeline Sisters keeping me company, along with a bottle of Don Q Victoria's dad had brought back from Puerto Rico for her. What was my plan? To crash and burn. To get so fucked up I'd be in a demicoma till the lunch was eaten, the reading read and dinner forgotten. I mean, fuck him. Really.

The fatal flaw in my plan was Victoria.

She didn't stay there to comfort me with her hair, her neat little zipper of a mouth and her mismatched breasts. No, she went to class, very big day, exams and papers and quizzes. So she said. But do I have to tell you where she really was? Can't you picture it? The fan, the diehard, somebody who supposedly cared about me, and there she was, camped outside his hotel in the Arctic wind with the snot crusted round her nose ring. They wouldn't tell her what room he was in, and when she took exception to the attitude of the girl behind the desk, they told her she'd have to wait outside—on the public sidewalk. While she was waiting and freezing and I was attempting to drink myself comatose, he was making phonecalls. Another hundred to my room and then to the registrar and the dean and anybody else who might have had a glimmer of my whereabouts, and of course they all fell over dead and contacted my professors, the local police—Christ, probably even the FBI, the CIA and TRW.

And then it was lunchtime and all the cheeses and honchos from the English Department wanted to break bread with him, so out the door he went, not with Judy on his arm or some more casual acquaintance who might have been last night's groin massager or the flight attendant who'd served him his breakfast, but his biographer. His biographer. Arm in arm with this bald guy half his height and a face depleted by a pair of glasses the size of the ones Elton John used to wear onstage, trailing dignitaries and toadies, and who does he run into?

Ten minutes later he's coming up the stairs at Victoria's place, and beneath the wailing of the Sisters and the thump of the organ I can hear his footsteps, his and nobody else's, and I know this: after all these years my father has come for me.

Lunch was at the Bistro, one of the few places in town that aspired to anything more than pizza, burgers and burritos. My father sat at the head of the table, of course, and I, three-quarters drunk on white rum, sat at his right hand. Victoria was next to me, her expression rapt, her hair snaking out behind me in the direction of the great man like the tendrils of some unkillable plant, and the biographer, sunk behind his glasses, hunched beside her with a little black notepad. The rest of the table, from my father's side down, was occupied by various members of the English Department I vaguely recognized and older lawyer types who must have been deans or whatever. There was an awkward moment when Dr. Delpino, my American Lit professor, came in, but her eyes, after registering the initial surprise and recalculating our entire relationship from the first day's roll call on, showed nothing but a sort of fawning, shimmering awe. And how did I feel about that? Sick. Just plain sick.

I drank desperate cups of black coffee and tried to detoxify myself with something called Coquilles Saint Jacques, which amounted to an indefinable rubbery substance sealed in an impenetrable layer of baked cheese. My father held forth, witty, charming, as pleased with himself as anybody alive. He said things like "I'm glad you're asking me to speak on the only subject I'm an authority on—me," and with every other breath he dropped the names of the big impressive actors who'd starred in the big impressive movie version of his last book. "Well," he'd say, "as far as that goes, Meryl once told me . . . ," or, "When we were on location in Barbados, Brad and Geena and I used to go snorkeling practically every afternoon, and then it was conch ceviche and this rum drink they call Mata-Mata, after the turtle, and believe me, kill you it does. . . ."

Add to this the fact that he kept throwing his arm round the back of my chair (and so, my shoulders) as if I'd been there with him through every scintillating tête-à-tête and sexual and literary score, and you might begin to appreciate how I felt. But what could I do? He was playing a role that would have put to shame any of the big-gun actors he named, and I was playing my role too, and though I was seething inside, though I felt betrayed by Victoria and him and all the stupid noshing doglike faces fawning round the table, I played the dutiful and proud son to Academy Award proportions. Or maybe I wasn't so great. At least I didn't jump up and flip the table over and call him a fraud, a cheat and a philanderer who had no right to call anybody his son, let alone me. But oh, how those deans and professors sidled up to me afterward to thoroughly kiss my ass while Dr. Delpino glowed over our little secret and tried to shoulder Victoria out of the way. And Victoria. That was another thing. Victoria didn't seem to recall that I was still alive, so enthralled was she by the overblown spectacle of my father the genius.

He took me aside just before we stepped back out into the blast of the wind, confidential and fatherly, the others peeling back momentarily in deference to the ties of the blood, and asked me if I was all right. "Are you all right?" he said.

Everything was in a stir, crescendoing voices, the merry ritual of the zippers, the gloves, the scarves and parkas, a string quartet keening through the speakers in some weird key that made the hair stand up on the back of my neck. "What do you mean?" I said.

I looked into his face then, and the oldness dropped away from him: he was my pal, my dad, the quick-blooded figure I remembered from the kitchen, den and bedroom of my youth. "I don't know," he said, shrugging. "Victoria said—that's her name, right, Victoria?"

I nodded.

"She said you were feeling sick, the flu or something," and he let it trail off. Somebody shouted, "You should have seen it in December!" and the string quartet choked off in an insectlike murmur of busy strings and nervous fingers. "Cute kid, Victoria," he said. "She's something." And then a stab at a joke: "Guess you inherited my taste, huh?"

But the dutiful son didn't smile, let alone laugh. He was feeling less like Achates than Oedipus.

"You need any money?" my father said, and he was reaching into the pocket of his jeans, an automatic gesture, when the rest of the group converged on us and the question fell dead. He threw an arm round me suddenly and managed to snag Victoria and the proud flag of her hair in the other. He gave a two-way squeeze with his skinny arms and said, "See you at the reading tonight, right?"

Everyone was watching, right on down to the busboys, not to mention the biographer, Dr. Delpino and all the by-now stunned, awed and grinning strangers squinting up from their coquilles and fritures. It was a real biographical moment. "Yeah," I said, and I thought for a minute they were going to break into applause, "sure."

The hall was packed, standing room only, hot and stifled with the crush of bodies and the coats and scarves and other paraphernalia that were like a second shadowy crowd gathered at the edges of the living and breathing one, students, faculty and townspeople wedged into every available space. Some of them had come from as far away as Vermont and Montreal, so I heard, and when we came through the big main double doors, scalpers were selling the $2.50 Student Activities Board–sponsored tickets for three and four times face value. I sat in the front row between my father's vacant seat and the biographer (whose name was Mal, as in Malcolm) while my father made the rounds, pumping hands and signing books, napkins, sheets of notebook paper and whatever else the adoring crowd thrust at him. Victoria, the mass of her hair enlarged to even more stupendous proportions thanks to some mysterious chemical treatment she'd undergone in the bathroom down the hall from her room, sat sprouting beside me.

I was trying not to watch my father, plunging in and out of the jungle of Victoria to make small talk, unconcerned, unflappable, no problem at all, when Mal leaned across the vacant seat and poked my arm with the butt of his always handy Scripto pen. I turned to him, Victoria's hand clutched tightly in mine—she hadn't let go, not even to unwrap her scarf, since we'd climbed out of the car—and stared into the reflected blaze of his glasses. They were amazing, those glasses, like picture windows, like a scuba mask grafted to his hairless skull. "Nineteen eighty-nine," he said, "when he wrecked the car? The BMW, I mean?" I sat there frozen, waiting for the rest of it, the man's voice snaking into my consciousness till it felt like the voice of my innermost self. "Do you remember if he was still living at home then? Or was that after he . . . after he, uh, moved out?"

Moved out. Wrecked the car.

"Do you remember what he was like then? Were there any obvious changes? Did he seem depressed?"

He must have seen from my face how I felt about the situation because his glasses suddenly flashed light, he tugged twice at his lower lip, and murmured, "I know this isn't the time or place, I was just curious, that's all. But I wonder, would you mind—maybe we could set up a time to talk?"

What could I say? Victoria clutched my hand like a trophy hunter, my fellow students rumbled and chattered and stretched in their bolted-down seats and my father squatted here, sprang up there, lifted his eyebrows and laid down a layer of witty banter about half a mile thick. I shrugged. Looked away. "Sure," I said.

Then the lights dimmed once, twice, and went all the way down, and the chairman of the English Department took the podium while my father scuttled into the seat beside me and the audience hushed. I won't bother describing the chairman—he was generic, and he talked for a mercifully short five minutes or so about how my father needed no introduction and et cetera, et cetera, before giving the podium over to Mal, as in Malcolm, the official hagiographer. Mal bounced up onto the stage like a trained seal, and if the chairman was selfless and brief, Mal was windy, verbose, a man who really craved an audience. He softened them up with half a dozen anecdotes about the great man's hyperinflated past, with carefully selected references to drug abuse, womanizing, unhinged driving and of course movies and movie stars. By the time he was done he'd made my father sound like a combination of James Dean, Tolstoy and Enzo Ferrari. They were thrilled, every last man, woman and drooling freshman—and me, the only one in the audience who really knew him? I wanted to puke, puke till the auditorium was filled to the balcony, puke till they were swimming in it. But I couldn't. I was trapped, just like in some nightmare. Right there in the middle of the front row.

When Mal finally ducked his denuded head and announced my father, the applause was seismic, as if the whole auditorium had been tipped on end, and the great man, in one of his own tour T-shirts and the omnipresent leather jacket, took the stage and engaged in a little high-fiving with the departing biographer while the thunder gradually subsided and the faces round me went slack with wonder. For the next fifteen minutes he pranced and strutted across the stage, ignoring the podium and delivering a preprogrammed monologue that was the equal of anything you'd see on late-night TV. At least all the morons around me thought so. He charmed them, out-hipped them, and they laughed, snorted, sniggered and howled. Some of them, my fellow freshmen, no doubt, even stamped their feet in thunderous unison as if they were at a pep rally or something. And the jokes—the sort of thing he'd come on with at lunch—were all so self-effacing, at least on the surface, but deep down each phrase and buttressed pause was calculated to remind us we were in the presence of one of the heroes of literature. There was the drinking-with-Bukowski story, which had been reproduced in every interview he'd done in the last twenty years, the travelling-through-Russia-with-nothing-but-a-pair-of-jeans-two-socks-and-a-leather-jacket-after-his-luggage-was-stolen story, the obligatory movie star story and three or four don't-ask-me-now references to his wild past. I sat there like a condemned man awaiting the lethal injection, a rigid smile frozen to my face. My scalp itched, both nostrils, even the crotch of my underwear. I fought for control.

And then the final blow fell, as swift and sudden as a meteor shrieking down from outer space and against all odds blasting through the roof of the auditorium and drilling right into the back of my reeling head. My father raised a hand to indicate that the jokes were over, and the audience choked off as if he'd tightened a noose around each and every throat. Suddenly he was more professorial than the professors—there wasn't a murmur in the house, not even a cough. He held up a book, produced a pair of wire-rim glasses—a prop if ever I saw one—and glanced down at me. "The piece I want to read tonight, from *Blood Ties*, is something I've wanted to read in public for a long time. It's a deeply personal piece, and painful too, but I read it tonight as an act of contrition. I read it for my son."

He spread open the book with a slow, sad deliberation I'm sure they all found very affecting, but to me he was like a terrorist opening a suitcase full of explosives, and I shrank into my seat, as miserable as I've ever been in my life. He can't be doing this, I thought, he can't. But he was. It was his show, after all.

And then he began to read. At first I didn't hear the words, didn't want to—I was in a daze, mesmerized by the intense weirdness of his voice, which had gone high-pitched and nasal all of a sudden, with a kind of fractured rhythm that made it seem as if he was translating from another language. It took me a moment, and then I understood: this was his reading voice, another affectation. Once I got past that, there were the words themselves, each one a little missile aimed at me, the hapless son, the victim who only wanted to be left lying in the wreckage where he'd fallen. He was reading a passage in which the guilt-racked but lusty father takes the fourteen-year-old son out to the best restaurant in town for a heart-to-heart talk about those lusts, about dreams, responsibilities and the domestic life that was dragging him down. I tried to close myself off, but I couldn't. My eyes were burning. Nobody in the auditorium was watching him anymore—how could they be? No, they were watching me. Watching the back of my head. Watching the fiction come to life.

I did the only thing I could. When he got to the part where the son, tears streaming into his chocolate mousse, asks him why, why, Dad, why, I stood up, right there, right in the middle of the front row, all those eyes drilling into me. I tore my hand away from Victoria's, stared down the biographer and Dr. Delpino and all the rest of them, and stalked straight out the nearest exit even as my father's amplified voice wavered, faltered, and then came back strong again, nothing wrong, nothing the matter, nothing a little literature wouldn't cure.

I don't know what happened between him and Victoria at the muted and minimally celebratory dinner later that night, but I don't suspect it was much, if anything. That wasn't the problem, and both of us—she and I, that is—knew it. I spent the night hiding out in the twenty-four-hour laundromat wedged between Brewskies Pub and Taco Bell, and in the morning I ate breakfast in a greasy spoon only the townies frequented and then caught up on some of Hollywood's distinguished product at the local cineplex for as long as I could stand it. By then, I was sure the great man would have gone on to his many other great appointments, all his public posturing aside. And that was just what happened: he cancelled his first flight and hung around till he could hang around no longer, flying out at four-fifteen with his biographer and all the sympathy of the deeply yearning and heartbroken campus. And me? I was nobody again. Or so I thought.

I too dropped out of Dr. Delpino's class—I couldn't stand the thought of that glazed blue look of accusation in her eyes—and though I occasionally spotted Victoria's hair riding the currents around campus, I avoided her. She knew where to find me if she wanted me, but all that was over, I could see that—I wasn't his son after all. A few weeks later I noticed her in the company of this senior who played keyboards in one of the local bands, and I felt something, I don't know what it was, but it wasn't jealousy. And then, at the end of a lonely semester in a lonely town in the lonely hind end of nowhere, the air began to soften and a few blades of yellow grass poked up through the rotting snow and my roommate took me downtown to Brewskies to celebrate.

The girl's name was Marlene, but she didn't pronounce it like the old German actress who was probably dead before she was born, but Mar-*lenna*, the second syllable banged out till it sounded as if she was calling herself Lenny. I liked the way her smile showed off the gold caps on her molars. The band I didn't want to mention earlier was playing through the big speakers over the bar, and there was a whole undercurrent of noise and excitement mixed with the smells of tap beer, Polish sausage and salt-and-vinegar chips. "I know you," she said. "You're, um, Tom McNeil's son, right?"

I never looked away from her, never blinked. All that was old news now, dead and buried, like some battle in the Civil War.

"That's right," I said. "How did you guess?"

MEXICO

He didn't know much about Mexico, not really, if you discount the odd margarita and a determined crawl through the pages of *Under the Volcano* in an alcoholic haze twenty years ago, but here he was, emerging pale and heavy from the sleek envelope of the airliner and into the fecund embrace of Puerto Escondido. All this—the scorching blacktop, the distant arc of the beach, the heat, the scent of the flowers and the jet fuel, and the faint lingering memory of yesterday's fish—was an accident. A happy accident. A charity thing at work—give five bucks to benefit the Battered Women's Shelter and win a free trip for two to the jewel of Oaxaca. Well, he'd won. And to save face and forestall questions he'd told everybody he was bringing his girlfriend along, for two weeks of R. and R.—Romance and Relaxation. He even invented a name for her—Yolanda—and yes, she was Mexican on her mother's side, gray eyes from her father, skin like burnished copper, and was she ever something in bed. . . .

There were no formalities at the airport—they'd taken care of all that in Mexico City with a series of impatient gestures and incomprehensible commands—and he went through the heavy glass doors with his carry-on bag and ducked into the first cab he saw. The driver greeted him in English, swivelling round to wipe an imaginary speck of dust from the seat with a faded pink handkerchief. He gave a little speech Lester couldn't follow, tossing each word up in the air as if it were a tight-stitched ball that had to be driven high over the fence, then shrank back into himself and said, "Where to?" in a diminished voice. Lester gave the name of his hotel—the best one in town—and sat back to let the ripe breeze wash over his face.

He was sweating. Sweating because he was in some steaming thick tropical place and because he was overweight, grossly over-weight, carrying fifty pounds too many and all of it concentrated in his gut. He was going to do something about that when he got back to San Francisco—join a club, start jogging, whatever—but right now he was just a big sweating overweight man with bare pale legs set like stanchions on the floor of the cab and a belly that soaked right through the front of his cotton-rayon open-necked shirt with the blue and yellow parrots cavorting all over it. And there was the beach, scalloped and white, chasing along beside the car, with palm trees and a hint of maritime cool, and before ten minutes had ticked off his watch he was at the hotel, paying the driver from a wad of worn velvety bills that didn't seem quite real. The driver had no problem with them—the bills, that is—and he accepted a fat velvety tip too, and seven and a half minutes after that Lester was sitting in the middle of a shady tiled dining room open to the sea on one side and the pool on the other, a room key in his pocket and his first Mexican cocktail clenched in his sweaty fist.

He'd negotiated the cocktail with the faintest glimmer of half-remembered high-school Spanish—jooze *naranja*, soda cloob and vodka, tall, with ice, *hielo*, yes, *hielo*—and a whole repertoire of mimicry he didn't know he possessed. What he'd really wanted was a Greyhound, but he didn't know the Spanish word for grape-fruit, so he'd fallen back on the orange juice and vodka, though there'd been some confusion over the meaning of the venerable Russian term for clear distilled spirits until he hit on the inspira-tion of naming the brand, Smirnoff. The waitress, grinning and nodding while holding herself perfectly erect in her starched white peasant dress, repeated the brand name in a creaking singsong voice and went off to fetch his drink. Of course, by the time she set it down, he'd already drunk the better half of it and he imme-diately ordered another and then another, until for the first twenty

minutes or so he had the waitress and bartender working in perfect synchronization to combat his thirst and any real or imagined
pangs he might have suffered on the long trip down.

After the fifth drink he began to feel settled, any anxiety over
travelling dissolved in the sweet flow of alcohol and juice. He was
pleased with himself. Here he was, in a foreign country, ordering
cocktails like a native and contemplating a bite to eat—guacamole
and nachos, maybe—and then a stroll on the beach and a nap
before dinner. He wasn't sweating anymore. The waitress was his
favorite person in the world, and the bartender came next.

He'd just drained his glass and turned to flag down the
waitress—one more, he was thinking, and then maybe the
nachos—when he noticed that the table at the far end of the veranda was occupied. A woman had slipped in while he was gazing out to sea, and she was seated facing him, bare-legged, in
a rust-colored bikini and a loose black robe. She looked to be
about thirty, slim, muscular, with a high tight chest and feathered
hair that showed off her bloodshot eyes and the puffed bow of
her mouth. There was a plate of something steaming at her
elbow—fish, it looked like, the specialty of the house, breaded,
grilled, stuffed, baked, fried, or sautéed with peppers, onion, and
cilantro—and she was drinking a Margarita rocks. He watched in
fascination—semi-drunken fascination—for a minute, until she
looked up, chewing, and he turned away to stare out over the water as if he were just taking in the sights like any other calm and
dignified tourist.

He was momentarily flustered when the waitress appeared to
ask if he wanted another drink, but he let the alcohol sing in his
veins and said, "Why not?"—"*¿Por qué no?*"—and the waitress
giggled and walked off with her increasingly admirable rump
moving at the center of that long white gown. When he stole another glance at the woman in the corner, she was still looking his
way. He smiled. She smiled back. He turned away again and bided
his time, but when his drink came he tossed some money on the
table, rose massively from the chair, and tottered across the room.

"Hi," he said, looming over the chewing woman, the drink

rigid in his hand, his teeth clenched round a defrosted smile. "I mean, *Buenos tardes*. Or *noches*."

He watched her face for a reaction, but she just stared at him.

"Uh, *¿Cómo está Usted?* Or *tú. ¿Cómo estás tú?*"

"Sit down, why don't you," she said in a voice that was as American as Hillary Clinton's. "Take a load off."

Suddenly he felt dizzy. The drink in his hand had somehow concentrated itself till it was as dense as a meteorite. He pulled out a chair and sat heavily. "I thought . . . I thought you were—?"

"I'm Italian," she said. "From Buffalo, originally. All four of my grandparents came from Tuscany. That's where I get my exotic Latin looks." She let out a short bark of a laugh, forked up a slab of fish, and began chewing vigorously, all the while studying him out of eyes that were like scalpels.

He finished his drink in a gulp and looked over his shoulder for the waitress. "You want another one?" he asked, though he saw she hadn't half finished her first.

Still chewing, she smiled up at him. "Sure."

When the transaction was complete and the waitress had presented them with two fresh drinks, he thought to ask her name, but the silence had gone on too long, and when they both began to speak at the same time he deferred to her. "So what do you do for a living?" she asked.

"Biotech. I work for a company in the East Bay—Oakland, that is."

Her eyebrows lifted. "Really? Is that like making potatoes that walk around the kitchen and peel themselves? Cloning sheep? Two-headed dogs?"

Lester laughed. He was feeling good. Better than good. "Not exactly."

"My name's Gina," she said, reaching out her hand, "but you might know me as the Puma. Gina (the Puma) Caramella."

He took her hand, which was dry and small and nearly lost in his own. He was drunk, gloriously drunk, and so far he hadn't been ripped off by the Federales or assailed by the screaming shits or leached dry by malarial mosquitoes and vampire bats or any of the other myriad horrors he'd been warned against, and that made him feel pretty near invulnerable. "What do you mean? You're an actress?"

She gave a little laugh. "I wish." Ducking her head, she chased the remnants of the fish around the plate with her fork and the plane of her left index finger. "No," she said. "I'm a boxer."

The alcohol percolated through him. He wanted to laugh, but he fought down the urge. "A boxer? You don't mean like *boxing*, do you? Fisticuffs? Pugilism?"

"Twenty-three, two, and one," she said. She took a sip of her drink. Her eyes were bright. "What I'm doing right now is agonizing over my defeat two weeks ago at the Shrine by one of the queen bitches in the game, DeeDee DeCarlo, and my manager thought it would be nice for me to just get away for a bit, you know what I mean?"

He was electrified. He'd never met a female boxer before—didn't even know there was such a thing. Mud-wrestling he could see—in fact, since his wife had died, he'd become a big fan, Tuesday nights and sometimes on Fridays—but boxing? That wasn't a woman's sport. Drunkenly, he scrutinized her face, and it was a good face, a pretty face, but for the bridge of her nose, a telltale depression there, just the faintest misalignment—and sure, sure, how had he missed it? "But doesn't it hurt? I mean, when you get punched in the . . . body punches, I mean?"

"In the tits?"

He just nodded.

"Sure it hurts, what do you think? But I wear a padded bra, wrap 'em up, pull 'em flat across the ribcage so my opponent won't have a clear target, but really, it's the abdominal blows that take it out of you," and she was demonstrating with her hands now, the naked slope of her belly and the slit of her navel, abs of steel, but nothing like those freakish female bodybuilders they threw at you on ESPN, nice abs, nice navel, nice, nice, nice.

"You doing anything for dinner tonight?" he heard himself say.

She looked down at the denuded plate before her, nothing left but lettuce, don't eat the lettuce, never eat the lettuce, not in Mexico. She shrugged. "I guess I could. I guess in a couple hours."

He lifted the slab of his arm and consulted his watch with a frown of concentration. "Nine o'clock?"

She shrugged again. "Sure."

"By the way," he said. "I'm Lester."

April had been dead two years now. She'd been struck and killed by a car a block from their apartment, and though the driver was a teenage kid frozen behind the wheel of his father's Suburban, it wasn't entirely his fault. For one thing, April had stepped out in front of him, twenty feet from the crosswalk, and, as if that wasn't bad enough, she was blindfolded at the time. Blindfolded and feeling her way with one of those flexible fiberglass sticks the blind use to register the world at their feet. It was for a psychology course she was taking at San Francisco State—"Strategies of the Physically Challenged." The professor had asked for two volunteers to remain blindfolded for an entire week, even at night, even in bed, no cheating, and April had been the first to raise her hand. She and Lester had been married for two years at the time—his first, her second—and now she was two years dead.

Lester had always been a drinker, but after April's death he seemed to enjoy drinking less and need it more. He knew it, and he fought it. Still, when he got back to his room, sailing on the high of his chance meeting with Gina—Gina the Puma—he couldn't help digging out the bottle of Herradura he'd bought in the duty-free and taking a good long cleansing hit.

There was no TV in the room, but the air conditioner worked just fine, and he stood in front of it a while before stripping off his sodden shirt and stepping into the shower. The water was tepid, but it did him good. He shaved, brushed his teeth, and repositioned himself in front of the air conditioner. When he saw the bottle standing there on the night table, he thought he'd have just one more hit—just one—because he didn't want to be utterly wasted when he took Gina the Puma out for dinner. But then he

looked at his watch and saw that it was only seven-twenty, and figured what the hell, two drinks, three, he just wanted to have a
good time. Too wired to sleep, he flung himself down on the bed
like a big wet dripping fish and began poking through the yellowed paperback copy of *Under the Volcano* he'd brought along because he couldn't resist the symmetry of it. What else was he
going to read in Mexico—Proust?

"*No se puede vivir sin amar,*" he read, "You can't live without love," and he saw April stepping out into the street with her
puny fiberglass stick and the black velvet sleep mask pulled tight
over her eyes. But he didn't like that picture, not at all, so he took
another drink and thought of Gina. He hadn't had a date in six
months, and he was ready. And who knew? Anything could
happen. Especially on vacation. Especially down here. He tipped
back the bottle, and then he flipped to the end of the book, where
the Consul, cored and gutted and beyond all hope, tumbles dead
down the ravine and they throw the bloated corpse of a dog down
after him.

The first time Lester had read it, he'd thought it was funny, in
a grim sort of way. But now he wasn't so sure.

Gina was waiting for him at the bar when he came down at quarter to nine. The place was lit with paper lanterns strung from the
thatched ceiling, there was the hint of a breeze off the ocean, the
sound of the surf, a smell of citrus and jasmine. All the tables were
full, people leaning into the candlelight over their fish and Margaritas and murmuring to each other in Spanish, French, German.
It was good. It was perfect. But as Lester ascended the ten steps
from the patio and crossed the room to the bar, his legs felt dead,
as if they'd been shot out from under him and then magically re-
attached, all in the space of an instant. Food. He needed food. Just
a bite, that was all. For equilibrium.

"Hey," he said, nudging Gina with his shoulder.

"Hey," she said, flashing a smile. She was wearing shorts and
heels and a blue halter top glistening with tiny blue beads.

He was amazed at how small she was—she couldn't have weighed more than a hundred pounds. April's size. April's size exactly.

He ordered a Herradura and tonic, his forearms laid out like bricks on the bar. "You weren't kidding before," he said, turning to her, "about boxing, I mean? Don't take offense, but you're so—well, small. I was just wondering, you know?"

She looked at him a long moment, as if debating with herself. "I'm a flyweight, Les," she said finally. "I fight other flyweights, just like in the men's division, you know? This is how big God made me, but you come watch me some night and you'll see it's plenty big enough."

She wasn't smiling, and somewhere on the free-floating periphery of his mind he realized he'd made a blunder. "Yeah," he said, "of course. Of course you are. Listen, I didn't mean to—but why boxing? Of all the things a woman could do."

"What? You think men have a patent on aggression? Or excellence?" She let her eyes sail out over the room, hard eyes, angry eyes, and then she came back to him. "Look, you hungry or what?"

Lester swirled the ice in his drink. It was time to defuse the situation, but quick. "Hey," he said, smiling for all he was worth, "I'd like to tell you I'm on a diet, but I like eating too much for that—and plus, I haven't had a thing since that crap they gave us on the plane, dehydrated chicken and rice that tasted like some sort of by-product of the vulcanizing process. So yeah, let's go for it."

"There's a place up the beach," she said, "in town. I hear it's pretty good—Los Crotos? Want to try it?"

"Sure," he said, but the deadness crept back into his legs. Up the beach? In town? It was dark out there, and he didn't speak the language.

She was watching him. "If you don't want to, it's no big deal," she said, finishing off her drink and setting the glass down with a rattle of ice that sounded like nothing so much as loose teeth spat into a cup. "We can just eat here. The thing is, I've been here two days now and I'm a little bored with the menu—you know, fish, fish, and more fish. I was thinking maybe a steak would be nice."

"Sure," he said. "Sure, no problem."

And then they were out on the beach, Gina barefoot at his side, her heels swinging from one hand, purse from the other. The night was dense and sustaining, the lights muted, palms working slowly in the breeze, empty *palapas* lined up along the high-water mark like the abandoned cities of a forgotten race. Lester shuffled through the deep sand, his outsized feet as awkward as snowshoes, while children and dogs chased each other up and down the beach in a blur of shadow against the white frill of the surf and knots of people stood in the deeper shadows of the palms, laughing and talking till the murmur of conversation was lost in the next sequence of breakers pounding the shore. He wanted to say something, anything, but his brain was impacted and he couldn't seem to think, so they walked in silence, taking it all in.

When they got to the restaurant—an open-air place set just off a shallow lagoon that smelled powerfully of sea-wrack and decay—he began to loosen up. There were tables draped in white cloth, the waiter was solicitous and grave, and he accepted Lester's mangled Spanish with equanimity. Drinks appeared. Lester was in his element again. "So," he said, leaning into the table and trying to sound as casual as he could while Gina squeezed a wedge of lime into her drink and let her shoe dangle from one smooth slim foot, "you're not married, are you? I mean, I don't see a ring or anything. . . ."

Gina hunched her shoulders, took a sip of her drink—they were both having top-shelf Margaritas, blended—and gazed out on the dark beach. "I used to be married to a total idiot," she said, "but that was a long time ago. My manager, Gerry O'Connell— he's Irish, you know?—him and me had a thing for a while, but I don't know anymore. I really don't." She focussed on him. "What about you?"

He told her he was a widower and watched her eyes snap to attention. Women loved to hear that—it got all their little wheels and ratchets turning—because it meant he wasn't damaged goods like all the other hairy-chested cretins out there, but tragic, just tragic. She asked how it had happened, a sink of sympathy and morbid female curiosity, and he told her the story of the kid in the Suburban and the wet pavement and how the student volunteers were supposed to have a monitor with them at all times, but not April, because she just shrugged it off—she wanted an authentic experience, and that was what she got, all right. His throat seemed to thicken when he got to that part, the irony of it, and what with the cumulative weight of the cocktails, the reek of the lagoon, and the strangeness of the place—Mexico, his first day in Mexico—he nearly broke down. "I wasn't there for her," he said. "That's the bottom line. I wasn't there."

Gina was squeezing his hand. "You must have really loved her."

"Yeah," he said. "I did." And he had loved her, he was sure of it, though he had trouble picturing her now, her image drifting through his consciousness as if blown by a steady wind.

Another drink came. They ordered dinner, a respite from the intensity of what he was trying to convey, and then Gina told him her own tale of woe, the alcoholic mother, the brother shot in the face when he was mistaken for a gang member, how she'd excelled in high-school sports and had nowhere to go with it, two years at the community college and a succession of mind-numbing jobs till Gerry O'Connell plucked her from anonymity and made her into a fighter. "I want to be the best," she said. "Number One—and I won't settle for anything less."

"You're beautiful," he said.

She looked at him. Her drink was half gone. "I know," she said.

By the time they were finished with dinner and they'd had a couple of after-dinner drinks, he was feeling unbeatable again. It was quarter past eleven and the solicitous waiter wanted to go home. Lester wanted to go home too—he wanted to take Gina up to his room and discover everything there was to know about her. He lurched suddenly to his feet and threw a fistful of money at the table. "Want to go?" he said, the words sticking to the roof of his mouth.

She rose unsteadily from her seat and leaned into him while she adjusted the strap of her right heel. "Think we should take a cab?" she said.

"A cab? We're just at the other end of the beach."

She was staring up at him, small as a child, her head thrown back to take in the spread and bulk of him. "Didn't you see that notice in your room—on the bathroom door? I mean, it sounds almost funny, the way they worded it, but still, I wonder."

"Notice? What notice?"

She fished around in her purse until she came up with a folded slip of paper. "Here," she said. "I wrote it down because it was so bizarre: 'The management regrets to inform you that the beach area is unsafe after dark because of certain criminal elements the local authorities are sadly unable to suppress and advises that all guests should take a taxi when returning from town.' "

"Are you kidding? Criminal elements? This place is a sleepy little village in the middle of nowhere—they ought to try the Tenderloin if they want to see criminal elements. And besides, besides"—he was losing his train of thought—"besides . . ."

"Yes?"

"There's nobody in the whole country taller than five-four, as far as I can see." He laughed. He couldn't help himself. *Criminal elements!* And he was still shaking his head as they stepped out into the night.

Call it hubris.

They hadn't gone two hundred yards, the night deepening, dogs howling in the hills, and every star set firmly in its track, when they were jumped. It was nothing like the way Lester had visualized it while stalking home after the bars closed on Twenty-fourth Street, half hoping some sorry shithead would come up to him so he could break him in two. There were no words, no warning, no "Give me your wallet" or "I've got a gun" or "This is a stickup." One minute he was trudging through the sand, a drunken arm draped hopefully over Gina's shoulder, and the next he was on the ground, two pairs of booted feet lashing diligently at his face and ribs while a whole fluttering rush of activity washed round him, as if a flock of birds had burst up off the ground in a panic. He heard a grunt, a curse, the unmistakable crack of bone and cartilage rearranging itself, and it was Gina, Gina the Puma, whaling away at the shadows with both fists as he shoved himself up out of the sand and the boots suddenly stopped kicking and fled.

"You all right?" she said, and he could hear her hard steady breathing over the hammering of the waves.

He was cursing into the night—"Sons of bitches! Mother-fuckers! I'll kill you!"—but it was all bluster, and he knew it. Worse, so did she.

"Yeah," he said finally, his chest heaving, the booze and adrenaline pulsing in his temples till the blood vessels there felt like big green garden hoses crawling up both sides of his head. "Yeah, I'm okay. . . . I took a few kicks in the face maybe . . . and I think—I think they got my wallet. . . ."

"Here," she said, her voice oddly calm, "are you sure?" And then she was crouching, feeling around in the sand with spread fingers.

He joined her, glad to be down on his hands and knees and relieved of the effort of holding himself up. His wallet? He didn't give a shit about any wallet. The sand was cool, and the regular thump of the waves conveyed itself to him in the most immediate and prescient way.

"Les?" She was standing now, obscuring the stars. He couldn't make out her face. "You sure you're all right?"

From a great reeling distance he heard himself say, "Yeah, I'm fine." Her voice was insistent, the voice of an intimate, a wife, a lover.

"Come on, Les, get up. You can't stay here. It's not safe."

"Okay," he said. "Sure. Just give me a minute."

Then there was a brightness, a burning-hot soldered light fused to the cracks of the blinds, and he woke to find himself in his bed—his Mexican bed, in his Mexican hotel, in Mexico. Alone. Without

Gina, that is. The first thing he did was check his watch. There it was, clinging like a manacle to his wrist, dividing his naked forearm from his meaty pale hand and indifferently announcing the time: two thirty-two. All right. He heaved himself up to a sitting position, drained the plastic water bottle he discovered behind the tequila on the night table, and took a minute to assess the situation.

There was a rumor of pain between his ribs, where, he began to recall, two pairs of sharp-toed boots had repeatedly inserted themselves in the waning hours of the previous night, but that was nothing compared with his face. It seemed to ache all over, from his hairline to his jaw. He reached a hand to his cheek and felt a tenderness there, and then he worked his jaw till the pain became too much for him. His right eye was swollen closed, there was a drumming in his head and a vague nauseous feeling creeping up the back of his throat. To top it off, his wallet was missing.

Now he'd have to call up and cancel his credit cards, and he was a fool and an idiot and he cursed himself twice over, but it wasn't the end of the world—he had ten thin crisp hundreds hidden away in his carry-on bag, or his shaving kit, actually, where no one would think to look for them. It could have been worse, he was thinking, but he couldn't get much beyond that. How had he managed to get himself back last night? Or had Gina managed it? The thought made him burn with shame.

He took a shower, clapped on a pair of coruscating silver-lensed sunglasses to mask the desecration of his eye, and limped down to the restaurant. She wasn't there, and that was all right for the moment—he needed time to pull himself together before he could face her. The waitress was there, though, eternally responsive to his needs, wearing another down-to-the-toes peasant dress, this time in a shade of blue so pale it barely registered. She smiled and chirped at him and he ordered two tall Smirnoff-and-*naranja* with soda cloob and three fried eggs with tortillas and a fiery serrano salsa that cleared his airways, no doubt about it. He ate and drank steadily, and when he looked up idly at the sea stretching beyond the veranda, he saw nothing but a desert of water. He had a third cocktail for equilibrium, then went down to the front desk and asked the attendant there if she knew which room Gina was staying in.

"Gina?" the woman echoed, giving him a blank look. "What family name, please?"

He had no idea. She'd told him, but it was gone now, obliterated by vodka, tequila, and half a dozen kicks to the head. All he could think of was her professional name. "The Puma," he tried. "Gina the Puma."

The woman's hair was pulled back in a bun, her blouse buttoned up to her throat. She studied him a long moment. "I'm sorry," she said. "I can't help you."

"Gina," he repeated, and his voice got away from him a bit. "How many Ginas could there be in this place, for Christ's sake?"

When she answered this time, she spoke in Spanish, and then she turned away.

He began a methodical search of the place, from pool to bar and back again, suddenly desperate. He had to explain last night to Gina, joke it away, rationalize, apologize, spin shit into gold; she had to understand that he was drunk and his judgment was impaired, and if the circumstances had been different he would have wiped the beach with those scumbags, he would have. Startled faces gaped up at him from the recliners round the pool, maids in pale-green uniforms flattened themselves to the walls. Then he was in the blast of the midday sun, searching through the *palapas* on the beach, hundreds of *palapas*, and practically every one with a sunburned tourist lounging beneath it. Soon he was sunburned himself, sweating rivulets and breathing hard, so he stripped off his shirt, threw himself into the waves, and came up dripping to the nearest unoccupied *palapa* and sent a skinny little girl scurrying away to provide him with a piss-warm beer.

Several piss-warm beers later, he began to feel like himself again—and so what if he'd lost his shirt somewhere in the surf? He was in Mexico and he was drunk and he was going to find Gina and make it up to her, ask her to dinner, take a cab—a whole fleet of cabs—and buy her all the steak and lobster she could hold. He drank a tequila with wedges of lime and some true, cold beers at a tourist bar, and when the shadows began to lengthen, he decided to continue up the beach to see if she'd maybe taken one of the water taxis over to Puerto Ángel or Carrizalillo and was only now coming back.

The sun was hanging on a string just over the horizon, pink and lurid, and the tourists were busy packing up their sunblock and towels and paperback novels while the dark people, the ones who lived here year-round and didn't know what a vacation was, began to drift out of the trees with their children and their dogs to reclaim their turf. He kept walking, intent on the way his toes grabbed and released the sand, and he'd got halfway to the boats before he realized he'd left his sunglasses somewhere. No matter. He never even broke stride. They were nothing to him, one more possession, one more thing he could slough off like so much dead skin, like April's desk and her clothes and the straw baskets and pottery she'd decorated the apartment with. Besides, there was hardly any glare off the water now, and these people, these coppery little grimacing Indians who seemed to sprout up all over the beach once the sun began to close down, they needed to see him, with his flaming belly and his crusted cheekbone and savage eye, because this was what their criminal elements had done to him and he was wearing the evidence of it like a badge. "Fuck you," he was muttering under his breath. "Fuck you all."

At some point, Lester looked up to orient himself and saw that he was just opposite the restaurant from last night. There it sat, squat among the trees, its lights reflected on the surface of the lagoon. A soft glow lit the bar, which he could just make out, figures there, movement, cocktail hour. He had a sudden intimation that Gina was in there, her dark head bent over a table in back, a drunken intimation that counted absolutely for nothing, but he acted on it, sloshing through the fetid lagoon in his sandals and shorts, mounting the three steps from the beach and drifting across the creaking floorboards to the bar.

It wasn't Gina seated at the table but a local woman, the proprietress no doubt, totting up figures in a ledger; she raised her head when he walked in, but looked right through him. There were three men at the bar, some sort of police, in black shirts and trousers, one of them wearing dark glasses though there was no practical reason to at this hour. They ignored him and went on smoking and talking quietly, in soft rapping voices. A plastic half-gallon jug of tequila stood before them on the bar, amid a litter of plates and three water glasses half-full of silvery liquid. Lester addressed the bartender. "Margarita rocks," he said. "With *hielo*."

He sipped his drink, profoundly drunk now, but drunk for a reason. Two reasons. Or three. For one thing, he had pain to kill, physical pain, and for another he was on vacation, and if you can't be legitimately wasted on your vacation, then when can you be? The third reason was Gina. He'd come so close, and then he'd blown it. *Criminal elements.* He glanced up at the cops with an idle curiosity that turned sour almost immediately: Where were they when he'd needed them?

And then he noticed something that made his heart skip a beat: the boots. These guys were wearing boots, sharp-toed boots with silver toe-caps, the only boots in town. Nobody in Puerto Escondido wore boots. They could barely afford sandals, fishermen who earned their living with a hook and thirty feet of line wrapped round an empty two-liter Pepsi bottle, maids and itinerant merchants, dirt farmers from the hills. Boots? They were as likely to have Armani blazers, silk shirts, and monogrammed boxer shorts. Understanding came down like a hammer. He had to find Gina.

Dusk now, children everywhere, dogs, fishermen up to their chests in the rolling water, bats swooping, sand fleas leaping away from the blind advance of his feet. The steady flow of alcohol had invigorated him—he was feeling no pain, none at all—though he realized he'd have to eat something soon, and clean himself up, especially if he was going to see Gina, because his whole body was seething and rushing, and everything, from the palms to the *palapas* to the rocks scattered along the shore, seemed to have grown fur. Or fuzz. Peach fuzz.

That was when he stepped in the hole and went down awkwardly on his right side, his face plowing a furrow in the loose sand, and the bad eye, wet with fluid, picking up a fine coating of sharp white granules. But it was no problem, no problem at all. He rolled over and lay on his back a while, laughing softly to himself. *Criminal elements*, he thought, and he was speaking the thought aloud as people stepped round him in the sand. "Sure, sure. And I'm the Pope in Rome."

When he finally got back to the hotel courtyard, he hesitated. Just stood there glistening in the muted light like a statue erected in honor of the befuddled tourist. On the one hand, he was struck by the impulse to go back to his room, wash the grit from his body, do something with his hair and fish another shirt out of his bag; on the other, he felt an equally strong urge to poke his head in the bar for a minute—just a minute—to see if Gina was there. Ultimately, it was no contest. There he went, feet thundering on the planks, the sand sparkling all over him as if he'd been dipped in sugar.

There. There was the waitress, giving him an odd look—a blend of hopefulness and horror—and the thicket of heads bent over plates and glasses, the air heavy as water, the bartender looking up sharply. Ever hopeful, Lester lurched out onto the floor.

This time he got lucky: Gina was sitting at a table just round the corner of the bar, the farthest table out on the veranda, her legs crossed at the knee, one shoe dangling from her toes. There was music playing somewhere, a faint hum of it leaking in out of the night, Mexican music, shot full of saccharine trumpets and weeping violins. It was a romantic moment, or it could have been. But Gina didn't see him coming—she was turned the other way, in profile, the sea crashing behind her, her hair hanging limp to her shoulders—and it wasn't till he'd rounded the end of the bar that he saw she wasn't alone. There was a man sitting across from her, a drink in one hand, cigarette in the other. Lester saw a dangle of red hair, muscles under a Lollapalooza T-shirt, the narrow face of an insect.

In the next instant he loomed up on the table, pulled out a chair, and dropped into it with a thump that reverberated the length of the dining room. "Gina, listen," he said, as if they were right in the middle of a conversation and the man with the insect face didn't exist, "about last night, and you're not going to believe this, but it was—"

And then he faltered. Gina's mouth was hanging open—and this was a mouth that could cushion any blow, a mouth that knew the taste of leather and the shock of the punch that came out of nowhere. "Christ, Les," she said. "What happened to you—you're a mess. Have you looked in the mirror?"

He watched her exchange a glance with the man across the table, and then he was talking again, trying to get it out, the night, the way they'd come at him, and they weren't just your average muggers, they were the law, for Christ's sake, and how could anybody expect him to defend her from that?

"Les," she was saying. "Les, I think you've had too much to drink."

"I'm trying to tell you something," he said, and his own voice sounded strange to him, distant and whining, the voice of a loser, a fat man, a maker of bad guesses and worse decisions.

That was when the red-haired man spoke up, his eyes twitching in his head. "Who is this jerk, anyway?"

Gina—Gina the Puma—gave him a look that was like a left jab. "Shut up, Drew," she said. And then, turning back to Lester: "Les, this is Drew." She tried to inject a little air into her voice, though he could see she wasn't up to it. "Drew wants to know where he can get a good steak around here."

Drew slouched in his chair. He had nothing to say. Lester looked from Gina to Drew and back again. He was very far gone, he knew that, but still, even through his haze, he was beginning to see something in those two faces that shut him out, that slammed the door with a bang and turned the key in the lock.

He had no right to Gina or this table or this hotel, either. He couldn't even make it through the first round.

Gina's voice came to him as if from a great distance—"Les, really, maybe you ought to go and lie down for a while"—and then he was on his feet. He didn't say "Yes" or "No" or even "See you later"—he just turned away from the table, wove his way through the restaurant, down the stairs and back out into the night.

It was fully dark now, black dark, and the shadows had settled under the skeletons of the trees. He wasn't thinking about Gina or Drew or even April and the kid in the Suburban. There was no justice, no revenge, no reason—there was just this, just the beach and the night and the criminal elements. And when he got to the place by the lagoon and the stink of decay rose to his nostrils, he went straight for the blackest clot of shadow and the rasping murmur at the center of it. "You!" he shouted, all the air raging in his lungs. "Hey, you!"

THE LOVE OF MY LIFE

They wore each other like a pair of socks. He was at her house, she was at his. Everywhere they went—to the mall, to the game, to movies and shops and the classes that structured their days like a new kind of chronology—their fingers were entwined, their shoulders touching, their hips joined in the slow triumphant sashay of love. He drove her car, slept on the couch in the family room at her parents' house, played tennis and watched football with her father on the big thirty-six-inch TV in the kitchen. She went shopping with his mother and hers, a triumvirate of tastes, and she would have played tennis with his father, if it came to it, but his father was dead. "I love you," he told her, because he did, because there was no feeling like this, no triumph, no high—it was like being immortal and unconquerable, like floating. And a hundred times a day she said it too: "I love you. I love you."

They were together at his house one night when the rain froze on the streets and sheathed the trees in glass. It was her idea to take a walk and feel it in their hair and on the glistening shoulders of their parkas, an otherworldly drumming of pellets flung down out of the troposphere, alien and familiar at the same time, and they glided the length of the front walk and watched the way the power lines bellied and swayed. He built a fire when they got back, while she towelled her hair and made hot chocolate laced with Jack Daniel's. They'd rented a pair of slasher movies for the ritualized comfort of them—"Teens have sex," he said, "and then they pay for it in body parts"—and the maniac had just climbed out of the heating vent, with a meat hook dangling from the recesses of his empty sleeve, when the phone rang.

It was his mother, calling from the hotel room in Boston where she was curled up—shacked up?—for the weekend with the man she'd been dating. He tried to picture her, but he couldn't. He even closed his eyes a minute, to concentrate, but there was nothing there. Was everything all right? she wanted to know. With the storm and all? No, it hadn't hit Boston yet, but she saw on the Weather Channel that it was on its way. Two seconds after he hung up—before she could even hit the Start button on the VCR—the phone rang again, and this time it was her mother. Her mother had been drinking. She was calling from a restaurant, and China could hear a clamor of voices in the background. "Just stay put," her mother shouted into the phone. "The streets are like a skating rink. Don't you even think of getting in that car."

Well, she wasn't thinking of it. She was thinking of having Jeremy to herself, all night, in the big bed in his mother's room. They'd been having sex ever since they started going together at the end of their junior year, but it was always sex in the car or sex on a blanket or the lawn, hurried sex, nothing like she wanted it to be. She kept thinking of the way it was in the movies, where the stars ambushed each other on beds the size of small planets and then did it again and again until they lay nestled in a heap of pillows and blankets, her head on his chest, his arm flung over her shoulder, the music fading away to individual notes plucked softly on a guitar and everything in the frame glowing as if it had been sprayed with liquid gold. That was how it was supposed to be. That was how it was going to be. At least for tonight.

She'd been wandering around the kitchen as she talked, dancing with the phone in an idle slow saraband, watching the frost sketch a design on the window over the sink, no sound but the soft hiss of the ice pellets on the roof, and now she pulled open the freezer door and extracted a pint box of ice cream. She was in her socks, socks so thick they were like slippers, and a pair of black leggings under an oversized sweater. Beneath her feet, the polished floorboards were as slick as the sidewalk outside, and she liked the feel of that, skating indoors in her big socks. "Uh-huh," she said into the phone. "Uh-huh. Yeah, we're watching a movie." She dug a finger into the ice cream and stuck it in her mouth.

"Come on," Jeremy called from the living room, where the maniac rippled menacingly over the Pause button. "You're going to miss the best part."

"Okay, Mom, okay," she said into the phone, parting words, and then she hung up. "You want ice cream?" she called, licking her finger.

Jeremy's voice came back at her, a voice in the middle range, with a congenital scratch in it, the voice of a nice guy, a very nice guy who could be the star of a TV show about nice guys: "What kind?" He had a pair of shoulders and pumped-up biceps too, a smile that jumped from his lips to his eyes, and close-cropped hair that stood up straight off the crown of his head. And he was always singing—she loved that—his voice so true he could do any song, and there was no lyric he didn't know, even on the oldies station. She scooped ice cream and saw him in a scene from last summer, one hand draped casually over the wheel of his car, the radio throbbing, his voice raised in perfect synch with Billy Corgan's, and the night standing still at the end of a long dark street overhung with maples.

"Chocolate. Swiss chocolate almond."

"Okay," he said, and then he was wondering if there was any whipped cream, or maybe hot fudge—he was sure his mother had a jar stashed away somewhere, *Look behind the mayonnaise on the top row*—and when she turned around he was standing in the doorway.

She kissed him—they kissed whenever they met, no matter where or when, even if one of them had just stepped out of the room, because that was love, that was the way love was—and then they took two bowls of ice cream into the living room and, with a flick of the remote, set the maniac back in motion.

It was an early spring that year, the world gone green overnight, the thermometer twice hitting the low eighties in the first week of March. Teachers were holding sessions outside. The whole school, even the halls and the cafeteria, smelled of fresh-mowed grass and the unfolding blossoms of the fruit trees in the development across the street, and students—especially seniors—were cutting class to go out to the quarry or the reservoir or to just drive the back streets with the sunroof and the windows open wide. But not China. She was hitting the books, studying late, putting everything in its place like pegs in a board, even love, even that. Jeremy didn't get it. "Look, you've already been accepted at your first-choice school, you're going to wind up in the top ten G.P.A.-wise, and you've got four years of tests and term papers ahead of you, and grad school after that. You'll only be a high-school senior once in your life. Relax. Enjoy it. Or at least *experience* it."

He'd been accepted at Brown, his father's alma mater, and his own G.P.A. would put him in the top ten percent of their graduating class, and he was content with that, skating through his final semester, no math, no science, taking art and music, the things he'd always wanted to take but never had time for—and Lit., of course, A.P. History, and Spanish 5. "*Tú eres el amor de mi vida,*" he would tell her when they met at her locker or at lunch or when he picked her up for a movie on Saturday nights.

"*Y tú también,*" she would say, "or is it '*yo también*'?"—French was her language. "But I keep telling you it really matters to me, because I know I'll never catch Margery Yu or Christian Davenport, I mean they're a lock for val and salut, but it'll kill me if people like Kerry Sharp or Jalapy Seegrand finish ahead of me—you should know that, you of all people—"

It amazed him that she actually brought her books along when they went backpacking over spring break. They'd planned the trip all winter and through the long wind tunnel that was February, packing away freeze-dried entrées, Power Bars, Gore-Tex windbreakers and matching sweatshirts, weighing each item on a handheld scale with a dangling hook at the bottom of it. They were going up into the Catskills, to a lake he'd found on a map, and they were going to be together, without interruption, without telephones, automobiles, parents, teachers, friends, relatives, and pets, for five full days. They were going to cook over an open fire, they were going to read to each other and burrow into the double sleeping bag with the connubial zipper up the seam he'd found in his mother's closet, a relic of her own time in the lap of nature. It smelled of her, of his mother, a vague scent of her perfume that had lingered there dormant all these years, and maybe there was the faintest whiff of his father too, though his father had been gone so long he didn't even remember what he looked like, let alone what he might have smelled like. Five days. And it wasn't going to rain, not a drop. He didn't even bring his fishing rod, and that was love.

When the last bell rang down the curtain on Honors Math, Jeremy was waiting at the curb in his mother's Volvo station wagon, grinning up at China through the windshield while the rest of the school swept past with no thought for anything but release. There were shouts and curses, T-shirts in motion, slashing legs, horns bleating from the seniors' lot, the school buses lined up like armored vehicles awaiting the invasion—chaos, sweet chaos—and she stood there a moment to savor it. "Your mother's car?" she said, slipping in beside him and laying both arms over his shoulders to pull him to her for a kiss. He'd brought her jeans and hiking boots along, and she was going to change as they drove, no need to go home, no more circumvention and delay, a stop at McDonald's, maybe, or Burger King, and then it was the sun and the wind and the moon and the stars. Five days. Five whole days.

"Yeah," he said, in answer to her question, "my mother said she didn't want to have to worry about us breaking down in the middle of nowhere—"

"So she's got your car? She's going to sell real estate in your car?"

He just shrugged and smiled. "Free at last," he said, pitching his voice down low till it was exactly like Martin Luther King's. "Thank God Almighty, we are free at last."

It was dark by the time they got to the trailhead, and they wound up camping just off the road in a rocky tumble of brush, no

place on earth less likely or less comfortable, but they were together, and they held each other through the damp whispering
hours of the night and hardly slept at all. They made the lake by
noon the next day, the trees just coming into leaf, the air sweet
with the smell of the sun in the pines. She insisted on setting up
the tent, just in case—it could rain, you never knew—but all he
wanted to do was stretch out on a gray neoprene pad and feel the
sun on his face. Eventually, they both fell asleep in the sun, and
when they woke they made love right there, beneath the trees, and
with the wide blue expanse of the lake giving back the blue of the
sky. For dinner, it was étouffée and rice, out of the foil pouch,
washed down with hot chocolate and a few squirts of red wine
from Jeremy's bota bag.

The next day, the whole day through, they didn't bother with
clothes at all. They couldn't swim, of course—the lake was too
cold for that—but they could bask and explore and feel the breeze
out of the south on their bare legs and the places where no breeze
had touched before. She would remember that always, the feel of
that, the intensity of her emotions, the simple unrefined pleasure
of living in the moment. Woodsmoke. Duelling flashlights in the
night. The look on Jeremy's face when he presented her with
the bag of finger-sized crayfish he'd spent all morning collecting.

What else? The rain, of course. It came midway through the
third day, clouds the color of iron filings, the lake hammered to
iron too, and the storm that crashed through the trees and beat
at their tent with a thousand angry fists. They huddled in the
sleeping bag, sharing the wine and a bag of trail mix, reading to
each other from a book of Donne's love poems (she was writing a
paper for Mrs. Masterson called "Ocular Imagery in the Poetry of
John Donne") and the last third of a vampire novel that weighed
eighteen-point-one ounces.

And the sex. They were careful, always careful—*I will never,
never be like those breeders that bring their puffed-up squalling little
red-faced babies to class*, she told him, and he agreed, got adamant
about it, even, until it became a running theme in their relationship, the breeders overpopulating an overpopulated world and

ruining their own lives in the process—but she had forgotten to pack her pills and he had only two condoms with him, and it wasn't as if there was a drugstore around the corner.

In the fall—or the end of August, actually—they packed their cars separately and left for college, he to Providence and she to Binghamton. They were separated by three hundred miles, but there was the telephone, there was E-mail, and for the first month or so there were Saturday nights in a motel in Danbury, but that was a haul, it really was, and they both agreed that they should focus on their course work and cut back to every second or maybe third week. On the day they'd left—and no, she didn't want her parents driving her up there, she was an adult and she could take care of herself—Jeremy followed her as far as the Bear Mountain Bridge and they pulled off the road and held each other till the sun fell down into the trees. She had a poem for him, a Donne poem, the saddest thing he'd ever heard. It was something about the moon. *More than moon*, that was it, lovers parting and their tears swelling like an ocean till the girl—the woman, the female—had more power to raise the tides than the moon itself, or some such. More than moon. That's what he called her after that, because she was white and round and getting rounder, and it was no joke, and it was no term of endearment.

She was pregnant. Pregnant, they figured, since the camping trip, and it was their secret, a new constant in their lives, a fact, an inescapable fact that never varied no matter how many home pregnancy kits they went through. Baggy clothes, that was the key, all in black, cargo pants, flowing dresses, a jacket even in summer. They went to a store in the city where nobody knew them and she got a girdle, and then she went away to school in Binghamton and he went to Providence. "You've got to get rid of it," he told her in the motel room that had become a prison. "Go to a clinic," he told her for the hundredth time, and outside it was raining—or, no, it was clear and cold that night, a foretaste of winter. "I'll find the money—you know I will."

She wouldn't respond. Wouldn't even look at him. One of the

Star Wars movies was on TV, great flat thundering planes of metal roaring across the screen, and she was just sitting there on the edge of the bed, her shoulders hunched and hair hanging limp. Someone slammed a car door—two doors in rapid succession— and a child's voice shouted, "Me! Me first!"

"China," he said. "Are you listening to me?"

"I can't," she murmured, and she was talking to her lap, to the bed, to the floor. "I'm scared. I'm so scared." There were footsteps in the room next door, ponderous and heavy, then the quick tattoo of the child's feet and a sudden thump against the wall. "I don't want anyone to know," she said.

He could have held her, could have squeezed in beside her and wrapped her in his arms, but something flared in him. He couldn't understand it. He just couldn't. "What are you thinking? Nobody'll know. He's a doctor, for Christ's sake, sworn to secrecy, the doctor-patient compact and all that. What are you going to do, keep it? Huh? Just show up for English 101 with a baby on your lap and say, 'Hi, I'm the Virgin Mary'?"

She was crying. He could see it in the way her shoulders suddenly crumpled and now he could hear it too, a soft nasal complaint that went right through him. She lifted her face to him and held out her arms and he was there beside her, rocking her back and forth in his arms. He could feel the heat of her face against the hard fiber of his chest, a wetness there, fluids, her fluids. "I don't want a doctor," she said.

And that colored everything, that simple negative: life in the dorms, roommates, bars, bullshit sessions, the smell of burning leaves and the way the light fell across campus in great wide smoking bands just before dinner, the unofficial skateboard club, films, lectures, pep rallies, football—none of it mattered. He couldn't have a life. Couldn't be a freshman. Couldn't wake up in the morning and tumble into the slow steady current of the world. All he could think of was her. Or not simply her—her and him, and what had come between them. Because they argued now, they wrangled and fought and debated, and it was no pleasure to see her in that motel room with the queen-size bed and the big color

TV and the soaps and shampoos they made off with as if they were treasure. She was pigheaded, stubborn, irrational. She was spoiled, he could see that now, spoiled by her parents and their standard of living and the socioeconomic expectations of her class—of his class—and the promise of life as you like it, an unscrolling vista of pleasure and acquisition. He loved her. He didn't want to turn his back on her. He would be there for her no matter what, but why did she have to be so *stupid?*

Big sweats, huge sweats, sweats that drowned and engulfed her, that was her campus life, sweats and the dining hall. Her dormmates didn't know her, and so what if she was putting on weight? Everybody did. How could you shovel down all those carbohydrates, all that sugar and grease and the puddings and nachos and all the rest, without putting on ten or fifteen pounds the first semester alone? Half the girls in the dorm were waddling around like the Doughboy, their faces bloated and blotched with acne, with crusting pimples and whiteheads fed on fat. So she was putting on weight. Big deal. "There's more of me to love," she told her roommate, "and Jeremy likes it that way. And, really, he's the only one that matters." She was careful to shower alone, in the early morning, long before the light had begun to bump up against the windows.

On the night her water broke—it was mid-December, almost nine months, as best as she could figure—it was raining. Raining hard. All week she'd been having tense rasping sotto voce debates with Jeremy on the phone—arguments, fights—and she told him that she would die, creep out into the woods like some animal and bleed to death, before she'd go to a hospital. "And what am I supposed to do?" he demanded in a high childish whine, as if he were the one who'd been knocked up, and she didn't want to hear it, she didn't.

"Do you love me?" she whispered. There was a long hesitation, a pause you could have poured all the affirmation of the world into.

"Yes," he said finally, his voice so soft and reluctant it was like the last gasp of a dying old man.

"Then you're going to have to rent the motel."

"And then what?"

"Then—I don't know." The door was open, her roommate framed there in the hall, a burst of rock and roll coming at her like an assault. "I guess you'll have to get a book or something."

By eight, the rain had turned to ice and every branch of every tree was coated with it, the highway littered with glistening black sticks, no moon, no stars, the tires sliding out from under her, and she felt heavy, big as a sumo wrestler, heavy and loose at the same time. She'd taken a towel from the dorm and put it under her, on the seat, but it was a mess, everything was a mess. She was cramping. Fidgeting with her hair. She tried the radio, but it was no help, nothing but songs she hated, singers that were worse. Twenty-two miles to Danbury, and the first of the contractions came like a seizure, like a knife blade thrust into her spine. Her world narrowed to what the headlights would show her.

Jeremy was waiting for her at the door to the room, the light behind him a pale rinse of nothing, no smile on his face, no human expression at all. They didn't kiss—they didn't even touch— and then she was on the bed, on her back, her face clenched like a fist. She heard the rattle of the sleet at the window, the murmur of the TV: *I can't let you go like this*, a man protested, and she could picture him, angular and tall, a man in a hat and overcoat in a black-and-white world that might have been another planet, *I just can't.* "Are you—?" Jeremy's voice drifted into the mix, and then stalled. "Are you ready? I mean, is it time? Is it coming now?"

She said one thing then, one thing only, her voice as pinched and hollow as the sound of the wind in the gutters: "Get it out of me."

It took a moment, and then she could feel his hands fumbling with her sweats.

Later, hours later, when nothing had happened but pain, a parade of pain with drum majors and brass bands and penitents crawling on their hands and knees till the streets were stained with their blood, she cried out and cried out again. "It's like *Alien*," she gasped, "like that thing in *Alien* when it, it—"

"It's okay," he kept telling her, "it's okay," but his face betrayed him. He looked scared, looked as if he'd been drained of blood in some evil experiment in yet another movie, and a part of her wanted to be sorry for him, but another part, the part that was so commanding and fierce it overrode everything else, couldn't begin to be.

He was useless, and he knew it. He'd never been so purely sick at heart and terrified in all his life, but he tried to be there for her, tried to do his best, and when the baby came out, the baby girl all slick with blood and mucus and the lumped white stuff that was like something spilled at the bottom of a garbage can, he was thinking of the ninth grade and how close he'd come to fainting while the teacher went around the room to prick their fingers one by one so they each could smear a drop of blood across a slide. He didn't faint now. But he was close to it, so close he could feel the room dodging away under his feet. And then her voice, the first intelligible thing she'd said in an hour: "Get rid of it. Just get rid of it."

Of the drive back to Binghamton he remembered nothing. Or practically nothing. They took towels from the motel and spread them across the seat of her car, he could remember that much . . . and the blood, how could he forget the blood? It soaked through her sweats and the towels and even the thick cotton bathmat and into the worn fabric of the seat itself. And it all came from inside her, all of it, tissue and mucus and the shining bright fluid, no end to it, as if she'd been turned inside out. He wanted to ask her about that, if that was normal, but she was asleep the minute she slid out from under his arm and dropped into the seat. If he focused, if he really concentrated, he could remember the way her head lolled against the doorframe while the engine whined and the car rocked and the slush threw a dark blanket over the windshield every time a truck shot past in the opposite direction. That and the exhaustion. He'd never been so tired, his head on a string, shoulders slumped, his arms like two pillars of concrete. And what if he'd nodded off? What if he'd gone into a skid and hurtled over an embankment into the filthy gray accumulation of the worst day of his life? What then?

She made it into the dorm under her own power, nobody even looked at her, and no, she didn't need his help. "Call me," she whispered, and they kissed, her lips so cold it was like kissing a steak through the plastic wrapper, and then he parked her car in the student lot and walked to the bus station. He made Danbury late that night, caught a ride out to the motel, and walked right through the Do Not Disturb sign on the door. Fifteen minutes. That was all it took. He bundled up everything, every trace, left the key in the box at the desk, and stood scraping the ice off the windshield of his car while the night opened up above him to a black glitter of sky. He never gave a thought to what lay discarded in the Dumpster out back, itself wrapped in plastic, so much meat, so much cold meat.

He was at the very pinnacle of his dream, the river dressed in its currents, the deep hole under the cutbank, and the fish like silver bullets swarming to his bait, when they woke him—when Rob woke him, Rob Greiner, his roommate, Rob with a face of crumbling stone and two policemen there at the door behind him and the roar of the dorm falling away to a whisper. And that was strange, policemen, a real anomaly in that setting, and at first—for the first thirty seconds, at least—he had no idea what they were doing there. Parking tickets? Could that be it? But then they asked him his name, just to confirm it, joined his hands together behind his back, and fitted two loops of naked metal over his wrists, and he began to understand. He saw McCaffrey and Tuttle from across the hall staring at him as if he were Jeffrey Dahmer or something, and the rest of them, all the rest, every head poking out of every door up and down the corridor, as the police led him away.

"What's this all about?" he kept saying, the cruiser nosing through the dark streets to the station house, the man at the wheel and the man beside him as incapable of speech as the seats or the wire mesh or the gleaming black dashboard that dragged them forward into the night. And then it was up the steps and into an explosion of light, more men in uniform, stand here, give me your hand, now the other one, and then the cage and the questions. Only then did he think of that thing in the garbage sack and the sound it had made—its body had made—when he flung it into the Dumpster like a sack of flour and the lid slammed down on it. He stared at the walls, and this was a movie too. He'd never been in trouble before, never been inside a police station, but he knew his role well enough, because he'd seen it played out a thousand times on the tube: deny everything. Even as the two detectives settled in across from him at the bare wooden table in the little box of the overlit room he was telling himself just that: *Deny it, deny it all.*

The first detective leaned forward and set his hands on the table as if he'd come for a manicure. He was in his thirties, or maybe his forties, a tired-looking man with the scars of the turmoil he'd witnessed gouged into the flesh under his eyes. He didn't offer a cigarette ("I don't smoke," Jeremy was prepared to say, giving them that much at least), and he didn't smile or soften his eyes. And when he spoke his voice carried no freight at all, not outrage or threat or cajolery—it was just a voice, flat and tired. "Do you know a China Berkowitz?" he said.

And she. She was in the community hospital, where the ambulance had deposited her after her roommate had called 911 in a voice that was like a bone stuck in the back of her throat, and it was raining again. Her parents were there, her mother red-eyed and sniffling, her father looking like an actor who's forgotten his lines, and there was another woman there too, a policewoman. The policewoman sat in an orange plastic chair in the corner, dipping her head to the knitting in her lap. At first, China's mother had tried to be pleasant to the woman, but pleasant wasn't what the circumstances called for, and now she ignored her, because the very unpleasant fact was that China was being taken into custody as soon as she was released from the hospital.

For a long while no one said anything—everything had already been said, over and over, one long flood of hurt and recrimination—and the antiseptic silence of the hospital held them in its grip while the rain beat at the windows and the machines at the foot of the bed counted off numbers. From down the hall came a snatch of TV dialogue, and for a minute China opened her eyes and thought she was back in the dorm. "Honey," her mother said, raising a purgatorial face to her, "are you all right? Can I get you anything?"

"I need to—I think I need to pee."

"Why?" her father demanded, and it was the perfect non sequitur. He was up out of the chair, standing over her, his eyes like cracked porcelain. "Why didn't you tell us, or at least tell your mother—or Dr. Fredman? Dr. Fredman, at least. He's been—he's like a family member, you know that, and he could have, or he would have . . . What were you *thinking*, for Christ's sake?"

Thinking? She wasn't thinking anything, not then and not now. All she wanted—and she didn't care what they did to her, beat her, torture her, drag her weeping through the streets in a dirty white dress with "Baby Killer" stitched over her breast in scarlet letters—was to see Jeremy. Just that. Because what really mattered was what he was thinking.

The food at the Sarah Barnes Cooper Women's Correctional Institute was exactly what they served at the dining hall in college, heavy on the sugars, starches, and bad cholesterol, and that would have struck her as ironic if she'd been there under other circumstances—doing community outreach, say, or researching a paper for her sociology class. But given the fact that she'd been locked up for more than a month now, the object of the other girls' threats, scorn, and just plain *nastiness*, given the fact that her life was ruined beyond any hope of redemption, and every newspaper in the country had her shrunken white face plastered across its front page under a headline that screamed MOTEL MOM, she didn't have much use for irony. She was scared twenty-four hours a day. Scared of the present, scared of the future, scared of the re-porters waiting for the judge to set bail so that they could swarm all over her the minute she stepped out the door. She couldn't concentrate on the books and magazines her mother brought her or even on the TV in the rec room. She sat in her room—it was a room, just like a dorm room, except that they locked you in at night—and stared at the walls, eating peanuts, M&M's, sunflower seeds by the handful, chewing for the pure animal gratification of it. She was putting on more weight, and what did it matter?

Jeremy was different. He'd lost everything—his walk, his smile, the muscles of his upper arms and shoulders. Even his hair lay flat now, as if he couldn't bother with a tube of gel and a comb. When she saw him at the arraignment, saw him for the first time since she'd climbed out of the car and limped into the dorm with the blood wet on her legs, he looked like a refugee, like a ghost. The room they were in—the courtroom—seemed to have grown up around them, walls, windows, benches, lights and radiators already in place, along with the judge, the American flag and the ready-made spectators. It was hot. People coughed into their fists and shuffled their feet, every sound magnified. The judge presided, his arms like bones twirled in a bag, his eyes searching and opaque as he peered over the top of his reading glasses.

China's lawyer didn't like Jeremy's lawyer, that much was evi-dent, and the state prosecutor didn't like anybody. She watched him—Jeremy, only him—as the reporters held their collective breath and the judge read off the charges and her mother bowed her head and sobbed into the bucket of her hands. And Jeremy was watching her too, his eyes locked on hers as if he defied them all, as if nothing mattered in the world but her, and when the judge said "First-degree murder" and "Murder by abuse or ne-glect," he never flinched.

She sent him a note that day—"I love you, will always love you no matter what, More than Moon"—and in the hallway, after-ward, while their lawyers fended off the reporters and the bailiffs tugged impatiently at them, they had a minute, just a minute, to themselves. "What did you tell them?" he whispered. His voice was a rasp, almost a growl; she looked at him, inches away, and hardly recognized him.

"I told them it was dead."

"My lawyer—Mrs. Teagues?—she says they're saying it was alive when we, when we put it in the bag." His face was composed, but his eyes were darting like insects trapped inside his head.

"It was dead."

"It looked dead," he said, and already he was pulling away from her and some callous shit with a camera kept annihilating them with flash after flash of light, "and we certainly didn't—I mean, we didn't slap it or anything to get it breathing. . . ."

And then the last thing he said to her, just as they were pulled apart, and it was nothing she wanted to hear, nothing that had any love in it, or even the hint of love: "You told me to get rid of it."

There was no elaborate name for the place where they were keeping him. It was known as Drum Hill Prison, period. No reform-minded notions here, no verbal gestures toward rehabilitation or behavior modification, no benefactors, mayors or role models to lend the place their family names, but then who in his right mind would want a prison named after him anyway? At least they kept him separated from the other prisoners, the gangbangers and dope dealers and sexual predators and the like. He was no longer a freshman at Brown, not officially, but he had his books and his course notes, and he tried to keep up as best he could. Still, when the screams echoed through the cellblock at night and the walls dripped with the accumulated breath of eight and a half thousand terminally angry sociopaths, he had to admit it wasn't the sort of college experience he'd bargained for.

And what had he done to deserve it? He still couldn't understand. That thing in the Dumpster—and he refused to call it human, let alone a baby—was nobody's business but his and China's. That's what he'd told his attorney, Mrs. Teagues, and his mother and her boyfriend, Howard, and he'd told them over and over again: "*I didn't do anything wrong.*" Even if it was alive, and it was, he knew in his heart that it was, even before the state prosecutor presented evidence of blunt-force trauma and death by asphyxiation and exposure, it didn't matter, or shouldn't have mattered. There was no baby. There was nothing but a mistake, a mistake clothed in blood and mucus. When he really thought about it, thought it through on its merits and dissected all his mother's pathetic arguments about where he'd be today if she'd felt as he did when she was pregnant herself, he hardened like a rock, like sand turning to stone under all the pressure the planet can bring to bear. Another unwanted child in an overpopulated world? They should have given him a medal.

It was the end of January before bail was set—three hundred and fifty thousand dollars his mother didn't have—and he was released to house arrest. He wore a plastic anklet that set off an alarm if he went out the door, and so did she, so did China, imprisoned like some fairy-tale princess at her parents' house. At first, she called him every day, but mostly what she did was cry— "I want to see it," she sobbed. "I want to see our daughter's *grave*." That froze him inside. He tried to picture her—her now, China, the love of his life—and he couldn't. What did she look like? What was her face like, her nose, her hair, her eyes and breasts and the slit between her legs? He drew a blank. There was no way to summon her the way she used to be or even the way she was in court, because all he could remember was the thing that had come out of her, four limbs and the equipment of a female, shoulders rigid and eyes shut tight, as if she were a mummy in a tomb . . . and the breath, the shuddering long gasping rattle of a breath he could feel ringing inside her even as the black plastic bag closed over her face and the lid of the Dumpster opened like a mouth.

He was in the den, watching basketball, a drink in his hand (7Up mixed with Jack Daniel's in a ceramic mug, so no one would know he was getting shit-faced at two o'clock on a Sunday afternoon), when the phone rang. It was Sarah Teagues. "Listen, Jeremy," she said in her crisp, equitable tones, "I thought you ought to know—the Berkowitzes are filing a motion to have the case against China dropped."

His mother's voice on the portable, too loud, a blast of amplified breath and static: "On what grounds?"

"She never saw the baby, that's what they're saying. She thought she had a miscarriage."

"Yeah, right," his mother said.

Sarah Teagues was right there, her voice as clear and present as his mother's. "Jeremy's the one that threw it in the Dumpster, and they're saying he acted alone. She took a polygraph test day before yesterday."

He could feel his heart pounding the way it used to when he plodded up that last agonizing ridge behind the school with the cross-country team, his legs sapped, no more breath left in his body. He didn't say a word. Didn't even breathe.

"She's going to testify against him."

Outside was the world, puddles of ice clinging to the lawn under a weak afternoon sun, all the trees stripped bare, the grass dead, the azalea under the window reduced to an armload of dead brown twigs. She wouldn't have wanted to go out today anyway. This was the time of year she hated most, the long interval between the holidays and spring break, when nothing grew and nothing changed—it didn't even seem to snow much anymore. What was out there for her anyway? They wouldn't let her see Jeremy, wouldn't even let her talk to him on the phone or write him anymore, and she wouldn't be able to show her face at the mall or even the movie theater without somebody shouting out her name as if she was a freak, as if she was another Monica Lewinsky or Heidi Fleiss. She wasn't China Berkowitz, honor student, not anymore—she was the punch line to a joke, a footnote to history.

She wouldn't mind going for a drive, though—that was something she missed, just following the curves out to the reservoir to watch the way the ice cupped the shore, or up to the turnout on Route 9 to look out over the river where it oozed through the mountains in a shimmering coil of light. Or to take a walk in the woods, just that. She was in her room, on her bed, posters of bands she'd outgrown staring down from the walls, her high school books on two shelves in the corner, the closet door flung open on all the clothes she'd once wanted so desperately she could have died for each individual pair of boots or the cashmere sweaters that felt so good against her skin. At the bottom of her left leg, down there at the foot of the bed, was the anklet she wore now, the plastic anklet with the transmitter inside, no different, she supposed, than the collars they put on wolves to track them across all those miles of barren tundra or the bears sleeping in their dens. Except that hers had an alarm on it.

For a long while she just lay there gazing out the window, watching the rinsed-out sun slip down into the sky that had no more color in it than a TV tuned to an unsubscribed channel, and then she found herself picturing things the way they were an eon ago, when everything was green. She saw the azalea bush in bloom, the leaves knifing out of the trees, butterflies—or were they cabbage moths?—hovering over the flowers. Deep green. That was the color of the world. And she was remembering a night, summer before last, just after she and Jeremy started going together, the crickets thrumming, the air thick with humidity, and him singing along with the car radio, his voice so sweet and pure it was as if he'd written the song himself, just for her. And when they got to where they were going, at the end of that dark lane overhung with trees, to a place where it was private and hushed and the night fell in on itself as if it couldn't support the weight of the stars, he was as nervous as she was. She moved into his arms, and they kissed, his lips groping for hers in the dark, his fingers trembling over the thin yielding silk of her blouse. He was Jeremy. He was the love of her life. And she closed her eyes and clung to him as if that were all that mattered.

RUST

That was the sky up above, hot, with a fried egg of a sun stuck in the middle of it, and this was the ground down here, hard, with a layer of parched grass and a smell of dirt and leaf mold, and no matter how much he shouted there didn't seem to be much else in between. What he could use was a glass of water. He'd been here, what—an hour, maybe?—and the sun hadn't moved. Or not that he could see, anyway. His lips were dry, and he could feel all that ultraviolet radiation cooking the skin off his face, a piece of meat on the grill, turkey skin, crisp and oozing, peeling away in strips. But he wasn't hungry—he was never hungry anymore. It was just an image, that was all. He could use a chair, though, and somebody to help him up and put him in it. And some shade. Some iced tea, maybe, beads of moisture sliding down the outside of the glass.

"Eunice!" he called out in a voice that withered in his throat. "Eunice, goddamnit, Eunice!" And then, because he was old and he was angry and he didn't give a damn anymore, he cried out for help. "Help!" he croaked. "Help!"

But nobody was listening. The sky hung there like a tattered curtain, shreds of cloud draped over the high green crown of the pepper tree he'd planted forty years ago, the day his son was born, and he could hear the superamplified rumble of the TV from behind the shut and locked windows and the roar of the air conditioner, and where was the damn dog, anyway? That was it. He remembered now. The dog. He'd come out to look for the dog—

she'd been gone too long, too long about her business, and Eunice had turned her parched old lampshade of a head away from the TV screen and said, "Where's the dog?" He didn't know where the dog was, though he knew where his first bourbon and water of the day was—right there on the TV tray in front of him—and it was 11:00 A.M. and plenty late enough for it. "How the hell would I know," he'd said, "you were the one let her out," and she'd come right back at him with something smart, like "Well you'd better just get yourself out there in the yard and see, hadn't you?"

He hadn't actually been out in the yard in a long while—years, it seemed—and when he went out the back door and down the steps he found himself gaping at the bushes all in flower, the trumpet vine smothering the back of the house, and he remembered a time when he cared about all that, about nature and flowers, steer manure and potting soil. Now the yard was as alien to him as the Gobi Desert. He didn't give a damn for flowers or trees or the stucco peeling off the side of the house and all the trim destroyed with the blast of the sun or anything else. "Booters!" he'd called, angry suddenly, angry at he didn't know what. "Booters! Here, girl!"

And that was when he fell.

Maybe the lawn dipped out from under him, maybe he stepped in a gopher hole or tripped over a sprinkler head—that must have been it—but the long and short of it was that he was here, on the grass, stretched out like a corpse under the pepper tree, and he couldn't for the life of him seem to get up.

I've never wanted anybody more in my life, from the minute I came home from Rutgers and laid eyes on you, and I don't care if you are my father's wife, I don't care about anything anymore. . . . Eunice sipped at her drink—vodka and soda, bland as all get-out, but juice gave her the runs—and nodded in complete surrender as the former underwear model–turned–actress fell into the arms of the clip-jawed actor with the ridge of glistening hair that stood up from his crown like a meat loaf just turned out of the pan. The screen faded for the briefest nanosecond before opening on a cheery ad for rectal suppositories, and she found herself drifting into a reverie about the first time Walt had ever taken her in his arms.

They were young then. Or younger. A whole lot younger. She was forty-three and childless, working the checkout desk at the library while her husband ran a slowly failing quick-printing business, and Walt, five years her junior and with the puffed-up chest and inflated arms of the inveterate body builder, taught phys ed at the local high school. She liked to stop in at the Miramar Hotel after work, just to see who was there and unwind a bit after a day of typing out three-by-fives for the card catalogue and collecting fifteen- and twenty-cent fines from born-nasty rich men's wives with beauty parlor hair and too much time on their hands. One day she came in out of the flaming nimbus of the fog and there was Walt, sitting at the bar like some monument to manhood, his tie askew and the sleeves of his white dress shirt rolled up to reveal the squared-off blocks of his forearms. She sat at one of the tables, ordered a drink—it was vodka and grapefruit in those days, tall— and lit a cigarette. When she looked up, he was standing over her. "Don't you know smoking's bad for your health?"

She took her time, crossed her legs under the table and squirmed her bottom around till she was comfortable. She'd seen Ava Gardner in the movies. And Lauren Bacall too. "Tell me that," she said, slow and languid, drawing it out with the smoke, "when I'm an old lady."

Well, he laughed and sat down and they got to talking and before long he was meeting her there every afternoon at five while her husband moaned and fretted over last-minute rush jobs and his wife drank herself into oblivion in her own kitchen. And when that moment came—their first embrace—she reached out for his arms as if she were drowning.

But now the screen flickered and *The Furious Hours* gave way to *Riddle Street* and she eased back in her chair, the vodka and soda at her lips like recirculated blood flowing back into her, and watched as the heroine—one of the towering sluts of daytime television— carved up another man.

/ / / / /

The funny thing was that nothing hurt, or not particularly or any more than usual, what with the arthritis in both knees and the unreconstructed hernia that felt as if some animal was living under his skin and clawing to get out—no, he hadn't broken anything, he was pretty sure of that. But there was something wrong with him. Desperately wrong. Or why else would he be lying here on his back listening to the grass grow while the clouds became ghosts in winding sheets and fled away to nothing and the sun burned the skin right off his face?

Maybe he was dying, maybe that was it. The thought didn't alarm him, not especially, not yet, but it was there, a hard little bolus of possibility lodged in his brain. He moved the fingers of his right hand, one by one, just to see if the signals still carried that far, and then he tried the other side, the left, and realized after a long moment that there was nothing there, nothing he could feel, anyway. Something whispered in his ear—a single word, *stroke*—and that was when he began to be afraid. He heard a car go by on the street out front of the house, the soughing of the tires, the clank of the undercarriage, the smooth fuel-injected suck of the engine. "Help!" he cried. "Somebody help!"

And then he was looking up into the lace of the pepper tree and remembering a moment on a bus forty-five years ago, some anonymous stop in Kansas or Nebraska, and he on his way to California for the first time and every good thing awaiting him. An old man got on, dazed and scrawny and with a long whittled pole of a neck and a tattered straw hat set way back on his head, and he just stood there in the middle of the aisle as if he didn't know where he was. Walt was twenty-nine, he'd been in the service and college too, and he wasn't acquainted with any old people or any dead people, either—not since the war, anyway. He lifted weights two hours every morning, rain or shine, hot or cold, sick or well, and the iron suffused him with its power like some magic potion.

He looked up at the old man and the old man looked right through him. That was when the driver, oblivious, put the bus in gear and the old man collapsed in his shiny worn suit like a puppet with the strings cut. No one seemed to know what to do, the mother with her mewling baby, the teenager with the over-sized shoes, the two doughy old hens with the rolled-in-butter smiles fixed on their faces, but Walt came up out of his seat automatically and pulled the old man to his feet, and it was as if the old guy wasn't even there, nothing more than a suit stuffed with wadding—he could have propped up ten old men, a hundred, because he was a product of iron and the iron flowed through his veins and swelled his muscles till there was nothing he couldn't do.

Eunice refreshed her drink twice during *Riddle Street*, and then she sat through the next program with her eyes closed, not asleep—she couldn't sleep anymore, sleep was a dream, a fantasy, the dimmest recollection out of an untroubled past—but in a state suspended somewhere between consciousness and its opposite. The sound of a voice, a strange voice, speaking right to her, brought her out of it—*It was amazing, just as if she knew me and my whole life and she told me I was going to come into some money soon, and I did, and the very next day I met the man of my dreams*—and the first thing she focused on was her husband's empty chair. Now where had he got himself off to? Maybe he'd gone to lie down, maybe that was it. Or maybe he was in the kitchen, his big arms that always seemed to be bleeding pinioning the wings of the newspaper, a pencil in his big blunt fingers, his drink like liquid gold in the light through the window and the crossword all scratched over with his black, glistening scrawl. Those were skin cancers on his arms, she knew that, tiny dots of fresh wet blood stippling the places where his muscles used to be, but he wouldn't do anything about it. He didn't care. It was like his hernia. "I'm going to be dead soon, any-way," he said, and that got her down, it did, that he should talk like that. "How can you talk like that?" she'd say, and he'd throw it right back at her. "Why not? What have I got to live for?" And she'd blink at him, trying desperately to focus, because if she couldn't focus she couldn't give him a look, all pouty and frowning, like Marlene Dietrich in *Destry Rides Again*. "For me, baby," she'd say. "For me."

The idea of the kitchen sent her there, a little shaky on her feet after sitting so long, and her ankles weren't helping, not at all—it felt as if somebody'd snuck in and wrapped truck tires around them while she sat watching her programs. The kitchen was glowing, the back windows glazed with sun, and all the clutter of their last few half-eaten meals invested with a purity and beauty that took her breath away and made her feel like crying, the caramel of the maple syrup bottle and the blue of the Windex and red of the ketchup as vibrant and natural there as flowers in a field. It was a pretty kitchen, the prettiest kitchen in the world. Or it had been once. They'd remodeled in '66—or was it '69? Double aluminum sink, self-cleaning oven, cabinets in solid oak and no cheap lamination, thank you very much. She'd loved that kitchen. It was a kitchen that made her feel loved in return, a place she could retreat to after all the personal nastiness and gossip at the library and wait for her man to come home from coaching football or basketball or whatever it was, depending on the season.

The thought came to her then—or not a thought, actually, but a feeling because feelings were what moved her now, not thoughts—that she ought to maybe fix a can of tomato soup for lunch, and wouldn't it be nice, for a change, to fix some for Walt too? Though she knew what his reaction would be. "I can't eat that," he'd say, "not with my stomach. What do you think, I'm still thirty-eight?"

Well, yes, she did, as a matter of fact. And when he was thirty-eight and he took her away from Stan Sadowsky and blackened both of his eyes for him when he tried to get rough about it, he'd eat anything she put down on the table in front of him, shrimp cocktail in horseradish sauce right out of the jar, pickled cherry peppers, her special Tex-Mex tamales with melted cheese and Tabasco. He loved her then too. Loved her like she'd never been loved before. His fingers—his fingers were magic, the fingers of a masseur, a man who knew what a deep rub was, who knew muscle and ligament and the finer points of erectile tissue and who could manipulate her till she was limp as a rag doll and tingling all over.

Sure, sure he could. But where in Lord's name was he?

The sun had moved. No doubt about it. He'd been asleep, unconscious, delirious, dehydrated, sun-poisoned—pick an adjective—and now he was awake again and staring up at that yellow blot in the sky that went to deep blue and then black if you stared at it too long. He needed water. He needed bourbon. Aspirin. Ibuprofen. Two of those little white codeine tablets the doctor gave him for the pain in his knees. More than anything, though, he needed to get up off this damn lawn before the grass grew through the back of his head. Furious suddenly, raging, he gave it everything he had and managed to lift his right shoulder and the dead weight of his head from the ground—and hold it there, hold it there for a full five seconds, as if he were bench-pressing his own body—before he sank back down again. It wasn't going to work, he could see that now, nothing was going to work, ever again, and he felt himself filling up with despair, a slow dark trickle of it leaking into the black pool that was already inside him.

With the despair came Jimmy. That was the way it always was. When he felt blue, when he felt that life was a disease and not worth the effort of drawing the next contaminated breath, Jimmy was there. Seven years, six months, and fourteen days old, sticks for legs, his head too big for his body and his hair like something you'd scour pans with. Jimmy. His son. The boy who grew up teething on a catcher's mitt and was already the fastest kid in the second grade. Walt had been at school the day he was killed, spotting for the gymnastics club as they went through their paces on the parallel bars. Somebody said there was smoke up the street—the paint store was on fire, the whole block going up, maybe even the bank—and the vaulted cathedral of the gym went silent. Then they smelled the smoke, musty and sharp at the same time, and then they heard the sirens. By the time Walt got out to the street, his gymnasts leading the way in a blur of flying heels, the fire engine was skewed across the sidewalk in the oddest way, three blocks at least from the fire, and he remembered thinking they must have been drunk or blind, one or the other. When he got there, to where the fire company was, smoke crowding the sky in the distance and the taste of it, acid and bitter, on his tongue, he asked the first person he saw—Ed Bakey, the assistant principal—what was the matter. "One of the kids," Ed said, and he was shaking so badly he could hardly get the words out, "one of the kids got hit by the truck."

He drifted off again, mercifully, and when he came to this time the sun was playing peekaboo with the crown of the pepper tree, and the field of shade, healing redemptive shade, spread almost to his feet. What time was it, anyway? Three, at least. Maybe four. And where the hell was Eunice? Inside, that's where she was, where time was meaningless, a series of half-hour slices carved out of the program guide, day melding into night, breakfast into dinner, the bright electrons dancing eternally across the screen. He dug his elbows into the lawn then, both of them, and yes, he could feel his left side all of a sudden and that was something, and he flexed every muscle in his body, pecs, delts, biceps, the long striated cords of his back and the lump of nothing that was his left leg, but he couldn't sit up, couldn't so much as put an inch between him and the flattened grass. That frustrated him. Made him angry. And he cried out again, the driest, faintest bleat of rage and bewilderment from the desert throat of a man who'd never asked anybody for anything.

She called him for lunch, went to the foot of the stairs and called out his name twice, but it was next to impossible to wake him once he went off, soundest sleeper in the world—you'd need a marching band just to get him to blink his eyes—so she heated the tomato soup, cleared a place at the table, and ate by herself. The soup was good, really hit the spot, but they put too much salt in it, they all did, didn't matter which brand you bought. It made her thirsty, all that salt, and she got up to make herself a fresh vodka and soda—there was no sense in traipsing round the house looking for the other glass, which, as she knew from experience, could be anywhere. She couldn't count the hours she'd spent shuffling through the bathroom, kitchen and living room on her feet that felt as if they'd been crimped in a vise, looking for one melted-down watery drink or another. So she took a fresh glass, and she poured, and she drank. Walt was up in the bedroom, that's where he was, napping, and no other possibility crossed her mind, because there was none.

There was the usual ebb and flow of afternoon programming, the stupid fat people lined up on a stage bickering about their stupid fat lives and too stupid to know the whole country was laughing at them, the game shows and teenage dance shows and the Mexican shows stocked with people as fat and stupid as the Americans, only bickering in Spanish instead of English. Then it was evening. Then it was dusk. She was watching a Mickey Rooney/Judy Garland picture on the classic movie channel when a dog began barking on the screen, and she was fooled, just for a second, into thinking it was Booters. That was when she noticed that Booters was gone. And Walt: whatever could he be doing all this time?

She went up the stairs, though each step seemed to rise up insidiously to snatch at her just as she lifted her foot, and saw that the bedroom was empty and that neither dog nor man was in the upstairs bathroom enjoying the monotonous drip-drip-drip of the faucet that never seemed to want to shut itself off. Twice more she went round the house, utterly bewildered, and she even looked in the pantry and the broom closet and the cabinet under the sink. It was nearly dark, the ice cubes of her latest vodka and soda tinkling like chimes in her hand, when she thought to look out back.

"Walt?" she called, thrusting her head out the door. "Booters?"

The frail bleating echo of her own voice came back to her, and then, slipping in underneath it, the faintest whisper of a sound, no louder than the hum of a mosquito's wings or the muffled cry of a bird strangled in the dark. "Help!" she heard, or thought she heard, a sound so weak and constrained it barely registered.

"Walt?" she tried again.

And then: "Eunice, goddamnit, over here!"

She was so startled she dropped her drink, the glass exploding on the flagstones at her feet and anointing her ankles with vodka. The light was fading, and she didn't see very well anymore, not without her glasses, anyway, and she was puzzled, truly puzzled, to hear her husband's voice coming out of nowhere. "Walt?" she murmured, moving across the darkened lawn as through a mine-field, and when she tripped, and fell, it wasn't over a sprinkler head or gopher's mound or a sudden rise in the lawn, it was over the long, attenuated shadow of her husband's still and recumbent form.

Eunice cried out when she went down, a sharp rising exhalation of surprise, followed by an aquiescent grunt and the almost in-evitable elision of some essential bone or joint giving way. He'd heard that sound before, too many times to count, on the football field, the baseball diamond, the basketball court, and he knew right away it was trouble. Or more trouble, if that was possible. "Eu-nice," he croaked, and his face was cooked right down to the bone, "are you hurt?"

She was right there, right there beside him, one of her legs thrust awkwardly over his, her face all but planted in the turf. She was trying to move, to turn over, to right herself—all that he could feel, though he couldn't for the life of him swivel his head to see—but she wasn't having much success. When finally, after a protracted effort, she managed to drag her living leg across his dead one, she took what seemed like an hour to gulp at the air before her lips, tongue and mouth could form a response. "Walt," she gasped, or moaned actually, that's what it was, moan-ing, "my . . . I think . . . oh, oh, it hurts . . ."

He heard a car race up the street, the swift progress of life, places to go, people to meet. Somewhere a voice called out and a door slammed.

"My hip, I think it's my hip—"

It was all he could do to keep from cursing, but he didn't have the strength to curse, and there was no use in it, not now. He gritted his teeth. "Listen, I can't move," he said. "And I've been laying here all day waiting for somebody to notice, but do you think anybody'd even poke their damn head out the door to see if their husband was dead yet and fried up in the sun like a damn pork rind?"

She didn't answer. The shadows thickened round them. The lawn went from gray to black, the color drained out of the treetops and the sky grew bigger by the minute, as if invisible forces were inflating it with the stuff of the universe. He was looking up at the emerging stars—he had no choice, short of closing his eyes. It had been a long time since he'd looked at the stars, indifferent to any space that didn't have a roof over it, and he was strangely moved to see that they were all still there. Or most of them, anyway, but who was counting? He could hear Eunice sobbing in the dark just to the left of him, and for a long while she didn't say anything, just sniffed and snuffled, gagging on every third or fourth breath. Finally her voice came at him out of the void: "You always blame me for everything."

Well, there was truth in that, he supposed, but no sense in getting into it now. "I don't know what's wrong with me, Eunice," he said, trying to keep his voice level, though his heart was hammering and he foresaw every disaster. "I can't get up. I can't even move. Do you understand what I'm saying?"

There was no response. A mosquito lighted on his lower eyelid, soft as a snowflake, and he didn't have the power to brush it away. "Listen," he said, speaking to the sky and all the spilled paint of the stars, "how bad are you? Can you—do you think you can crawl?"

"It hurts," she gasped, "Walt, it hurts," and then she was sobbing again, a broken dry nagging rasp that cut into him like the teeth of a saw.

He softened his voice. "It's okay, Eunice. Everything's going to be okay, you'll see."

It was then, just as the words passed his lips, that the familiar music of Booters' jingling tags rang out ecstatically from the far corner of the yard, followed by a joyful woof and the delirious patter of approaching paws. "Booters!" they cried out simultaneously. "Good girl, Booters. Come here, come here, girl!"

Eunice was expecting a miracle, nothing less—she was an optimist, always was, always would be—and the minute she heard the dog she thought of all the times Lassie had come to the rescue, Rin Tin Tin, Old Yeller, Buck, Toto and she didn't know who else. She was lying face-down on the lawn, and her cheek had begun to itch where it was pressed into the grass and the grass made its snaking intaglio in the flesh, but she didn't dare move because of the pain in her hip and lower back that made her feel as if she were being torn in two. She was scared, of course she was, for herself and for Walt, but when Booters stood over her and began to lick the side of her face, she felt a surge of hope. "That's a girl," she said. "Now speak, Booters, speak!"

Booters didn't speak. She settled her too-big paws down in the grass beside Eunice's head and whined in a soft, puppyish way. She wasn't much more than a puppy, after all, a big lumpish stupid dog of indeterminate breed that couldn't seem to resist soiling the carpet in the hallway no matter how many times she was punished for it. The last dog they'd had, Booters the First, the original Booters, now that was a dog. She was a border collie, her eyes bright with alertness and suspicion, and so smart you could have taught her the multiplication tables if you had a mind to. It was a sad day when they had to have her put down, fifteen years old and so stiff it was like she was walking on stilts, and Walt felt it as much as she did herself, but all he said was "You measure your life in dogs, and if you're lucky you'll get five or six of them," and then he threw the dirt in the hole.

For the next hour, while the mosquitoes had a field day with her face and the back of her neck and her unprotected legs, Eunice kept trying. "Speak, girl!" she said. "Go get help. Get help! Speak!" At first, Walt did his part too, growling out one command after another, but all Booters did was whine through her slushy jowls and shift position to be near whichever one of them was exhorting her the most passionately. And when the automatic sprinklers came on with a hiss of air and the first sputtering release of subterranean pressure, the dog sprang up and trotted over to the porch, smart enough at least to come in out of the rain.

He was dozing when the sprinklers came on. He'd long since given up on the dog—what did Eunice expect her to do, flag down an ambulance?—and he was dreaming about nothing more complicated than his bed, his bed and a glass of water, half a glass, anything to soothe his throat, when the deluge began. It was a mixed blessing. He'd never been so thirsty in his life, baked and bleached under the sun till he felt mummified, and he opened his mouth reflexively. Unfortunately, none of the sprinklers had been adjusted to pinpoint the gaping maw of a supine old man stretched out in the middle of the lawn, and while the odd drop did manage to strike his lips and even his tongue, it did nothing to relieve his thirst, and he was soon soaked through to the skin and shivering. And yet still the water kept coming like some sort of Oriental water torture until finally the pipes heaved a sigh and the flow cut off as abruptly as it had begun.

He felt bad for Eunice, felt powerless and weak, felt dead, but he fought down the despair and tried to sit up again. Or his brain tried. The rest of him, aside from the sting of his sun-scorched face and the persistent ache of his knees and the shivers that shook him like a rag, seemed to belong to somebody else, some stranger he couldn't communicate with. After a while, he gave it up and called out softly to his wife. There was no response. Then he was asleep, and the night came down to lie on him with all its crushing weight.

Toward morning he woke and saw that Eunice had managed to crawl a few feet away; if he rolled his eyes all the way to the left, he could just make her out, a huddled lump in the shining grass. He held his breath, fearing the worst, but then he heard her breathing—or snoring, actually—a soft glottal insuck of air followed by an even softer puff of exhalation. The birds started in then, recommencing their daily argument, and he saw that the sky had begun to grow light, a phenomenon he hadn't witnessed in ages, not since he was in college and stayed up through the night bullshitting about women and metaphysics and gulping beer from the can.

He could shake it off then. Push himself up out of the damp grass, plow through ten flapjacks and half a dozen sausage links, and then go straight to class and after that to the gym to work out. He built himself up then, every day, with every repetition and every set, and there was the proof of it staring back at him in the weight-room mirror. But there was no building now, no collecting jazz albums and European novels, no worrying about brushing between meals or compound interest or life insurance or anything else. Now there was only this, the waiting, and whether you waited out here on the lawn like breakfast for the crows or in there in the recliner, it was all the same. Nothing mattered anymore but this. This was what it all came down to: the grass, the sky, the trumpet vine and the pepper tree, the wife with her bones shot full of air and her hip out of joint, the dog on the porch, the sun, the stars.

Stan Sadowsky had tried to block the door on him the day he came to take Eunice away, but he held his ground because he'd made up his mind and when he made up his mind he was immovable. "She doesn't want to be with you anymore, Stan," he said. "She's not going to be with you."

"Yeah?" Stan's neck was corded with rage and his eyes leaped right out of his head. Walt didn't hate him. He didn't feel anything for him, one way or the other. But there behind him, in the soft light of the hall, was Eunice, her eyes scared and her jaw set, wearing a print dress that showed off everything she had. "Yeah?" Stan repeated, barking it like a dog. "And what the fuck do you know about it?"

"I know this," Walt said, and he hit him so hard he went right through the screen door and sprawled out flat on his back in the hallway. And when he got up, Walt hit him again.

But now, now there was the sun to contend with, already burning through the trees. He smelled the rich wet chlorophyll of the grass and the morning air off the sea, immemorial smells, ancient as his life, and when he heard the soft annunciatory thump of the paper in the front drive, he called out suddenly, but his voice was so weak he could scarcely hear it himself. Eunice was silent. Still and silent. And that worried him, because he couldn't hear her snoring anymore, and when he found his voice again, he whispered, "Eunice, honey, give me your hand. Can you give me your hand?"

He could have sworn he saw her lift her shoulder and swivel toward him, her face alive and glowing with the early light, but he must have been fooling himself. Because when he summoned everything he had left in him and somehow managed to reach out his hand, there was nothing there.

PEEP HALL

I like my privacy. My phone is unlisted, my mailbox locks with a key, and the gate across the driveway automatically shuts behind me when I pull in. I've got my own little half-acre plot in the heart of this sunny little university town, and it's fenced all the way round. The house is a Craftsman-era bungalow, built in 1910, and the yard is lush with mature foliage, including the two grand old oaks that screen me from the street out front, a tsunami of Bougainvillea that long ago swallowed up the chainlink on both sides of the place, half a dozen tree ferns in the fifteen-foot range, and a whole damp, sweet-earth-smelling forest of Pittosporum, acacia, and blue gum eucalyptus crowding out what's left of the lawn.

When I sit on the porch in the afternoon, all I see is twenty shades of green, and when someone bicycles by or the couple across the way get into one of their biweekly wrangles, I'm completely invisible, though I'm sitting right here with my feet propped up, taking it all in. I haven't been to a concert or a sporting event for as long as I can remember, or even a play or the movies, because crowds irritate me, all that jostling and hooting, the bad breath, the evil looks, not to mention the microbes hanging over all those massed heads like bad money on a bad bet. And no, I'm not a crank. I'm not crazy. And I'm not old, or not particularly (I'll be forty-one in November). But I do like my privacy, and I don't think there's any crime in that, especially when you work as hard as I do. Once I pull my car into the driveway, I just want to be left alone.

Six nights a week, and two afternoons, I stir *Mojitos* and shake martinis at the El Encanto Hotel, where I wear a bowtie and a frozen smile. I don't have any pets, I don't like walking, my parents are dead, and my wife—my *ex*-wife—may as well be. When I'm not at the El Encanto, I read, garden, burn things in a pan, clean spasmodically, and listen to whatever the local arts station is playing on the radio. When I feel up to it, I work on my novel (working title, *Grandma Rivers*)—either that or my Master's thesis, "Claustrophobia in Franz Kafka's Fictive Universe," now eleven years behind schedule.

I was sitting on the porch late one afternoon—a Monday, my day off, the sun suspended just above the trees, birds slicing the air, every bud and flower entertaining its individual bee—when I heard a woman's voice raised in exasperation from the porch next door. She was trying to reel herself in, fighting to keep her voice from getting away from her, but I couldn't quite make out what she was saying. The woman's voice rose and fell, and then I recognized the voice of my next-door neighbor saying something in reply, something curt and dismissive, punctuated by the end stop of the front door slamming shut.

Next it was the sharp hammer-and-anvil ring of spike heels on pavement—*toing, toing, toing*—as they retreated down the Schusters' macadam driveway, turned left on the sidewalk, and halted at my gate, which was, of course, locked. I was alert now in every fiber. I slipped a finger between the pages of the novel I'd been reading and held my breath. I heard the gate rattle, my eyes straining to see through the dense leathery mass of the oaks, and then the voice called, "Hello, hello, *hello!*" It was a young voice, female, a take-charge and brook-no-nonsense sort of voice, a very attractive voice, actually, but for some reason I didn't reply. Habit, I suppose. I was on my own porch in my own yard, minding my own business, and I resented the intrusion, no matter what it turned out to be, and I had no illusions on that score either. She was selling something, circulating a petition, organizing a

Neighborhood Watch group, looking for a lost cat; she was out of gas, out of money, out of luck. I experienced a brief but vivid recollection of the time the gardener had left the gate ajar and a dark little woman in a sari came rushing up the walk holding a balsawood replica of the *Stars & Stripes* out in front of her as if it were made of sugar-frosted air, looked me in the eye, and said, "P'raps maybe you buy for a hunnert dollah good coin monee?"

"I'm your neighbor," the voice called, and the gate rattled again. "Come on," she said, "I can see you, you know—I can see your feet—and I know you're there. I just want to take a minute of your time, that's all, just a minute—"

She could see me? Self-consciously I lifted my feet from the floorboards and propped them up on the rail. "I can't," I said, and my voice sounded weak and watered down, "I'm busy right now."

The fraction of a moment passed, all the sounds of the neighborhood butting up against one another—crows cursing in the trees, a jet revealing itself overhead with the faintest distant whine of its engines, a leaf blower starting up somewhere—and then she sang out, "I like your shoes. Where'd you get them? Not in this town, right?"

I said nothing, but I was listening.

"Come on, just a minute, that's all I ask."

I may live alone, by preference, but don't get me wrong, I'm no eunuch. I have the same needs and urges as other men, which I've been able to satisfy sporadically with Stefania Porovka, the assistant pastry chef at the hotel. Stefania is thirty-two, with a smoky deep Russian voice that falls somewhere in the range between magnetic and aphrodisiacal and two children in elementary school. The children are all right, as children go, aside from a little caterwauling when they don't get their way (which seems to be about a hundred percent of the time), but I can't manage to picture them in my house, and by the same token, I can't picture myself in Stefania's psychotically disordered two-bedroom walk-up. So what I'm saying is that I got up from the porch and ambled down the walk to the gate and the girl of twenty or so standing there in blue jeans, heels and a V-neck top.

She was leaning over the gate, her arms crossed at the wrists, rings glinting from her fingers. Her eyes and hair were the exact same shade of brown, as if the colors had been mixed in the same vat, which in a sense I guess they were, and she had unusually thick and expressive eyebrows of the same color. From where I was standing, five feet back from the locked gate, I could see down the front of her blouse. She wasn't wearing a brassiere. "Hello," I said, regaling her with a cautious nod and the same approximation of a smile I put on for my customers at the bar.

"Oh, *hi*," she returned, giving it the sort of emphasis that said she was surprised and impressed and very, very friendly. "I'm Samantha. I live up at the end of the block—the big white house with the red trim?"

I nodded. At this point I was noncommittal. She was attractive—pretty and beyond, actually—but too young for me to be interested in anything more than a neighborly way, and as I say, I wasn't especially neighborly to begin with.

"And you are—?"

"Hart," I said, "Hart Simpson," and I put my hands on my hips, wondering if she could translate body language.

She never moved, but for a slight readjustment of her hands that set her bracelets ajingle. She was smiling now, her eyebrows arching up and away from the sudden display of her teeth. "Hart," she repeated, as if my name were a curious stone she'd found in the street and was busy polishing on the sleeve of her blouse. And then: "Hart, are we bothering you? I mean, are we really bothering you all that much?"

I have to admit the question took me by surprise. Bothering me? I never even knew she existed until thirty seconds ago—and who was this *we* she was referring to? "*We?*" I said.

The smile faded, and she gave me a long, slow look. "So you're not the one who complained—or one of the ones?"

"You must have me confused with somebody else. I don't have the faintest idea what you're talking about."

"Peep Hall—" she said, "you know, like *peephall.com*?"

It was warm, midsummer, the air charged with the scent of

rosemary and lavender and the desiccated menthol of the eucalyptus trees. I felt the sun on my face. I slowly shook my head.

She rubbed the palms of her hands together as if she were washing with soap and water, shifted her eyes away, and then came back to me again. "It's nothing dirty," she said. "It's not like it's some sleazoid club with a bunch of Taiwanese businessmen shoving dollar bills up our crotches or we're lap-dancing or anything like that—we don't even take our clothes off that much, because that totally gets old—"

I still had no idea what she was talking about, but I was beginning to warm to the general drift of it. "Listen," I said, trying to unhinge my smile a bit, "do you want to come in for a beer or maybe a glass of wine or something?"

My house—not the one I grew up in, but this one, the one I inherited from my grandmother—is a shrine to her conventional, turn-of-the-last-century taste, as well as a kind of museum of what my parents left behind when they died. There isn't too much of me in it, but I'm not one for radical change, and the Stickley furniture, the mica lamps, and even the ashtrays and bric-a-brac are wearing well, as eternal as the king's ankus or the treasure buried with Tutankhamen. I keep the place neat—my parents' books commingled with my own on the built-in bookshelves, rugs squared off against the couches and chairs, cups and dishes neatly aligned in the glass-front cabinets—but it's not particularly clean, I'm afraid. I'm not much for dusting. Or vacuuming. The toilets could use a little more attention. And the walls on either side of the fireplace feature long, striated, urine-colored stains where the water got in around the chimney flashing last winter.

"Nice place," Samantha breathed as I handed her a beer and led her into the living room, the house as dark and cool as a wine cellar though it must have been ninety out there in the sun. She settled into the big oak chair by the window, kicked off her heels and took first one foot, then the other, into her hands and slowly rubbed it. "I hate heels," she said, "especially these. But that's what they want us to wear."

I was having a beer too, and I cradled it in my lap and watched her.

"No running shoes—they hate running shoes—and no sweats. It's in our contract." She laughed. "But you don't know what I'm talking about, do you?"

I was thinking about Stefania and how long it had been since I'd had her over, how long it had been since she'd sat in that chair and done something as unselfconscious as rubbing her bare white feet and laughing over a beer. "Tell me," I said.

It was a long story, involving so many digressions that the digressions became stories in themselves, but finally I began to gather that the big white house on the corner, where she lived with six other girls, was meant to represent a college dorm—that's where the "Peep Hall" designation came in—and that the business of the place was to sell subscriptions on the Internet to over-lathered voyeurs who could click on any time of day or night to watch the girls going about their business in living color. "So you've got all these video cameras around," I said, trying to picture it. "Like at the bank or the 7-Eleven—that sort of thing?"

"Yeah, but much better quality, and instead of just like two of them or whatever, you've got cameras all over the place."

"Even in the bathroom?"

Another laugh. "*Especially* the bathroom, what do you think?"

I didn't have anything to say to that. I guess I was shocked. I *was* shocked. I definitely was. But why not admit it? I was titillated too. Women in the shower, I was thinking, women in the tub. I drained my beer, held the bottle up to the light, and asked her if she'd like another one.

She was already slipping her feet back into the shoes. "No, no thanks—I've got to go," she said, rising to her feet. "But thanks for the beer and all—and if they do come around with a petition, you tell them we're not doing anything wrong, okay?" She was smiling, swaying slightly over her heels. "And I don't know if you're into it—you're on-line, right?—but you should check us out, see for yourself."

We were at the door. She handed me the empty beer bottle,

still warm from the embrace of her hand. "You really should," she said.

After she left, I opened another beer and wandered through the downstairs rooms, picking up magazines and tossing them back down again, opening and shutting doors for no good reason, until I found myself in the kitchen. There were dishes in the sink, pans encrusted with one thing or another on the stove. The drainboard looked like an artifact, the one incomprehensible object left behind by a vanished civilization, and was it merely decorative or was it meant for some utilitarian purpose? The windows were a smudge of light. The plants needed water. I'd been planning to make myself an omelet and then go up to the university for the Monday Night Film Society's showing of *The Seventh Seal*, a film so bleak it always brought tears of hysterical laughter to my eyes, but instead, on an impulse, I dialed Stefania's number. When she answered, there was an edge to her voice, all the Russian smoke blown right out of it by the winds of complexity and turmoil, and in the background I could hear the children shrieking as if the skin were being peeled from their bodies in long, tapering strips. "Hello?" Stefania demanded. "Who is it? Is anybody there? Hello?" Very carefully, though my hand was trembling, I replaced the receiver in its cradle.

And this was strange: it was my day off, the only day of the week when I could really relax, and yet I was all worked up, as if I'd had one too many cups of coffee. I found myself drifting through the house again, thoughtfully pulling at my beer, studying a lamp or a painting or an old family photo as if I'd never seen it before, all the while making a wide circuit around the little room off the front hall where the computer sat on my desk like a graven idol. I resisted it for half an hour or more, until I realized I was resisting it, and then I sat down, booted it up and clicked on *www.peephall.com*.

A Web page gradually took shape on the screen. I saw the house on the corner, a big shapeless stucco box against a neutral background, and in front of it, as the image filled in from top to bottom, the girls began to materialize. There were seven of them, squeezed shoulder-to-shoulder to fit in the frame, and they were dressed in low-cut tops and smiling as if they were selling lip gloss or plaque remover. Samantha was second from the left, staring right at me. *"Twenty-four hours a day!"* screamed the teaser. *"Watch our young sexy College Girls take bubble baths, throw sexy Lingerie parties and sunbathe Nude poolside! You'll never miss an Intimate Moment!"* To the left, in a neat pulsating sidebar, were come-ons for related sites, like *See Me Pee* and *Hot Sexy Teen Vixens*. The subscription fee was $36 a month. I never hesitated.

Once I was in, I was presented with an array of choices. There were forty cameras in all, and I could choose among the two bathrooms, three bedrooms, the pool, kitchen, living room and deck. I was working on my third beer—on an empty stomach, no less—and I wasn't really thinking, just moving instinctively toward something I couldn't have defined. My pulse was racing. I felt guilty, paranoiac, consumed with sadness and lust. The phrase *dirty old man* shot through my head, and I clicked on "The Kitchen" because I couldn't go to "Upstairs Bath," not yet anyway.

The room that came into view was neat, preternaturally neat, like the set for a cooking show, saucepans suspended from hooks, ceramic containers of flour, sugar, tea and coffee lined up along a tile counter, matching dishtowels hanging from two silver loops affixed to the cabinet beneath the sink. But of course it *was* a set, the whole house was a set, because that was what this was all about: seeing through walls like Superman, like God. I clicked on Camera 2, and suddenly a pair of shoulders appeared on the screen, female shoulders, clad in gray and with a blond ponytail centered in the frame. The shoulders ducked out of view, came back again, working vigorously, furiously, over something, and now the back of a blond head was visible, a young face in profile, and I experienced my first little *frisson* of discovery: she was beating eggs in a bowl. The sexy young teen college vixens were having omelets for dinner, just like me . . . but no, another girl was there now, short hair, almost boyish, definitely not Samantha, and she had a cardboard box in her hand, and they were—what were they doing?—they were making brownies. *Brownies*. I could have cried for the simple sweet irreducible beauty of it.

That night—and it was a long night, a night that stretched on past the declining hours and into the building ones—I never got out of the kitchen. Samantha appeared at twenty past six, just as the blonde (Traci) pulled the brownies from the oven, and in the next five minutes the entire cast appeared, fourteen hands hovering over the hot pan, fingers to mouths, fat dark crumbs on their lips, on the front of their T-shirts and clingy tops, on the unblemished tiles of the counter and floor. They poured milk, juice, iced tea, Coke, and they flowed in and out of chairs, propped themselves up against the counter, the refrigerator, the dishwasher, every movement and gesture a revelation. And more: they chattered, giggled, made speeches, talked right through one another, their faces animated with the power and fluency of their silent words. What were they saying? What were they thinking? Already I was spinning off the dialogue ("Come on, don't be such a pig, leave some for somebody else!"; "Yeah, and who you think went and dragged her ass down to the store to pick up the mix in the first place?"), and it was like no novel, no film, no experience I'd ever had. Understand me: I'd seen girls together before, seen them talk, overheard them, and men and women and children too, but this was different. This was for me. My private performance. And Samantha, the girl who'd come up my walk in a pair of too-tight heels, was the star of it.

The next morning I was up at first light, and I went straight to the computer. I needed to shave, comb my hair, dress, eat, micturate; I needed to work on my novel, jog up and down the steps at the university stadium, pay bills, read the paper, take the car in for an oil change. The globe was spinning. People were up, alert, ready for the day. But I was sitting in a cold dark house, wrapped in a blanket, checking in on Peep Hall.

Nobody was stirring. I'd watched Samantha and the short-haired girl (Gina) clean up the kitchen the night before, sweeping up the crumbs, stacking plates and glasses in the dishwasher, setting the brownie pan out on the counter to soak, and then I'd watched the two of them sit at the kitchen table with their books and a boombox, turning pages, taking notes, rocking to the beat of the unheard music. Now I saw the pan sitting on the counter, a peach-colored band of sunlight on the wall behind it, plates stacked in the drainboard, the silver gleam of the microwave—and the colors weren't really true, I was thinking, not true at all. I studied the empty kitchen in a kind of trance, and then, without ceremony, I clicked on "Upstairs Bath." There were two cameras, a shower cam and a toilet cam, and both gazed bleakly out on nothing. I went to "Downstairs Bath" then, and was rewarded by a blur of motion as the stone-faced figure of one of the girls—it was Cyndi, or no, Candi—slouched into the room in a flannel nightdress, hiked it up in back, and sat heavily on the toilet. Her eyes were closed—she was still dreaming. There was the sleepy slow operation with the toilet paper, a perfunctory rinsing of the fingertips, and then she was gone. I clicked on the bedrooms then, all three of them in succession, until I found Samantha, a gently respiring presence beneath a quilt in a single bed against the far wall. She was curled away from me, her hair spilled out over the pillow. I don't know what I was feeling as I watched her there, asleep and oblivious, every creep, sadist, pervert and masturbator with thirty-six dollars in his pocket leering at her, but it wasn't even remotely sexual. It went far beyond that, far beyond. I just watched her, like some sort of tutelary spirit, watched her till she turned over and I could see the dreams invade her eyelids.

I was late for work that day—I work lunch on Tuesdays and Thursdays, then come back in at five for my regular shift—but it was slow and nobody seemed to notice. A word on the hotel: it's a pretty little place on the European model, perched at the top of the tallest hill around, and it has small but elegant rooms, and a cultivated—or at least educated—staff. It features a restaurant with pretensions to three-star status, a cozy bar and a patio with a ten-million-dollar view of the city and the harbor spread out beneath it. The real drinkers—university wives, rich widows, department heads entertaining visiting lecturers—don't come in for lunch till one o'clock or later, so in my absence the cocktail waitress was able to cover for me, pouring two glasses of sauvignon blanc and uncapping a bottle of non-alcoholic beer all on her own. Not that I didn't apologize profusely—I might have been eleven years late with my thesis, but work I took seriously.

It was a typical day on the South Coast, seventy-two at the beach, eighty or so on the restaurant patio, and we did get busy for a while there. I found myself shaking martinis and Manhattans, uncorking bottles of merlot and viognier, cutting up whole baskets of fruit for the sweet rum drinks that seemed to be in vogue again. It was work—simple, repetitive, nonintellectual—and I lost myself in it. When I looked up again, it was ten of three and the lunch crowd was dispersing. Suddenly I felt exhausted, as if I'd been out on some careening debauch the night before instead of sitting in front of my computer till my eyes began to sag. I punched out, drove home and fell into bed as if I'd been hit in the back of the head with a board.

I'd set the alarm for four-thirty, to give myself time to run the electric razor over my face, change my shirt and get back to work, and that would have been fine, but for the computer. I checked the walnut clock on the mantel as I was knotting my tie—I had ten minutes to spare—and sat down at my desk to have a quick look at Peep Hall. For some reason—variety's sake, I guess—I clicked on "Living Room Cam 1," and saw that two of the girls, Mandy and Traci, were exercising to a program on TV. In the nude. They were doing jumping jacks when the image first appeared on the screen, hands clapping over their heads, breasts flouncing, and then they switched, in perfect unison, to squat thrusts, their faces staring into the camera, their arms flexed, legs kicking out behind. It was a riveting performance. I watched, in awe, as they went on to aerobics, some light lifting with three-pound dumbbells and what looked to be a lead-weighted cane, and finally concluded by toweling each other off. I was twenty minutes late for work.

This time it wasn't all right. Jason, the manager, was behind the bar when I came in, and the look on his face told me he wasn't especially thrilled at having this unlooked-for opportunity to dole out cocktail onions and bar mix to a roomful of sunburned hotel guests, enchanted tourists and golfers warming up for dinner. He didn't say a word. Just dropped what he was doing (frothing a mango margarita in the blender), brushed past me and hurried down the corridor to his office as if the work of the world awaited him there. He was six years younger than I, he had a Ph.D. in history from a university far more prestigious than the one that ruled our little burg, and he wielded a first-rate vocabulary. I could have lived without him. At any rate, I went around to each customer with a smile on my face—even the lunatic in tam-o'-shanter and plus fours drinking rum and Red Bull at the far end of the bar—and refreshed drinks, bar napkins and the bowls of pretzels and bar mix. I poured with a heavy hand.

Around seven, the dining room began to fill up. This was my favorite hour of the day, the air fragrant and still, the sun picking out individual palms and banks of flowers to illuminate as it sank into the ocean, people bending to their hors d'oeuvres with a kind of quiet reverence, as if for once they really were thankful for the bounty spread out before them. Muted snatches of conversation drifted in from the patio. Canned piano music—something very familiar—seeped out of the speakers. All was well, and I poured myself a little Irish whiskey to take some of the tightness out of my neck and shoulders.

That was when Samantha walked in.

She was with two other girls—Gina, I recognized; the other one, tall, athletic, with a nervous, rapid-blinking gaze that seemed to reduce the whole place and everything in it to a series of snapshots, was unfamiliar. All three were wearing sleek ankle-length dresses that left their shoulders bare, and as they leaned into the hostess' stand there was the glint of jewelry at their ears and throats. My mouth went dry. I felt as if I'd been caught out at something desperate, something furtive and humiliating, though they were all the way across the room and Samantha hadn't even so much as glanced in my direction. I fidgeted with the wine key and tried not to stare, and then Frankie, the hostess, was leading them to a table out on the patio.

I realized I was breathing hard, and my pulse must have shot up like a rocket, and for what? She probably wouldn't even recognize me. We'd shared a beer for twenty minutes. I was old enough to be her—her what? Her uncle. I needed to get a grip. She wasn't the one watching *me* through a hidden lens. "Hart? Hart, are you there?" a voice was saying, and I looked up to see Megan, the cocktail waitress, hovering over her station with a drink order on her lips.

"Yeah, sure," I said, and I took the order and started in on the drinks. "By the way," I said as casually as I could, "you know that table of three—the girls who just came in? Tell me when you take their order, okay? Their drinks are on me."

As it turned out, they weren't having any of the sweet rum drinks garnished with fruit and a single orange nasturtium flower or one of our half dozen margaritas or even the house chardonnay by the glass. "I carded them," Megan said, "and they're all legal, but what they want is three sloe gin fizzes. Do we even have sloe gin?"

In the eight years I'd been at the El Encanto, I doubt if I'd mixed more than three or four sloe gin fizzes, and those were for people whose recollections of the Eisenhower administration were still vivid. But we did have a vestigial bottle of sloe gin in the back room, wedged between the peppermint schnapps and the Benedictine, and I made them their drinks. Frankie had seated them around the corner on the patio, so I couldn't see how the fizzes went over, and then a series of orders came leapfrogging in, and I started pouring and mixing and forgot all about it. The next time I looked up, Samantha was coming across the room to me, her eyebrows dancing over an incipient smile. I could see she was having trouble with her heels and the constriction of the dress— or gown, I suppose you'd call it—and I couldn't help thinking how young she looked, almost like a little girl playing dress-up. "Hart," she said, resting her hands on the bar so that I could admire her sculpted fingers and her collection of rings—rings even on her thumbs—"I didn't know you worked here. This place is really nice."

"Yeah," I said, grinning back at her while holding the picture of her in my head, asleep, with her hair splayed out over the pillow. "It's first-rate. Top-notch. Really fantastic. It's a great place to work."

"You know, that was really sweet of you," she said.

I wanted to say something like "Aw, shucks" or "No problem," but instead I heard myself say, "The gesture or the drink?"

She looked at me quizzically a moment, and then let out a single soft flutter of a laugh. "Oh, you mean the gin fizzes?" And she laughed again—or giggled, actually. "I'm legal today, did you know that? And my gramma made me promise to have a sloe gin fizz so she could be here tonight in spirit—she passed last winter?—but I think we're having like a bottle of white wine or something with dinner. That's my sister I'm with—she's taking me out for my birthday, along with Gina—she's one of my roommates? But you probably already know that, right?"

I shot my eyes left, then right, up and down the bar. All the drinks were fresh, and no one was paying us the least attention. "What do you mean?"

Her eyebrows lifted, the silky thick eyebrows that were like two strips of mink pasted to her forehead, and her hair was like some exotic fur too, rich and shining and dark. "You didn't check out the Web site?"

"No," I lied.

"Well, you ought to," she said. The air was a stew of smells—a couple at the end of the bar were sharing the warm spinach and scallop salad, there was the sweet burnt odor of the Irish whiskey I was sipping from a mug, Samantha's perfume (or was it Megan's?) and a medley of mesquite-grilled chops and braised fish and Peter Oxendine's famous sauces wafting in from the kitchen. "Okay," she said, shaking out her hair with a flick of her head and running a quick look around the place before bringing her eyes back to me. "Okay, well—I just wanted to say thanks." She shrugged. "I guess I better be getting back to the girls."

"Yeah," I said. "Nice seeing you again. And hey, happy birthday."

She'd already turned away from the bar, earrings swaying, face composed, but she stopped to give me a smile over her shoulder, and then she made her way across the room and out onto the darkened patio.

And that would have been it, at least until I could get home and watch her shimmy out of that gown and paint her toenails or gorge on cake or whatever it was she was going to do in the semi-privacy of her own room, but I couldn't let it go and I sent over dessert too, a truly superior raspberry-kiwi tart Stefania had whipped up that afternoon. That really put them in my debt, and after dessert the three of them came to the bar to beam at me and settle in for coffee and an after-dinner drink. "You're really just twenty-one today?" I said, grinning at Samantha till the roots of my teeth must have showed. "You're sure I don't have to card you, now, right?"

I watched the hair swirl round her shoulders as she braced herself against the bar and reached down to ease off her heels, and then she was fishing through her purse till she came up with her driver's license and laid it out proudly on the bar. I picked it up and held it to the light—there she was, grinning wide out of the bottom right-hand corner, date of birth clearly delineated, and her name, Jennifer B. Knickish, spelled out in bold block letters. "Jennifer?" I said.

She took the card back with a frown, her eyebrows closing ranks. "Everybody calls me Samantha," she said. "Really." And to her companions: "Right, guys?" I watched them nod their glossy heads. The older one, the sister, giggled. "And besides, I don't want any of the creeps to know my real name—even my first name—you know what I mean?"

Oh, yes, yes I did. And I smiled and bantered and called up reserves of charm I hadn't used in years, and the drinks were on me all night long. It was Samantha's birthday, wasn't it? And her twenty-first, no less—a rite of passage if ever there was one. I poured Grand Marnier and Rémy till the customers disappeared and the waiters and busboys slipped out the back and the lights drew down to nothing.

I woke with a headache. I'd matched them, round for round, and, as I say, I'd started in on the Irish whiskey earlier in the night—and yes, I'm all too well aware that the concrete liver and stumbling tongue are hazards of the profession, but I'm pretty good at keeping all that in check. I do get bored, though, and wind up over-doing it from time to time, especially when the novel isn't going well, and it hadn't been going well in a long while. The problem was, I couldn't get past the initial idea—the setup—which was a story I'd come across in the newspaper two or three years ago. It had to do with an old woman's encounter with the mysterious forces of nature (I don't recall her real name, not that it would matter, but I called her Grandma Rivers, to underscore the irony that here was a woman with eight children, thirty-two grandchildren and six great-grandchildren and she was living alone in a trailer park in a part of the country so bleak no one who wasn't condemned to it would ever even deign to glance down on it from the silvered window of a jetliner at thirty-five thousand feet). One night, when the wind was sweeping up out of the south with the smell of paradise on it and all her neighbors were mewed up in their aluminum boxes lulled by booze, prescription drugs and the somnolent drone of the tube, she stepped outside to take in the scent of the night and indulge in a cigarette (she always smoked outside so as not to pollute the interior of her own little aluminum box set there on the edge of the scoured prairie). No sooner had she lit up than a fox—a red fox, *Vulpes fulva*—shot out of the shadows and latched onto her ankle. In the shock and confusion of that moment, she lurched back, lost her balance and fell heavily on her right side, dislocating her hip. But the fox, which later proved to be rabid, came right back at her, at her face this time, and the only thing she could think to do in her panic was to seize hold of it with her trembling old arms and pin it beneath her to keep the snapping jaws away from her.

Twelve hours. That's how long she lay there, unable to move, the fox snarling and writhing beneath her, its heartbeat joined to hers, its breathing, the eloquent movement of its fluids and juices and the workings of its demented little vulpine brain, until somebody—a neighbor—happened to glance beyond the hedge and the hump of the blistered old Jeep Wagoneer her late husband had left behind to see her there, stretched out in the gravel drive like a strip of discarded carpet. Yes. But what then? That was what had me stumped. I thought of going back and tracing her life up to that point, her girlhood in the Depression, her husband's overseas adventures in the war, the son killed in Vietnam . . . or maybe just to let her sink into the background while I focused on the story of the community, the benighted neighbors and their rat-faced children, so that the trailer park itself became a character. . . .

But, as I say, I woke with a headache, and when I did sit down at the computer, it wasn't to call up Grandma Rivers and the imperfect dream of her life, but to click onto *peephall.com* and watch another sort of novel unfold before my eyes, one in which the plot was out of control and the details were selected and shaped only by the anonymous subscriber with his anonymous mouse. I went straight to Samantha's bedroom, but her bed was empty save for the jumbled topography of pillows and bedclothes, and I stared numbly at the shadows thickening round the walls, at the limp form of the gown tossed over a chair, and checked my watch. It was ten-thirty. *Breakfast*, I thought. I clicked on "Kitchen," but that wasn't her staring into the newspaper with a cup of coffee clenched in one hand and a Power Bar in the other, nor was that her bent at the waist and peering into the refrigerator as if for enlightenment. I went to the living room, but it was empty, a dully flickering static space caught in the baleful gaze of my screen. Had she gone out already? To an early class maybe?

But then I remembered she was taking only one class— "Intermediate Sketching," paid for by the Web site operators, who were encouraging the Sexy Teen College Coeds actually to enroll so that all the voyeurs out there could live the fantasy of seeing them hitting the books in their thong bikinis and lacy push-up bras—and that the class met in the afternoon. She was getting paid too, incidentally—five hundred dollars a month, plus the rent-free accommodations at Peep Hall and a food allowance—and all for allowing the world to watch her live hot sexy young life through each scintillating minute of the over-inflated day, the orotund month and the full, round year. I thought of the girls who posed naked for the art classes back when I was an undergraduate (specifically, I thought of Nancy Beckers, short, black hair, balls of muscle in her calves and upper arms and a look in her eyes that made me want to strip to my socks and join her on the dais), and then I clicked on "Downstairs Bath," and there she was.

This wasn't a hot sexy moment. Anything but. Samantha—my Samantha—was crouched over the toilet on her knees, the soles of her feet like single quotes around the swell of her buttocks, her hair spilling over the bright rim of the porcelain bowl. I couldn't see her face, but I watched the back of her head jerk forward as each spasm racked her, and I couldn't help playing the sound track in my mind, feeling sorrowful and guilty at the same time. Her feet—I felt sorry for her feet—and the long sudden shiver of her spine and even the dangling wet ends of her hair. I couldn't watch this. I couldn't. My finger was on the mouse—I took one more look, watched one last shudder ascend her spine and fan out across her shoulder blades, watched her head snap forward and her hair slide loose, and then I clicked off and left her to suffer in private.

A week rolled by, and I hardly noticed. I wasn't sleeping well, wasn't exercising, wasn't sitting on the porch with a book in my hand and the world opening up around me like a bigger book. I was living the life of the screen, my bones gone hollow, my brain dead. I ate at my desk, microwave pizza and chili-cheese burritos, nachos, whiskey in a glass like a slow, sweet promise that was never fulfilled. My scalp itched. My eyes ached. But I don't think I spent a waking moment outside work when I wasn't stalking the rooms of Peep Hall, clicking from camera to camera in search of a new angle, a better one, the view that would reveal all. I watched Gina floss her teeth and Candi pluck fine translucent hairs from the mole at the corner of her mouth, sat there in the upstairs bath with Traci as she bleached her roots and shaved her legs, hung electrified over the deck as Cyndi perched naked on the railing with a bottle of vodka and a cigarette lighter, breathing fire into the gloom of the gathering night. Mainly, though, I watched Samantha. When she was home, I followed her from room to room, and when she picked up her purse and went out the door, I felt as if Peep Hall had lost its focus. It hurt me, and it was almost like a physical hurt, as if I'd been dealt an invisible blow.

I was pulling into the drive one afternoon—it must have been a Monday or Wednesday, because I'd just worked lunch—when a rangy, tall woman in a pair of wraparound sunglasses came out of nowhere to block my way. She was wearing running shorts and a T-shirt that advertised some fund-raising event at the local elementary school, and she seemed to be out of breath or out of patience, as if she'd been chasing after me for miles. I was trying to place her as the gate slowly cranked open on its long balky chain to reveal the green depths of the yard beyond—she was someone I knew, or was expected to know. But before I could resolve the issue, she'd looped around the hood of the car and thrust her face in the open window, so close to me now I could see the fine hairs catching the light along the parabola of her jawbone and her shadowy eyes leaping at the lenses of her sunglasses. "I need you to sign this," she said, shoving a clipboard at me.

The gate hit the end of the chain with a clank that made the posts shudder. I just stared at her. "It's me," she said, removing the sunglasses to reveal two angry red welts on the bridge of her nose and a pair of impatient eyes, "Sarah. Sarah Schuster—your next-door neighbor?"

I could smell the fumes of the car as it rumbled beneath me, quietly misfiring. "Oh, yeah," I said, "sure," and I attempted a smile.

"You need to sign this," she repeated.

"What is it?"

"A petition. To get rid of them. Because this is a residential neighborhood—this is a *family* neighborhood—and frankly Steve and I are outraged, just outraged, I mean, as if there isn't enough of this sort of thing going on in town already—"

"Get rid of who?" I said, but I already knew.

I watched her face as she filled me in, the rolling eyes, the clamp and release of the long mortal jaws, moral outrage under-scored by a heavy dose of irony, because she was an educated woman, after all, a liberal and a Democrat, but this was just—well, it was just too much.

I didn't need this. I didn't want it. I wanted to be in my own house minding my own business. "All right, yeah," I said, pushing the clipboard back at her, "but I'm real busy right now—can you come back later?"

And then I was rolling up the driveway, the gate already rum-bling shut behind me. I was agitated and annoyed—*Sarah Schuster*, who did she think she was?—and the first thing I did when I got in the house was pull the shades and turn on the computer. I checked Peep Hall to be sure Samantha was there—and she was, sunk into the couch in T-shirt and jeans, watching TV with Gina—and then I smoothed back my hair in the mirror and went out the front door. I looked both ways before swinging open the gate, wary of Sarah Schuster and her ilk, but aside from two kids on bikes at the far end of the block, the street was deserted.

Still, I started off in the opposite direction from the big white house on the corner, then crossed the street and kept going—all the way up the next block over—so as to avoid any prying eyes. The sun was warm on my face, my arms were swinging, my feet knew just what to do—I was walking, actually walking through the neighborhood, and it felt good. I noticed things the view from the car window wouldn't have revealed, little details, a tree in fruit here, a new flowerbed there, begonias blooming at the base of three pale silvery eucalypti at the side of a neighbor's house, and all that would have been fine but for the fact that my heart seemed to be exploding in my chest. I saw myself ringing the doorbell, mounting the steps of the big white house and ringing the bell, but beyond that I couldn't quite picture the scene. Would Samantha—or Traci or Candi or whoever—see me as just another one of the creeps she had to chat with on-line for two hours each week as part of her job description? Would she shut the door in my face? Invite *me* in for a beer?

As it turned out, Cyndi answered the door. She was shorter than I'd imagined, and she was dressed in a red halter top and matching shorts, her feet bare and toenails painted blue—or aquamarine, I suppose you'd call it. I couldn't help thinking of the way she looked without her clothes on, throwing back her head and spewing flames from her lips. "Hi," I said, "I was looking for Samantha? You know, *Jennifer*," I added, by way of assuring her I was on intimate terms here and not just some psychotic who'd managed to track them all down.

She didn't smile. Just gave me a look devoid of anything—love, hate, fear, interest, or even civility—turned her head away and shouted, "Sam! Sammy! It's for you!"

"Tell her it's Hart," I said, "she'll know who—" but I broke off because I was talking to myself: the doorway was empty. I could hear the jabber and squawk of the TV and the thump of bass-heavy music from one of the upstairs bedrooms, then a whisper of voices in the hall.

In the next moment a shadow fell across the plane of the open door, and Samantha slid into view, her face pale and tentative. "Oh," she said, and I could hear the relief in her voice. "Oh, hi."

"I've got something to tell you," I said, coming right out with it, "—bad news, I think. This woman just stopped me when I was pulling into the driveway—my next-door neighbor—and they're circulating a petition." I watched her eyebrows, her eyes, saw the glint of the rings on her right hand as she swept it through her hair. "But I didn't sign. I blew her off."

She looked distracted, staring out over my shoulder as if she hadn't heard me. "Louis warned us there might be trouble," she said finally, "but it really isn't fair. I mean, do I look like some kind of slut to you? Do I?"

I wanted to make a speech, or at least a confession, and now was the time for it, now, but the best I could do was shake my head slowly and emphatically. *Louis?* Who was Louis?

Her eyes were burning. I heard a blast of gunfire from the TV, and then the volume went dead. "I'm sorry, Hart," Samantha said, lifting one bare foot from the floor to scratch the other with a long casual stroke of her instep, "but do you want to come in? You want a beer?"

And then I was in, following the sweep of Samantha's shoulders and hair and the sweet balsam scent of her into the living room I knew so well—and that was strange, surpassing strange, to know a place in its every apparent detail and yet never to have been there in the flesh. It was like a dream made concrete, a vision come to life. I felt like a character in a play, walking onto the set for the first time—and I was, I *was*. Don't look at the camera, isn't that what they tell you on TV? I glanced up, and there it was, staring me in the face. Gina stuck her head through the swinging door to the kitchen. "Hi," she said, for form's sake, and then she disappeared—out onto the deck, I supposed, to tan her hot sexy young limbs. I sat in the chair facing the dead TV screen and Samantha went out of the frame and into the kitchen for the beer, and I couldn't help wondering how many hundreds of perverts went with her.

She came back with two beers and sat opposite me, in the armchair facing "Living Room Cam 2," and gave me a smile as she settled into the chair.

I took a sip of beer, smiled back, and said, "Who's Louis?"

Samantha was sitting with one leg tucked under her, her back arched, the beer pinioned between her legs. "He's one of the operators—of the site? He's got something like thirty of them around the country, and he's like—"

"A cyber-pimp?" It was out before I could think.

She frowned and looked down into the neck of the bottle a minute, then brought her head back up and flicked the hair out of her face. "I was going to say he's like used to this sort of thing, people hassling him over zoning laws and sex-oriented businesses and all that, but really, I mean, what's the big deal?"

"I watch," I said suddenly, looking directly into her eyes. "I watch you."

Her smile blossomed into a grin. "You do?"

I held her eyes. I nodded.

"Really? Well, that's—that's great. But you've never seen me do anything dirty, have you? Some of the girls get off on it, but I figure I'm just going to live, you know, and get my end out of it—it's a good deal. I need the money. I *like* the money. And if I'm nude in the shower or when I'm changing clothes and all these guys are jerking off or whatever, I don't care, that's life, you know what I mean?"

"You know when I like to watch you best? When you're asleep. You look so—I don't want to say angelic, but that's part of it—you just look so peaceful, I guess, and I feel like I'm right there with you, watching over you."

She got up from the chair then and crossed the room to me. "That's a sweet thing to say," she said, and she set her beer down on the coffee table and settled into the couch beside me. "Really sweet," she murmured, slipping an arm round my neck and bringing her face in for a close-up. Everything seemed transformed in that moment, every object in the room coming into sudden focus, and I saw her with a deep and revelatory clarity. I kissed her. Felt the soft flutter of her lips and tongue against mine and forgot all about Stefania, my ex-wife, Sarah Schuster and Grandma Rivers. I broke away and then kissed her again, and it was a long, slow, sweet, lingering kiss and she was rubbing my back and I had my hands on her hips, just dreaming and dreaming. "Do you want to—?" I breathed. "Can you—?"

"Not here," she said, and she looked right into the camera. "They don't like it. They don't even like this."

"All right," I said, "all right," and I looked up too, right into the glassy eye of Camera 1. "What do we do now?"

"I don't know," she said. "Just hold me."

GOING DOWN

He started the book at two-fifteen on a Saturday afternoon in early December. There were other things he'd rather be doing—watching the Notre Dame game, for instance, or even listening to it on the radio—but that was freezing rain slashing down outside the window, predicted to turn to snow by nightfall, and the power had been out for over an hour. Barb was at the mall, indulging her shopping disorder, Buck was away at college in Plattsburgh, and the dog lay in an arthritic bundle on the carpet in the hall. He'd built a fire, checked the hurricane lamps for fuel and distributed them round the house, washed up the breakfast dishes by hand (the dishwasher was just an artifact now, like the refrigerator and the furnace), and then he'd gone into Buck's room in search of reading material.

His son's room was another universe, an alien space contained within the walls of the larger, more familiar arena of the house he knew in all its smallest details, from the corroding faucet in the downstairs bathroom to the termite-riddled front porch and the balky light switch in the guest bedroom. Nobody had been in here since September, and the place smelled powerfully of mold—refrigerated mold. It was as cold as a meat locker, and why not? Why heat an unoccupied room? John felt for the light switch and actually flicked it twice, dumbfounded, before he realized it wasn't working for the same reason the dishwasher wasn't working. That was what he was doing in here in the first place, getting a book to read, because without power there was no TV, and without TV, there was no Notre Dame.

He crossed the faintly glutinous carpet and cranked open the blinds; a bleak pale rinsed-out light seeped into the room. When he turned back round he was greeted by the nakedly ambitious faces of rap and rock stars leering from the walls and the collages of animals, cars and various body parts with which Buck had decorated the ceiling. One panel, just to the left of the now-useless overhead light, showed nothing but feet and toes (male, female, androgyne), and another, the paws of assorted familiar and exotic animals, including what seemed to be the hooked forefeet of a tree sloth. Buck's absence was readily apparent—the heaps of soiled clothes were gone, presumably soiled now in Plattsburgh. In fact, the sole sartorial reminder of his son was a pair of mud-encrusted hiking boots set against the wall in the corner. Opposite them, in the far corner, a broken fly rod stood propped against the bed above a scattering of yellowed newspapers and the forlorn-looking cage where a hamster had lived out its days. The bed itself was like a slab in the morgue. And that was it: Buck was gone now, grown and gone, and it was a fact he'd just have to get used to.

For a long moment John stood there at the window, taking it all in, and then he shivered, thinking of the fire in the living room, the inoperative furnace and the storm. And then, almost as an afterthought, he bent to the brick-and-board bookcase that climbed shakily up the near wall.

Poking through his son's leftover books took him a while, longer than he would have thought possible, and it gave him time to reflect on his own adolescent tastes in literature, which ran basically in a direct line from Heinlein to Vonnegut and detoured from there into the European exotica, like *I Jan Cremer* and *Death on the Installment Plan*, which he'd never finished. But books were a big factor in his life then, the latest news, as vital to day-to-day existence as records and movies. He never listened to music anymore, though—it seemed he'd heard it all before, each band a regurgitation of the last, and he and Barb rarely had the time or energy to venture out to the wasteland of the cineplex. And books—well, he wasn't much of a reader anymore, and he'd be the first to admit it. Oh, he'd find himself stuck in an airport someplace, and like anybody else he'd duck apologetically into the bookshop for something fat and insipid to kill the stupefying hours on the ground and in the air, but whatever he seemed to choose, no matter how inviting the description on the cover, it was invariably too fat and too insipid to hold his attention. Even when he was strapped in with two hundred strangers in a howling steel envelope thirty-five thousand feet above the ground and there was no space to move or think or even shift his weight from one buttock to the other.

Finally, after he'd considered and rejected half a dozen titles, a uniform set of metallic spines caught his eye—gold, silver, bronze, a smooth gleaming polished chromium—and he slid a shining paperback from the shelf. The title, emblazoned in a hemoglobic shade of red that dripped off the jacket as if gravity were still at work on it, was *The Ravishers of Pentagord*. He'd never heard of the author, a man by the name of Filéncio Salmón, described on the inside flap as "The preeminent Puerto Rican practitioner of speculative fiction," which, as even John knew, was the preferred term for what he and his dormmates used to call sci-fi. He looked over each of the glittering metallic books that constituted the Salmón oeuvre and settled finally on one called *Fifty Going Down (Cincuenta y retrocetiendo)*. And why that one? Well, because he'd just turned fifty himself, an age fraught with anxiety and premonitory stirrings, and the number in the title spoke to him. He'd always been attracted to titles that featured numbers—*One Hundred Years of Solitude; Two Years Before the Mast; 2001: A Space Odyssey*—and maybe that was because of his math background. Sure it was. He felt safe with numbers, with the order they represented in a disordered world—that was all.

When he reemerged from the narcotic gloom of Buck's sanctuary, he had the book clutched in his hand, and there was a nostalgic feel to it—to the book and the whole business of it, opening the cover and seeing the title there in bold black letters, and the epigraph ("Death is something I only want to do once"—Oliver Niles)—and he opened a can of chicken corn chowder, thought briefly of heating it in the fireplace, then dismissed the idea and settled into the couch to spoon it up cold and attack the book. It was quiet, preternaturally quiet, no hum of the household machinery or drone of the TV to distract him, and he began, as if it were the most natural thing in the world, to read.

My mother was my child. I mean this in no metaphoric sense, but literally, because my universe is not strictly like yours, the universe of decay and decrepitude, in which one sinks each day closer and closer to the yawning mouth of the grave. I loved my mother—she raised me and then I raised her—and my memories of her are inextricably bound up with the cradle, the nursery, toys and playthings and the high ecstatic thrill of juvenile laughter. And sadness. Infinite sadness. But it is not my mother I wish to tell you about, but my wife and lover, Sonia, the mature woman of fifty with the voice of smoke and the eyes of experience, the silky girl of twenty who would bound ahead of me along the banks of the Río Luminoso as if she had been granted a second childhood. Which she had.

Let me explain. You see, in our scheme of things the Creator has been much more generous than in yours. In His wisdom, He has chosen the age of fifty as the apex of existence, and not a debilitated and toothless ninety or an even more humbling ninety-five or a hundred. (And what is more obscene than the wasted old man with his mouth full of mush and crumbs on his lapels, or the gaping hag staring round her in the street as if she's misplaced some vital part of herself?) We do not progress inexorably in age as you do, but when we reach the magical plateau, that golden age of fifty, we begin, as we say, to go down. That is, one is forty-nine the year before one turns fifty, and one is forty-nine the year after.

When Sonia was forty-nine for the second time, I was thirty-one for the first. She had been a dancer, a model, a photographer and a sculptress, and she was looking forward to going down, and, as I presumed, doing it all over again. She'd known some of the great younging minds of her day—they were history now, all of them—and I admired her for that and for her accomplishments too, but I wanted a wife who would stand by me, fix me paella and roast veal in the languorous evenings and hand me a crisply ironed shirt each morning. I broached the subject one afternoon just after our engagement. We were sitting at an outdoor café, sipping aperitifs and nibbling at a plate of fried squid. "Sonia," I murmured, reaching across the table to entwine my fingers in hers, "I want a wife, not a career woman. Can you be that for me?"

Her eyes seemed to grow until they ate up her face. Her cheekbones were monuments, her lips like two sweet desert fruits. "Oh, Faustito," she murmured, "poor little boy. Of course I'll be a wife to you. I have no interest in society anymore, really I don't—I'm retired from all that now." She sighed. Patted her lips with a snowy napkin and leaned forward to kiss me. "I just want to be young again, that's all—young and carefree."

The room had grown cold and the darkness was coming down when John next looked up. It was the darkness, more than anything, that did it: he couldn't see to read. He woke as if from a dream and saw that the windows had gone pale with the storm—it was snow now, and no doubt about it. The can of soup, the spoon still transfixed in a bit of congealed goop at the bottom, stood frigidly on the end table beside him. When he let out a breath, he could see it condense in a cloud at the tip of his nose. Stirring himself—this was a crisis, the pipes would freeze, and just look at that fire, nothing but embers and ash—he stoked the fire impatiently, laid on an armful of kindling and two massive slabs of split oak. It was four forty-five, he was a hundred pages into the book and the snow was raging down over the slick heart of the ice that lay beneath it. And where was Barb? Stuck in a drift somewhere? Abandoned in a darkened mall? Dead? Mutilated? Laid out on a slab at the county hospital?

The anxiety came up in him like a sort of fuel, pure-burning and high of octane, and he'd actually lifted the phone to his ear before he realized it was dead. There was no dial tone, no sound of any kind, just the utter nullity of the void. He went to the window again. The sky was dark now, moiling with the flecks and bits of itself it was shedding over the earth. He could barely see to the end of the drive, and the lightless houses across the street were invisible. He thought of the car then—his car, the compulsively restored MGA roadster with the fifteen-hundred-dollar paint job in British racing green—but he couldn't risk that on streets as slick as these were bound to be. He hardly drove it in winter at all—just enough to keep it in trim—and it certainly wouldn't get him far on a night like this, even in an emergency. And he couldn't call Barb's absence an emergency, not yet. They were having a storm. The lines were down. There was no way she could get to him or he to her. He couldn't call the police, couldn't call her sister or that restaurant in the mall or that store, Things & Oddments, that featured so prominently in his monthly credit card bill. He was powerless. And like the pioneers before him, he would just have to batten down the hatches—the doors and windows, that is—and wait out the storm.

And where better to do it than stretched out on the sofa in front of the fireplace, with a hurricane lamp and a book? He gave the fire a poke, spread a comforter over his legs, and settled back to read.

"Sonia," I cried, exasperated, "you're behaving like a child!"

She was dancing through the town square, riding high up off the lithe and juvenile stems of her legs, laughing in the astonished faces of the shopkeepers and making rude flatulent noises with her tongue and her pouting underlip. Even Don Pedro C———, the younging commandant of our fair city, who was in that moment taking the air with his aging bride of twenty, had to witness this little scene. "I am a child!" Sonia shrieked, tailing the phrase with a cracked and willful schoolgirl's laugh that mounted the walls to tremble in every fishbowl and flowerpot on the square. "And you're an old tightwad!" And then she was off again, singing it through the side streets and right on up to the house where my mother had been twice an infant: "Don Fausto's a tightwad, Don Fausto's a tightwad!"

It was my fault, actually—at least partly—because I'd denied her a bauble at the jewelry merchant's, but still, you can imagine my consternation, not to mention my embarrassment. I bit my lip and cursed myself. I should have known better, marrying a woman going down when I was going up. But I'd always been attracted to maturity, and when I was a young, aging man of thirty, I found her fifty-year-old's wrinkles and folds as attractive as her supple wit and her voice of authority and experience. Then she was forty-five and I was thirty-five and we were closer than ever, till we celebrated our fortieth birthdays together and I thought I had found heaven, truly and veritably.

But now, now she's running through the streets like a little wanton, fifteen years old and you'd think she'd never been fifteen before, her slip showing, her feet a mad dancing blur and something in her hair—chocolate, the chocolate she ate day and night and never mind the pimples sprouting in angry red constellations all over her face and pretty little chin. And there she is, just ahead of me, running her hands through all the bowls of fighting fish poor Leandro Mopa has put out on display—and worse, upsetting Benedicta Moreno's perfectly proportioned pyramid of mangoes.

And what am I thinking, all out of breath and my lungs heaving like things made of leather? When we get home—this is what I am thinking—when we get home, I will spank her.

There was a sudden thump on the front porch, an ominous thump, ponderous and reverberative, and it resounded through the empty house like the clap of doom. John sat up, startled. It sounded as if someone had dropped down dead on the planks—or been murdered. But there it was again, not just a single thump now but a whole series of them, as if the local high school were staging a sack race on his front porch. He glanced at the clock on the mantel—eight-forty already, and where had the time gone?—then set the book down and rose from the couch to investigate.

As he approached the front door, the thumping became louder and more insistent, as if someone were kicking snow from their boots—that was it, yes, of course. It was Barb, the car was stuck in a drift someplace and she'd walked the whole way, he could see it already, and she'd be annoyed, of course she would, but not too annoyed, because of the magic and romance of the storm, and she'd warm herself by the fire, share a brandy with him and some-

thing they could heat over the open flames—hot dogs, whatever—
and then, then he could go back to his book. But all that, the
elaborate vision called up by the sound of thumping feet, the comfort and rationalization of it, went for nothing. Because at that
moment, just as he reached his hand out for the doorknob, he
heard the murmur of a man's voice and the high assaultive giggle
of a female, definitely not Barb.

And then the door stood open, the keen knife of the air, the
immemorial smell of the snow and the whole world transformed
and transforming still, and there was Buck, home from college in a
snow-shrouded ski jacket and a girl with him, a girl with fractured
blue eyes and a knit cap pulled down to her eyebrows. "Hey,
Dad," Buck breathed in passing, and then he and the vigorously
stomping girl were in the hall and the old dog was wagging her
tail and attempting a puppyish yip of greeting.

"Jesus"—and Buck was shouting suddenly, his voice gone high
with enthusiasm—"you ever see anything like this? Must've taken
us twelve hours from Plattsburgh and the only thing moving on
the Northway was the bus. Good old Greyhound, huh?"

John wasn't thinking clearly. He was still in the book, or part of
him was. "You didn't flunk out, did you?" he said, throwing his
hands out, as if for balance.

Buck gave him a look, the narrow eyes he'd inherited from his
mother, the beak of the nose and the cheeks flushed with the
cold—or drink, hard liquor, and that was all they did up in Plattsburgh, as far as John had heard, anyway. "No," Buck said finally,
a hurt and sorrowful expression clouding his features, "I just
thought I'd come home for the weekend, you know, see how
everybody was . . . oh, this is Bern." He indicated the girl, who
reached up to tear off the knit cap and shake out a blazing head of
white-blond hair.

John was impressed. He snatched a quick look at her breasts
and her slim legs rising out of a pair of slick red boots. This was
the sort of girl he'd wanted in college, lusted after, howled to the
moon over, but to no avail. He'd been a nerd, a math nerd, the
kind of guy who got excited over cryptography and differential

equations, and he'd wound up with Barb. Thankfully. And he wasn't complaining. But his son, look at his son: Buck was no nerd, no sir, not with a girl like— "What was your name?" he heard himself asking.

A final shake of the hair, a soft cooed greeting for the reeking old dog. "Bern," she said evenly, and she had a smile for him, wonderful teeth, staggering lips, pink and youthful gums.

The door was shut now. The hallway was cold. And dark. He was smiling till his own teeth must have glowed in the dim glancing light of the fire in the other room. "Short for Bernadette?" he ventured.

They were moving instinctively, as a group, toward the fire— even the dog. "Nope," she said. "Just Bern."

Well, fine. And would she like a drink? Suddenly, for some reason, it was vitally important to John that she have a drink, crucial even. No, she said, looking to Buck, no, she didn't drink. There was a silence. "And how's school?" he asked finally, just to say something.

Neither of them rushed to answer. Buck, alternately warming his hands over the fire and stroking the old dog, just shrugged, and the girl, Bern, turned to John and said, "Frankly, it sucks."

"That's why we're here," Buck murmured.

John was puzzled. "You mean—?"

"Aw, shit." Buck spoke with real vehemence, but softly, almost under his breath, and he rose tumultuously from his place by the fire. "We're going to hang in my room for a while, okay, Dad?" His arm found Bern's shoulder and they were gone, or almost, two shadows touching and melding and then slowly receding down the dark hall. But then Buck hung back a moment, the shadows separating, and his face was floating there in the unsteady light of the hurricane lamp. "Where's Mom?" he said.

When she was twelve, she began to lose her breasts. I would put my arm round her in a restaurant and feel like a child molester, and when we went to bed together I had to keep reminding myself that she was a younging twelve, which actually gave her some eighty-eight years of worldly wiles and experience, at least seventy-five of them enlivened by venereal pleasures. (I never fooled myself into thinking I was the only one, though I wanted to be. She'd been married and separated before I met her, and when she was young the first time, there had been a succession of lovers, a whole mighty tide of them.) She'd begun taking a rag doll to bed—and crunching hard candy between her dwindling molars or snapping gum in my face whenever I began to feel amorous—and this just intensified my feelings of jealousy and resentment.

"Tell me about your first," I would demand. "What was his name, Eduardo, wasn't it?"

"Don't!" She would giggle, because I was stroking the soft white doeskin of her belly or the silk of her upper arm, and then, blowing a pink bubble with her gum, she would correct me. "It wasn't Eduardo, silly, it was Armando. I told you. Silly." And it would become a chant—"Silly, silly, silly!"—till I sprang up off the bed and chased her round the room, through the apartments and past the maid's quarters, and only then, when I was out of breath and half spent, would she give me my pleasure.

And then came the day, the inevitable day, when she was no longer a woman. Her breasts had disappeared entirely, not even the tiniest bud left, and between her legs she was as bald as an apple. Of course, I'd known all along the day was coming, and I'd tried to prepare myself as so many before me had done, watching soap operas and reading the great tragedies, but the pain and disillusionment were more than I could bear—yes, disillusionment. Here was the woman I loved, the woman who could talk all day of the books of Mangual and Garci-Crespo, make love all night to the sensual drone of Rodriguez's Second Cello Concerto and cry out in joy at the dawn as if she'd created it herself. And now, now she sat Indian style in the middle of the bed and called out for me in a piping little singsong voice that made my blood boil. And what did she call me? Fausto, or even Faustito? No, she called me Daddy. "Daddy, Daddy," she called, "read me a story."

Buck's question was a good one: where *was* Barb? Though Buck hardly seemed concerned—irritated was more like it, as if he'd expected his mother to spring out of the woodwork and wash his socks or whip him up a lemon meringue pie from scratch. John had already sunk back into the couch, the book clutched like a living thing in his hand, and he just stared up at the glowing ball of his son's face. "I don't know," he said, drawing up his lip and shrugging a little more elaborately than was necessary, "—she went shopping."

Buck's face just hung there at the mouth of the dark hallway as if it had been sliced from his shoulders. "Shopping?" he repeated, knitting his brows and working a querulous edge into his voice. "When? When did she leave?"

John felt guilty now—he was the accused, the accused on the witness stand and the district attorney hammering away at him—and he felt afraid suddenly too, afraid for his wife and his son and the whole withering masquerade of his second-rate engineer's life, numbers turned vile and accusatory, job shopping, one deadening plant after another. "I don't know," he said. "Sometime this afternoon—or this morning, I mean. Late this morning."

"This morning? Jesus, Dad, are you losing your mind? That's a blizzard out there—she could be dead for all we know."

And now he was standing, his son's face shining fiercely with the reds and ambers of combustion, and he was ordering his apologies and excuses, ever rational, ever precise, till he realized that Buck was no longer there—he'd receded down the hallway to the refrigerated room, where even now the door slammed behind him in finality. That was when John struggled with himself, when it all came to the surface—his fears, his needs, his love for Barb, or respect for her, or whatever you wanted to call it—and he actually threw on his coat, muffler and hat and went to the little jade box on the mantel for the keys to the MG, before he caught himself. It was a fool's errand. A recipe for disaster. How could he go out in this—there must have been two and a half feet of snow out there, and it was drifting—and in a car made for summer roads, no less? It was crazy. Irresponsible. And she could be anywhere—what was he supposed to do, go house to house and shop to shop?

Finally, and it was past nine now, he convinced himself that the only rational thing was to wait out the storm. He'd been through blizzards before—he was fifty years old, after all—and they'd always come out right, aside from maybe a fender bender here or there, or a minor case of back strain from leaning into the snow shovel, running out of bread and milk and the like. But the storms always blew themselves out and the sun came back and the snow receded from the roads. No, he'd been right all along—there was nothing to do but wait, to curl up with a good book, and just, well, see what developed, and he'd shrugged off his coat, found his place on the couch and taken up the book again, when he heard the creak of the floorboards in the hall and glanced up.

Bern was standing there, hands at her sides. The primitive light attacked her hair, hair so white it reminded him of death, and she showed him her palms in a humble gesture of submission, amicability, engagement. "Buck's asleep," she said.

"Already?" The book was in his lap, his left index finger marking the place. "That was fast."

"It was a long trip."

"Yes," he said, and he didn't know why he was saying it, "yes." The wind came up suddenly and twisted round the corner of the house, spraying the windowpanes with compact pellets of snow.

She was in the room now, hovering over the couch. "I was just—I mean, I'm not sleepy at all, and I thought it would be nice, you know, just to sit by the fire . . . for a while, I mean."

"Sure," he said, and she squatted by the fire and threw her head back to curb her hair, and a long moment went by—five minutes, ten, he couldn't tell—before she spoke again. He'd just folded back the page of the book when she turned round and said, in a low murmur, "Buck's been very depressed. I mean, like clinically."

Her face was broad and beautiful, with a high forehead and the nose of a legislator or poet. That face stunned him, so beautiful and new and floating there like an apparition in his living room, and he couldn't think of how to respond. The snow ticked at the windows. The old dog let out an audible fart. "He can't—" John began, and then he faltered. "What do you mean, depressed? How? Why?"

She'd been watching him, focusing a clear, steady gaze on him that seemed to say all sorts of things—erotic things, crazy things—but now she dropped her eyes. "He thinks he's going to die."

Something clutched suddenly at him, something deep, but he ignored it. He was going to say, "Don't be ridiculous," but aimed for something lighter instead. "Well, he is," he said. "I mean, it's a rational fear. We're all going to die." He stared into her eyes, a pillar of strength and wisdom. "Eventually," he added, and tried for a smile. "Look at me—I'm fifty already. But Buck—you kids, the two of you—what have you got to worry about? It's a long way off. Forget about it, enjoy yourselves, dance to the music of life." *Dance to the music of life?* The phrase had just jumped into his head, and now he felt a little silly, a little quaint, but seductive too and wise and so full of, of love and maybe fear that he was ready to get up from the couch and embrace her.

The only problem was, she was no longer there. She'd heard something—and he'd heard it too, Buck calling out, the wind dragging its nails across the windowpane—and had risen like a ghost and silently vanished into the black hole of the hallway. John looked round him a moment, listening for the smallest sounds. The snow ticked away at the roof, the gutters, the window frame. The dog groaned in her sleep. He glanced down absently and saw the book there in his lap, turned back the page with a single autonomous sweep of his hand, and began, again, to read.

I'd never wanted to be a father—it was enough to have been father to my own diminishing parents, and I vowed I would never repeat the experience. Sonia felt as I did, and we took precautions to avoid any chance of conception, especially as she began younging and found herself menstruating again. I'd seen my own beloved mother dwindle to the size of a doll, a glove, an acorn, to nothing recognizable except to a scientist with a high-powered microscope, and the idea of it—of parenthood, little people, babies—terrified me.

But what could I do? I loved Sonia with all my being and I'd sworn before the Creator and Father Benitez to minister to her in sickness and health, if not in age and youth. It was my duty and my obligation to care for her when she could no longer care for herself—some would say it was my privilege, and perhaps it was, but it made me no less miserable for all that. For, you see, the inevitable had come to pass and she was an infant now, my Sonia, a baby, a squally, colicky, wide-eyed, little niñita sucking greedily on a bottle of formula and howling through the sleepless nights with miniature tears of rage and impotence rolling down her ugly red cheeks.

"Sonia!" I would cry. "Sonia, snap out of it! I know you're in there, I know you understand me—now just stop that bawling, stop it right now!"

But, of course, she didn't. How could she? She was only a baby, eight months old, six months, two. I held her in my arms, my lover, my Sonia, and watched her shrink away from me day by day. I picked her up by her naked ankles as if she were nothing more than a skinned rabbit ready for the pan, and I laid her out on a clean diaper after swabbing her privates and the little cleft that had once been my joy and my life.

Don't think I didn't resent it. Oh, I knew the rules, we all did, but this was cruel, too cruel, and I wept to see her reduced to this sucking, grasping, greedy little thing. "Sonia!" I cried. "Oh, Sonia!" And for all that she just stared at me out of her eyes the color of hazelnuts, eyes as brimming and lucid as her adult eyes, eyes that must have seen and known and felt. I lost weight. I couldn't sleep. My boss at the Banco Nacional, an eminently reasonable man, took me aside and informed me in so many words that I was in danger of losing the position I'd held for nearly sixty years.

Then one evening, after Sonia had soiled herself so thoroughly and repulsively I had no choice but to draw her a bath, there came a knock at the door. I had her in my arms, Sonia, my Sonia, the water in the tub as mild as a breeze and only two inches deep, but rising, rising, and she gave me a look that ate right through to my soul. It was a plea, a very particular and infinitely sad request that sprang like fire from the depths of her wide and prescient hazelnut eyes. . . .

The knock came again, louder and more insistent now, and I set her down on her back in the slowly accumulating water, all the while watching her eyes as her spastic little legs kicked out and her fists clenched. Then I rose—just for a second, only a second—wiped my hands on my pants, and called, "I'm coming, I'm . . . coming!"

The knock at the door roused John momentarily—Good God, it was past one in the morning, the fire was dead, and Barb, where was Barb?—but he was caught up in something here, and he tried to fight down his anxiety, compartmentalize it, tuck it away in a corner of his brain for future reference. When the knock came again, he didn't hear it, or not consciously, and *Sonia,* he was thinking, *what's going to become of Sonia?* till Buck was there and the door stood open like the mouth of a cave, freezing, absolutely freezing, and a figure loomed in the doorway in a great wide-brimmed felt hat above a gaunt and harried face.

"Dad," Buck was saying, "Dad, there's been an accident—"

John barely heard him. He held the book to his face like a screen, and over the tumult and the confusion and the sudden slashing movement that swept up the room in a hurricane of shouts and moans and the frantic sobbing bark of the old dog, he finally found his voice. "Fifteen pages," he said, waving a frantic hand to fend them off, all of them, even the dog. "I've just got fifteen pages to go."

FRIENDLY SKIES

When the engine under the right wing began to unravel a thin skein of greasy, dark smoke, Ellen peered out the abraded Plexiglas window and saw the tufted clouds rising up and away from her and knew she was going to die. There was a thump from somewhere in the depths of the fuselage, the plane lurched like a balsawood toy struck by a rock, and the man in the seat in front of her lifted his head from the tray table and cried, "Mama!" in a thin, disconsolate wail. On went the "Fasten Seat Belts" sign. The murmur of the cabin became a roar. Every muscle in her body seized.

She thought distractedly of cradling her head—isn't that what you were supposed to do, cradle your head?—and then there was a burst of static, and the captain's voice was chewing calmly through the loudspeakers: "A little glitch there with engine number three, I'm afraid, folks. Nothing to worry about." The plane was obliterating the clouds with a supersonic howl, and every inanimate fold of metal and crease of plastic had come angrily to life, sloughed shoes, pieces of fruit, pretzels, paperback books, and handbags skittering by underfoot. Ellen stole a glance out the window: the smoke was dense now, as black and rich as the roiling billows rising from a ship torpedoed at sea, and stiff raking fingers of yellow flame had begun to strangle the massive cylinder of the engine. The man in the seat next to hers—late twenties, with a brass stud centered half an inch beneath his lower lip, and hair the exact color and texture of meringue—turned a slack face to her. "What is that? Smoke?"

She was so frightened that she could only nod, her head filled with the sucking dull hiss of the air jets and the static of the speakers. The man leaned across her and squinted through the gray aperture of the window to the wing beyond. "Fuck, that's all we need. There's no way I'm going to make my connection now."

She didn't understand. Connection? Didn't he realize they were all going to die?

She braced herself and murmured a prayer. Voices rose in alarm. Her eyes felt as if they were going to implode in their sockets. But then the flames flickered and dimmed, and she felt the plane lifted up as if in the palm of some celestial hand, and for all the panic, the dimly remembered prayers, the cries and shouts, and the sudden, potent reek of urine, the crisis was over almost as soon as it had begun. "I hate to do this to you, folks," the captain drawled, "but it looks like we're going to have to turn around and take her back into LAX."

And now there was a collective groan. The man with the meringue hair let out a sharp, stinging curse and slammed the back of the seat in front of him with his fist. Not LAX. Not that. They'd already been delayed on the ground for two and a half hours because of mechanical problems, and then they'd sat on the runway for another forty minutes because they'd lost their slot for takeoff—or at least that's what the pilot had claimed. Everyone had got free drinks and peanuts, but nobody wanted peanuts, and the drinks tasted like nothing, like kerosene. Ellen had asked for a Scotch-and-soda—she was trying to pace herself, after sitting interminably at the airport bar nursing a beer that had gone stale and warm—but the man beside her and the woman in the aisle seat had both ordered doubles and flung them down wordlessly. "Shit!" the man cursed now, and slammed his fist into the seat again, pounding it as if it were a punching bag, until the man in front of him lifted a great, swollen dirigible of a head over the seat back and growled, "Give it a rest, asshole. Can't you see we got an emergency here?"

Ellen caught a glimpse of his face, blunt and oblivious, as he swung ponderously into his seat, and then the line shuffled forward and she saw that her prayer had been answered—she was three rows ahead of him. She'd been assigned a middle seat, of course, as had most of the passengers bumped from the previous flight, but at least it wasn't a middle seat beside him. She waited as the woman in the aisle seat (mid-fifties, with a saddlebag face and a processed pouf of copper hair) unfastened her seat belt and laboriously rose to make way for her. There was no one in the window seat—not yet, at least—and even as she settled in, elbow to elbow with the saddlebag woman, Ellen was already coveting it.

Could she be so lucky? No, no, she couldn't, and here was another layer of superstition rising up out of the murk of her subconscious, as if luck had anything to do with her or what she'd been through already today or in the past week or month or year—or, for that matter, through the whole course of her vacant and constricted life. A name came to her lips then, a name she'd been trying, with the help of the prescription the doctor had given her, to suppress. She held it there for a moment, enlarged by her grief until she felt like the heroine of some weepy movie, a raped nun, an airman's widow, sloe-eyed and wilting under the steady gaze of the camera. She shouldn't have had the beer, she told herself. Or the Scotch, either. Not with the pills.

The plane quieted. The aisles cleared. She fought down her exhaustion and kept her eyes fixed on the far end of the aisle, where the last passenger—a boy in a reversed baseball cap—was fumbling into his seat. Surreptitiously, with her feet only, she shifted her bag from the space under her seat to the space beneath the window seat, and then, after a moment, she unfastened her seat belt and slipped into the unoccupied seat. She stretched her legs, adjusted her pillow and blanket, watched the flight attendants work their way up the aisle, easing shut the overhead bins. She was thinking that she should have called her mother with the new flight information—she'd call her from Chicago, that's what she'd do—when there was movement at the front of the plane and one final passenger came through the door, even as the attendants stood by to screw it shut. Stooping to avoid the TV monitors, he came slowly down the aisle, sweeping his eyes right and left to check the row numbers, an overcoat over one arm, a soft computer bag slung over the opposite shoulder. He was dressed in a sport coat and a T-shirt, his hair cut close, after the fashion of the day, and his face seemed composed despite what must have been a mad dash through the airport. But what mattered most about him was that he seemed to be coming straight to her, to 18A, the seat she'd appropriated. And what went through her mind? A curse, that was all. Just a curse.

Sure enough, he paused at Row 18, glanced at the saddlebag woman, and then at Ellen, and said, "Excuse me, I believe I'm in here?"

Ellen reddened. "I thought . . ."

"No, no," he said, holding Ellen's eyes even as the saddlebag woman rolled up and out of her seat like a rock dislodged from a crevice, "stay there. It's okay. Really."

The pilot said something then, a garble of the usual words, the fuselage shuddered, and the plane backed away from the gate with a sudden jolt. Ellen put her head back and closed her eyes.

She woke when the drinks cart came around. There was a sour taste in her mouth, her head was throbbing, and the armrest gouged at her ribs as if it had come alive. She'd been dreaming about Roy, the man who had dismembered her life like a boy pulling the legs off an insect, Roy and that elaborate, humiliating scene in the teachers' lounge, her mother there somehow to witness it, and then she and Roy were in bed, the stiff insistence of his erection (which turned out to be the armrest), and his hand creeping across her rib cage until it was Waldo, Waldo the tarantula, closing in on her breast. "Something to drink?" the broad-faced flight attendant was asking, and both Ellen's seatmates seemed to be hanging on her answer. "Scotch-and-soda," she said, without giving it a second thought.

The man beside her, the new man, the one who had offered up

his seat to her, was working on his laptop, the gentle blue glow of the screen softly illuminating his lips and eyes. He looked up at the flight attendant, his fingers still poised over the keys, and murmured, "May I have a chardonnay, please?" Then it was the saddlebag woman's turn. "Sprite," she said, the dull thump of her voice swallowed up in the drone of the engines.

The man flattened himself against the seat back as the flight attendant leaned in to pass Ellen her drink, then he typed something hurriedly, shut down the computer, and slipped it into his lap, beneath the tray table. He took the truncated bottle, the glass, napkin and peanuts from the attendant, arranged them neatly before him, and turned to Ellen with a smile. "I never know where to put my elbows on these things," he said, shrinking away from the armrest they shared. "It's kind of like being in a coffin—or one of those medieval torture devices, you know what I mean?"

Ellen took a sip of her drink and felt the hot smoke of the liquor in the back of her throat. He was good-looking, handsome—more than handsome. At that moment, the engines thrumming, the flat, dull earth fanning out beneath the plane, he was shining and beautiful, as radiant as an archangel come flapping through the window to roost beside her. Not that it would matter to her. Roy was handsome too, but she was done with handsome, done with fifth graders, done with the whole failed experiment of living on her own in the big, smoggy, palm-shrouded city. Turn the page, new chapter. "Or maybe a barrel," she heard herself say, "going over Niagara Falls."

"Yeah," he said, laughing through his nose. "Only in the barrel you don't get your own personal flotation device."

Ellen didn't know what to say to that. She took another pull at her drink for lack of anything better to do. She was feeling it, no doubt about it, but what difference would it make if she were drunk or sober as she wandered the labyrinthine corridors of O'Hare, endlessly delayed by snow, mechanical failure, the hordes of everybody going everywhere? Three sheets to the wind, right—isn't that what they said? And what, exactly, did that mean? Some old sailing expression, she supposed, something from the days of the clipper ships, when you vomited yourself from one place to another.

Their meals had come. The broad-faced flight attendant was again leaning in confidentially, this time with the eternal question— "Chicken or pasta?"—on her lips. Ellen wasn't hungry—food was the last thing she wanted—but on an impulse she turned to her neighbor. "I'm not really very hungry," she said, her face too close to his, their elbows touching, his left knee rising up out of the floor like a stanchion, "but if I get a meal, would you want it—or some of it? As an extra, I mean?"

He gave her a curious look, then said, "Sure, why not?" The flight attendant was waiting, the sealed-in smile beginning to crack at the corners with the first fidgeting of impatience. "Chicken for me," the man said, "and pasta for the lady." And then, to Ellen, as he shifted the tray from one hand to the other: "You sure, now? I know it's not exactly three-star cuisine, but you've got to eat, and the whole reason they feed you is to make the time pass so you don't realize how cramped and miserable you are."

The smell of the food—salt, sugar, and animal fat made palpable—rose to her nostrils, and she felt nauseated again. Was it the pills? The alcohol? Or was it Roy—Roy, and life itself? She thought about that, and the instant she did, there he was—Roy— clawing his way back into her mind. She could see him now, his shoulders squared in his black polyester suit with the little red flecks in it—the suit she'd helped him pick out, as if he had any taste or style he could call his own—his eyes swollen out of their sockets, his lips reduced to two thin, ungenerous flaps of skin grafted to his mouth. *Shit-for-brains.* That's what he'd called her, right there in the teachers' lounge with everybody watching— Lynn Bendall and Lauren McGimpsey and that little teacher's aide, what was her name? He was shouting, and she was shouting back, no holds barred, not anymore. *So what if I am sleeping with her? What's it to you? You think you own me? Do you? Huh, shit-for-brains? Huh?* Lauren's face was dead, but Ellen saw Lynn exchange a smirk with the little teacher's aide, and that smirk said it all, because Lynn, it seemed, knew more about who he was sleeping with than Ellen did herself.

The man beside her—her neighbor—was eating now. He was hungry, and that was good. She felt saintly, watching him eat and listening to him chatter on about his work—he was some sort of writer or journalist, on his way to Philadelphia for the holidays. She'd renounced the pasta and given it to him, and he was grateful—he hadn't eaten all day, and he was a growing boy, he said, with a smile, though he must have been in his early thirties. And unmarried, judging from his naked fingers. When the drinks cart came by, Ellen ordered another Scotch.

They were talking about movies, maybe the only subject people had in common these days, when Ellen glanced up to see Lercher, his face twisted in a drunken scowl, looming over them as he made his unsteady way to the forward lavatories. She and her companion—his name was Michael, just Michael, that was all he offered—had struck a real chord when it came to the current cinema (no movies with explosions, no alien life-forms, no geriatric lovers, no sappy kids), and she'd begun to feel something working inside her. She was interested, genuinely interested in something, for maybe the first time in months. Michael. She held the name on her tongue like the thinnest wafer, repeating it silently, over and over. And then it came to her: he was the anti-Roy, that's who he was, so polite and unassuming, a soul mate, somebody who could care, really care—she was sure of it.

"You see that man?" she asked, lowering her voice. "The one with the hair? He was sitting right next to me on the last flight, the one where, well, I was telling you, I was looking out the window and the engine caught fire? And I've never been so scared in my life."

The wind shrieked along the length of the fuselage, the lights dimmed and went up again, Michael poured himself a second glass of wine and made sympathetic noises. "You actually saw this? Flames? Or was it like sparks or something?"

She went cold with the memory of it. "Flames," she said, pursing her lips and nodding her head. "I was so scared I started praying." She glanced out the window, as if to reassure herself. "You're not religious, are you?" she said, turning back to him.

"No," he said, and he raised his hand to cut the throat of the subject before it could take hold of him. "I'm an atheist. I mean, we had no set religion in our house, that's just the way my parents were."

"Me too," she said, remembering religious instruction, the icy dip of the holy water, her mother in a black veil, and the priest intoning the sleepy immemorial phrases of her girlhood, "but we went to church when I was little."

He didn't ask what church, and a silence fell between them as the plane rocked gently and the big man oscillated back from the lavatory. Ellen closed her eyes again, for just a moment, the swaying of the cabin and the pills and the Scotch pulling her down toward some inky dark place that was like the mouth of an abandoned well, like a cave deep in the earth. . . .

She was startled awake by a sudden explosion of voices behind her. "The fuck I will!" snarled a man's voice, and even through the fog of her waking she recognized it.

"But, sir, I've already told you, the plane is full. You can see for yourself."

"Then put me up front—and don't try to tell me that's full, because I was up there to use the rest room, and there's all sorts of space up there. This is bullshit. I'm not going to sit here squeezed in like a rat. I paid full fare, and I'm not going to take this shit anymore, you hear me?"

Heads had begun to turn. Ellen glanced at Michael, but he was absorbed with his computer, some message she couldn't read, some language she didn't know; for a moment she stared at the ranks of dark symbols floating across the dull firmament of the screen, then she craned her neck to see over the seat back. Lercher was standing in the aisle, his shoulders hunched, his head cocked forward against the low ceiling. Two flight attendants, the broad-faced woman and another, slighter woman with her hair in a neat French braid, stood facing him.

"There's nothing we can do, sir," the slight woman said, an

edge of hostility in her voice. "I've already told you, you don't qualify for an upgrade. Now, I'm going to have to ask you to take your seat."

"This is bullshit," he reiterated. "Two and a half fucking hours on the ground, and then we get sent back to LAX, and now I'm stuck in this cattle car, and you won't even serve me a fucking drink? Huh? What do you call this?" He flailed his arms, appealing to the people seated around him; to a one, they looked away. "Well, I call it bullshit!" he roared.

The women held their ground. "Sit down, sir. Now. Or we'll have to call the captain."

The big man's face changed. The crease between his eyes deepened; his lips drew back as if he were about to spit down the front of the first woman's crisp blue jacket. "All right," he said ominously, "if that's how you want to play it," and he was already swinging around and staggering toward the rear of the plane, the flight attendants trailing along helplessly in his wake. Ellen shifted in her seat so she could follow their progress, her hips straining against the seat belt, her right hand inadvertently braced against Michael's forearm. "Oh, I'm sorry," she murmured, even as Lercher disappeared into the galley at the rear and she turned her face to Michael's. He looked startled, his eyes so blue and electric they reminded her of the fish in the classroom aquarium—the neon tetras, with their bright lateral stripes. "Did you see that? I mean, did you hear him—the man, the one I was telling you about?"

He hesitated a moment, just staring into her eyes. "No," he said finally, "I didn't notice. I was—I guess I was so absorbed in my work I didn't know where I was."

Ellen's face darkened. "He's the worst kind of trash," she said. "Just mean, that's all, like the bullies on the playground."

And now there was the sound of a commotion from the rear of the plane, and Ellen turned to see Lercher emerge from the galley on the far side of the plane, the flight attendants cowering behind him. In each hand he wielded a gleaming stainless-steel coffeepot, and he was moving rapidly up the aisle, his eyes gone hard with hate. "Out of my way!" he screamed, elbowing a tottering old lady aside. "Anybody fucks with me gets scalded, you hear me?"

People awoke with a snort. A hundred heads ducked down protectively, and on every face was an expression that said *not now, not here, not me.* No one said a word. And then, suddenly, a male flight attendant came hurtling down the aisle from the first-class section and attempted to tackle the big man, gripping him around the waist, and Ellen heard a woman cry out as hot coffee streamed down the front of her blouse. Lercher held his ground, bludgeoning the flight attendant to the floor with the butt of the wildly splashing pot he clutched in his right fist, and then the two female attendants were on him, tearing at his arms, and a male passenger, heavyset and balding, sprang savagely up out of his seat to enter the fray.

For a moment, they achieved a sort of equilibrium, surging forward and falling back again, but Lercher was too much for them. He stunned the heavyset man with a furious, slashing blow, then flung off the flight attendants as if they were nothing. The scalded woman screamed again, and Ellen felt as if a knife were twisting inside her. She couldn't breathe. Her arms went limp. Lercher was dancing in the aisle, shouting obscenities, moving backward now, toward the galley, and God only knew what other weapons he might find back there.

Where was the captain? Where were the people in charge? The cabin was in an uproar, babies screaming, voices crying out, movement everywhere—and Lercher was in the galley, dismantling the plane, and no one could do anything about it. There was the crash of a cart being overturned, a volley of shouts, and suddenly he appeared at the far end of Ellen's aisle, his face contorted until it was no human face at all. "Die!" he screamed. "Die, you motherfuckers!" The rear exit door was just opposite him, and he paused in his fury to kick at it with a big booted foot, and then he was hammering at the Plexiglas window with one of the coffeepots as if he could burst through it and sail on out into the troposphere like some sort of human missile.

"You're all going to die!" he screamed, pounding, pounding. "You'll be sucked out into space, all of you!" Ellen thought she could hear the window cracking—wasn't anybody going to do anything?—and then he dropped both coffeepots and made a rush up the aisle for the first-class section.

Before she could react, Michael rose in a half-crouch, swung his laptop out across the saddlebag lady's tray table, and caught Lercher in the crotch with the sharp, flying corner of it. She saw his face then, Lercher's, twisted and swollen like a sore, and it came right at Michael, who could barely maneuver in his eighteen inches of allotted space. In a single motion, the big man snatched the laptop from Michael's hand and brought it whistling down across his skull, and Ellen felt him go limp beside her. At that point, she didn't know what she was doing. All she knew was that she'd had enough, enough of Roy and this big, drunken, testosterone-addled bully and the miserable, crimped life that awaited her at her mother's, and she came up out of her seat as if she'd been launched—and in her hand, clamped there like a flaming sword, was a thin steel fork that she must have plucked from the cluttered dinner tray. She went for his face, for his head, his throat, enveloping him with her body, the drug singing in her heart and the Scotch flowing like ichor in her veins.

They made an emergency stop in Denver, and they sat on the ground in a swirling light snow as the authorities boarded the plane to take charge of Lercher. He'd been overpowered finally and bound to his seat with cloth napkins from the first-class dining service, a last napkin crammed into his mouth as a gag. The captain had come on the loudspeaker with a mouthful of apologies, and then, to a feeble cheer from the cabin, pledged free headphones and drinks on the house for the rest of the flight. Ellen sat, dazed, over yet another Scotch, the seat beside her vacant. Even before the men in uniforms boarded the plane to handcuff and shackle Lercher, the paramedics had rushed down the aisle to evacuate poor Michael to the nearest hospital, and she would never forget the way his eyes had rolled back in his head as they laid him out on the stretcher. And Lercher, big and bruised, his head drunkenly bowed and the dried blood painted across his cheek where the fork had gone in and gone in again, as if she'd been carving a roast with a dull knife, Lercher led away like Billy Tindall or Lucas Lopez in the grip of the principal on a bad day at La Cumbre Elementary.

She sipped her drink, her face gone numb, eyes focused on nothing, as the whole plane murmured in awe. People stole glances at her, the saddlebag woman offered up her personal copy of the January *Cosmopolitan*, the captain himself came back to pay homage. And the flight attendants—they were so relieved they were practically genuflecting to her. It didn't matter. Nothing mattered. There would be forms to fill out, a delay in Chicago, an uneventful flight into New York, eight hours behind schedule. Her mother would be there, with a face full of pity and resignation, and she'd be too delicate to mention Roy, or teaching, or any of the bleak details of the move itself, the waste of a new microwave, and all that furniture tossed in a Dumpster. She would smile, and Ellen would try to smile back. "Is that it?" her mother would say, eyeing the bag slung over her shoulder. "You must have some baggage?" And then, as they were heading down the carpeted corridor, two women caught in the crush of humanity, with the snow spitting outside and the holidays coming on, her mother would take her by the arm, smile up at her, and just to say something, anything, would ask, "Did you have a nice flight?"

THE BLACK AND WHITE SISTERS

I used to cut their lawn for them, before they paved it over, that is. It was the older one, Moira, the one with the white hair and vanilla skirt, who gave me the bad news. "Vincent," she said, "Caitlin and I have decided to do without the lawn—and the shrubs and flowers too." (We were in her kitchen at the time, a place from which every hint of color had been erased, Caitlin was hovering in the doorway with her vulcanized hair and cream-pie face, and my name is Larry, not Vincent—just to give you some perspective.)

I shuffled my feet and ducked my head. "So you won't be needing a gardener anymore then?"

Moira exchanged a look with her sister, who was my age exactly: forty-two. I know, because we were in school together, all three of us, from elementary through junior high, when their parents took them to live in New York. Not long after that the parents died and left them a truckload of money, and eventually they made their way back to California to take up residence in the family manse, which has something like twenty rooms and two full acres of lawns and flowerbeds, which I knew intimately. Moira wasn't much to look at anymore—too pinned-back and severe— but Caitlin, if you caught her in the right light, could be very appealing. She had a sort of retro-ghoulish style about her, with her dead black clinging dress and Kabuki skin and all the rest of it. Black fingernails, of course. And toenails. I could just see the glossy even row of them peeping out from beneath the hem of her dress.

"Well," Moira demurred, coming back to me in her brisk grandmotherly way, though she wasn't a grandmother, never even married, and couldn't have been more than forty-four or -five, "I wouldn't be too hasty. We're going to want all the shrubs and trees removed—anything that shows inside the fence, that is."

I'd been around in my time (in and out of college, stint in the merchant marine, twice married and twice divorced, and I'd lived in Poughkeepsie, Atlanta, Juneau, Cleveland and Mazatlán before I came home to California and my mother), and nothing surprised me. Or not particularly. I studied Moira's face, digging the toe of my workboot into the square of linoleum in front of me. "I don't know," I said finally, "it's going to be a big job—the trees, anyway. I can handle the shrubs and flowers myself, but the treework's going to have to go to a professional. I can make some calls, if you want."

Moira came right back at me, needling and sharp. "You know the rule: black jeans, white T-shirt, black caps. No exceptions."

I was wearing black jeans myself—and a white T-shirt and black cap, from which I'd removed the silver Raiders logo at her request. I was clear on the parameters here. But the money was good, very good, and I was used to dealing with the eccentric rich—that was pretty much all we had in this self-consciously quaint little town by the sea. And eccentric, as we all know, is just a code word for pure cold-water crazy. "Sure," I said. "No problem."

"You'll bill us?" Moira asked, smoothing down her skirt and crossing the room in a nervous flutter to pull open the refrigerator and peer inside.

Ten percent, I could see it already—and the treework would be eleven or twelve thousand, easy, maybe more. It wasn't gouging, not really, just my commission for catering to their whims—or needs. Black jeans and white T-shirts. Sure. I just nodded.

"And no Mexicans. I know there's practically nothing but on any work crew these days, and I have nothing against them, nothing at all, but you know how I feel, Vincent, I think. Don't you?"

She removed a clear glass pitcher of milk from the refrigerator and took a glass from the cupboard. "A black crew I'd have no objection to—or a white one, either. But it's got to be one or the other, no mixing, and you know"—she paused, the glass in one hand, the pitcher in the other—"if it's a black crew, I think I'd like to see them in *white* jeans and *black* T-shirts. Would there be a problem with that, if the question should arise?"

"No," I said, slowly shaking my head, as if I could barely sustain the weight of it, "no problem at all."

"Good," she said, pouring out a clean white glass of milk and setting it down on the counter beside the pitcher as if she were arranging a still life. She clasped her hands over her breast, flashed a look at her sister, and then smiled as if I'd just carved up the world like a melon and handed it to her, piece by dripping piece. "We'll begin A.S.A.P. then, hmm? The sooner the better?"

"Sure," I said.

"All right, then. Do you have anything to add, Caitlin?"

Caitlin's voice, soft as the beat of a cabbage moth's wing: "No, nothing."

I started digging out the bushes myself—fuchsia, oleander, mock orange—but I had to go pretty far afield for the tree crew. There were three grand old oaks in the front yard, a mature Australian tea tree on the east side of the house, and half a dozen citrus trees in the back. It would take a crew of ten at least, with climbers, a cherry picker, shredder and cleanup, and as I say, it was going to be expensive. And wasteful. A real shame, really, to strip and pave a yard like that, but if that was what they wanted, I was in no position to argue. I stood to make eleven hundred or so on the trees and another five digging out the shrubs and tilling up the lawn.

The problem, though, as Moira had foreseen, was in finding a non-Mexican crew in San Roque. It just didn't exist. Nor were there many white guys on the dirty end of the tree business—they basically just bid the jobs and sent you the bill—and there were no blacks in town at all. Finally, I drove down to Los Angeles and talked to Walt Tremaine, of Walt's Stump & Tree, and he agreed to come up and bid the job, writing in three hundred extra for the aesthetic considerations—i.e., the white jeans and black T-shirts.

Walt Tremaine was a man of medium size with a firm paunch and a glistening bald sweat-speckled crown. He looked to be in his fifties, and he was wearing a pair of cutoff blue jeans and one of those tight-fitting shirts with the little alligator logo over the left nipple. The alligator was green, and the shirt was the color of a crookneck squash—a bright, glowing, almost aniline yellow. We were both contemplating the problem of the tea tree, a massive snaking thing that ran its arms out into a tangle of neglected Victorian Box, when the two women appeared round the corner of the house. Moira was in white—high-heeled boots, ankle-length dress and sweater, though it was a golden temperate day, like most days here—and Caitlin was in her customary black. Both of them had parasols, but Caitlin had taken the white one and Moira the black for some reason—maybe they were trying to impress Walt Tremaine with their improvisatory daring.

I introduced them, and Moira, beaming, took Walt Tremaine's hand and said, "So, you're a black man."

He just stared at the picture of her white-gloved hand in the shadow of his for a minute and then corrected her. "African-American."

"Yes," Moira said, still beaming, "exactly. And I very much like the color of your shirt, but you do understand I hope that it's much too much of an excitation and will simply have to go. Yes?" And then she turned to me. "Vincent, have you explained to this gentleman what we require?"

Walt Tremaine gave me a look. It was a look complicated by the fact that I'd introduced myself as Larry when he climbed out of his pickup truck, not to mention Moira's comment about his shirt and the dead white of Moira's dress and the nullifying black of her sister's lipstick, but it went further than that too—it was the way Moira was talking, taking elaborate care with each syllable, as if she were an English governess with a board strapped to her back. He operated out of Van Nuys, and I figured he didn't run across many women like Moira in an average day. But he was equal to the challenge, no problem there.

"Sure," he said, pressing a little smile onto his lips. "Your man here—whatever his name is—outlined the whole thing for me. I can do the job for you, but I have to say I'm an equal-opportunity employer, and I have eight Mexicans, two Guatemalans, a Serb and a Fiji Islander working for me, as well as my African-Americans. And I don't particularly like it, but I can split off one crew of black men and bring them up here, if that's what you want." He paused. Toed the grass a minute, touched a finger to his lips. When he spoke, it was with a rising inflection, and his eyes rolled up like loose windowshades and then came back down again: "White jeans?"

Caitlin gave a little laugh and gazed out across the lawn. Her sister shot her a fierce look and then clamped the grandmotherly smile back on her face. "Indulge us," she said. "We're just trying to—well, let's say we're trying to simplify our environment."

Later that afternoon, sweating buckets, I stopped to strip off my soaked-through T-shirt and hose some of the grit off me. I stood there a moment, my mind blank, the scent of everything that lives and grows rising to my nostrils, the steady stream of the hose now dribbling from my fingertips, now distending my cheeks, when the front gate cranked open and Caitlin's black Mercedes rolled up the drive and came to a silent, German-engineered halt beside me. I'd been hacking away at an ancient plumbago bush for the past half hour, and I wasn't happy. It seemed wrong to destroy all this living beauty, deeply wrong, a desecration of the yard and the neighborhood and a violation of the principles I try to live by—I hadn't started up a gardening business to maim and uproot things, after all. I wanted to nurture new growth. I wanted healing. Rebirth. All of that. Because I'd seen some bad times, especially with my second wife, and all I can say is thank God we didn't have any children.

Anyway, there I was and there she was, Caitlin, stepping out of the car with a panting dog at her heels (no, it wasn't a Scottie or a black Lab, but a Hungarian puli that was so unrelievedly black it cut a moving hole out of the scenery). She lifted two bulging plastic sacks from the seat beside her—groceries—and I remember wondering if the chromatic obsession extended to foods too. There would be eggplant in one of those bags, I was thinking, vanilla ice cream in another, devil's food cake, Béchamel, week-old bananas, coffee, Crisco . . . but inspiration began to fail me when I realized she was standing two feet from me, watching the water roll off my shoulders and find its snaking way down my chest and into the waist of my regulation black jeans.

"Hi, Larry," she murmured, smiling at me with as sweet an expression as you could expect from a woman with black-rimmed eyes and lips the color of a dead streetwalker's. "How's it going?"

I tried to wipe every trace of irritation from my face—as I say, I wasn't too pleased with what she and her sister were doing here, but I tried to put things in perspective. I'd had crazier clients by a long shot. There was Mrs. Boutilier du Plessy, for one, who had me dig a pond twenty feet across for a single goldfish she'd been handed by a stranger at the mall, and Frank and Alma Fortressi, who paid me to line the floor of their master bedroom with Visquine and then dump thirty bags of planting mix on top of it so I could plant peonies right at the foot of the bed. I smiled back at Caitlin. "All right, I guess."

She shaded her eyes from the sun and squinted at me. "Is that sweat? All over you, I mean?"

"It was," I said, holding her eyes. I was remembering her as a child, black hair in braids, like Pocahontas, dimpled knees, the plain constricting chute of a little girl's dress, but a dress that was pink or moss-green or Lake Tahoe blue. "I just hosed off."

"Hard work, huh?" she said, looking off over my shoulder as if she were addressing someone behind me. And then: "Can I get you something to drink?"

"It wouldn't be milk, would it?" I said, and she laughed.

"No, no milk, I promise. I can give you juice, soda, beer—would you like a beer?"

The dog sniffed at my leg—or at least I hope he was sniffing, since he was so black and matted you couldn't tell which end of him was which. "A beer sounds real nice," I said, "but I don't know how you and your sister are supposed to feel about it—I mean, beer's not white." I let it go a beat. "Or black."

She held her smile, not fazed in the least. "For one thing," she said, "Moira always takes a nap after lunch, so she won't be involved. And for another"—she was looking right into my eyes now, the smile turned up a notch—"we only serve Guinness in this house."

We sat in the kitchen—black-and-white tile, white cabinets, black appliances—and had three bottles each while the sun slid across the windowpanes and the plumbago withered over its hacked and naked roots. I don't know what it was—the beer, the time of day, the fact that she was there and listening—but I really opened up to her. I told her about Janine, my second wife, and how she picked at me all the time—I was never good enough for her, no matter what I did—and I got off on a tangent about a transformative experience I'd had in Hawaii, when I first realized I wanted to work with the earth, with the whole redemptive process of digging and planting, laying out flowerbeds, running drip lines, setting trees in the ground. (I was on top of Haleakala Crater, in the garden paradise of the world, and there was nothing but volcanic debris all around me, a whole sour landscape of petrified symbols. It was dawn and I hadn't slept and Janine and I stood there in the wind, bleary tourists gazing out on all that nullity, and suddenly I understood what I wanted in life. I wanted things to be green, that was all. It was as simple as that.)

Caitlin was a good listener, and I liked the way she tipped the glass back in delicate increments as she drank, her eyes shining and her free hand spread flat on the tabletop, as if we were at sea and she needed to steady herself. She kept pushing the hair away from her face and then leaning forward to let it dangle loose again, and whenever I touched on anything painful or sensitive (and practically everything about Janine fell into that category), a sympathetic little crease appeared between her eyebrows and she clucked her tongue as if there were something stuck to the roof of her mouth. After the second beer, we turned to less personal topics: the weather, gardening, people we knew in common. When we cracked the third, we began reminiscing about the lame, halt and oddball teachers we'd had in junior high and some of the more memorable disasters from those days, like the time it rained day and night for the better part of a week and boulders the size of Volkswagens rolled up out of the streambeds and into the passing lane of the freeway.

I was having a good time, and good times had been in precious short supply since my divorce. I felt luxurious and calm. The shrubs, I figured, could wait until tomorrow—and the trees and the grass and the sky too. It was nice, for a change, to let the afternoon stretch itself over the window like a thin skin and not have to worry about a thing. I was drunk. Drunk at three in the afternoon, and I didn't care. We'd just shared a laugh over Mr. Clemens, the English teacher who wore the same suit and tie every day for two years and pronounced *poem* as "poim," when I set my glass down and asked Caitlin what I'd been wanting to ask since I first left my card in her mailbox six months back. "Listen, Caitlin," I said, riding the exhilaration of that last echoing laugh, "I hope you won't take this the wrong way, but what is it with the black and white business—I mean, is it some sort of political statement? A style? A religious thing?"

She leaned back in her chair and made an effort to hold on to her smile. The dog lay asleep in the corner, as shabby and formless as an old alpaca coat slipped from a hanger. He let out a long, heaving sigh, lifted his head briefly, and then dropped it again. "Oh, I don't know," she said, "it's a long story—"

That was when Moira appeared, right on cue. She was wearing a gauzy white pantsuit she might have picked up at a beekeepers' convention, and she hesitated at the kitchen door when she saw me sitting there with her sister and a thick black beer, but only for an instant. "Why, Vincent," she said, more the governess than ever, "what a nice surprise."

/ / / / /

The next morning, at eight, Walt Tremaine showed up with seven black men in white jeans, black T-shirts and white caps and enough heavy machinery to take down every tree within half a mile before lunch. "And how are you this fine morning, Mr. Vincent Larry," he said, "—or is it Larry Vincent?"

I blew the steam off a cup of McDonalds's coffee and worked my tongue round the remnants of an Egg McMuffin. "Just call me Larry," I said. "It's her," I added, by way of explanation. "Moira, the older one. I mean, she's . . . well, I don't have to tell you—I'm sure you can draw your own conclusions."

Walt Tremaine planted his feet and wrapped his arms round his chest. "Oh, I don't know," he said, waxing philosophical as his crew scuttled past us with ropes, chainsaws, blowers and trimmers. "Sometimes I wish I could get a little simplicity in *my* life, if you know what I mean. Up in a tree half the day, sawdust in my hair, and when I come home to my wife she expects me to mow the lawn and break out the hedge clippers." He looked down at his feet and then out across the lawn. "Hell, I'd like to pave my yard over too."

I was going to say *I know what you mean*, because that's the sort of thing you say in a situation like that, but that would have implied agreement, and I didn't agree, not at all. So I just shrugged noncommittally and watched Walt Tremaine's eyes follow his climbers up the biggest, oldest and most venerable oak in the yard.

Later, when the tree was in pieces and the guy I'd hired for the day and I had rototilled the lawn and raked the dying fragments into three top-heavy piles the size of haystacks, Moira, in her bee-keeper's regalia, appeared with a pitcher of milk and a tray of Oreo cookies. It was four in the afternoon, the yard was raw with dirt, and the air shrieked with the noise of Walt Tremaine's shredder as his men fed it the remains of the oak's crown. The other two oaks, smaller but no less grand, had been decapitated preparatory to taking them down, and the tea tree had been relieved of its limbs. All in all, it looked as if a bomb had hit the yard while miraculously sparing the house (white, of course, with whiter trim and a dead black roof). I watched Moira circulate among the bewildered sweating men of Walt Tremaine's crew, pouring out milk, offering cookies.

When she got around to me and Greg (black jeans, white T-shirt, black cap, white skin), she let her smile waver and flutter twice across her lips before settling in. We were taking a hard-earned break, stretched out in comfort on the last besieged patch of grass and trying to muster the energy to haul all that yellowing turf out to my pickup. We'd really humped it all afternoon, so caught up in the rhythm of destruction we never even stopped for a drink from the hose, but we couldn't help but look guilty now—you always do when the client catches you on your rear end. I introduced her to Greg, who didn't bother to get up.

"I'm very pleased to meet you," she said, and Greg just grunted in return, already tucking a cookie inside his cheek. I passed on the cookies myself, and the milk too—I was beginning to resent being reduced to a figure in some crazy composition. She smiled at me, though, a full-on interplanetary dreamer's smile that really made me wonder if there was anyone home, at least for that instant, and then she turned back to Greg. "You're, uh, how can I put this?" she murmured, studying his deeply tanned face and arms. "You're not Mexican, by any chance, are you?"

Greg looked surprised and maybe a bit shocked too—she might as well have asked him if he was a Zulu. He gave me a quick glance, then shifted his gaze to Moira. "My last name's Sorenson," he said, struggling to keep his voice under control, and he took off his cap to show her the blond highlights in his hair. He replaced the cap indignantly and held out his arms. "I'm a surfer," he said, "every chance I get. This is what's known as a *tan*."

I watched the sun touch her hair as she straightened up with the tray and struggled with her smile. She must bleach her hair, I was thinking, because nobody under seventy has hair that white—and it was amazing hair, white right on through to the scalp, sheep-white, bone-white, paper-white—when she squared her shoulders and looked down at Greg as if he were some panting animal she'd discovered in a cage at the zoo. "Well, that's nice," she said finally. "Very nice. It's a nice sport. Will you be working here long? For us, I mean?"

"We'll be done this time tomorrow, Moira," I said, cutting in before Greg could say something I might wind up regretting. "We've just got to rake out the lawn—the dirt, that is—for the blacktop guy, and take out the rest of the Pittosporum under the tea tree. Walt Tremaine and his people are going to need two more days."

Moira wavered on the cusp of this news, the gauzy beekeeper's outfit inflating with a sudden breath of wind. She held the tray of milk and cookies rigidly before her, and I noticed her hands for the first time, a young woman's hands, sleek and unlined, the fingernails heavily enamelled in cake-frosting white. "Vincent," she said after a moment, raising her voice to be heard over the dopplering whine of the shredder out on the street, "could I have a word with you in private?" She moved off then without waiting for an answer, and I was left to push myself up and tag after her, like the hired help I was.

We'd marched forty feet across the ravaged yard before she turned to me. "This Sorenson," she said. "Your associate?"

"Yeah?"

"I presume he's just casual labor?"

I nodded.

She glanced up toward the house and I followed her line of sight to one of the second-story windows. Caitlin was there, in her funereal black, looking down on the wreckage of the yard with a fixed stare. "I don't want to put you out, Vincent," Moira was saying, and she was still staring up at the image of her sister, "but couldn't you find someone a little less *sallow* for tomorrow?"

There wouldn't be any gardening going on around here for some time to come, and I didn't really have to kowtow to this woman anymore—or humor her, either—but I went along with her just the same. Call it a reflex. "Sure," I said, and I had to keep myself from tipping my hat. "No problem."

/ / / / /

A week later the yard was an empty parking lot surrounded by a ten-foot-high clapboard fence (whitewashed, of course). From inside you couldn't see a trace of green anywhere—or yellow, red, pink or tangerine, for that matter. I wondered how they felt, Moira and her sweet sad sister, when they stepped outside on their perfectly contoured blacktop plateau and looked up into the airy blue reaches of the sky with that persistent golden sun hanging in the middle of it. Disappointed? Frustrated? Sorry. God hadn't made us all as color-blind as dogs? Maybe they ought to just go ahead and dome the place—sure, just like a baseball stadium, and they could paint the underside of the thing Arctic white. Or avoid daylight altogether. A good starlit night wouldn't interfere with the scheme at all.

Do I sound bitter? I was bitter—and disgusted with myself for being party to the whole fiasco. It was so negative, so final, so life-quenching and drab. Moira was sick, and her heart and mind must have been as black as her sister's dresses, but Caitlin—I couldn't believe she was that far gone. Not after the day we'd spent drinking beer and reminiscing or the way she smiled at me and spoke my name, my real name, and not some bughouse invention (and who *was* Vincent, I'd like to know?). No, there was feeling there, I was sure of it, and sensitivity and sweetness too. And need. A whole lot of need. That was why I found myself slowing outside their fence as I came and went from one job or another, hoping to catch a glimpse of Caitlin backing her Mercedes out into the street or collecting the mail, but all I ever saw was the blank white field of the fence.

Then, early one evening as I lay soaking in the tub, trying to scrub the deep verdigris stains of Miracle-Gro off my hands and forearms, the phone rang. I got to it, dripping, on the fifth ring. Caitlin was on the other end. "Larry," she said, "hi. Listen," she said, her voice soft and breathy, "I kind of miss you, I mean, not seeing you around. I'd like to offer you a beer sometime—"

"Be right over," I said.

It was high summer and still light out when I got there, the streets bathed in a soft, milky luminescence, swallowtails leaping in the air, Bougainvillea, hibiscus, Euryops and oleander blazing against the fall of night. I'd automatically thrown on a pair of black jeans and an unadorned white T-shirt, but as I was going out the door I reached in the coat closet and pulled out a kelly-green sport coat I'd bought for St. Patrick's Day one year, the sort of thing you regret having spent good money on the minute the last beer is drained and the fiddler stops fiddling. But by my lights, what Caitlin needed was a little color in her life, and I was the man to give it to her. I stopped by the florist's on my way and got her a dozen long-stemmed roses, and I didn't look twice at the white ones. No, the roses I picked were as deep and true as everything worth living for, red roses, bright red roses, roses that flowed up out of their verdant stems like blood from an open artery.

I punched in the code at the gate and wheeled my pickup into the vast parking lot that was their yard and parked beside the front steps (the color of my truck, incidentally, is white, albeit a beat-up, battered and very dirty shade of it). Anyway, I climbed out of my white truck in my black jeans, white shirt and kelly-green jacket and moved across the blacktop and up the white steps with the blood-red roses clutched under one arm.

Caitlin answered the door. "Larry," she murmured, letting her eyes stray from my face to the jacket and back again, "I'm glad you could come. Did you eat yet?"

I had. A slime burger, death fries and a side dish of fermented slaw at the local greasy spoon. I could have lied, trying to hold the picture of her whipping up a mud pie or blackened sole with mashed potatoes or black beans, but food wasn't what I'd come for. "Yeah," I said, "on my way home from work. Why? You want to go out?"

We were in the front hall now, in a black and white world, no shade of gray even, the checkered tiles gleaming, ebony chairs, a lacquered Japanese cabinet. She gave me her black-lipped smile. "Me?" she said. "Uh-uh. No. I don't want to go out." A pause. "I want to go to bed."

In bed, after I discovered she was black and white without her clothes on too, we sipped stout and porter and contemplated the scintillating roses, set in a white vase against a white wall like a trompe l'oeil. And we talked. Talked about love and need and loss, talked about the world and its tastes and colors, and talked round and round the one subject that stood between us. We'd become very close for the second time and were lying in each other's arms, all the black lipstick kissed off her, when I came back to the question I'd posed in the kitchen the last time we'd talked. "So," I said. "Okay. It's a long story, but the night's long too, and I tell you, I don't feel the least bit sleepy. Come on, the black and white. Tell me."

It would make a better story if there was some sort of "Rose for Emily" thing going on, if Moira had been left at the altar in her white satin and veil or seduced and abandoned by some neon hippie in an iridescent pink shirt and tie-dyed jacket, but that wasn't it at all. She was just depressed. Afraid of the world. In need of control. "But what about you?" I said, searching Caitlin's eyes. "You feel that way too?"

We were naked, in each other's arms, stretched the length of the bed. She shrugged. "Sort of," she said. "When we were girls, before we moved to New York, Moira and I used to watch TV, everything in black and white, Fred MacMurray, Donna Reed, *Father Knows Best*, and we had a game, a competition really, to see who could make her room like that, like the world of those shows, where everything turned out right in the end. I wanted white, but Moira was older, so I got black."

There was more, but the next line—"Our parents didn't like it, of course"—didn't come from Caitlin, but her sister. Maybe I'd closed my eyes a minute, I don't know, but suddenly there she was, all in white and perched at the end of the bed. Her mouth was drawn up in a little bow, as if the whole scene was distasteful to her, but she looked at me without blinking. "In New York, everything was pink, chiffon and lace, peach, champagne, the pink of little girls and blushing maidens. That was what Daddy wanted—and his wife too. Little girls. Normal, sweet, curtsying and respectfully whispering little girls who'd climb up into his lap for a

bedtime story. I was sixteen at the time, Vincent; Caitlin was fourteen. Can you see? Can you?"

I pulled the black sheets up to my hips, trying to calm the
pounding in my chest. This was an unusual situation, to say the
least—as I say, I'd been around, but this was out of my league altogether. I wanted to say something, but I couldn't for the life of me
guess what that might be. My right arm lay under the luxurious
weight of Caitlin's shoulders; I gave them a squeeze to reassure
myself.

"Oh, it's nothing like that, Larry," Caitlin said, anticipating
me. "Nothing dirty. But Daddy wanted an end to black and white,
and we—we didn't. Did we, Moira?"

Moira was staring off across the room to where the night hung
in the windows, absolute and unadulterated. "No, Caitly, we
didn't. And we showed them, didn't we?"

I felt Caitlin tense beside me. I wanted nothing in that moment
but to leap up out of the bed, pull the ridiculous green jacket over
my head and sprint for my truck. But instead I heard myself asking, "How?"

Both sisters laughed then, a low rasping laugh caught deep in
their throats, and there wasn't a whole lot of hilarity in it. "Oh,
I don't know, Vincent," Moira said, throwing her head back to
laugh again, and then coming back to me with a hand pattering at
her breast. "Let's just say that colors can get out of hand sometimes, if you know what I mean."

"Fire is our friend," Caitlin said, leaving a little hiatus after the
final syllable.

"If you *respect* it," Moira chimed in, and they both laughed
again. I pulled the sheet up a little farther. Caitlin had lit a pair of
tapering black candles when the sky had gone dark, and I stared
into the unsteady flame of them now, watching the yellow ribbons
of light die back and re-create themselves over and over. There
wasn't a sound in the world.

"And Vincent," Moira said, turning back to me, "if you're going to be seeing my sister on any sort of regular basis, I have to tell

you you're simply not white enough. There'll be no more outdoor work, that's out of the question." She let out another laugh, but this one at least had a little life in it. "You wouldn't want to end up looking like your surfer friend, would you?"

The silence held. I could hear the two sisters breathing gently, almost in unison, and it was as if they were breathing for me, and I'd never felt so tranquil and volitionless in my life. Whiteness loomed, the pale ethereality of nothingness, and blackness too, the black of a dreamless sleep. I closed my eyes. I could feel my head sinking into the pillow as if into the ancient mud of an untracked forest.

"Oh, and Vincent, one more thing," Moira said, and I opened my eyes long enough to see her cross the room and dump the roses in the wastebasket. "Dye your hair, will you?"

DEATH OF THE COOL

First there were the kids on the beach. What were they, fifteen, sixteen? Big ugly kids in big shorts with haircuts right out of a 1963 yearbook, all thatch and no shag, but what did they know about 1963? They were drunk, one-thirty in the afternoon, and they'd lifted a pint of tequila and a forty-ouncer from the convenience store or raided somebody's mother's liquor cabinet, and so what if he'd done the same sort of thing himself when he was their age, so *what?*—that was then and this was now. Drunk, and they had a dog with them, a retriever that had something else in it around the ears and snout and in the frantic splay of the rear legs. They were throwing a stick—an old scrap of flotsam spotted with tar and barnacles—and the dog was bringing it back to them. Every time the exchange was made and the stick went hurtling back into the ribbon of the surf, they collapsed with the hilarity of it, pounded each other's freshly tattooed shoulders and melted right into the sand, because there was nothing under the sun funnier than this. Come to think of it, they were probably stoned too.

"You want to buy a dog?" they were shouting at everybody who came up the beach. "Cheap. He's real cheap."

They asked him—they asked Edison, Edison Banks—as he kicked through the sand to lay out his towel in the place tucked into the rocks where he'd been coming every afternoon for a week now to stretch out and ease the ache in his knee. He'd just had arthroscopic surgery on the right knee and it was weak and the Tylenol-codeine tabs they'd given him were barely scratching the surface of the pain. But walking in the sand was a good thing—it strengthened the muscles, or so the surgeon told him. "Hey, man," the ugliest of the three kids had shouted, "you want to buy a dog?"

Edison was wearing a pair of shorts nearly as big as the stiffened shrouds they'd somehow managed to prop up on their nonexistent hips, and he had his Lakers cap on backwards and an oversized T-shirt and beads, the beads he'd been wearing since beads were invented back in 1969. "No, thanks," he said, a little ruffled, a little pissed off at the world in general and these three kids in particular, "—I had one for breakfast."

That was the end of the exchange, and on a better day, that would have been the end of the encounter and let's turn the page and get on with it. Edison wanted to lie in the sun, shuffle through the deep sand above tideline for maybe a hundred yards in each direction, thrash his arms in the surf a bit and let the codeine work on the pain till cocktail hour, and that was it, that was the day he was envisioning, with dinner out and maybe a movie after that. But the kids wouldn't let it rest. They didn't recognize Edison as one of their own, didn't appreciate his wit, his graying soul beard and the silver stud in his left ear. They saw him as a gimpy, pinchfaced old relic, in the same camp as their facially rejuvenated mothers, vanished fathers, and the various teachers, principals, deputy sheriffs and dance club bouncers who washed through their lives each day like some stinking red tide. They gave him a cold sneer and went back to the dog.

And *that* would have been it, but no sooner had Edison stretched out on his towel and dug out the sunblock and his book than the stick came rocketing his way. And after the stick, half a beat later, came the dog, the wet dog, the heaving, whimpering, sand-spewing whipcrack of a wet dog with a wet smell all its own. The stick vanished, only to come thumping back at him, this time landing no more than two feet away, so that the sand kicked up in his face. Were they trying to provoke him, was that it? Or were they just drunk and oblivious? Not that it mattered. Because if that stick came his way one more time, he was going to go ballistic.

He tried to focus on the page, his eyes stinging with sweat, the smell of the sunblock bringing him back to the beaches of the past, the sun like a firm, hot hand pressing down on his shoulders and the heavy knots of his calves. The book wasn't much—some tripe about a one-armed lady detective solving crimes in a beach town full of rich people very much like the one he was living in— but it had been there on the hall table when he was limping out the door, a relic of Kim. Kim had been gone three weeks now, vanished along with the Z3 he'd bought her, an armload of jewelry and a healthy selection of off-the-shoulder dresses and open-toed shoes. He expected to hear from her lawyer any day now. And the credit card company. Them too, of course.

When it came this time, the final time, the stick was so close it whirred in his ears like a boomerang, and before he could react— or even duck—it was there, right at his elbow, and the black panting form of the dog was already hurtling over him in an explosion of sand and saliva. He dropped the book and shoved himself up out of the sand, the tide pulling back all along the beach with a long, slow sigh, gulls crying out, children shrieking in the surf. They were smirking, the three of them, laughing at him, though now that he was on his feet, now that he was advancing on them, the line of his mouth drawn tight and the veins pounding in his neck, the smirks died on their faces. "Hey, Jack," he snarled in his nastiest New York–transplanted–to–California voice, "would you mind throwing that fucking stick someplace else? Or do I have to shove it up your ass?"

They were kids, lean and loose, flat stomachs, the beginner's muscles starting to show in their upper arms and shoulders like a long-delayed promise, just kids, and he was a man—and a man in pretty good shape too, aside from the knee. He had the authority here. This was his beach—or the community's, and he was a member of the community, paying enough in taxes each year to repave all the roads personally and buy the entire police force new uniforms and gold-capped nightsticks to boot. There were no dogs allowed on this beach, unless they were leashed (*Dogs Required on Leash*, the sign said, and he would joke to Kim that they had to get a dog and leash him or they were out of compliance with the law), and there was no drinking here either, especially underage drinking.

One of the kids, the one with the black crewcut and dodgy eyes, murmured an apology—"We didn't realize," or something to that effect—but the big one, the ugly one, the one who'd started all this in the first place by giving him that wiseass crap about did he want to buy a dog, just stood his ground and said, "My name isn't Jack."

Nobody moved. Edison swayed over the prop of his good leg, the right knee still red and swollen, and the two blond kids—they were brothers, he saw that in a flash, something in the pinched mouths and the eyes that were squeezed too close together, as if there weren't enough room on the canvas—crossed their arms over their tanned chests and gave him a look of contempt.

"All right," he said, "fine. Maybe you want to tell me what your name is then, huh?"

Up on the street, on the ridge behind the beach, a woman in an aquamarine Porsche Boxster swung into the last open spot in a long line of parked cars, pausing to let a trio of cyclists glide silently past. The palms rose rigid above her. There was no breath of wind. "I don't have to tell you nothing," the kid said, and his hands were shaking as he drew the stub of a joint out of one of the pouches in his shorts and put a match to it. "You know what I say? I say fuck you, Mister."

And here was the dog, trembling all over, a flowing rill of muscle, dropping the stick at the kid's feet, and "No," Edison said, his voice like an explosion in his own ears, "no, fuck *you!*"

He was ten feet from them, fifteen maybe, so imprisoned in the moment he couldn't see the futility of it, standing there on the public beach trading curses with a bunch of drunk and terminally disaffected kids, kids a third his age, mere kids. What was it? What did they see in him? And why him? Why him and not one of the real geeks and geezers strung out up and down the beach with their potbellies and skinny pale legs and the Speedos that clung to their cracks like geriatric diapers?

That was when the tall kid snatched the stick out of the dog's mouth and flung it directly at Edison with everything he had, a savage downward chop of the arm that slammed the thing into his chest with so much force he found himself sprawling backwards in the sand even as the kids took to their feet and the harsh, high laughter rang in his ears.

Then it was the bar, the scene at the bar at four o'clock in the afternoon, when the sun was still high and nobody was there. Edison didn't even bother to go home and change. He hadn't gone near the water—he was too furious, too pissed off, burned up, rubbed raw—and aside from a confectioner's sprinkle of dry sand on his ankle and the dark stain in the center of his T-shirt, no one would have guessed he'd been to the beach, and what if they did? This was California, beach city, where the guy sitting next to you in the bleached-out shirt and dollar-twenty-nine Kmart flip-flops was probably worth more than the GNP of half a dozen third world countries. But there was nobody sitting next to him today— the place was deserted. There was only the bartender, the shrine to booze behind him, and a tall slim cocktail waitress with blue eyes, dimples, and hair that glistened like the black specks of tar on the beach.

He ordered a top-shelf margarita on the rocks, no salt, and morosely chewed a handful of bar mix that looked and tasted like individual bits of laminated sawdust, his dark blood-flecked eyes sweeping the room, from TV to waitress to the mirror behind the bar and back again. His heart was still pounding, though he'd left the beach half an hour ago, humiliated, decrepit, feeling like the thousand-year-old man as he gathered up his things and limped up the steps to his car. It was irrational, he knew it, a no-win situation, but all he could think about was revenge—Revenge? Murder was more like it—and he methodically combed the street along the beach, up one narrow lane and down another, looking for any sign of his three antagonists. Every time he came round a bend and saw movement up ahead, he was sure it would be them, drunk and stoned and with their guard down, whacking one another with rolled-up towels, shoving and jostling, crowing at the world. He'd take them by surprise, jerk the wheel, and slice in at the curb to cut them off, and then he'd be on them, slamming the tall kid's face, over and over, till there was no more smirk left in him. . . .

"You want another one?" the bartender was asking. Edison had seen him before—he was the day man and Edison didn't know his name and he didn't know Edison's—and he had no opinion about him one way or the other. He was young, twenty-eight, thirty maybe, with a deep tan and the same basic haircut as the kids on the beach, though it wasn't cut so close to the scalp. Edison decided he liked him, liked the look of him, with his surfer's build and the streaks of gold in his hair and the smile that said he was just enjoying the hell out of every goddamned minute of life on this earth.

"Yeah, sure," Edison said, and he found that the first drink, in combination with the codeine, had made his words run down like an unoiled machine, all the parts gummed up and locked in place, "and let me maybe see the bar menu. You got a bar menu?"

The cocktail waitress—she was stunning, she really was, a tall girl, taller than the bartender, with nice legs and outstanding feet perched up high on a pair of black clogs—flashed her dimpled smile when Edison cocked his head to include her in the field of conversation.

Sure they had a bar menu, sure, but they really wouldn't have anything more than crudités or a salad till the kitchen opened up for dinner at six—was that all right, or would he rather wait? Edison caught sight of himself in the mirror in back of the bar then, and it shook him. At first he didn't even recognize himself, sure that some pathetic older guy had slipped onto the stool beside him while he was distracted by the waitress, but no, there was the backwards Lakers cap and the shades and the drawn-down sink-hole of his mouth over the soul beard and the chin that wasn't nearly as firm as it should have been. And his skin—how had his skin got so yellow? Was it hepatitis? Was he drinking too much?

The bartender moved off down the bar to rub at an imaginary speck on the mahogany surface and convert half a dozen limes into neat wedges, and the cocktail waitress was suddenly busy with the cash register. On the TV, just above the threshold of sound, somebody was whispering about the mechanics of golf while the camera flowed over an expanse of emerald fairways and a tiny white ball rose up into the sky in a distant looping trajectory. A long moment hung suspended, along with the ball, and Edison was trying not to think about what had happened on the beach, but there it was, nagging at him like grief, and then the bartender was standing in front of him again. "You decide yet?"

"I think I'll," Edison began, and at that moment the door swung open and a woman with a wild shag of bleached hair slipped in and took a seat three stools down, "I'll . . . I don't know, I think I'll wait."

Who was she? He'd seen her around town, he was sure of it.

"Hi, Carlton," she said, waving two fingers at the bartender while simultaneously swinging round to chirp "Hi, Elise" at the waitress. And then, shifting back into position on the stool, she gave Edison a long cool look of appraisal and said hi to him too. "Martini," she instructed the bartender, "three olives, up. And give me a water back. I'm dying."

She was a big girl, big in the way of the jeans model who'd married that old tottering cadaver of a millionaire a few years back and then disappeared from the face of the earth, big but sexy, very sexy, showing off what she had in a tight black top—and how long had it been since Kim had left? Edison, the T-shirt still damp over his breastbone, smiled back.

He initiated the conversation. He'd seen her around, hadn't he? Yes, she had a condo just down the street. Did she come in here often? A shrug. The roots of her hair were black, and she dug her fingers deep into them, massaging as she talked. "Couple times a week maybe."

"I'm Edison," he said, smiling like he meant it, and he did. "And you're—?"

"I'm Sukie."

"Cool," Edison said, in his element now, smiling, smiling, "I've never known anybody named Sukie. Is that your real name?"

She dug her fingers into her scalp, gave her head a snap so that the whole towering shako of her hair came to life. "No," she said.

"It's a nickname?"

"No."

"You don't want to tell me your real name? Is that it?"

She shrugged, an elegant big-shouldered gesture that rippled all the way down her body and settled in one gently rocking ankle. She was wearing a long blue print skirt and sandals. Earrings. Makeup. And how old was she? Thirty-five, he figured. Thirty-five and divorced. "What about you?" she said. "What kind of name is Edison?"

Now it was his turn. He lifted both hands and flashed open the palms. "My father thought I was going to be an inventor. But maybe you've heard of me, my band, I mean—I had an eponymous rock band a few years back."

She just blinked.

"*Edison Banks.* You ever hear of them—of us, I mean? Early eighties? Warner Brothers? The *Downtown* LP?"

No, she hadn't heard of anything.

All right. He knew how to play this, though he was out of practice. Back off—"We weren't all that big, really, I don't know"—and then a casual mention of the real firepower he could bring to the table. "That was before I got into TV."

And now the scene shifted yet again, because before she could compress her lips in a little moue and coo "Tee-vee?" the door swung open, loudly, and brought in the sun and the street and three guys in suits, all of them young, with haircuts that chased them around the ears and teeth that should have been captured on billboards for the dental hygienists' national convention. One of them, as it turned out, would turn out to be Lyle, and when she saw him come through the door, Sukie froze just for the briefest slice of an instant, but Edison saw it, and registered it, and filed it away.

The roar went down the other end of the bar, and Edison asked her if she'd like another drink. "No," she said, "I don't think so. But it's been nice talking to you," and already she was shifting away from the stool to reach for her purse.

"How about a phone number?" he said. "We could do dinner or something—sometime, I mean."

She was on her feet now, looking down at him, the purse clutched in her hand. "No," she said, and she shook her head till her hair snatched up all the light in the room, "no, I don't think so."

Edison had another drink. The sun slid down the sky to where it should have been all along. He gazed out idly across the street and admired the way the sunlight sat in the crowns of the palms and sank into the grip of the mountains beyond. Cars drifted lazily by. He watched a couple turn the corner and seat themselves under a green umbrella on the patio of the restaurant across the way. For the briefest moment the face of his humiliation rose up in his mind—the kid's face, the poised stick—but he fought it down and thumbed through a copy of the village paper, just to have something to do while he sucked at his sweet-sour drink and chewed his way through another dish of sawdust pellets.

He read of somebody's elaborate wedding ("fifteen thousand dollars on sushi alone"), the booming real estate market, and the latest movie star to buy up one of the estates in the hills, browsed the wine column ("a dramatic nose of dried cherries and smoked meat with a nicely defined mineral finish"), then settled on an item about a discerning burglar who operated by daylight, entering area homes through unlocked doors and ground-floor windows to make off with all the jewelry he could carry—as long as it was of the very highest quality, that is. Paste didn't interest him, nor apparently did carpets, electronics, vases, or artwork. Edison mulled that over: a burglar, a discerning burglar. The brazenness it must take—just strolling up the walk and knocking on the front door, hello, is anybody home? And if they were, he was selling magazine subscriptions or looking for a lost cat. What a way to make a living. Something for those little shits on the beach to aspire to.

By the time he looked up to order his fourth drink, the place had begun to fill up. The cocktail waitress—Elise, he had to remember her name, and the bartender's too, but what was it?—was striding back and forth on her long legs, a tray of drinks held high above the jostling crowd. Up on the TV in the corner the scene had shifted from golf to baseball, fairways and greens giving way to the long, dense grass of the outfield—or was it artificial turf, a big foam mat with Easter basket fluff laid over it? He was thinking he should just eat and get it over with, ask what's his name for the menu and order something right at the bar and then hang out for a while and see what developed. Home was too depressing. All that was waiting for him at home was the channel changer and a thirty-two-ounce packet of frozen peas to wrap around his bad knee. And that killed him: where was Kim when he needed her, when he was in pain and could barely get around? What did she care? She had her car and her credit cards and probably by now some new sucker to take to the dance—

"Excuse me," somebody was saying at his elbow, and he looked up into the face of one of the men who'd come in earlier, the one the big blonde had reacted to. "I don't mean to bother you, but aren't you Edison Banks?"

The codeine was sludge in his veins, and his knee—he'd forgotten he had a knee—but he peeled off his sunglasses and gave the man a smile. "That's right," he said, and he would never admit to himself that he was pleased, but he was. He'd lived here three years now, and nobody knew who he was, not even the mailman or the girl who counted out his money at the bank.

"I'm Lyle," the man was saying, and then they were locked palm to palm in a rollicking soul shake, "Lyle Hansen, and I can't tell you how cool this is. I mean, I'm a big fan. *Savage Street* was the coolest thing in the history of TV, and I mean that—it got me through high school, and that was a bad time for me, real adolescent hell, with like all the rules and the regimentation and my parents coming down on me for every little minor thing—shit, *Savage Street* was my *life*."

Edison took hold of his drink, the comforting feel of the glass in his hand, the faces at the bar, dark blue shadows leaning into the building across the street. There was a trip-hop tune playing on the jukebox, a languid slow female vocal over an industrial storm of guitars and percussion that managed to be poignant and ominous at the same time, and it felt right. Just right.

"Listen, I didn't mean to intrude or anything—"

Edison waved a hand. "No problem, man, it's cool, it's all right."

Lyle looked to be about the same age as the bartender, which meant he would have been out of high school for ten or twelve years. He wore his hair longer than the bartender's, combed back up off his forehead with enough mousse to sustain it and the odd strand dangling loose in front. He kept shifting from foot to foot, rattling the keys in his pocket, tugging at his tie, and his smile flashed and flashed again. "Hey, Carlton," he spoke into the din, "give me another one, will you—and one for Mr. Banks here too. On me."

"No, no," Edison protested, "you don't have to do that," but the money was on the bar, and the drink appeared in a fresh glass.

"So you wrote *and* produced that show, right?"

"Shit, I *created* it. You know, when you see the titles and it says 'Created By'? I wrote the first two seasons, then left it to them. Why work when you can play, right?"

Lyle was drinking shooters of Herradura out of a slim tube of a glass. He threw back the current one, then slapped his forehead as if he'd been stung. "I can't believe it. Here I am talking to Edison Banks. You know, when you moved into town, like what was it, three, four years ago?"

"Three."

"Yeah, I read that article in the paper about you and I thought wow—you were the guitarist for Edison Banks too, right? I had both their albums, New Wave, right? But what I really dig is jazz. Miles Davis. Monk. That era stuff."

Edison felt a weight lift off him. "I've been a jazz fan all my life," he said, the alcohol flaring up in him till the whole place was on fire with it, mystical fire, burning out of the bottles and the light fixtures and the golden shining faces lined up at the bar. "Since I was a kid of fifteen, anyway, hopping the subway up to Harlem and bullshitting my way into the clubs. I've got everything—*Birth of the Cool, Sketches*, all the Coltrane stuff, Sonny Rollins, Charles Lloyd, Ornette, Mulligan—and all of it on the original LPs too."

Lyle set both hands down on the bar, as if to brace himself. He was wearing a pinkie ring that featured a silver skull, and the rough edge of a tattoo showed at the base of his left wrist where the cuff climbed up his arm. "You might think I'm just some suit or something," he said, "but that's not me at all." He plucked at his lapels. "See this? This is my first day on the job. Real estate. That's where the money is. But I tell you, I'd love to hear some of that shit with you—I mean, *Miles*. Wow. And I know what you're saying—CDs just don't cut it like vinyl."

And Edison, in the shank of a bad evening that had begun to turn clement after all, turned to him and said, "I'm up at the corner of Dolores and San Ignacio—big Spanish place with the tile roof? Come by anytime, man—anytime, no problem." And then he looked up to see the waitress—Elise—glide by like a ballerina, that's what she was like, a ballerina, with her bare arms held high and the tray levitating above her head. He had to get home. Had to eat. Feed the cat. Collapse in front of the tube. "Just don't come between maybe one and four—that's when I'm down at the beach."

In the morning, the dryness in the back of his throat told him he'd drunk too much the night before—that and a fuzziness between his ears, as if his head were a radio caught between stations—and he took two of the Tylenol-codeine tabs to ease his transition into the day. Theoretically, he was working on a screenplay about the adventures of a rock band on the road as seen through the eyes of the drummer's dog, but the work had stalled even before Kim walked out, and now there was nothing there on the screen but words. He took the newspaper and a glass of orange juice out on the patio, and then he swam a couple of laps and began to feel better. The maid came at eleven and fixed him a plate of eggs and chorizo before settling into her routine with the bucket, the mop and the vacuum cleaner. Two hours later, as he sat frozen at his desk, playing his eighteenth game of computer solitaire, there was a tap at the door.

It was Orbalina, the maid. "Mr. Banks," she said, poking her head into the room, "I don't want to bother you, but I can't, I can't—" He saw that she was crying, her face creased with the geography of her grief, tears wetting her cheeks. This was nothing new—she was always sobbing over one thing or another, the tragedies that constantly befell her extended family, the way a man on TV had looked right at her as if he'd come alive right there in her own living room, the hollowness of the sky over the graveyard in Culiacán where her mother lay buried under a wooden cross. Kim used to handle her moods with a mixture of compassion and firmness that bordered on savagery; now it was up to him. "What is it?" he said. "What's the matter?"

She was in the room now, a whittled-down woman in her thirties whose weight had migrated to her haunches. "The elephants," she sobbed.

"Elephants? What elephants?"

"You know what they do to them, to the elephants?" She buried her face in her hands, then looked up at him out of eyes that were like two pools of blood. "Do you?" she demanded, her frame shaken with the winds of an unceasing emotional storm.

He didn't. His knee hurt. He had a headache. And his screenplay was shit.

"They beat them. With big, with big *sticks!*" Her hands flailed at the air. "Like this! And this! And when they get too old to work, when they fall down in the jungle with their big trees in their noses, you know what they do then? They beat them more! They do! They do! And I know what I'm saying because I saw it on the, on the"—and here her voice failed her, till her final words were so soft and muted they might have been a prayer—"on the TV."

He was on his feet now, the screen behind him displaying seven neat rows of electronic cards, a subtle crepitating pain invading his knee, as if a rodent were trapped beneath the patella and gnawing to get out. "Listen," he said, "it's okay, don't worry about it." He wanted to take her in his arms and press her to him, but he couldn't do that because she was the maid and he the employer, so he limped past her to the door and said, "Look, I'm going to the beach, okay? You finish up here and take the rest of the day off—and tomorrow, tomorrow too."

The morning haze had burned off by the time he stepped out into the drive. The sky was a clear, depthless blue, the blue of childhood adventures, picnics, outings to Bear Mountain and the Island, the blue of good times, and he was thinking of his first wife, Sarah, thinking of Cap d'Antibes, Isla Mujeres, Molokai. They traveled in those days, on the beaten path and off it. There was no end to what he wanted to see: the Taj Mahal, the snow monkeys of Hokkaido, prayer wheels spinning idly on the naked slopes above Lhasa. They went everywhere. Saw it all. But that turned sour too, like everything else. He took a minute to duck behind a bank of Bougainvillea and empty his bladder—there was no place to pee on the beach, unless you did it surreptitiously in the flat water beyond the breakers, and since he'd hit forty he couldn't seem to go more than an hour at a time without feeling that nagging pressure in his lower abdomen. And was that cool? No, no part of it was even remotely cool—it was called getting old.

There was a discolored place on the floor of the garage where Kim's car had been, a kind of permanent shadow, but he didn't dwell on it. He decided to take the sports car—a mint Austin-Healey 3000 he'd bought from a guy in the movie business with a garage full of them—because it made him feel good, and feeling good had been in short supply lately. The top was down, so he took a moment to rub a palmful of sunblock into the soft flesh under his eyes—no reason to wind up looking like one of the unwrapped mummies nodding over their white wine and appetizers in every café and trattoria in town. Then he adjusted his sunglasses, turned his cap backwards, and shot down the street with a modulated roar.

He'd nearly got to the beach—had actually turned into the broad, palm-lined boulevard that fronted it—before he remembered the three kids from yesterday. What if they showed up again? What if they were already there? The thought made him brake inappropriately, and the next thing he knew some jerk in a 4x4 with the frame jacked up eight feet off the ground was giving him the horn—and the finger. Normally, he would have had a fit—it was a New York thing, turf wars, attitude—but he was so put out he just pulled over meekly and let the jerk go by.

But then he told himself he wasn't about to be chased off his own beach by anybody, especially not some punk-ass kids who wouldn't know one end of hip from the other. He found a spot to park right across from the steps down to the beach and pulled his things out of the trunk with a quick angry jerk of his arm—if he could run, if he could only run, he'd chase them down till their stinking weed-choked little punk lungs gave out, even if it took miles. The shits. The little shits. He was breathing hard, sweating under the band of the cap.

Then he was on the concrete steps, the Pacific opening up before him in an endless array of waves, that cool, fathomless smell on the air, the white crescent of the beach, blankets and umbrellas spread out across the sand as far as he could see in either direction. There was something about the scene that always lightened his mood, no matter how sorry for himself he was feeling. That was one thing he could never understand about Kim. Kim didn't like the beach. Too much sun. Bad for the skin. And the sand—the sand was just another kind of grit, and she always bitched when she found a white spill of it on the carpet in the hall. But she liked it when he came home to her all aflame because he'd just watched a hundred women strip down to the essentials and rub themselves all over with the sweetest unguents and emollients an eight-ounce tube could hold. She liked that, all right.

He was halfway down the steps, studying a pair of girls descending ahead of him, when he heard the high, frenzied barking of the dog. There they were, the three of them, in their boxcar shorts and thatch haircuts, laughing and jiving, throwing the stick as if nothing had happened. And nothing had, not to them, anyway. Edison froze, right there, six steps down. It was as if he were paralyzed, as if he'd suffered a stroke as he reached for the iron rail and set one gimpy leg down in front of the other. An older couple, trainwrecks of the flesh, brushed past him, then a young mother trailing kids and plastic buckets. He could not move. The dog barked. There was a shout from down the beach. The stick flew.

And then, patting down his pockets as if he'd forgotten something, he swung slowly round and limped up the steps. For a long moment he sat in the car, fiddling with the tuner until he found a rap station, and he cranked it as loud as it would go, though he hated the music, hated it. Finally he slammed the car in gear and took off with a lurch, the thunderous bass and hammering lyrics thrusting a dagger into the corpse of the afternoon, over and over, all the way down the street.

He thought of the bar—of lunch at the bar and a cocktail to pull the codeine up out of whatever hole it was hiding in—but he didn't have the heart for it. He was Edison Banks. He'd had his own band. He'd created *Savage Street*. He didn't eat lunch at one-thirty in the afternoon, and he didn't eat lunch alone, either—or drink anything, even wine, before five o'clock. That was what the rest of them did, all his hopeless washed-out diamond-encrusted neighbors: they ate lunch. And then they had a couple of cocktails and bought flowers from the flower girl in the short skirt before picking up their prescriptions at the drugstore, and by then it was cocktail hour and they drank cocktails and ate dinner. Or ordered it, anyway.

He burned up the tires for the next half hour, taking the turns like a suicide—or a teenager, a thatch-headed, flat-stomached, stick-throwing teenager—and then the engine started to overheat and he switched off the radio and crawled back home like one of the living dead in their ancient Jags and Benzes. A nap, that was what he was thinking, elevate the knee, wrap the frozen peas round it, and doze over a book by the pool—where at least it was private. He winced when he climbed out of the car and put some weight on his right leg, but the peas and another codeine tab would take care of that, and he came up the back walk feeling nothing. He was digging for his keys, the sun pushing down like a weight on his shoulders while a pair of hummingbirds stitched the air with iridescent feints and dodges and the palms along the walk nodded in the faintest stirrings of a breeze, when he saw that the back door was open

And that was odd, because he was sure he'd shut and locked it when he left. Kim might have been clueless about security, leaving her handbag on the front seat of the car where anybody could see it, running out of the house with her makeup half on and never thinking twice about the door gaping behind her, but he was a rock. He never forgot anything, even when his brain was fuzzed with the little white pills the doctor kept feeding him. He wouldn't have left the door open. He couldn't have. His next thought was for the maid—she must not have left yet. But then he glanced over his shoulder, down the slope and past the fence to the spot out on the public road where she always parked her dirt-brown Corolla. It wasn't there.

He shut the door behind him, thinking he'd have to talk to her about that, about walking off and leaving the place wide open— there was no excuse for it, even if she was distraught about the fate of the elephants or her sister's latest lumpectomy. In the kitchen, he fought the childproof cap of the prescription bottle and chased down a pill with a glass of cranberry juice. He'd just pulled open the freezer to reach for the peas when a sound from above made him catch his breath. It was a furtive sound, the soft friction of wood on wood—as of a dresser drawer, antique oak, slightly balky, sliding open. He didn't breathe again until he heard the faint squeal of the drawer going back in, and the answering echo of the next one falling open.

Edison kept three guns in the house, identical Smith & Wesson 9mm stainless steel pistols, two of which had never been fired, and he went now for the one he kept in a cubicle in the pantry, behind the old telephone books. He held it in his hand a long while, listening, then made sure it was loaded, flicked off the safety, and started up the stairs. It was very quiet. Shadows collided on the walls above him, and the air was thick with motes of dust and the lazy circling attentions of the flies at the upstairs window. He was in his own house, among familiar things, but everything seemed distorted and unfamiliar, because he'd never before gone up these stairs with a gun in his hand—and yet he didn't feel nervous or tense, or not particularly. He felt like a hunter in an air-conditioned forest.

When he crept into the bedroom—the master bedroom, the place where he'd slept alone in the big antique bed for the past three weeks—there was a man there, his back to the door, his arms and shoulders busy with the work at hand. A phrase came into Edison's head: *rifling the drawers.* And then another one, one he'd heard on TV a thousand times—used himself in too many episodes of *Savage Street* to count: *Freeze.* And that's what he said now, in a kind of bark, and he couldn't help appending an epithet to it, for maximum effect. "Freeze, motherfucker," that's what he said. "Freeze, motherfucker!"

That was when Lyle, dressed in the same pale European-cut suit he'd been wearing the night before, turned around, his hands at his sides. "Hey, man," he said, all the sunshine in the world distilled in his voice, no worries, no problems, and how do you spell California? "I just stopped by to see you, take you up on your invitation, you know? Cool house. I really dig your antiques—you the collector, or is it your wife?"

Edison had a gun in his hand. A gun he'd fired just once, at the indoor firing range, twelve bucks an hour, no target big enough for him to nail—or maybe it wasn't this gun at all. Maybe it was the one under the sink in the master bath or the one behind the drapes in the front hall. The gun was cold. It was heavy. He didn't know what to do with it now that he was holding it there in his hand like some party favor.

"Hey, come on, man, put that thing away, all right? You're scaring me." Lyle was wearing two-tone shoes and a hand-painted tie, very cool. He swept the hair back from his brow with a hand that betrayed him—a hand that was shaking. "I mean I knocked and all, but nobody answered, right? So I came in to wait for you, so we could maybe spin some sides—isn't that what you say, 'spin some sides'?"

It came to him then that Lyle was exactly like the kid on the beach, the kid grown up, all mockery and hate, all attitude. "You're the guy," Edison said. "You're the guy, aren't you?"

And there it was, the curled lip, the dead blue vacancy of the eyes. "What guy? I don't know what you're talking about, man—I mean, I come over, at *your* invitation, to, to—"

"The jewelry thief. 'The discerning burglar.' You're him, aren't you?" The knowledge went right through him, hot knowledge, knowledge like the burning needle his mother would use to probe his flesh when he came in screaming with a splinter embedded in his finger. "Let me see your pockets. Pull out your pockets."

"Spin some sides," Lyle said, but the phrase was bitter now, nasal and venomous. "Isn't that what you hepcats say, you hipsters and thin white dukes? Too cool, right?" And he pulled a necklace out of his pocket, one of the things Kim, in her haste, had left behind. He held it out for a moment, a gentle silken dangle of thin hammered gold with a cluster of jewels, and let it drop to the carpet. "Let me tell you something, *Edison*—your show sucked. Even back then it was a joke—me and my buds'd get stoned and laugh at it, you know that? And your band—your pathetic band—was even worse."

Outside, beyond Lyle, beyond the blinds and the curtains, the sun was spread over everything like the richest cream, and the window that framed it all was like nothing so much as an outsized TV screen. Edison felt something in him die, droop down and die like some wilted plant, and he wondered if it was the codeine or what it was. It came almost as a surprise to him to glance down and see that he was still holding on to the gun.

Lyle leaned back against the dresser and fumbled in his pocket for a cigarette, stuck it between his lips, and lit it with a quick flick of his lighter. "So what are you going to do, shoot me?" he said. "Because it's my word against yours. I mean, where's your witness?

Where's the stolen property? You invited me over, right? 'Anytime, man,' isn't that what you said? And here I am, an honored guest, and maybe we had an argument and you got a little crazy— old guys are like that, aren't they? Don't they go a little crazy every once in a while?" He exhaled a blue veil of smoke. "Or shit, I mean I was just up here checking out my listings, I thought this was going to be an open house, and I wander in, innocent, totally innocent, and suddenly there's this guy with a gun . . . and who is it? It's you."

"That's right," Edison said, "it's me. Edison Banks. And who the fuck are you? What did you ever write? How many albums did you record? Huh?"

Lyle put the cigarette to his lips, and Edison watched the coal go red with the rush of oxygen. He had nothing to say, but his look—it was the look of the kid on the beach all over again. Exactly. Exactly that. But this time there would be no footrace, because Edison had already caught up.

MY WIDOW

CAT PERSON

My widow likes cats. No one knows exactly how many cats inhabit the big solid old redwood house I left her, but after several generations of inbreeding and depositing fecal matter in select corners and in an ever-growing mound on the mantelpiece, their numbers must reach into the thirties, perhaps even the forties. There are cats draped like bunting over every horizontal surface in the house, and when they mew in concert for their cat chow and their tins of mashed fish heads, the noise is enough to wake the dead, if you'll pardon the expression. She sleeps with these cats, my widow does, or at least as many of them as the antique bed, with its questionable sheets and cat-greased quilt, can accommodate, and all night and into the burgeoning sun-dappled hours of the early morning, there is a ceaseless movement of limb and tongue and the lazy twitching of feline tails. In addition to the cats, my widow once had a pair of vocal and energetic little dogs, of a breed whose name I could never remember, but both have long since run off or been crushed to marrow out on the busy street that winds up from the village and past the rear gate of the house. She had a ferret too, for a while, though ferrets are illegal in the state of California. It didn't last long. After throttling and partially dismembering a litter of week-old kittens, the animal secreted itself in the crawl space under the house, where it took sick and died. Even now, its mummified corpse subsides gradually into the immemorial dust beneath the floorboards of the kitchen, just under the place where the refrigerator rests, going quietly about its work.

One afternoon, a day or two after the first rain of the winter has converted the dry creek bed out back into a sluice of braided, sepia-colored ripples and long, trailing ropes of eucalyptus bark, my widow is startled by a persistent thumping from the far end of the house. She is, as always, in the kitchen, peering into a steaming pot of chicken-vegetable soup, the only thing she ingests these days, aside from the odd slab of indifferently grilled flank steak and coffee so acidic it's taken the glaze off the ceramic cup our son made her when he was in the sixth grade. The doorbell, which in my day chimed a carillon from Beethoven's "Ode to Joy," is long since defunct, and so my widow takes a while to register the notion that someone is knocking at the front door. The front door, is, after all, a good sixty paces from the kitchen, out the kitchen door and down the long L-shaped hall that leads to the entryway and the grand room beyond it, now a refuge for cats. Still, that is unmistakably the sound of knocking, and you can see the alertness come into her eyes—it could be the postman, she's thinking, who just the other day (or was it the other week?) brought her a letter from our son, who lives and works in Calcutta, dispensing corn-meal mush and clean bandages to the mendicants there. "I'm coming!" my widow calls in her creaking, octave-challenged voice, and she sets down the stirring spoon amidst the debris of what once was the kitchen counter, wipes her hands on her flannel nightgown, and moves slowly but resolutely down the hall to answer the door.

Standing on the brick doorstep, plainly visible through the ancient flowing glass of the front door, is a young woman in shorts, leggings and some sort of athletic jersey, with stringy black hair, terrible posture, and what appears to be a fur muff tucked under one arm. As my widow gets closer and the indefinite becomes concrete, she sees that the young woman's eyes are heavily made up, and that the muff has become a kitten of indeterminate breed—black, with a white chest and two white socks. Curious, and pursing her lips in the way she used to when she was a young woman herself, my widow swings open the door and stands there blinking and mute, awaiting an explanation.

"Oh, hi," the young woman says, squeezing the words through an automatic smile, "sorry to disturb you, but I was wondering . . ." Unaccountably, the young woman trails off, and my widow, whose hearing was compromised by the Velvet Underground and Nico during a period of exuberance in the last century, watches her lips for movement. The young woman studies my widow's face a moment, then decides to change tack. "I'm your neighbor, Megan Capaldi?" she says finally. "Remember me? From the school-lunch drive last year?"

My widow, dressed in an old flannel shirt over the faded and faintly greasy flannel nightgown, does not, in fact, remember her. She remains noncommittal. Behind her, from the depths of the house, a faint mewling arises.

"I heard that you were a real cat person, and I just thought— well, my daughter April's cat had kittens, and we're looking for good homes for them, with people who really care, and this one— we call her Sniggers—is the last one left."

My widow is smiling, her face transformed into a girl's, the striations over her lip pulling back to reveal a shining and perfect set of old lady's teeth—the originals, beautifully preserved. "Yes," she says, "yes," before the question has been asked, already reaching out for the kitten with her regal old hands. She holds it to her a moment, then looks up myopically into the young woman's face. "Thanks for thinking of me," she says.

THE ROOF

The roof, made of a composite material guaranteed for life, leaks. My widow is in the bedroom, in bed, crocheting neat four-inch granny squares against some larger need while listening to the murmur of the TV across the room and the crashing impact of yet another storm above her, when the dripping begins. The cats are the first to notice it. One of them, a huge, bloated, square-headed tom with fur like roadkill, shifts position to avoid the cold stinging drops, inadvertently knocking two lesser cats off the west slope of the bed. A jockeying for space ensues, the cats crowding my widow's crocheting wrists and elbows and leaving a vacant spot at the foot of the bed. Even then, she thinks nothing of it. A voice emanating from the TV cries out, *They're coming—they're coming through the walls!*, followed by the usual cacophony of screams, disjointed music and masticatory sounds. The rain beats at the windows.

A long slow hour hisses by. Her feet are cold. When she rubs them together, she discovers that they are also wet. Her first thought is for the cats—have they been up to their tricks again? But no, there is a distinct patter now, as of water falling from a height, and she reaches out her hand to confront the mystery. There follows a determined shuffle through the darkened arena of the house, the close but random inspection of the ceilings with a flashlight (which itself takes half an hour to find), and then the all-night vigil over the stewpot gradually filling itself at the foot of the bed. For a while, she resumes her crocheting, but the steady mesmeric drip of the intruding rain idles her fingers and sweeps her off into a reverie of the past. She's revisiting other roofs—the attic nook of her girlhood room, the splootching nightmare of her student apartment with the dirty sit-water drooling down the wall into the pan as she heated brown rice and vegetables over the stove, the collapse of the ceiling in our first house after a pipe burst when we were away in Europe—and then she's in Europe herself, in the rain on the Grand Canal, with me, her first and most significant husband, and before long the stewpot is overflowing and she's so far away she might as well exist in another dimension.

The roofer, whose name emerged from the morass of the Yellow Pages, arrives some days later during a period of tumultuous weather and stands banging on the front door while rain drools from the corroded copper gutters (which, incidentally, are also guaranteed for life). My widow is ready for him. She's been up early each day for the past week, exchanging her flannel nightgown for a pair of jeans and a print blouse, over which she wears an old black cardigan decorated with prancing blue reindeer she once gave me for Christmas. She's combed out her hair and put on a dab of lipstick. Like Megan Capaldi before him, the roofer pounds at the redwood frame of the front door until my widow appears in the vestibule. She fumbles a moment with the glasses that hang from a cord around her neck, and then her face assumes a look of bewilderment: *Who is this infant banging at the door?*

"Hello!" calls the roofer, rattling the doorknob impatiently as my widow stands there before him on the inside of the glass panel, looking confused. "It's me—the roofer?" He's shouting now: "You said you had a leak?"

The roofer's name is Vargas D'Onofrio, and the minute he pronounces it, it's already slipped her mind. He has quick, nervous eyes, and his face is sunk into a full beard of tightly wound black hairs threaded with gray. He's in his early forties, actually, but any-one under seventy looks like a newborn to my widow, and under-standably so.

"You're all wet," she observes, leading him into the house and up the slow heaving stairs to reveal the location of the leak. She wonders if she should offer to bake him cookies and maybe fix a pouch of that hot chocolate that only needs microwaved water to complete it, and she sees the two of them sitting down at the kitchen table for a nice chat after he's fixed the roof—but does she have any hot chocolate? Or nuts, shortening, brown sugar? How long has it been since she remembered to buy flour, even? She had a five-pound sack of it in the pantry—she distinctly remembers that—but then wasn't that the flour the weevils got into? She's seeing little black bugs, barely the size of three grains of pepper cobbled together, and then she understands that she doesn't want to chat with this man—or with anybody else, for that matter. She just wants the roof repaired so she can go back to the quiet seep of her old lady's life.

"Rotten weather," the roofer breathes, thumping up the stairs in his work boots and trundling on down the upper hallway to the master bedroom, scattering cats as he goes.

My widow has given up on the stewpot and has been sleeping

downstairs, in what was once our son's room. As a result, the antique bed is now soaked through to the springs and oozing water the color of tobacco juice.

"I can patch it," the roofer says, after stepping out onto the sleeping porch and assaying the roof from the outside, "but you really should have the whole thing replaced once summer comes—and I can do that for you too, and give you a good price. Best price in town, in fact." The roofer produces a wide bearded closer's grin that is utterly lost on my widow.

"But that roof," she says, "was guaranteed for life."

The roofer just shrugs. "Aren't they all?" he sighs, and disappears through the door to the sleeping porch. As she pulls the door shut, my widow can smell the keen working scent of the rain loosening the earth around the overgrown flowerbeds and the vaguely fishy odor of wet pavement. The air is alive. She can see her breath in it. She watches the roofer's legs ride up past the window as he hoists himself up the ladder and into the pall of the rain. And then, as she settles into the armchair in the bedroom, she hears him up there, aloft, his heavy tread, the pounding of nails, and through it all a smell of hot burning tar.

SHOPPING

In her day my widow was a champion shopper. She'd been a student of anthropology in her undergraduate years, and she always maintained that a woman's job—her need, calling and compulsion—was to accumulate things against the hard times to come. Never mind that we didn't experience any hard times—aside from maybe having to pinch a bit in grad school or maxing out our credit cards when we were traveling in Japan back in the eighties—my widow was ready for anything. She shopped with a passion matched by few women of her generation. Her collections of antique jewelry, glassware, china figurines and the like would, I think, be truly valuable if she could ever find them in the cluttered caverns and dark byways of the house and basement, and the fine old Craftsman-era couches and chairs strewn through the main rooms are museum pieces, or would be, if the cats hadn't gotten to them. Even now, despite the fact that she's become increasingly withdrawn and more than a bit impatient with the fuss and hurry of the world, my widow can still get out and shop with the best of them.

On a day freshened by a hard cold breeze off the ocean, she awakens in my son's narrow bed to a welter of cats and a firm sense of purpose. Her sister, Inge, ten years her junior and unmarried, is driving up from Ventura to take her shopping at the mall for the pre-Christmas sales, and she is galvanized into action. Up and out of bed at first light, cats mewling at her feet, the crusted pot set atop the crusted burner, coffee brewing, and she slips into a nice skirt and blouse (after a prolonged search through the closet in the master bedroom, where the mattress, unfortunately, continues to ooze a brownish fluid), pulls her hair back in a bun and sits down to a breakfast of defrosted wheat bread, rancid cream cheese and jam so old it's become a culture medium. In my time, there were two newspapers to chew through and the morning news on the radio, but my widow never bothered herself much with the mechanism of receiving and paying bills (the envelope, the check, the stamp), and the newspapers have been discontinued. As for the radio, my widow prefers silence. She is thinking nothing, staring into space and slowly rotating the coffee cup in her hands, when there is a sharp rap at the kitchen door and Inge's face appears framed there in the glass panel.

Later, hours later, after lunch at the Thai Palace, after Pic 'n Save, Costco, Ruby's Thrift Shoppe and the Bargain Basement, my widow finds herself in the midst of a crush of shoppers at Macy's. She doesn't like department stores, never has—no bargains to be had, or not usually—but her sister was looking at some tableware for one of their grandnieces, and she finds herself, unaccountably, in the linen department, surrounded by women poking through sheets and pillowcases and little things for the bathroom. There will be a white sale in January, she knows that as well as she knows there will be valentines for Valentine's Day and lilies for Easter, and since the maid died ten years back she really hasn't had much need of linens—nobody to change the beds, really—but she can't help herself. The patterns are so unique, the fabric so fresh and appealing in its neat plastic packaging. Voices leap out around her. Christmas music settles on the air. My widow looks round for a salesperson.

SECOND HUSBAND

His name is—*was*—Roland Secourt. He was one of those types who never really strain themselves with such trivialities as earning a living during their younger years, and he wound up being a pretty impressive old man, replete with teeth, hair and the ability to walk unaided from the car to the house. I remember him only slightly—he used to give piano lessons to our son a thousand years ago, and I think he managed a parking lot or something like that. At any rate, five years after I bowed out, he began showing up at the front door with one excuse or another—he was driving past and saw the gate was open; he'd picked up six cases of cranberry juice at a sale and didn't know what to do with it all; he was just wondering if my widow might want to go down to the village for maybe a cocktail and dinner—and before long, my widow, who'd succumbed to the emptiness that afflicts us all, took him in.

She never loved him, though. He was a man, a presence in a deteriorating house full of cats, my shadowy simulacrum. What did he bring with him? Three cardboard boxes full of out-of-date shoes, belt buckles, underwear, a trophy he'd once won in a piano competition. Nine months into the marriage he sucked up his afflatus to crack the holy living hell out of a golf ball on the fourth tee at La Cumbre Country Club (he was golf-fixated, another strike against him), felt a stab under his arm as if someone had inserted one of those gleaming biopsy needles between his ribs, and fell face forward into the turf, dead, without displacing the ball from the tee.

That was a long time ago. My widow didn't have him around long enough to really get used to him in the way she was used to the walls and the furniture and the cats, so his death, though a painful reminder of what awaits us all, wasn't the major sort of dislocation it might have been. He was there, and then he was gone. I have no problem with that.

HER PURSE

Her purse was always a bone of contention between us—or her *purses*, actually. She seemed to have a limitless number of them, one at least for every imaginable occasion, from dining at the White House to hunting boar in Kentucky, and all of them stuffed full of ticket stubs, charge card receipts, wadded-up tissues, cat collars, gum wrappers, glasses with broken frames, makeup in various states of desiccation, crushed fortune cookies, fragments of our son's elementary school report cards, dice, baby teeth, empty Tic Tac cases, keychains, cans of Mace and a fine detritus of crumbs, dandruff, sloughed skin and chipped nail polish. Only one of these, however, contained her checkbook and wallet. That was the magical one, the essential one, the one she spent a minimum of half an hour looking for every time we left the house, especially when we were on our way to the airport or the theater or a dinner date with A-type personalities like myself who'd specified *eight P.M., sharp*.

Not that I'm complaining. My widow lived a placid, unhurried existence, no slave to mere schedules, as so many of us were. She radiated calm in a crisis. When things went especially bad— during the '05 earthquake, for instance—she would fix herself a nice meal, some stir-fry or chicken-vegetable soup, and take a nap in order to put things in their proper perspective. And so what if the movie started at 7:45 and we arrived at 8:30? It was all the more interesting for having to piece together what must have transpired with this particular set of characters while we were looking for purses, parking the car and sprinting hand in hand down the crowded street. The world could wait. What was the hurry?

At any rate, it is that very same totemic purse that turns up missing after her shopping trip. She and her sister arrive at home in a blizzard of packages, and after sorting them out in the driveway and making three trips from car to house, they part just as dusk is pushing the birds into the trees and thickening the shadows in the fronds of the tree ferns I planted thirty years ago. Inge won't be staying for dinner, nor will she be spending the night. She is eager to get home to her own house, where a pot of chicken-vegetable soup and her own contingent of cats await her. "Well," she says, casting a quick eye over the welter of packages on the table, "I'm off," and the door closes on silence.

Days pass. My widow goes through her daily routine without a thought to her purse, until, with the cat food running low, she prepares for a trip to the market in the ancient, battered, *hennarot* BMW M3 that used to be my pride and joy, and discovers that none of the purses she is able to locate contains her wallet, her keys, her glasses (without which she can't even see the car, let alone drive it). While the cats gather round her, voicing their complaint, she attempts to retrace her steps of the past few days and concludes finally that she must have left the purse in her sister's car. Certainly, that's where it is. Of course it is. Unless she left it on the counter at Ruby's or the Bargain Basement or even Macy's. But if she had, they would have called, wouldn't they?

She tries her sister, but Inge isn't much for answering the phone these days, a quirk of her advancing years. Why bother?, that's what she thinks. Who is there she wants to hear from? At her age, is there any news that can't wait? Any news that could even vaguely be construed as good? My widow is nothing if not persistent, however, and on the twelfth ring Inge picks up the phone. "Hello?" she rasps in a voice that was never especially melodious but is now just a deflated ruin. My widow informs her of the problem, accepts a scolding that goes on for at least five minutes and incorporates a dozen ancient grievances, and then she waits on the line for another fifteen minutes while Inge hobbles out to the garage to check the car. *Click, click,* she's back on the line and she has bad news for my widow: the purse is not there. Is she sure? Yes, yes, she's sure. She's no idiot. She still has two eyes in her head, doesn't she?

For the next two hours my widow searches for the phone book. Her intention is to look up the phone number of the stores they'd visited, and the Thai Palace too—she's concerned, and the cats are hungry. But the phone book is elusive. After evicting a dozen cats from the furniture in the main room, digging through the pantry and the closet and discovering any number of things she'd misplaced years ago, she loses track of what she's looking for, lost in a reverie over an old photo album that turns up in the cabinet under the stove, amidst the pots and pans. She sits at the table, a crescent of yellow lamplight illuminating her features, and studies the hard evidence of the way things were. There are pictures of the two of us, smiling into the camera against various exotic backdrops, against Christmas trees and birthday cakes, minarets and mountains, a succession of years flipping by, our son, his dog, the first cat. Her heart—my widow's heart—is bursting. It's gone, everything is gone, and what's the sense of living, what's it all about? The girlhood in Buffalo, the college years, romance and love and hope and the prospect of the future—what was the sense in it, where had it gone? The pictures cry out to her. They scream from the page. They poke her and prod her till she's got no breath left in her body. And just then, when the whole world seems to be closing down, the phone rings.

BOB SMITH, A.K.A. SMYTHE ROBERTS, ROBERT P. SMITHEE, CLAUDIO NORIEGA AND JACK FROUNCE

"Hello?" my widow answers, her voice like the clicking of the tumblers in an old lock.

"Mrs. B.?" a man's voice inquires.

My widow is cautious but polite, a woman who has given out her trust, time and again, and been rewarded, for the most part, with kindness and generosity in return. But she hates telephone solicitors, especially those boiler-room types that prey on the elderly—the TV news has been full of that sort of thing lately, and the A.A.R.P. newsletter too. She hesitates a moment, and then, in a barely audible voice, whispers, "Yes?"

"My name is Bob Smith," the caller returns, "and I've found your purse. Somebody apparently dumped it in a trash bin outside of Macy's—no cash left, of course, but your credit cards are intact, and your license and whatnot. Listen, I was wondering if I might bring it to you—I mean, I could mail it, but who can trust the mail these days, right?"

My widow makes a noise of assent. She doesn't trust the mail, either. Or, actually, she's never really thought about it one way or another. She shuts her eyes and sees the mailman in his gray-blue shorts with the black stripe up the side, his neatly parted hair cut in the old-fashioned way, his smile, and the way his eyes seem to register everything about everybody on his route as if he took it personally, as if he were policing the streets out front and back of her house and stuffing mailboxes at the same time. Maybe she does trust the mail. Maybe she does.

Bob Smith says, "The mail'd take three days, and I'd have to find a box for the thing—"

My widow says what Bob Smith has been hoping she'll say: "Oh, you don't have to go to all that bother. Honestly, I'd come to you, but without my driving glasses—they're in the purse, you see, and I do have another pair, several pairs, but I can't seem to, I can't—"

"That's all right," he croons, his voice flowing like sugar water into a child's cup, "I'm just glad to help out. Now, is this address on your driver's license still current?"

My widow is waiting at the door for him when he steps through the front gate, a pair of legs like chopsticks in motion, his hair a dyed fluff of nothing combed straight up on his head as if he were one of those long-pants comedians of her father's era, a face gouged with wrinkles and a smile that makes his eyes all but disappear into two sinkholes of flesh. He wouldn't have got any farther than the gate if I was around, and I don't care how old I might have been, or how frail—this man is trouble, and my widow doesn't know it. Look out, honey, I want to say. Watch out for this one.

But she's smiling her beautiful smile, the smile that even after all these years has the two puckered dimples in it, her face shining and serene, and "Hello, hello, Mr. Smith," she's saying, "won't you come in?"

He will. He ducks reflexively on stepping through the door, as if his head would crack the doorframe, a tall man with dangling hands, a grubby white shirt and a tie that looks as if it'd been used to swab out the deep fryer at McDonald's. In his left hand, a plain brown shopping bag, and as she shuts the door behind him and six or seven cats glance up suspiciously from their perch on the mantel, he holds it out to her. "Here it is," he says, and sure enough, her purse is inside, soft black leather with a silver clasp and the ponzu sauce stain etched into the right panel like an abstract design. She fumbles through the purse for her wallet, thinking to offer him a reward, but then she remembers that there's no money in it—hadn't he said on the phone that the money was gone? "I wanted to—" she begins, "I mean, you've been so nice, and I—"

Bob Smith is not listening. He's wandered out into the arena of the grand room, hands clasped behind his back, dodging mounds of discarded magazines, balled-up skeins of yarn, toppled lamps and a cat-gutted ottoman. He has the look of a prospective buyer, interested, but not yet committed. "Pretty old place," he says, taking his time.

My widow, plumped with gratitude, is eager to accommodate him. "Nineteen-oh-nine," she says, working the purse between her hands. "It's the only Prairie style—"

"The rugs and all," he says, "they must be worth something. And all this pottery and brass stuff—you must have jewelry too."

"Oh, yes," my widow says, "I've been collecting antique jewelry for, well, since before I was an antique myself," and she appends a little laugh. What a nice man, she's thinking, and how many out there today would return a lady's purse? Or anything, for that matter? They'd stolen the lawn mower right out of the garage, stripped the tires off the car that time she'd broken down in Oxnard. She's feeling giddy, ready to dial Inge the minute he leaves and crow about the purse that's come back to her as if it had wings.

"Your husband here?" Bob Smith asks, picking his way back to her like a man on the pitching deck of a ship. There seems to be something stuck to the bottom of his left shoe.

"My husband?" Another laugh, muted, caught deep in her throat. "He's been gone twenty years now. Twenty-one. Or no, twenty-two."

"Kids?"

"Our son, Philip, lives in Calcutta, India. He's a doctor."

"So there's nobody here but you," Bob Smith says, and that's when my widow feels the first faint stirring of alarm. A cat rises slowly on the periphery of her vision, stretching itself. The sun slants through the windows, irradiating the skeleton of the dead palm in the big pot in the corner. Everything is still. She just nods her head in response to the question and clutches the purse to her, thinking, It's all right, just show him to the door now, and thank him, tell him the reward's coming, in the mail, just leave an address . . .

But Bob Smith isn't ready to leave. In fact, he's hovering over her now, his face as rucked and seamed as an old mailbag, his eyes glittering like something that's been crushed in the street. "So where's the jewelry then?" he says, and there's nothing of the good Samaritan left in his voice now, no bonhomie, no fellow feeling or even civility. "Can you even find it in this shithole? Huh?"

My widow doesn't say a word.

He has a hand on her wrist suddenly, clamped there like a manacle, and he's tugging at her, shouting in her face. "You stupid old bitch! You're going to pay—shit, yes, you're going to pay. Any cash? Huh? Cash? You know what that is?" And then, before she has time to answer, he snakes out his other hand, the right one, and slaps her till she jerks back from the grip of him like an animal caught in the jaws of a trap.

My widow hasn't been slapped in seventy-odd years, not since she got into a fight with her sister over a pan of brownies when their mother stepped out of the kitchen to answer the phone. She's in shock, of course—everything's happened so fast—but she's tough, my widow, as tough in the core of her as anybody on earth. Nobody slaps her. Nobody comes into her house on false pretenses and—well, you get the picture. And in the next instant her free hand comes up out of the purse with an ancient can of Mace clutched in it, and because this is a good and fitting universe I'm constructing here, the aerosol spray still works despite an expiration date ten years past, and before she can think, Bob Smith is writhing on the floor in a riot of cat feces, dust balls and lint, cursing and rubbing at his eyes. And more: when my widow turns for the door, ready to scurry out onto that brick porch and scream till her dried-up old lungs give out, who should be standing there at the door but Megan Capaldi, screaming herself.

IN HER OWN WORDS

As I say, my widow doesn't get the newspaper, not anymore. But Megan Capaldi brings her two copies the next day, because her picture is on the front page under the caption, "FEISTY OCTOGENARIAN THWARTS BURGLARY." There she is, hunched and squinting into the camera, arm in arm with Megan Capaldi, who dialed 911 on her cell phone and escorted my widow to safety while the San Roque Municipal Police handcuffed Bob Smith and secured him in the back of their cruiser. In the photograph, which shows off the front of the house to real advantage, I think, the windows especially, with their intricate design and the wooden frames I scraped, sanded and painted at least three times in the course of my tenure here, my widow is smiling. So too is Megan Capaldi, who wouldn't be bad-looking at all if only she'd stand up straight. Posed there, with the house mushrooming over them in grainy black and white, you can hardly tell them apart.

On page 2, at the end of the article, my widow is given an

opportunity to reflect on her ordeal. "It's a shame, is what it is," she is quoted as saying, "the way people like this prey on the elderly—and don't forget the telemarketers, they're just as bad. It didn't used to be this way, before everybody got so suspicious of everybody else, and you didn't have to triple-lock your doors at night, either."

There was more, much more, because the young woman reporter they sent out to the house had been so sympathetic—a cat person herself—but there were space limitations, and the story, while novel, didn't have the sort of grit and horror the paper's readers had come to expect. Any number of times during the interview, for instance, my widow had begun with the phrase "When my husband was alive," but none of that made the cut.

NIGHT

It is Christmas, a clear cold night, the sky above the house staggering under the weight of the stars. My widow doesn't know about the stars—or if she does, it's only theoretically. She doesn't leave the house much, except for shopping, of course, and shopping is almost exclusively a daytime activity. At the moment, she is sitting in the grand room, on the cherrywood couch in front of the fireplace, where the ashes lie heaped, twenty-two years cold. She has been knitting, and the electric blue needles and balls of yarn lie in her lap, along with three or four cats. Her head is thrown back, resting on the broad wooden plane of the couch, and she is staring up at the high sloping ceiling above her, oblivious to the sky beyond and the cold pinpoints of light crowding the plane of the ecliptic. She's not thinking about the roof, or the roofer, or rain. She's not thinking about anything.

There is little evidence of the holidays here—a few Christmas cards scattered across the end table, a wreath of artificial pine she draped over one of the light sconces six years ago. She doesn't bother anymore with the handcrafted elves and angels from Gstaad, the crèche made of mopane wood, or even the colored lights and bangles. All that was peerless in its time, the magic of the season, our son coming down the stairs in his pajamas, year after year, growing taller and warier, the angels tarnished, the pile of gift-wrapped presents growing in proportion, but that time is past. She and Inge had planned to get together and exchange gifts in the afternoon, but neither of them had felt much enthusiasm for it, and besides, Inge's car wouldn't start. What I'd wanted here was for our son to pull up front in a cab, having flown in all the way from the subcontinent to be with his mother for Christmas—and he'd been planning on it too, planning to surprise her, but a new and cruelly virulent strain of cholera swept through the refugee camps, and he couldn't get away.

So she sits there by the ashes of the cold fire, listening to the furtive groans and thumps of the old house. The night deepens, the stars draw back, higher and higher, arching into the backbone of the sky. She is waiting for something she can't name, a beautiful old lady clothed in cats, my widow, just waiting. It is very still.

THE UNDERGROUND GARDENS

But you do not know me if you think I am afraid. . . .

—Franz Kafka, "The Burrow"

All he knew, really, was digging. He dug to eat, to breathe, to live and sleep. He dug because the earth was there beneath his feet, and men paid him to move it. He dug because it was a sacrament, because it was honorable and holy. As a boy in Sicily he stood beside his brothers under the sun that was like a hammer and day after day stabbed his shovel into the skin of the ancient venerable earth of their father's orchards. As a young man in Boston and New York he burrowed like a rodent beneath streets and rivers, scouring the walls of subway tubes and aqueducts, dropping his pick, lifting his shovel, mining dirt. And now, thirty-two years old and with the deed to seventy bleak and hard-baked acres in his back pocket, he was in California. Digging.

> FRIENDS! COME TO THE LAND OF FERTILITY WHERE THE SUN SHINES THE YEAR ROUND AND THE EARTH NEVER SUBMITS TO FROST! COME TO THE LAND THE ANGELS BLESSED! COME TO CALIFORNIA! WRITE NOW, C/O EUPHRATES MEAD, Box 9, Fresno, California.

Yes, the land never froze, that was true and incontrovertible. But the sun scorched it till it was like stone, till it was as hard and impenetrable as the adobe brick the Indians and Mexicans piled up to make their shabby, dusty houses. This much Baldasare discovered in the torporific summer of 1905, within days of disembarking from the train with his pick and shovel, his cardboard suitcase, and his meager supply of dried pasta, flour, and beans. He'd come all the way across the country to redeem the land that would bloom with the serrate leaves and sweetly curling tendrils of his own grapes, the grapes of the Baldasare Forestiere Vineyards.

When he got down off the train, the air hot and sweet with the scent of things growing and multiplying, he was so filled with hope it was a kind of ecstasy. There were olive trees in California, orange and lemon and lime, spreading palms, fields of grapes and cotton that had filled the rushing windows of the train with every kind of promise. No more sleet and snow for him, no more wet feet and overshoes or the grippe that took all the muscle out of your back and arms, but heat, good Sicilian heat, heat that baked you right down to the grateful marrow of your happy Sicilian bones.

The first thing he did was ask directions at the station, his English a labyrinth of looming verbs and truncated squawks that sounded strange in his ears, but was serviceable for all that, and he soon found himself walking back in the direction he'd come, following the crucified grid of the tracks. Three miles south, then up a dry wash where two fire-scarred oaks came together like a pair of clasped arms, he couldn't miss it. At least that was what the man on the platform had told him. He was a farmer, this man, unmistakably a farmer, in faded coveralls and a straw hat, long of nose and with two blue flecks for eyes in a blasted face. "That's where all the Guineas are," he said, "that's where Mead sold 'em. Seventy acres, isn't it? That's what I figured. Same as the rest."

When he got there and set his cardboard suitcase in the dust, he couldn't help but pace off the whole seventy acres with the surveyor's map Euphrates Mead had sent in the mail held out before him like a dowsing stick. The land was pale in a hundred shades of brown and a sere gray-green, and there was Russian thistle everywhere, the decayed thorny bones of it already crushed to chaff in his tracks. It crept down the open neck of his shirt and into his socks and shoes and the waist of his trousers, an itch of the land, abrasive and unforgiving. Overhead, vultures rose on the air currents like bits of winged ash. Lizards scuttered underfoot.

That night he ate sardines from a tin, licking the oil from his fingers and dipping soda crackers in the residue that collected in the corners, and then he spread a blanket under one of his new oak trees and slept as if he'd been knocked unconscious. In the morning he walked into town and bought a wheelbarrow. He filled the wheelbarrow with provisions and two five-gallon cans that had once held olive oil and now contained water—albeit an oleaginous and tinny-tasting variant of what he knew water to be. Then he hefted the twin handles of the new wheelbarrow till he felt the familiar flex of the muscles of his lower back, and he guided it all the long way back out to the future site of the Baldasare Forestiere Vineyards.

He'd always thought big, even when he was a boy wandering his father's orchards, the orchards that would never be his because of a simple confluence of biology and fate—his brothers had been born before him. If, God forbid, either Pietro or Domenico should die or emigrate to Argentina or Australia, there was always the other one to stand in his way. But Baldasare wasn't discouraged—he knew he was destined for greatness. Unlike his brothers, he had the gift of seeing things as they would one day be, of seeing himself in America, right here in Fresno, his seventy acres buried in grapes, the huge oak fermenting barrels rising above the cool cellar floors, his house of four rooms and a porch set on a hill and his wife on the porch, his four sons and three daughters sprinting like colts across the yard.

He didn't even stop to eat, that first day. Sweating till his eyes burned with the sting of salt, his hands molded to the shape of the wheelbarrow's polished handles, he made three more trips into town and back—twelve miles in all, and half of them pushing the overladen wheelbarrow. People saw him there as they went about their business in carriages and farm wagons, a sun-seared little man in slept-in clothes following the tread of a single sagging tire along the shoulder of the broad dirt road. Even if he'd looked up, they probably wouldn't have nodded a greeting, but he never took his eyes off the unwavering line the tire cut in the dirt.

By the end of the week a one-room shanty stood beneath the oak, a place not much bigger than the bed he constructed of planks. It was a shelter, that was all, a space that separated him from the animals, that reminded him he was a man and not a beast. *Men are upright,* his father had told him when he was a boy, *and they have dominion over the beasts. Men live in houses, don't they? And where do the beasts live,* mio figlio? *In the ground, no? In a hole.*

It was some day of the following week when Baldasare began digging (he didn't have a calendar and he didn't know Sunday from Monday, and even if he did, where was the church and the priest to guide him?). He wanted the well to be right in front of the shack beneath the tree where his house would one day stand, but he knew enough about water to know that it wouldn't be as easy as that. He spent a whole morning searching the immediate area, tracing dry watercourses, observing the way the hill of his shack and the one beside it abutted each other like the buttocks of a robust and fecund woman, until finally, right there, right in the cleft of the fundament, he pitched his shovel into the soil.

Two feet down he hit the hardpan. It didn't disconcert him, not at all—he never dreamed it would extend over all of the seventy acres—and he attacked the rocky substrate with his pick until he was through it. As he dug deeper, he squared up the sides of his excavation with mortared rock and devised a pulley system to haul the buckets of superfluous earth clear of the hole. By the close of the second day, he needed a ladder. A week later, at thirty-two feet, he hit water, a pure sweet seep of it that got his shoes wet and climbed up the bottom rungs of his homemade ladder to a depth of four feet. And even as he set up the hand pump and exulted over the flow of shimmering sun-struck water, he was contriving his irrigation system, his pipes, conduits, and channels, a water tank, a reservoir. Yes. And then, with trembling hands, he dug into the earth in the place where the first long row of canes would take root, and his new life, his life of disillusionment, began.

Three months later, when his savings began to dwindle down to nothing, Baldasare became a laboring man all over again. He plowed another man's fields, planted another man's trees, dug irrigation channels and set grape canes for one stranger after another. And on his own property, after those first few weeks of feverish activity, all he'd managed, after working the soil continuously and amending it with every scrap of leaf-mold and bolus of chicken manure he could scrounge, was a vegetable garden so puny and circumscribed a housewife would have been ashamed of it. He'd dreamed of independence—from his father and brothers, from the hard-nosed Yankee construction bosses of Boston and Manhattan Island—and what had he gotten but wage slavery all over again?

He was depressed. Gloomy. Brooding and morose. It wasn't so much Mr. Euphrates Mead who'd betrayed him, but the earth, the earth itself. Plying his shovel, sweating in a long row of sweating men, he thought of suicide in all its gaudy and elaborate guises, his eyes closed forever on his worthless land and his worthless life. And then one rainy afternoon, sitting at the counter in Siagris' Drugstore with a cup of coffee and a hamburger sandwich, he had a vision that changed all that. The vision was concrete, as palpable as flesh, and it moved with the grace and fluidity of a living woman, a woman he could almost reach out and . . . "Can I get you anything else?" she asked.

He was so surprised he answered her in Italian. Olive eyes, hair piled up on her head like a confection, skin you could eat with a spoon—and hadn't it been old Siagris, the hairy Greek, who'd fried his hamburger and set it down on the counter before him? Or was he dreaming?

She was giving him a look, a crease between her eyebrows, hands on hips. "What did you say?"

"I mean"—fumbling after his English—"no, no, thank you . . . but who, I mean . . . ?"

She was serene—a very model of serenity—though the other customers, men in suits, two boys and their mother lingering over their ice cream, were all watching her and quietly listening for her answer. "I'm Ariadne," she said. "Ariadne Siagris." She looked over her shoulder to the black-eyed man standing at the grill. "That's my uncle."

Baldasare was charmed—and a bit dazed too. She was beautiful—or at least to his starved eyes she was—and he wanted to say something witty to her, something flirtatious, something that would let her know that he wasn't just another sorrowful Italian laborer with no more means or expectations than the price of the next hamburger sandwich, but a man of substance, a landowner, future proprietor of the Baldasare Forestiere Vineyards. But he couldn't think of anything, his mind impacted, his tongue gone dead in the sleeve of his mouth. Then he felt his jaws opening of their own accord and heard himself saying, "Baldasare Forestiere, at your service."

He would always remember that moment, through all the digging and lifting and wheelbarrowing to come, because she looked hard at him, as if she could see right through to his bones, and then she turned up the corners of her mouth, pressed two fingers to her lips, and giggled.

That night, as he lay in his miserable bed in his miserable shack that was little more than a glorified chicken coop, he could think of nothing but her. Ariadne Siagris. She was the one. She was what he'd come to America for, and he spoke her name aloud as the rain beat at his crude roof and insinuated itself through a hundred slivers and cracks to drizzle down onto his already damp blankets, spoke her name aloud and made the solemnest pledge that she would one day be his bride. But it was cold and the night beyond the walls was limitless and black and his teeth were chattering so forcefully he could barely get the words out. He was mad, of course, and he knew it. How could he think to have a chance with her? What could he offer her, a girl like that who'd come all the way from Chicago, Illinois, to live with her uncle, the prosperous Greek—a school-educated girl used to fine things and books? Yes, he'd made inquiries—he'd done nothing but inquire since he'd left the drugstore that afternoon. Her parents were dead, killed at a railway crossing, and she was nineteen years old, with two younger sisters and three brothers, all of them farmed out to relatives. Ariadne. Ariadne Siagris.

The rain was relentless. It spoke and sighed and roared. He was wearing every stitch of clothing he possessed, wrapped in his blankets and huddled over the coal-oil lamp, and still he froze, even here in California. It was an endless night, an insufferable night, but a night in which his mind was set free to roam the universe of his life, one thought piled atop another like bricks in a wall, until at some point, unaccountably, he was thinking of the grand tunnels he'd excavated in New York and Boston, how clean they were, how warm in winter and cool in summer, how they smelled, always, of the richness of the earth. Snow could be falling on the streets above, the gutters frozen, wind cutting into people's eyes, but below ground there was no weather, none at all. He thought about that, pictured it—the great arching tubes carved out of the earth and the locomotive with a train of cars standing there beneath the ground and all the passengers staring placidly out the windows—and then he was asleep.

The next morning, he began to dig again. The rain had gone and the sun glistened like spilled oil over his seventy acres of mire and hardpan. He told himself he was digging a cellar—a proper cellar for the house he would one day build, because he hadn't given up, not yet, not Baldasare Forestiere—but even then, even as he spat on his hands and raised the pick above his head, he knew there was more to it than that. The pick rose and fell, the shovel licked at the earth with all the probing intimacy of a tongue, and the wheelbarrow groaned under one load after another. Baldasare was digging. And he was happy, happier than he'd been since the day he stepped down from the train, because he was digging for her, for Ariadne, and because digging was what he'd been born to do.

But then the cellar was finished—a fine deep vaulted space in which he could not only stand erect—at his full height of five feet and four inches—but thrust his right arm straight up over his head and still only just manage to touch the ceiling—and he found himself at a loss for what to do next. He could have squared up the corners and planed the walls with his spade till all the lines were rectilinear, but he didn't want that. That was the fashion of all the rooms he'd ever lived in, and as he scraped and smoothed and tamped, he realized it didn't suit him. No, his cellar was dome-shaped, like the apse of the cathedral in which he'd worshipped as a boy, and its entrance was protected from the elements by a long broad ramp replete with gutters that drained into a small reflecting pool just outside the wooden door. And its roof, of course, was of hardpan, impervious to the rain and sun, and more durable than any shingle or tile.

He spent two days smoothing out the slope of the walls and tidying and leveling the floor, working by the light of a coal-oil lantern while in the realm above the sky threw up a tatter of cloud and burned with a sun in the center of it till the next storm rolled in to snuff it out like a candle. When the rain came, it seemed like the most natural thing in the world to move his clothes and his bed and his homemade furniture down into the new cellar, which was snug and watertight. Besides, he reasoned, even as he fashioned himself a set of shelves and broke through the hardpan to run a stovepipe out into the circumambient air, what did he need a cellar for—a strict cellar, that is—if he couldn't grow the onions, apples, potatoes, and carrots to store in it?

Once the stove was installed and had baked all the moisture out of the place, he lay on the hard planks of his bed through a long rainy afternoon, smoking one cigarette after another and thinking about what his father had said—about the animals and how they lived in the ground, in holes. His father was a wise man. A man of character and substance. But he wasn't in California and he wasn't in love with Ariadne Siagris and he didn't have to live in a shack the pigeons would have rejected. It took him a while, but the conclusion Baldasare finally reached was that he was no animal—he was just practical, that was all—and he barely surprised himself when he got up from the bed, fetched his shovel and began to chip away at the east wall of his cellar. He could already see a hallway there, a broad grand hallway, straight as a plumb line and as graceful and sensible as the arches the Romans of antiquity put to such good use in their time. And beyond that, as the dirt began to fall and the wheelbarrow shuddered to receive it, he saw a kitchen and bedroom opening onto an atrium, he saw grape and wisteria vines snaking toward the light, camellias, ferns, and impatiens overflowing clay pots and baskets—and set firmly in the soil, twenty feet below the surface, an avocado tree, as heavy with fruit as any peddler's cart.

The winter wore on. There wasn't much hired work this time of year—the grapes had been picked and pressed, the vines cut back, the fig trees pruned, and the winter crops were in the ground. Baldasare had plenty of time on his hands. He wasn't idle—he just kept right on digging—nor was he destitute. Modest in his needs and frugal by habit, he'd saved practically everything he'd earned through the summer and fall, repairing his own clothes, eating little more than boiled eggs and pasta, using his seventy acres as a place to trap rabbits and songbirds and to gather wood for his stove. His one indulgence was tobacco—that, and a weekly hamburger sandwich at Siagris' Drugstore.

Chewing, sipping coffee, smoking, he studied his future bride there, as keen as any scholar intent on his one true subject. He made little speeches to her in his head, casual remarks he practiced over and over till he got them right—or thought he did, anyway. Lingering over his coffee after cleaning the plate of crumbs with a dampened forefinger, he would wait till she came near with a glass or washcloth in hand, and he would blurt: "One thinks the weather will change, is that not true?" Or: "This is the most best sandwich of hamburger my mouth will ever receive." And she? She would show her teeth in a little equine smile, or she would giggle, then sometimes sneeze, covering her nose and mouth with one hand as her late mother had no doubt taught her to do. All the while, Baldasare feasted on the sight of her. Sometimes he would sit there at the counter for two or three hours till Siagris the Greek would make some impatient remark and he would rise in confusion, his face suffused with blood, bowing and apologizing till he managed to find his way to the door.

It was during this time of close scrutiny that he began to detect certain small imperfections in his bride-to-be. Despite her education, for instance, she seemed to have inordinate difficulty in making change or reading off the menu from the chalkboard on the wall behind her. She'd begun to put on weight too, picking at bits of doughnut or fried potatoes the customers left on their plates. If she'd been substantial when Baldasare first laid eyes on her, she was much more than that now—stout, actually. As stout as Signora Cardino back home in Messina, who was said to drink olive oil instead of wine and breakfast on sugared cream and cake. And then there were her eyes—or rather, her right eye. It had a cast in it, and how he'd missed that on the day he was first smitten, he couldn't say. But he had to look twice to notice the hairs on her chin—as stiff as a cat's whiskers and just as translucent—and as far as he was concerned, the red blotches that had begun to appear on the perfect skin of her hands and throat might have been nothing more than odd splashes of marinara sauce, as if she'd gotten too close to the pot.

Another lover, less blinded by the light of certitude than Baldasare, might have found these blemishes a liability, but Baldasare treasured them. They were part of her, part of that quiddity that made her unique among women. He watched with satisfaction as her hips and buttocks swelled so that even at nineteen she had to walk with a waddle, looked on with a soaring heart as the blotches spread from her throat to her cheeks and brow and her right eye stared out of her head, across the room and out the window, surer each day that she was his. After all, who else would see in her what he saw? Who else could love her the way he did? Who but Baldasare Forestiere would come forward to declare himself? And he would declare himself soon—as soon as he finished digging.

Two years passed. He worked for other men and saved every cent of his wages, worse than any miser, and in his free time, he dug. When he completed a passage or a room or carved his way to the sky for light, he could already see the next passage and the next room beyond that. He had a vision, yes, and he had Ariadne to think of, but even so, he wasn't the sort to sit around idle. He didn't have the gift of letters, he didn't play violin or mouth organ, and he rarely visited among his neighbors. The vaudeville theater was a long way off, too far to walk, and he went there only once, with Lucca Albanese, a vineyard worker with whom he'd struck up a friendship. There were comedians and jugglers and pretty women all dancing like birds in flight, but all the while he was regretting the two cents the streetcar had cost him and the fifteen-cent admission, and he never went back. No, he stayed home with his shovel and his vision, and many days he didn't know morning from night.

Saturdays, though, he kept sacred. Saturday was the day he walked the three and a half miles to Siagris' Drugstore, through winter rains and summer heat that reached a hundred and sixteen degrees Fahrenheit. He prided himself on his constancy, and he was pleased to think that Ariadne looked forward to his weekly visits as much as he did. His place at the end of the counter was always vacant, as if reserved for him, and he relished the little smiles with which she greeted him and the sweet flow of familiar phrases that dropped so easily from her supple American lips: "So how've you been?" "Nice day." "Think it's coming on to rain?"

As time went on, they became increasingly intimate. She told him of her uncle's back pain, the illness of her cat, the ascension of her oldest brother to assistant floor supervisor at the Chicago Iron Works, and he told her of his ranch and of the elegance and spaciousness of his living quarters. "Twelve room," he said. "Twelve room, and all to myself." And then came the day when he asked her, in his runaway English, if she would come with him to the ranch for a picnic. "But not just the picnic," he said, "but also the scene, how do you say, the scene of the place, and my, my house, because I want—I need—you see, I . . ."

She was leaning over the counter, splotchy and huge. Her weight had stabilized in the past year—she'd reached her full growth, finally, at the age of twenty-one—and she floated above her feet like one of the airships the Germans so prized. "Yes," she said, and she giggled and sneezed, a big mottled hand pressed to her mouth, "I'd love to."

The following Sunday he came for her, lightly ascending the sun-bleached steps to the walkup above the drugstore where she lived with uncle and aunt and their five children. It was a hot September morning, all of Fresno and the broad dusty valley beyond held in the grip of something stupendous, a blast of air so sere and scorching you would have thought the whole world was a pizza oven with the door open wide. Siagris the Greek answered his knock. He was in his shirtsleeves and the sweat had made a washcloth of his garments, the white field of his shirt stuck like a postage stamp to the bulge of his belly. He didn't smile but he didn't look displeased either, and Baldasare understood the look: Siagris didn't like him, not one bit, and in other circumstances might have gone out of his way to squash him like a bug, but then he had a niece who took up space and ate like six nieces, and Baldasare could just maybe deliver him from that. "Come in," he said, and there was Baldasare, the cave-dweller, in a room in a house two stories above the ground.

Up here, inside, it was even hotter. The Siagris children lay about like swatted flies, and Mrs. Siagris, her hair like some wild beast clawing at her scalp, poked her head around the corner from the kitchen. It was too hot to smile, so she grimaced instead and pulled her head back out of sight. And then, in the midst of this suffocating scene, the voice of a ventriloquist cried out, "He's here," and Ariadne appeared in the hallway.

She was all in white, with a hat the size of a tabletop perched atop the mighty pile of her hair. He was melting already, from the heat, but when she focussed her wild eye on him and turned up her lips in the shyest of smiles, he melted a little more.

Outside, in the street, she gave him her arm, which was something of a problem because she was so much taller than he was, and he had to reach up awkwardly to take it. He was wearing his best suit of clothes, washed just the evening before, and the unfamiliar jacket clung to him like dead skin while the new celluloid collar gouged at his neck and the tie threatened to throttle him. They managed to walk the better part of a block before she put her feet together and came to a halt. "Where's your carriage?" she asked.

Carriage? Baldasare was puzzled. He didn't have any carriage— he didn't even have a horse. "I no got," he said, and he strained to give her his best smile. "We walk."

"Walk?" she echoed. "In this heat? You must be crazy."

"No," he said, "we walk," and he leaned forward and exerted the most delicate but insistent pressure on the monument of her arrested arm.

Her cheeks were splotched under the crisp arc of shadow the hat brim threw over her face and her olive eyes seemed to snatch at his. "You mean," and her voice was scolding and intemperate, "you ain't even got a wagon? You, with your big house you're always telling me about?"

The following Sunday, though it wounded him to throw his money away like some Park Avenue millionaire, he pulled up to Siagris' Drugstore in a hired cabriolet. It was a clear day, the sun high and merciless, and the same scenario played itself out in the walkup at the top of the stairs, except that this time Baldasare seemed to have things in hand. He was as short with Siagris as Siagris was with him, he made a witticism regarding the heat for the benefit of the children, and he led Ariadne (who had refused the previous week to go farther than a bench in the park at the end of the street) out the door, down the steps, and into the carriage like a *cavaliere* of old.

Baldasare didn't like horses. They were big and crude and expensive and they always seemed to need grooming, shoeing, doctoring, and oats—and the horse attached to the cabriolet was no exception. It was a stupid, flatulent, broad-flanked, mouse-colored thing, and it did its utmost to resist every touch of the reins and thwart every desire of the man wielding them. Baldasare was in a sweat by the time they reached his property, every square inch of his clothing soaked through like a blotter, and his nerves were frayed raw. Nor had he made any attempt at conversation during the drive, so riveted was he on the task at hand, and when they finally pulled up in the shade of his favorite oak, he turned to Ariadne and saw that she hadn't exactly enjoyed the ride either.

Her hat was askew, her mouth set in a thin unyielding line. She was glistening with sweat, her hands like doughballs fried in lard, and a thin integument of moistened dust clung to her features. She gave him a concentrated frown. "Well, where is it?" she demanded. "Why are we stopping here?"

His tongue ran ahead of him, even as he sprang down from the carriage and scurried to her side to assist her in alighting. "This is what I have want for to show you, and so long, because—well, because I am making it for you."

He studied the expression of her face as she looked from the disreputable shack to the hummock of the well and out over the heat-blasted scrub to where the crown of his avocado tree rose out of the ground like an illusion. And then she saw the ramp leading down to the cellar. She was stunned, he could see it in her face and there was no denying it, but he watched her struggle to try on a smile and focus her eyes on his. "This is a prank, ain't it? You're just fooling with me and your house is really over there behind that hill"—pointing now from her perch atop the carriage—"ain't it?"

"No, no," he said, "no. It's this, you see?" And he indicated the ramp, the crown of the avocado, the bump where the inverted cone of a new atrium broke the surface. "Twelve room, I tell you, twelve room." He'd become insistent, and he had his hand on her arm, trying to lead her down from the carriage—if only she would come, if only she would see—and he wanted to tell her how cool and fresh-smelling it was down there beneath the earth, and how cheap it was to build and expand, to construct a nursery, a sewing room, anything she wanted. All it took was a strong back and a shovel, and not one cent wasted on nails and lumber and shingles that fell apart after five years in the sun. He wanted to tell her, but the words wouldn't come, and he tried to articulate it all through the pressure of his hand on her arm, tugging, as if the whole world depended on her getting down from that carriage—and it did, it did!

"Let go!" she cried, snatching her arm away, and then she was sobbing, gasping for breath as if the superheated air were some other medium altogether and she was choking on it. "You said . . . you said . . . *twelve rooms!*"

He tried to reach for her again—"Please," he begged, "please"—but she jerked back from him so violently the carriage nearly buckled on its springs. Her face was furious, streaked with tears and dirt. "You bully!" she cried. "You Guinea, Dago, Wop! You, you're no better than a murderer!"

Three days later, in a single paragraph set off by a black border, the local paper announced her engagement to Hiram Broadbent, of Broadbent's Poultry & Eggs.

An engagement wasn't a marriage, that's what Baldasare was thinking when Lucca Albanese gave him the news. An engagement could be broken, like a promise or a declaration or even a contract. There was hope yet, there had to be. "Who is this Hiram Broadbent?" he demanded. "Do you know him?"

They were sharing a meal of beans and vermicelli in Baldasare's subterranean kitchen, speaking in a low tragic Italian. Lucca had just read the announcement to him, the sharp-edged English words shearing at him like scissors, and the pasta had turned to cotton wadding in his throat. He was going to choke. He was going to vomit.

"Yeah, sure," Lucca said. "I know him. Big, fat man. Wears a straw hat winter and summer. He's a drunk, mean as the devil, but his father owns a chicken farm that supplies all the eggs for the local markets in Fresno, so he's always got money in his pocket. Hell, if you ever came out of your hole, you'd know who I'm talking about."

"You don't think—I mean, Ariadne wouldn't really . . . would she?"

Lucca ducked his head and worked his spoon in the plate. "You know what my father used to say? When I was a boy in Catania?"

"No, what?"

"There's plenty of fish in the sea."

But that didn't matter to Baldasare—he wanted only one fish. Ariadne. Why else had he been digging, if not for her? He'd created an underground palace, with the smoothest of corners and the most elegant turnings and capacious courtyards, just to give her space, to give her all the room she could want after having to live at her uncle's mercy in that cramped walkup over the drugstore. Didn't she complain about it all the time? If only she knew, if only she'd give him a chance and descend just once into the cool of the earth, he was sure she'd change her mind, she had to.

There was a problem, though. An insurmountable problem. She wouldn't see him. He came into the drugstore, hoping to make it all up to her, to convince her that he was the one, the only one, and she backed away from the counter, exchanged a word with her uncle, and melted away through the sun-struck mouth of the back door. Siagris whirled round like some animal startled in a cave, his shoulders hunched and his head held low. "We don't want you in here anymore, understand?" he said. There was the sizzle of frying, the smell of onions, tuna fish, a row of startled white faces staring up from pie and coffee. Siagris leaned into the counter and made his face as ugly as he could. *"Capiche?"*

Baldasare Forestiere was not a man to be easily discouraged. He thought of sending her a letter, but he'd never learned to write, and the idea of having someone write it for him filled him with shame. For the next few days he brooded over the problem, working all the while as a hired laborer, shoveling, lifting, pulling, bending, and as his body went through the familiar motions his mind was set free to achieve a sweated lucidity. By the end of the third day, he'd decided what he had to do.

That night, under cover of darkness, he pushed his wheelbarrow into town along the highway and found his way to the vacant lot behind the drugstore. Then he started digging. All night, as the constellations drifted in the immensity overhead until one by one they fled the sky, Baldasare plied his shovel, his pick, and his rake. By morning, at first light, the outline of his message was clearly visible from the second-story window of the walkup above the store. It was a heart, a valentine, a perfectly proportioned symbol of his love dug three feet deep in the ground and curving gracefully over the full area of what must have been a quarter-acre lot.

When the outline was finished, Baldasare started on the interior. In his mind's eye, he saw a heart-shaped crater there in the lot, six feet deep at least, with walls as smooth as cement, a hole that would show Ariadne the depth of the vacancy she'd left in him. He was coming up the ramp he'd shaped of earth with a full wheelbarrow to spread over the corners of the lot, when he glanced up to see Siagris and two of his children standing there peering down at him. Siagris' hands were on his hips. He looked more incredulous than anything else. "What in Christ's name do you think you're doing?" he sputtered.

Baldasare, swinging wide with his load of dirt so that Siagris and the children had to take a quick step back, never even hesitated. He just kept going to a point in the upper corner of the frame where he was dumping and raking out the dirt. "Digging," he said over his shoulder.

"But you can't. This is private property. You can't just dig up people's yards, don't you know that? Eh? Don't you know anything?"

Baldasare didn't want a confrontation. He was a decent man, mild and pacifistic, but he was determined too. As he came by again with the empty wheelbarrow and eased it down the ramp, he said, "Tell her to look. She is the one. For her, I do this."

After that, he was deaf to all pleas, threats, and remonstrations, patiently digging, shoring up his walls, spreading his dirt. The sun climbed in the sky. He stopped only to take an occasional drink from a jug of water or to sit on his overturned wheelbarrow and silently eat a sandwich from a store of them wrapped in butcher's paper. He worked through the day, tireless, and though the sheriff came and threatened him, even the sheriff couldn't say with any certainty who owned the lot Baldasare was defacing—couldn't say, that is, without checking the records down at the courthouse, which he was going to do first thing in the morning, Baldasare could be sure of that. Baldasare didn't respond. He just kept digging.

It began to get dark. Baldasare had cleared the entire cutout of his heart to a depth of three feet, and he wasn't even close to quitting. Six feet, he was thinking, that's what it would take, and who could blame him if he kept glancing up at the unrevealing window of the apartment atop the drugstore in the hope of catching a glimpse of his inamorata there? If she was watching, if she knew what he was doing for love of her, if she saw the lean muscles of his arms strain and his back flex, she gave no sign of it. Undeterred, Baldasare dug on.

And then there came a moment, and it must have been past twelve at night, the neighborhood as silent as the grave and Baldasare working by the light of a waxing moon, when two men appeared at the northern edge of the excavation, right where the lobes of the heart came together in a graceful loop. "Hey, Wop," one of them yelled down to where Baldasare stood with his shovel, "I don't know who you think you are, but you're embarrassing my fiancée, and I mean to put an end to it."

The man's shadow under that cold moon was immense—it could have been the shadow of a bear or buffalo. The other shadow was thinner, but broad across the shoulders, where it counted, and it danced on shadowy feet. There was no sound but for the slice of Baldasare's shovel and the slap of the dirt as it dropped into the wheelbarrow.

He was a small man, Baldasare, but the hundreds of tons of dirt he'd moved in his lifetime had made iron of his limbs, and when they fell on him he fought like a man twice his size. Still, the odds were against him, and Hiram Broadbent, fueled by good Kentucky bourbon and with the timely assistance of Calvin Tompkins, a farrier and amateur boxer, was able to beat him to the ground. And once he was down, Broadbent and Tompkins kicked him with their heavy boots till he stirred no more.

/ / / / /

When Baldasare was released from the hospital, he was a changed man—or at least to the degree that the image of Ariadne Siagris no longer infested his brain. He went back home and sat in a bentwood rocker and stared at the sculpted dirt walls of the kitchen that gave onto the atrium and the striated trunk of its lone avocado tree. His right arm was in a sling, with a cast on it from the elbow down, and he was bound up beneath his shirt like an Egyptian mummy with all the tape it took to keep his cracked ribs in place. After a week or so—his mourning period, as he later referred to it—he found himself one evening in the last and deepest of his rooms, the one at the end of the passage that led to the new atrium where he was thinking of planting a lemon tree or maybe a quince. It was preternaturally quiet. The earth seemed to breathe with and for him.

And then suddenly he began to see things, all sorts of things, a rush of raw design and finished image that flickered across the wall before him like one of Edison's moving pictures. What he saw was a seventy-acre underground warren that beckoned him on, a maze like no other, with fishponds and gardens open to the sky above, and more, much more—a gift shop and an Italian restaurant with views of subterranean grottoes and a lot for parking the carriages and automobiles of the patrons who would flock there to see what he'd accomplished in his time on earth. It was a complete vision, more eloquent than any set of blueprints or elevations, and it staggered him. He was a young man still, healing by the day, and while he had a long way to go, at least now he knew where he was going. *Baldasare Forestiere's Underground Gardens*, he said to himself, trying out the name, and then he said it aloud: "Baldasare Forestiere's Underground Gardens."

Standing there in the everlasting silence beneath the earth, he reached out a hand to the wall in front of him, his left hand, pronating the palm as if to bless some holy place. And then, awkwardly at first, but with increasing grace and agility, he began to dig.

AFTER THE PLAGUE

After the plague—it was some sort of Ebola mutation passed from hand to hand and nose to nose like the common cold—life was different. More relaxed and expansive, more natural. The rat race was over, the freeways were clear all the way to Sacramento, and the poor dwindling ravaged planet was suddenly big and mysterious again. It was a kind of miracle really, what the environmentalists had been hoping for all along, though of course even the most strident of them wouldn't have wished for his own personal extinction, but there it was. I don't mean to sound callous—my parents are long dead and I'm unmarried and siblingless, but I lost friends, colleagues and neighbors, the same as any other survivor. What few of us there are, that is. We're guessing it's maybe one in ten thousand, here in the States anyway. I'm sure there are whole tribes that escaped it somewhere in the Amazon or the interior valleys of Indonesia, meteorologists in isolated weather stations, fire lookouts, goatherds and the like. But the president's gone, the vice president, the cabinet, Congress, the joint chiefs of staff, the chairmen of the boards and CEOs of the Fortune 500 companies, along with all their stockholders, employees and retainers. There's no TV. No electricity or running water. And there won't be any dining out anytime soon.

Actually, I'm lucky to be here to tell you about it—it was sheer serendipity, really. You see, I wasn't among my fellow human beings when it hit—no festering airline cabins or snaking supermarket lines for me, no concerts, sporting events or crowded

restaurants—and the closest I came to intimate contact was a telephone call to my on-and-off girlfriend, Danielle, from a gas station in the Sierra foothills. I think I may have made a kissing noise
over the wire, my lips very possibly coming into contact with the
molded plastic mouthpiece into which hordes of strangers had
breathed before me, but this was a good two weeks before the first
victim carried the great dripping bag of infection that was himself
back from a camcorder safari to the Ngorongoro Crater or a con-
ference on economic development in Malawi. Danielle, whose
voice was a drug I was trying to kick, at least temporarily, promised to come join me for a weekend in the cabin after my six weeks
of self-imposed isolation were over, but sadly, she never made it.
Neither did anyone else.

I *was* isolated up there in the mountains—that was the whole
point—and the first I heard of anything amiss was over the radio.
It was a warm, full-bodied day in early fall, the sun caught like a
child's ball in the crown of the Jeffrey pine outside the window,
and I was washing up after lunch when a smooth melodious voice
interrupted *Afternoon Classics* to say that people were bleeding
from the eyeballs and vomiting up bile in the New York subways
and collapsing en masse in the streets of the capital. The authorities were fully prepared to deal with what they were calling a
minor outbreak of swine flu, the voice said, and people were cau-
tioned not to panic, but all at once the announcer seemed to
chuckle deep in his throat, and then, right in the middle of the
next phrase, he sneezed—a controlled explosion hurtling out
over the airwaves to detonate ominously in ten million trembling
speakers—and the radio fell silent. Somebody put on a CD of
Richard Strauss' *Death and Transfiguration*, and it played over and
over through the rest of the afternoon.

    I didn't have access to a telephone—not unless I hiked two and
a half miles out to the road where I'd parked my car and then
drove another six to Fish Fry Flats, pop. 28, and used the public phone at the bar/restaurant/gift shop/one-stop grocery/gas
station there—so I ran the dial up and down the radio to see

if I could get some news. Reception is pretty spotty up in the mountains—you never knew whether you'd get Bakersfield, Fresno, San Luis Obispo or even Tijuana—and I couldn't pull in anything but white noise on that particular afternoon, except for the aforementioned tone poem, that is. I was powerless. What would happen would happen, and I'd find out all the sordid details a week later, just as I found out about all the other crises, scandals, scoops, coups, typhoons, wars and cease-fires that held the world spellbound while I communed with the ground squirrels and woodpeckers. It was funny. The big events didn't seem to mean much up here in the mountains, where life was so much more elemental and immediate and the telling concerns of the day revolved around priming the water pump and lighting the balky old gas stove without blowing the place up. I picked up a worn copy of John Cheever's stories somebody had left in the cabin during one of its previous incarnations and forgot all about the news out of New York and Washington.

Later, when it finally came to me that I couldn't live through another measure of Strauss without risk of permanent impairment, I flicked off the radio, put on a light jacket and went out to glory in the way the season had touched the aspens along the path out to the road. The sun was leaning way over to the west now, the shrubs and ground litter gathering up the night, the tall trees trailing deep blue shadows. There was the faintest breath of a chill in the air, a premonition of winter, and I thought of the simple pleasures of building a fire, preparing a homely meal and sitting through the evening with a book in one hand and a scotch and Drambuie in the other. It wasn't until nine or ten at night that I remembered the bleeding eyeballs and the fateful sneeze, and though I was half-convinced it was a hoax or maybe one of those fugitive terrorist attacks with a colorless, odorless gas—sarin or the like—I turned on the radio, eager for news.

There was nothing, no Strauss, no crisp and efficient NPR correspondent delivering news of riots in Cincinnati and the imminent collapse of the infrastructure, no right-wing talk, no hip-hop, no jazz, no rock. I switched to AM, and after a painstaking search I hit on a weak signal that sounded as if it were coming from the bottom of Santa Monica Bay. *This is only a test*, a mechanical voice pronounced in what was now just the faintest whispering squeak, *in the event of an actual emergency please stay tuned to* . . . and then it faded out. While I was fumbling to bring it back in, I happened upon a voice shouting something in Spanish. It was just a single voice, very agitated, rolling on tirelessly, and I listened in wonder and dread until the signal went dead just after midnight.

I didn't sleep that night. I'd begun to divine the magnitude of what was going on in the world below me—this was no hoax, no casual atrocity or ordinary attrition; this was the beginning of the end, the Apocalypse, the utter failure and ultimate demise of all things human. I felt sick at heart. Lying there in the fastness of the cabin in the absolute and abiding dark of the wilderness, I was consumed with fear. I lay on my stomach and listened to the steady thunder of my heart pounding through the mattress, attuned to the slightest variation, waiting like a condemned man for the first harrowing sneeze.

Over the course of the next several days, the radio would sporadically come to life (I left it switched on at all times, day and night, as if I were going down in a sinking ship and could shout "Mayday!" into the receiver at the first stirring of a human voice). I'd be pacing the floor or spooning sugar into my tea or staring at a freshly inserted and eternally blank page in my ancient manual typewriter when the static would momentarily clear and a harried newscaster spoke out of the void to provide me with the odd and horrific detail: an oceanliner had run aground off Cape Hatteras and nothing left aboard except three sleek and frisky cats and various puddles of flesh swathed in plaid shorts, polo shirts and sunglasses; no sound or signal had come out of South Florida in over thirty-six hours; a group of survivalists had seized Bill Gates' private jet in an attempt to escape to Antarctica, where it was thought the infection hadn't yet reached, but everyone aboard vomited black bile and died before the plane could leave the ground. Another announcer broke down in the middle of an unconfirmed report that every man, woman and child in Minneapolis was dead, and yet another came over the air early one morning shouting, "It kills! It kills! It kills in three days!" At that point, I jerked the plug out of the wall.

My first impulse, of course, was to help. To save Danielle, the frail and the weak, the young and the old, the chairman of the social studies department at the school where I teach (or taught), a student teacher with cropped red hair about whom I'd had several minutely detailed sexual fantasies. I even went so far as to hike out to the road and take the car into Fish Fry Flats, but the bar/restaurant/gift shop/one-stop grocery/gas station was closed and locked and the parking lot deserted. I drove round the lot three times, debating whether I should continue on down the road or not, but then a lean furtive figure darted out of a shed at the corner of the lot and threw itself—himself—into the shadows beneath the deck of the main building. I recognized the figure immediately as the splay-footed and pony-tailed proprietor of the place, a man who would pump your gas with an inviting smile and then lure you into the gift shop to pay in the hope that the hand-carved Tule Indian figurines and Pen-Lite batteries would prove irresistible. I saw his feet protruding from beneath the deck, and they seemed to be jittering or trembling as if he were doing some sort of energetic new contra-dance that began in the prone position. For a long moment I sat there and watched those dancing feet, then I hit the lock button, rolled up the windows and drove back to the cabin.

What did I do? Ultimately? Nothing. Call it enlightened self-interest. Call it solipsism, self-preservation, cowardice, I don't care. I was terrified—who wouldn't be?—and I decided to stay put. I had plenty of food and firewood, fuel for the generator and propane for the stove, three reams of twenty-five percent cotton fiber bond, correction fluid, books, board games—Parcheesi and Monopoly—and a complete set of *National Geographic*, 1947–1962. (By way of explanation, I should mention that I am—or was—a social studies teacher at the Montecito School, a preparatory academy in a pricey suburb of Santa Barbara, and that the serendipity that spared me the fate of nearly all my fellow men and women was as simple and fortuitous a thing as a sabbatical leave. After fourteen years of unstinting service, I applied for and was granted a one-semester leave at half-salary for the purpose of writing a memoir of my deprived and miserable Irish-Catholic upbringing. The previous year a high school teacher from New York—the name escapes me now—had enjoyed a spectacular *succès d'estime*, not to mention *d'argent*, with a memoir about his own miserable and deprived Irish-Catholic boyhood, and I felt I could profitably mine the same territory. And I got a good start on it too, until the plague hit. Now I ask myself what's the use—the publishers are all dead. Ditto the editors, agents, reviewers, booksellers and the great congenial book-buying public itself. What's the sense of writing? What's the sense of anything?)

At any rate, I stuck close to the cabin, writing at the kitchen table through the mornings, staring out the window into the ankles of the pines and redwoods as I summoned degrading memories of my alcoholic mother, father, aunts, uncles, cousins and grandparents, and in the afternoons I hiked up to the highest peak and looked down on the deceptive tranquillity of the San Joaquin Valley spread out like a continent below me. There were no planes in the sky overhead, no sign of traffic or movement anywhere, no sounds but the calling of the birds and the soughing of the trees as the breeze sifted through them. I stayed up there past dark one night and felt as serene and terrible as a god when I looked down at the velvet expanse of the world and saw no ray or glimmer of light. I plugged the radio back in that night, just to hear the fading comfort of man-made noise, of the static that emanates from nowhere and nothing. Because there was nothing out there, not anymore.

It was four weeks later—just about the time I was to have ended my hermitage and enjoyed the promised visit from Danielle—that I had my first human contact of the new age. I was at the kitchen window, beating powdered eggs into a froth for dinner, one ear half-attuned to the perfect and unbroken static hum of the radio, when there was a heavy thump on the deteriorating planks of the front deck. My first thought was that a branch had dropped out of the Jeffrey pine—or worse, that a bear had got wind of the corned beef hash I'd opened to complement the powdered eggs—but I was mistaken on both counts. The thump was still reverberating through the floorboards when I was surprised to hear a moan and then a curse—a distinctly human curse. "Oh, shit-fuck!" a woman's voice cried. "Open the goddamned door! Help, for shit's sake, help!"

I've always been a cautious animal. This may be one of my great failings, as my mother and later my fraternity brothers were always quick to point out, but on the other hand, it may be my greatest virtue. It's kept me alive when the rest of humanity has gone on to a quick and brutal extinction, and it didn't fail me in that moment. The door was locked. Once I'd got wind of what was going on in the world, though I was devastated and the thought of the radical transformation of everything I'd ever known gnawed at me day and night, I took to locking it against just such an eventuality as this. "Shit!" the voice raged. "I can hear you in there, you son of a bitch—I can *smell* you!"

I stood perfectly still and held my breath. The static breathed dismally through the speakers and I wished I'd had the sense to disconnect the radio long ago. I stared down at the half-beaten eggs.

"I'm dying out here!" the voice cried. "I'm starving to death— hey, are you deaf in there or what? I said, I'm *starving!*"

And now of course I was faced with a moral dilemma. Here was a fellow human being in need of help, a member of a species whose value had just vaulted into the rarefied atmosphere occupied by the gnatcatcher, the condor and the beluga whale by virtue of its rarity. Help her? Of course I would help her. But at the same time, I knew if I opened that door I would invite the pestilence in and that three days hence both she and I would be reduced to our mortal remains.

"Open up!" she demanded, and the tattoo of her fists was the thunder of doom on the thin planks of the door.

It occurred to me suddenly that she couldn't be infected— she'd have been dead and wasted by now if she were. Maybe she was like me, maybe she'd been out brooding in her own cabin or hiking the mountain trails, utterly oblivious and immune to the general calamity. Maybe she was beautiful, nubile, a new Eve for a new age, maybe she would fill my nights with passion and my days with joy. As if in a trance, I crossed the room and stood at the door, my fingers on the long brass stem of the bolt. "Are you alone?" I said, and the rasp of my own voice, so long in disuse, sounded strange in my ears.

I heard her draw in a breath of astonishment and outrage from the far side of the thin panel that separated us. "What the hell do you think, you son of a bitch? I've been lost out here in these stinking woods for I don't know how long and I haven't had a scrap for days, not a goddamn scrap, not even bark or grass or a handful of soggy trail mix. *Now will you fucking open this door?!*"

Still, I hesitated.

A rending sound came to me then, a sound that tore me open as surely as a surgical knife, from my groin to my throat: she was sobbing. Gagging for breath, and sobbing. "A frog," she sobbed, "I ate a goddamn slimy little putrid *frog!*"

God help me. God save and preserve me. I opened the door.

Sarai was thirty-eight years old—that is, three years older than I—and she was no beauty. Not on the surface, anyway. Even if you discounted the twenty-odd pounds she'd lost and her hair that was like some crushed rodent's pelt and the cuts and bites and suppurating sores that made her skin look like a leper's, and tried, by a powerful leap of the imagination, to see her as she once might have been, safely ensconced in her condo in Tarzana and surrounded by all the accoutrements of feminine hygiene and beauty, she still wasn't much.

This was her story: she and her live-in boyfriend, Howard, were nature enthusiasts—at least Howard was, anyway—and just before the plague hit they'd set out to hike an interlocking series of trails in the Golden Trout Wilderness. They were well provisioned, with the best of everything—Howard managed a sporting goods store—and for the first three weeks everything went according to plan. They ate delicious freeze-dried fettuccine Alfredo and shrimp couscous, drank cognac from a bota bag and made love wrapped in propylene, Gore-Tex and nylon. Mosquitoes and horseflies sampled her legs, but she felt good, born again, liberated from the traffic and the smog and her miserable desk in a miserable corner of the electronics company her father had founded. Then one morning, when they were camped by a stream, Howard went off with his day pack and a fly rod and never came back. She waited. She searched. She screamed herself hoarse. A week went by. Every day she searched in a new direction, following the stream both ways and combing every tiny rill and tributary, until finally she got herself lost. All streams were one stream, all hills and ridges alike. She had three Kudos bars with her and a six-ounce bag of peanuts, but no shelter and no freeze-dried entrées—all that was back at the camp she and Howard had made in happier times. A cold rain fell. There were no stars that night, and when something moved in the brush beside her she panicked and ran blindly through the dark, hammering her shins and destroying her face, her hair and her clothes. She'd been wandering ever since.

I made her a package of Top Ramen, gave her a towel and a bar of soap and showed her the primitive shower I'd rigged up above the ancient slab of the tub. I was afraid to touch her or even come too close to her. Sure I was skittish. Who wouldn't be when ninety-nine percent of the human race had just died off on the tailwind of a simple sneeze? Besides, I'd begun to adopt all the habits of the hermit—talking to myself, performing elaborate rituals over my felicitous stock of foodstuffs, dredging bursts of elementary school songs and beer jingles out of the depths of my impacted brain—and I resented having my space invaded. *Still.* Still, though, I felt that Sarai had been delivered to me by some higher power and that she'd been blessed in the way that I was— we'd escaped the infection. We'd survived. And we weren't just errant members of a selfish, suspicious and fragmented society, but the very foundation of a new one. She was a woman. I was a man.

At first, she wouldn't believe me when I waved a dismissive

hand at the ridge behind the cabin and all that lay beyond it and informed her that the world was depeopled, that the Apocalypse had come and that she and I were among the solitary survivors—and who could blame her? As she sipped my soup and ate my flapjacks and treated her cuts and abrasions with my Neosporin and her hair with my shampoo, she must have thought she'd found a lunatic as her savior. "If you don't believe me," I said, and I was gloating, I was, sick as it may seem, "try the radio."

She looked up at me out of the leery brooding eyes of the one sane woman in a madhouse of impostors, plugged the cord in the socket and calibrated the dial as meticulously as a safecracker. She was rewarded by static—no dynamics even, just a single dull continuum—but she glared up at me as if I'd rigged the thing to disappoint her. "*So,*" she spat, skinny as a refugee, her hair kinked and puffed up with my shampoo till it devoured her parsimonious and disbelieving little sliver of a face, "that doesn't prove a thing. It's broken, that's all."

When she got her strength back, we hiked out to the car and drove into Fish Fry Flats so she could see for herself. I was half-crazy with the terrible weight of the knowledge I'd been forced to hold inside me, and I can't describe the irritation I felt at her utter lack of interest—she treated me like a street gibberer, a psychotic, Cassandra in long pants. She condescended to me. She was *humoring* me, for God's sake, and the whole world lay in ruins around us. But she would have a rude awakening, she would, and the thought of it was what kept me from saying something I'd regret—I didn't want to lose my temper and scare her off, but I hate stupidity and willfulness. It's the one thing I won't tolerate in my students. Or wouldn't. Or didn't.

Fish Fry Flats, which in the best of times could hardly be mistaken for a metropolis, looked now as if it had been deserted for a decade. Weeds had begun to sprout up through invisible cracks in the pavement, dust had settled over the idle gas pumps and the windows of the main building were etched with grime. And the animals—the animals were everywhere, marmots waddling across the lot as if they owned it, a pair of coyotes asleep in the shade of an abandoned pickup, ravens cawing and squirrels chittering. I cut the engine just as a bear the color of cinnamon toast tumbled stupendously through an already shattered window and lay on his back, waving his bloodied paws in the air as if he were drunk, which he was. As we discovered a few minutes later— once he'd lurched to his feet and staggered off into the bushes—a whole host of creatures had raided the grocery, stripping the candy display right down to the twisted wire rack, scattering Triscuits and Doritos, shattering jars of jam and jugs of port wine and grinding the hand-carved Tule Indian figurines underfoot. There was no sign of the formerly sunny proprietor or of his dancing feet—I could only imagine that the ravens, coyotes and ants had done their work.

But Sarai—she was still an unbeliever, even after she dropped a quarter into the public telephone and put the dead black plastic receiver to her ear. For all the good it did her, she might as well have tried coaxing a dial tone out of a stone or a block of wood, and I told her so. She gave me a sour look, the sticks of her bones briefly animated beneath a sweater and jacket I'd loaned her—it was the end of October and getting cold at seventy-two hundred feet—and then she tried another quarter, and then another, before she slammed the receiver down in a rage and turned her seething face on me. "The lines are down, that's all," she sneered. And then her mantra: "It doesn't prove a thing."

While she'd been frustrating herself, I'd been loading the car with canned goods, after entering the main building through the broken window and unlatching the door from the inside. "And what about all this?" I said, irritated, hot with it, sick to death of her and her thick-headedness. I gestured at the bloated and lazy coyotes, the hump in the bushes that was the drunken bear, the waddling marmots and the proprietary ravens.

"I don't know," she said, clenching her jaws. "And I don't care." Her eyes had a dull sheen to them. They were insipid and bovine, exactly the color of the dirt at her feet. And her lips—thin and stingy, collapsed in a riot of vertical lines like a dried-up mud puddle. I hated her in that moment, godsend or no. Oh, how I hated her.

"What are you *doing?*" she demanded as I loaded the last of the groceries into the car, settled into the driver's seat and turned the engine over. She was ten feet from me, caught midway between the moribund phone booth and the living car. One of the coyotes lifted its head at the vehemence of her tone and gave her a sleepy, yellow-eyed look.

"Going back to the cabin," I said.

"You're *what?*" Her face was pained. She'd been through agonies. I was a devil and a madman.

"Listen, Sarai, it's all over. I've told you time and again. You don't have a job anymore. You don't have to pay rent, utility bills, don't have to make car payments or remember your mother's birthday. It's over. Don't you get it?"

"You're insane! You're a shithead! I hate you!"

The engine was purring beneath my feet, fuel awasting, but there was infinite fuel now, and though I realized the gas pumps would no longer work, there were millions upon millions of cars and trucks out there in the world with full tanks to siphon, and no one around to protest. I could drive a Ferrari if I wanted, a Rolls, a Jag, anything. I could sleep on a bed of jewels, stuff the mattress with hundred-dollar bills, prance through the streets in a new pair of Italian loafers and throw them into the gutter each night and get a new pair in the morning. But I was afraid. Afraid of the infection, the silence, the bones rattling in the wind. "I know it," I said. "I'm insane. I'm a shithead. I admit it. But I'm going back to the cabin and you can do anything you want—it's a free country. Or at least it used to be."

I wanted to add that it was a free world now, a free universe, and that God was in the details, the biblical God, the God of famine, flood and pestilence, but I never got the chance. Before I could open my mouth she bent for a stone and heaved it into the windshield, splintering me with flecks and shards of safety glass. "Die!" she shrieked. "*You* die, you shit!"

That night we slept together for the first time. In the morning, we packed up a few things and drove down the snaking mountain road to the charnel house of the world.

I have to confess that I've never been much of a fan of the apocalyptic potboiler, the doomsday film shot through with special effects and asinine dialogue or the cyberpunk version of a grim and relentless future. What these entertainments had led us to expect—the roving gangs, the inhumanity, the ascendancy of machines and the redoubled pollution and ravaging of the earth—wasn't at all what it was like. There were no roving gangs—they were all dead, to a man, woman and tattooed punk—and the only machines still functioning were the automobiles and weed whippers and such that we the survivors chose to put into prosaic action. And a further irony was that the survivors were the least likely and least qualified to organize anything, either for better or worse. We were the fugitive, the misfit, the recluse, and we were so widely scattered we'd never come into contact with one another, anyway—and that was just the way we liked it. There wasn't even any looting of the supermarkets—there was no need. There was more than enough for everybody who ever was or would be.

Sarai and I drove down the mountain road, through the deserted small town of Springville and the deserted larger town of Porterville, and then we turned south for Bakersfield, the Grapevine and Southern California. She wanted to go back to her apartment, to Los Angeles, and see if her parents and her sisters were alive still—she became increasingly vociferous on that score as the reality of what had happened began to seep through to her—but I was driving and I wanted to avoid Los Angeles at all costs. To my mind, the place had been a pit before the scourge hit, and now it was a pit heaped with seven million moldering corpses. She carped and moaned and whined and threatened, but she was in shock too and couldn't quite work herself up to her usual pitch, and so we turned west and north on Route 126 and headed toward Montecito, where for the past ten years I'd lived in a cottage on one of the big estates there—the DuPompier place, *Mírame*.

By the way, when I mentioned earlier that the freeways were clear, I was speaking metaphorically—they were free of traffic, but cluttered with abandoned vehicles of all sorts, take your pick, from gleaming choppers with thousand-dollar gold-fleck paint jobs to sensible family cars, Corvettes, Winnebagos, eighteen-wheelers and even fire engines and police cruisers. Twice, when Sarai became especially insistent, I pulled alongside one or another of these abandoned cars, swung open her door and said, "Go ahead. Take this Cadillac"—or BMW or whatever—"and drive yourself any damn place you please. Go on. What are you waiting for?" But her face shrank till it was as small as a doll's and her eyes went stony with fear: those cars were catacombs, each and every one of them, and the horror of that was more than anybody could bear.

So we drove on, through a preternatural silence and a world that already seemed primeval, up the Coast Highway and along the frothing bright boatless sea and into Montecito. It was evening when we arrived, and there wasn't a soul in sight. If it weren't for that—and a certain creeping untended look to the lawns, shrubs and trees—you wouldn't have noticed anything out of the ordinary. My cottage, built in the twenties of local sandstone and draped in wisteria till it was all but invisible, was exactly as I'd left it. We pulled into the silent drive with the great house looming in the near distance, a field of dark reflective glass that held the blood of the declining sun in it, and Sarai barely glanced up. Her thin shoulders were hunched and she was staring at a worn place on the mat between her feet.

"We're here," I announced, and I got out of the car.

She turned her eyes to me, stricken, suffering, a waif. "Where?"

"Home."

It took her a moment, but when she responded she spoke slowly and carefully, as if she were just learning the language. "I have no home," she said. "Not anymore."

So. What to tell you? We didn't last long, Sarai and I, though we were pioneers, though we were the last hope of the race, drawn together by the tenacious glue of fear and loneliness. I knew there wouldn't be much opportunity for dating in the near future, but we just weren't suited to each other. In fact, we were as unsuited as any two people could ever be, and our sex was tedious and obligatory, a ballet of mutual need and loathing, but to my mind at least, there was a bright side—here was the chance to go forth and be fruitful and do what we could to repopulate the vast and aching sphere of the planet. Within the month, however, Sarai had disabused me of that notion.

It was a silky, fog-hung morning, the day deepening around us, and we'd just gone through the mechanics of sex and were lying exhausted and unsatisfied in the rumple of my gritty sheets (water was a problem and we did what laundry we could with what we were able to haul down from the estate's swimming pool). Sarai was breathing through her mouth, an irritating snort and burble that got on my nerves, but before I could say anything, she spoke in a hard shriveled little nugget of a voice. "You're no Howard," she said.

"Howard's dead," I said. "He deserted you."

She was staring at the ceiling. "Howard was gold," she mused in a languid, reflective voice, "and you're shit."

It was childish, I know, but the dig at my sexual performance really stung—not to mention the ingratitude of the woman—and I came back at her. "You came to me," I said. "I didn't ask for it—I was doing fine out there on the mountain without you. And where do you think you'd be now if it wasn't for me? Huh?"

She didn't answer right away, but I could feel her consolidating in the bed beside me, magma becoming rock. "I'm not going to have sex with you again," she said, and still she was staring at the ceiling. "Ever. I'd rather use my finger."

"You're no Danielle," I said.

She sat up then, furious, all her ribs showing and her shrunken breasts clinging to the remains of them like an afterthought. "Fuck Danielle," she spat. "And fuck you."

I watched her dress in silence, but as she was lacing up her hiking boots I couldn't resist saying, "It's no joy for me either, Sarai, but there's a higher principle involved here than our likes and dis-likes or any kind of animal gratification, and I think you know what I'm talking about—"

She was perched on the edge of a leather armchair I'd picked up at a yard sale years ago, when money and things had their own reality. She'd laced up the right boot and was working on the left, laces the color of rust, blunt white fingers with the nails bitten to the quick. Her mouth hung open slightly and I could see the pink tip of her tongue caught between her teeth as she worked mind-lessly at her task, reverting like a child to her earliest training and her earliest habits. She gave me a blank look.

"Procreation, I mean. If you look at it in a certain way, it's— well, it's our duty."

Her laugh stung me. It was sharp and quick, like the thrust of a knife. "You idiot," she said, and she laughed again, showing the gold in her back teeth. "I hate children, always have—they're little monsters that grow up to be uptight fussy pricks like you." She paused, smiled, and released an audible breath. "I had my tubes tied fifteen years ago."

That night she moved into the big house, a replica of a Moor-ish castle in Seville, replete with turrets and battlements. The paintings and furnishings were exquisite, and there were some twelve thousand square feet of living space, graced with carved wooden ceilings, colored tiles, rectangular arches, a loggia and formal gardens. Nor had the DuPompiers spoiled the place by being so thoughtless as to succumb inside—they'd died, Julius, Eleanor and their daughter, Kelly, under the arbor in back, the white bones of their hands eternally clasped. I wished Sarai good use of the place. I did. Because by that point I didn't care if she moved into the White House, so long as I didn't have to deal with her anymore.

Weeks slipped by. Months. Occasionally I would see the light of Sarai's Coleman lantern lingering in one of the high windows of *Mírame* as night fell over the coast, but essentially I was as solitary—and as lonely—as I'd been in the cabin in the mountains. The rains came and went. It was spring. Everywhere the untended gardens ran wild, the lawns became fields, the orchards forests, and I took to walking round the neighborhood with a baseball bat to ward off the packs of feral dogs for which Alpo would never again materialize in a neat bowl in the corner of a dry and warm kitchen. And then one afternoon, while I was at Von's, browsing the aisles for pasta, bottled marinara and Green Giant asparagus spears amid a scattering of rats and the lingering stench of the perished perishables, I detected movement at the far end of the next aisle over. My first thought was that it must be a dog or a coyote that had somehow managed to get in to feed on the rats or the big twenty-five-pound bags of Purina Dog Chow, but then, with a shock, I realized I wasn't alone in the store.

In all the time I'd been coming here for groceries, I'd never seen a soul, not even Sarai or one of the six or seven other survivors who were out there occupying the mansions in the hills. Every once in a while I'd see lights shining in the wall of the night—someone had even managed to fire up a generator at Las Tejas, a big Italianate villa half a mile away—and every so often a car would go helling up the distant freeway, but basically we survivors were shy of one another and kept to ourselves. It was fear, of course, the little spark of panic that told you the contagion was abroad again and that the best way to avoid it was to avoid all human contact. So we did. Strenuously.

But I couldn't ignore the squeak and rattle of a shopping cart wheeling up the bottled water aisle, and when I turned the corner, there she was, Felicia, with her flowing hair and her scared and sorry eyes. I didn't know her name then, not at first, but I recognized her—she was one of the tellers at the Bank of America branch where I cashed my checks. Formerly cashed them, that is. My first impulse was to back wordlessly away, but I mastered it— how could I be afraid of what was human, so palpably human, and appealing? "Hello," I said, to break the tension, and then I was going to say something stupid like "I see you made it too" or "Tough times, huh?" but instead I settled for "Remember me?"

She looked stricken. Looked as if she were about to bolt—or die on the spot. But her lips were brave and they came together and uttered my name. "Mr. Halloran?" she said, and it was so ordinary, so plebeian, so real.

I smiled and nodded. My name is—was—Francis Xavier Halloran III, a name I've hated since Tyrone Johnson (now presumably dead) tormented me with it in kindergarten, chanting "Francis, Francis, Francis" till I wanted to sink through the floor. But it was a new world now, a world burgeoning and bursting at the seams to discover the lineaments of its new forms and rituals. "Call me Jed," I said.

Nothing happens overnight, especially not in plague times. We were wary of each other, and every banal phrase and stultifying cliché of the small talk we made as I helped her load her groceries into the back of her Range Rover reverberated hugely with the absence of all the multitudes who'd used those phrases before us. Still, I got her address that afternoon—she'd moved into Villa Ruscello, a mammoth place set against the mountains, with a creek, pond and Jacuzzi for fresh water—and I picked her up two nights later in a Rolls Silver Cloud and took her to my favorite French restaurant. The place was untouched and pristine, with a sweeping view of the sea, and I lit some candles and poured us each a glass of twenty-year-old Bordeaux, after which we feasted on canned crab, truffles, cashews and marinated artichoke hearts.

I'd like to tell you that she was beautiful, because that's the way it should be, the way of the fable and the fairy tale, but she wasn't—or not conventionally, anyway. She was a little heavier than she might have been ideally, but that was a relief after stringy Sarai, and her eyes were ever so slightly crossed. Yet she was decent and kind, sweet even, and more important, she was available.

We took walks together, raided overgrown gardens for lettuce, tomatoes and zucchini, planted strawberries and snow peas in the middle of the waist-high lawn at Villa Ruscello. One day we drove to the mountains and brought back the generator so we could have lights and refrigeration in the cottage—ice cubes, now there was a luxury—and begin to work our way through the eight thousand titles at the local video store. It was nearly a month before anything happened between us—anything sexual, that is. And when it did, she first felt obligated, out of a sense of survivor's guilt, I suppose, to explain to me how she came to be alive and breathing still when everyone she'd ever known had vanished off the face of the earth. We were in the beamed living room of my cottage, sharing a bottle of Dom Pérignon 1970, with the three-hundred-ten-dollar price tag still on it, and I'd started a fire against the gathering night and the wet raw smell of rain on the air. "You're going to think I'm an idiot," she said.

I made a noise of demurral and put my arm round her.

"Did you ever hear of a sensory deprivation tank?" She was peering up at me through the scrim of her hair, gold and red highlights, health in a bottle.

"Yeah, sure," I said. "But you don't mean—?"

"It was an older one, a model that's not on the market anymore—one of the originals. My roommate's sister—Julie Angier?—she had it out in her garage on Padaro, and she was really into it. You could get in touch with your inner self, relax, maybe even have an out-of-body experience, that's what she said, and I figured why not?" She gave me a look, shy and passionate at once, to let me know that she was the kind of girl who took experience seriously. "They put salt water in it, three hundred gallons, heated to your body temperature, and then they shut the lid on you and there's nothing, absolutely nothing there—it's like going to outer space. Or inner space. Inside yourself."

"And you were in there when—?"

She nodded. There was something in her eyes I couldn't read—pride, triumph, embarrassment, a spark of sheer lunacy. I gave her an encouraging smile.

"For days, I guess," she said. "I just sort of lost track of everything, who I was, where I was—you know? And I didn't wake up till the water started getting cold"—she looked at her feet—"which I guess is when the electricity went out because there was nobody left to run the power plants. And then I pushed open the lid and the sunlight through the window was like an atom bomb, and then, then I called out Julie's name, and she . . . well, she never answered."

Her voice died in her throat and she turned those sorrowful eyes on me. I put my other arm around her and held her. "Hush," I whispered, "it's all right now, everything's all right." It was a conventional thing to say, and it was a lie, but I said it, and I held her and felt her relax in my arms.

It was then, almost to the precise moment, that Sarai's naked sliver of a face appeared at the window, framed by her two uplifted hands and a rock the size of my Webster's unabridged. "What about *me*, you son of a bitch!" she shouted, and there it was again, everlasting stone and frangible glass, and not a glazier left alive on the planet.

I wanted to kill her. It was amazing—three people I knew of had survived the end of everything, and it was one too many. I felt vengeful. Biblical. I felt like storming Sarai's ostentatious castle and wringing her chicken neck for her, and I think I might have if it weren't for Felicia. "Don't let her spoil it for us," she murmured, the gentle pressure of her fingers on the back of my neck suddenly holding my full attention, and we went into the bedroom and closed the door on all that mess of emotion and glass.

In the morning, I stepped into the living room and was outraged all over again. I cursed and stomped and made a fool of myself over heaving the rock back through the window and attacking the shattered glass as if it were alive—I admit I was upset out of all proportion to the crime. This was a new world, a new beginning, and Sarai's nastiness and negativity had no place in it. Christ, there were only three of us—couldn't we get along?

Felicia had repaired dozens of windows in her time. Her little brothers (dead now) and her fiancé (dead too) were forever throwing balls around the house, and she assured me that a shattered window was nothing to get upset over (though she bit her lip and let her eyes fill at the mention of her fiancé, and who could blame her?). So we consulted the Yellow Pages, drove to the nearest window glass shop and broke in as gently as possible. Within the hour, the new pane had been installed and the putty was drying in the sun, and watching Felicia at work had so elevated my spirits I suggested a little shopping spree to celebrate.

"Celebrate what?" She was wearing a No Fear T-shirt and an Anaheim Angels cap and there was a smudge of off-white putty on her chin.

"You," I said. "The simple miracle of you."

And that was fine. We parked on the deserted streets of downtown Santa Barbara and had the stores to ourselves—clothes, the latest (and last) bestsellers, CDs, a new disc player to go with our newly electrified house. Others had visited some of the stores before us, of course, but they'd been polite and neat about it, almost as if they were afraid to betray their presence, and they always closed the door behind them. We saw deer feeding in the courtyards and one magnificent tawny mountain lion stalking the wrong way up a one-way street. By the time we got home, I was elated. Everything was going to work out, I was sure of it.

The mood didn't last long. As I swung into the drive, the first thing I saw was the yawning gap where the new window had been, and beyond it, the undifferentiated heap of rubble that used to be my living room. Sarai had been back. And this time she'd done a thorough job, smashing lamps and pottery, poking holes in our cans of beef stew and chili con carne, scattering coffee, flour and sugar all over everything and dumping sand in the generator's fuel tank. Worst of all, she'd taken half a dozen pairs of Felicia's panties and nailed them to the living room wall, a crude X slashed across the crotch of each pair. It was hateful and savage—human, that's what it was, human—and it killed all the joy we'd taken in the afternoon and the animals and the infinite and various riches of the mall. Sarai had turned it all to shit.

"We'll move to my place," Felicia said. "Or any place you want. How about an oceanfront house—didn't you say you'd always wanted to live right on the ocean?"

I had. But I didn't want to admit it. I stood in the middle of the desecrated kitchen and clenched my fists. "I don't want any other place. This is my home. I've lived here for ten years and I'll be damned if I'm going to let *her* drive me out."

It was an irrational attitude—again, childish—and Felicia convinced me to pack up a few personal items (my high school yearbook, my reggae albums, a signed first edition of *For Whom the Bell Tolls*, a pair of deer antlers I'd found in the woods when I was eight) and move into a place on the ocean for a few days. We drove along the coast road at a slow, stately pace, looking over this house or that, until we finally settled on a grand modern place that was all angles and glass and broad sprawling decks. I got lucky and caught a few perch in the surf, and we barbecued them on the beach and watched the sun sink into the western bluffs.

The next few days were idyllic, and we thought about little beyond love and food and the way the water felt on our skin at one hour of the day or another, but still, the question of Sarai nagged at me. I was reminded of her every time I wanted a cold drink, for instance, or when the sun set and we had to make do with candles and kerosene lanterns—we'd have to go out and dig up another generator, we knew that, but they weren't exactly in demand in a place like Santa Barbara (in the old days, that is) and we didn't know where to look. And so yes, I couldn't shake the image of Sarai and the look on her face and the things she'd said and done. And I missed my house, because I'm a creature of habit, like anybody else. Or more so. Definitely more so.

Anyway, the solution came to us a week later, and it came in human form—at least it appeared in human form, but it was a miracle and no doubt about it. Felicia and I were both on the beach—naked, of course, as naked and without shame or knowledge of it as Eve and Adam—when we saw a figure marching resolutely up the long curving finger of sand that stretched away into the haze of infinity. As the figure drew closer, we saw that it was a man, a man with a scraggly salt-and-pepper beard and hair the same color trailing away from a bald spot worn into his crown. He was dressed in hiking clothes, big-grid boots, a bright blue pack riding his back like a second set of shoulders. We stood there, naked, and greeted him.

"Hello," he said, stopping a few feet from us and staring first at my face, then at Felicia's breasts, and finally, with an effort, bending to check the laces of his boots. "Glad to see you two made it," he said, speaking to the sand.

"Likewise," I returned.

Over lunch on the deck—shrimp salad sandwiches on Felicia-baked bread—we traded stories. It seems he was hiking in the mountains when the pestilence descended—"The mountains?" I interrupted. "Whereabouts?"

"Oh," he said, waving a dismissive hand, "up in the Sierras, just above this little town—you've probably never heard of it—Fish Fry Flats?"

I let him go on a while, explaining how he'd lost his girlfriend and wandered for days before he finally came out on a mountain road and appropriated a car to go on down to Los Angeles—"One big cemetery"—and how he'd come up the coast and had been wandering ever since. I don't think I've ever felt such exhilaration, such a rush of excitement, such perfect and inimitable a sense of closure.

I couldn't keep from interrupting him again. "I'm clairvoyant," I said, raising my glass to the man sitting opposite me, to Felicia and her breasts, to the happy fishes in the teeming seas and the birds flocking without number in the unencumbered skies. "Your name's Howard, right?"

Howard was stunned. He set down his sandwich and wiped a fleck of mayonnaise from his lips. "How did you guess?" he said, gaping up at me out of eyes that were innocent and pure, the newest eyes in the world.

I just smiled and shrugged, as if it were my secret. "After lunch," I said, "I've got somebody I want you to meet."

In fourteen smart, funny, and richly crafted works,
T. C. Boyle strips away the veneer of respectability
draped across the American psyche, and
exposes the comical truths beneath.

AFTER THE PLAGUE

These sixteen stories display an astonishing range, as Boyle zeroes in on everything from air rage to abortion doctors to the story of a 1920s Sicilian immigrant who constructs an amazing underground mansion in an effort to woo his sweetheart. By turns mythic and realistic, farcical and tragic, ironic and moving, these new stories find "one of the most inventive and verbally exuberant writers" (*The New York Times*) at the top of his form.   *ISBN 0-14-200141-4*

BUDDING PROSPECTS

All Felix and his friends have to do is harvest a crop of *Cannabis Sativa* and half a million tax-free dollars will be theirs. But as their beloved buds wither under assault from ravenous scavengers, human caprice, and a drug-busting state trooper named Jerpbak, their dreams of easy money go up in smoke. "Consistently, effortlessly, intelligently funny." —*The New York Times*   *ISBN 0-14-029996-3*

DESCENT OF MAN

A primate-center researcher becomes romantically involved with a chimp. A Norse poet overcomes bard-block. These and other strange occurrences come together in Boyle's collection of satirical stories that brilliantly express just what the "evolution" of mankind has wrought. "Madness that hits you where you live." —*Houston Chronicle*
ISBN 0-14-029994-7

EAST IS EAST

Young Japanese seaman Hiro Tanaka jumps ship off the coast of Georgia and swims into a net of rabid rednecks, genteel ladies, descendants of slaves, and the denizens of an artists' colony. *The New York Times* called this sexy, hilarious tragicomedy a "pastoral version of *The Bonfire of the Vanities.*"   *ISBN 0-14-013167-1*

GREASY LAKE AND OTHER STORIES

Mythic and realistic, these masterful stories are, according to *The New York Times*, "satirical fables of contemporary life, so funny and acutely observed that they might have been written by Evelyn Waugh as sketches for . . . *Saturday Night Live.*"
ISBN 0-14-007781-2

IF THE RIVER WAS WHISKEY

Boyle, winner of the 1999 PEN/Malamud award for short fiction, tears through the walls of contemporary society to reveal a world at once comic and tragic, droll and horrific, in these sixteen magical and provocative stories. "Writing at its very, very best." —*USA Today*   *ISBN 0-14-011950-7*

RIVEN ROCK

With his seventh novel to date, T. C. Boyle pens a heartbreaking love story taken from between the lines of history. Millionaire Stanley McCormick, diagnosed as a schizophrenic and sexual maniac shortly after his marriage, is forbidden the sight of women, but his strong-willed, virginal wife Katherine Dexter is determined to cure him. "As romantic as it is informative, as colorful as it is convincing. Boyle combines his gift for historical re-creation with his dazzling powers as a storyteller."—*The Boston Globe*

ISBN 0-14-027166-X

THE ROAD TO WELLVILLE

Centering on John Harvey Kellogg and his turn-of-the-century Battle Creek Spa, this wickedly comic novel brims with a Dickensian cast of characters and is laced with wildly wonderful plot twists. "A marvel, enjoyable from the beginning to end." —Jane Smiley, *The New York Times Book Review*

ISBN 0-14-016718-8

T. C. BOYLE STORIES

"Boyle has the tale-teller's gift in abundance," writes the *Chicago Tribune*. And nowhere is that more evident than in this collection of sixty-eight short stories—all of the work from his four previous collections, as well as seven tales that have never before appeared in book form—that comprise a virtual feast of the short story. "Seven hundred flashy, inventive pages of stylistic and moral acrobatics."—*The New York Times Book Review*

ISBN 0-14-028091-X

THE TORTILLA CURTAIN

Winner of France's Prix Medicis Etranger for best foreign-language novel, *The Tortilla Curtain* illuminates the many potholes along the road to the elusive American Dream. Illegal immigrants Candido and America cling to life at the bottom of Topanga Canyon, dreaming of a privileged existence of the sort endured by L.A. liberals Delaney and Kyra. When a freak accident brings these two couples together, darkly comic events leave them wondering what the world is coming to.

ISBN 0-14-023828-X

WATER MUSIC

Funny, bawdy, and full of imaginative and stylistic fancy, *Water Music* follows the wild adventures of Ned Rise, thief and whoremaster, and Mungo Park, explorer, from London to Africa. "*Water Music* does for fiction what *Raiders of the Lost Ark* did for film . . . Boyle is an adept plotter, a crazed humorist, and a fierce describer." —*The Boston Globe*

ISBN 0-14-006550-4

WITHOUT A HERO

With fierce, comic wit and uncanny accuracy, Boyle zooms in on an astonishingly wide range of American phenomena in this critically-applauded collection of stories. "Gloriously comic . . . vintage Boyle . . . [these] stories are more than funny, better than wicked. They make you cringe with their clarity." —*The Philadelphia Inquirer*

ISBN 0-14-017839-2

WORLD'S END

Walter Van Brunt is about to have a collision with history that will lead him to search for his long-lost father. This fascinating novel, for which Boyle won the prestigious PEN/Faulkner Award for American Fiction, showcases the author's "ability to work all sorts of magical variations of literature and history" (*The New York Times*).

ISBN 0-14-029993-9